DAZZLING REVIEWS FOR
SUE-ELLEN WELFONDER
AND HER NOVELS

BRIDE FOR A KNIGHT

"4 Stars! Welfonder's love of Scotland shines through on every page of this medieval romance, where sexual tension is an integral part of a dramatic story. She skillfully draws you into a suspenseful mystery with wonderful atmosphere."

—*Romantic Times BOOKreviews Magazine*

"Once again, Welfonder's careful scholarship and attention to detail vividly re-create the lusty, brawling days of medieval Scotland with larger-than-life chivalrous heroes and the dainty but spirited maidens chosen by the old gods and blessed by the saints to partner them."

—*Booklist*

"Wonderful historical romance. Lots of romance and intrigue with some danger and suspense as well. I would never have guessed as to whom the enemy was or why. Recommended!"

—**HuntressReviews.com**

"The paranormal and mystery elements blend nicely into the story line as those segues enhance a fine historical romance."

—*Midwest Book Review*

more . . .

"This is not just a love story, but one of mystery as well. Sue-Ellen Welfonder has a beautiful way of spinning a story."

—*FreshFiction.com*

"Again Sue-Ellen Welfonder uses surprises and special twists and turns as she tells a poignant love story."

—*NovelTalk.com*

"I've read tons of Scottish historicals, but loved the added ghostly intrigue and superstitions present in Scotland—the ancient histories, legends, and fascinating lore that Sue-Ellen Welfonder intertwines with the sensual Highlander romance in *Bride for a Knight*."

—*WritersAndReaders.com*

UNTIL THE KNIGHT COMES

"To lovers of all things Scottish, [Welfonder] writes great tales of passion and adventure. There's magic included along with the various ghosts and legends only Scotland could produce. It's almost better than a trip there in person."

—**RomanceReviewsMag.com**

"Welfonder's storytelling skill and medieval scholarship shine in her latest Kintail-based Scottish romance with magical elements."

—*Booklist*

"Will win your heart. It's a romantic treasure. If you love Scottish tales, this one is for you."

—**FreshFiction.com**

ONLY FOR A KNIGHT

"Hooked me from the first page . . . larger-than-life characters and excellent descriptions bring this story . . . to vivid life."
—Rendezvous

"Captivating . . . fast-moving . . . steamy, sensual, and utterly breathtaking . . . will win your heart."
—FreshFiction.com

"4½ Stars! Enthralling . . . Welfonder brings the Highlands to life with her vibrant characters, impassioned stories, and vivid description."
—Romantic Times BOOKreviews Magazine

"A book I highly recommend for those who enjoy sexy Scotsmen. A wonderful tale of love."
—TheRomanceReadersConnection.com

"As usual, Welfonder gives her many fans another memorable historical read."
—ReadertoReader.com

WEDDING FOR A KNIGHT

"TOP PICK! You couldn't ask for a more joyous, loving, smile-inducing read . . . Will win your heart!"
—Romantic Times BOOKreviews Magazine

more . . .

"With history and beautiful details of Scotland, this book provides romance, spunk, mystery, and courtship . . . a must-read!"
—*Rendezvous*

"A very romantic story . . . extremely sexy. I recommend this book to anyone who loves the era and Scotland."
—TheBestReviews.com

MASTER OF THE HIGHLANDS

"Welfonder does it again, bringing readers another powerful, emotional, highly romantic medieval that steals your heart and keeps you turning the pages."
—*Romantic Times BOOKreviews Magazine*

"Vastly entertaining and deeply sensual medieval romance . . . for those of us who like our heroes moodly, *ultrahot,* and *sexy* . . . this is the one for you!"
—HistoricalRomanceWriters.com

"Yet another bonny Scottish romance to snuggle up with and inspire pleasantly sinful dreams."
—*Heartstrings*

BRIDE OF THE BEAST

"Larger-than-life characters and a scenic setting . . . Welfonder pens some steamy scenes."
—*Publishers Weekly*

"Thrilling . . . so sensual at times, it gives you goose bumps . . . Welfonder spins pure magic."
—ReaderToReader.com

"4½ Stars! . . . A top pick . . . powerful emotions, strong and believable characters, snappy dialogue, and some humorous moments add depth to the plotline and make this a nonstop read."

—Romantic Times BOOKreviews Magazine

KNIGHT IN MY BED

"Exciting, action-packed . . . a strong tale that thoroughly entertains."

—Midwest Book Review

"Steamy . . . sensual."

—Booklist

"Ripe with sexual tension . . . breathtaking!"

—RoadtoRomance.dhs.org

DEVIL IN A KILT

"A lovely gem of a book. Wonderful characters and a true sense of place make this a keeper."

—PATRICIA POTTER, author of *The Heart Queen*

"As captivating as a spider's web, and the reader can't get free until the last word . . . tense, fast-moving."

—Rendezvous

"4½ Stars! This dynamic debut has plenty of steaming sensuality . . . You'll be glued to the pages by the fresh, vibrant voice and strong emotional intensity."

—Romantic Times BOOKreviews Magazine

Books by Sue-Ellen Welfonder

Devil in a Kilt
Knight in My Bed
Bride of the Beast
Master of the Highlands
Wedding for a Knight
Only for a Knight
Until the Knight Comes
Bride for a Knight
Seducing a Scottish Bride

SEDUCING A SCOTTISH BRIDE

SUE-ELLEN WELFONDER

FOREVER

NEW YORK   BOSTON

Copyright © 2009 by Sue-Ellen Welfonder
Excerpt from *A Highlander's Temptation* copyright © 2009 by Sue-Ellen Welfonder
All rights reserved. Except as permitted under the U.S. Copyright Act of 1976, no part of this publication may be reproduced, distributed, or transmitted in any form or by any means, or stored in a database or retrieval system, without the prior written permission of the publisher.

Cover design by Claire Brown
Book design by Giorgetta Bell McRee

Forever
Hachette Book Group
237 Park Avenue
New York, NY 10169
Visit our Web site at www.HachetteBookGroup.com

Forever is an imprint of Grand Central Publishing.
The Forever name and logo is a trademark of Hachette Book Group, Inc.

Printed in the United States of America

First Printing: March 2009

10 9 8 7 6 5 4 3 2 1

This one is for Judy DeWitt.

A special soul in my life, she's a long-time friend and champion, a bookseller extraordinaire, and a staunch supporter of the romance genre.

She's been there for me since before I wrote the first line of *Devil in a Kilt*. And she's there still, always ready with an encouraging word or a go-get-'em squeeze.

To me, she's a Knightess.

A thousand blessings on you, my friend. The world would be a better place if there were more like you!

Acknowledgments

Inspiration can come from a thousand places, but for me there's only one such place: Scotland, land of my ancestors and home of my heart. I visit as often as I can, each time returning with my soul replenished. Being there refills my creative well, and the only difficulty is deciding which special place or tantalizing bit of lore to weave into the next book.

Several such places found their way into this book, and although I'm always ready to strike off on my own in search of Scotland's truly wild and remote corners, I'd miss the real gems without the insider knowledge of my very special Highland friends.

Too many to name, most of them live in my favorite Highland town of Nairn. Glen Dare, almost a character in this book, is a combination of a few truly magical places they've either sent me to or taken me to visit. Dark and mysterious Glenelg, the wild moors of Drynachen, and the sweetest of Highland lochs, Loch Muick.

The Tomnavernie stone circle, a fraction of the size of Stonehenge, but so much more special for its nontouristy remoteness. To visit Tomnavernie on a cold, misty day, touching the stones and absorbing the quiet, is to live and breathe the wonder of Scotland's past.

That wonder stays with me as I write my books. It's as real as my last walk in soft Highland rain or the echo of wind racing across the moors. It's definitely in the earthy sweet scent of peat, especially on a chill and damp autumn afternoon. To me it's all Highland magic, and when I can't be there in person, I love returning in the guise of my characters.

Three very special women make that possible: Roberta M. Brown, my agent and dearest of friends. She knows what she means to me. Karen Kosztolnyik, my much-appreciated editor. She always has just the right sprinkling of fairy dust to bring my books to life. And Celia Johnson, an absolute gem, whose unflagging support I'll always appreciate.

As ever, much appreciation and love to my very handsome husband, Manfred, who thought he was marrying a stewardess and ended up with a Scotophile bookworm whose greatest goal in life is to board the next plane to Glasgow. He's a wonderfully good sport about that particular quirk of mine, and he's also great at keeping marauders away from my turret. I am more than grateful. And my little dog, Em, my four-legged soulmate who makes the journey so worthwhile. There aren't words for how much I love him.

The Legacy of the Raven

❧

Since the earliest memories of time, the chieftains of the great house of MacKenzie have called Kintail their own. A vast territory of extraordinary beauty, its splendors have been known to bring a shine to the eye of even the most battle-hardened Highlander. Blessed with sparkling lochs and deep inlets, wild heather hills, and endless whispering moors, Kintail's grandeur is legend.

No stretch of land in all the Western Highlands can equal its glory.

And no Highland chieftain is more respected — or feared — than Clan MacKenzie's puissant leader, Duncan MacKenzie, the formidable Black Stag of Kintail.

A man of iron will and incomparable strength, his name alone can inflame the hearts of those who follow him. And those who don't know to stay away, for it is said he fears nothing and has no mercy.

Only a fool would dare allow that there might be corners of Kintail untouched by the Black Stag's sway.

But there was one deeply shadowed corner of that land, haunted by the doomed aspirations of a man best forgotten. Maldred the Dire was his name, and although he has long since disappeared from history, his clan, the MacRuaris, still bear the shame of his nefarious deeds.

The shame, and the sorrow.

Keeping to themselves, the blighted clan dwell unseen in the fair land of Kintail, their quiet presence unnoted by man, until one amongst them grows weary of the shadows, unwilling to accept a fate written long before he or his heir, the Raven, ever thought to tread these hills.

Aging chief of the MacRuaris, *his* days might be numbered, his life's journey nearing its end. But the Raven is young and vital, a man of valor and passion who does not deserve to be alone.

But before the Raven can find happiness, old debts must be repaid.

The hidden past unrolled and brought to the fore.

A past that inextricably binds the fates of the Black Stag and the man called the Raven. An unwanted turn of events that even the mighty Duncan MacKenzie cannot escape, for the truth of it cuts to the marrow, trapping him by means of his one great weakness.

His honor.

Chapter One

✦

EILEAN CREAG CASTLE,
THE WESTERN HIGHLANDS, AUTUMN 1348

Let us speak plainly, my sister. What you would have us do is pure folly."

Lady Gelis MacKenzie dismissed her elder sister's opinion with an impatient flip of one hand. Scarce able to contain her own excitement, she ignored the other's lack of enthusiasm and stepped closer to the arch-topped windows of their tower bedchamber.

A bedchamber she hoped she wouldn't be sharing with Lady Arabella much longer.

Not that she didn't love her sister.

She did.

Just as she adored their lovely room, appointed as it was with every comfort and luxury their father, the Black Stag of Kintail, chose to lavish on them. Elegant trappings met the eye no matter where one gazed, and those trusted enough to gain entry saw immediately that the room's sumptuous finery rivaled even that of the Black Stag's own privy quarters. But Gelis cared little for the splendor of the hooded fireplace and matching pair of carved oaken armchairs, or the jewel-toned tapestries and extravagant bed hangings of richest brocade, each costly thread glowing in the light of fine wax candles.

Flicking a speck of lint off her sleeve, she cast a glance at her sister. Even if some stubborn souls refused to admit it, *she* knew that life held greater treasures.

Wax candles and hanging oil lamps might banish shadows and a well-doing log fire surely took the worst bite out of a chill Highland morn, but such things did little to warm a woman's heart.

Enflame her passion and make her breath catch with wonder.

Wonder, and love.

Such were Gelis's dreams.

And all her sister's purse-lipped protestations weren't going to stop her from chasing them.

Apparently bent on doing just that, Arabella joined her in the window embrasure. "Such nonsense will bring you little joy," she contended. "Only a dim—"

"I am not light-minded." Gelis whipped around to face her. "Even Father wouldn't deny Devorgilla of Doon's wisdom."

Arabella sniffed. "There's a difference between spelling charms and herb-craft and expecting moon-infused water to reveal the face of one's future mate."

"Future *love*," Gelis corrected, unable to prevent a delicious shiver of anticipation. "Love as in a girl's one true heart-mate."

Looking unconvinced, Arabella moved closer to the window arch and peered down into the bailey. "Och, to be sure," she quipped, "we shall hasten below, stare into the bowl you hid in the lee of the curtain wall last night, and then we shall see our true loves' faces there in the water."

"So Devorgilla said."

Arabella lifted a brow with predictable skepticism. "And you believe everything you are told?"

Gelis puffed a curl off her forehead. "I believe everything *Devorgilla* says. She has ne'er been known to err. Or can you prove otherwise?"

"I—" Arabella began, only to close her mouth as quickly. Turning aside, she trailed her fingers along the edge of a small table. "'Tis only that you've so much fancy," she said at last, a slight furrow creasing her brow. "I would not see you disappointed."

"Bah!" Gelis tried not to convulse with laughter. "My only disappointment is when Father refuses a bonny suitor! I do not mind him naesaying the toads, but some have been more than appealing."

"Then why bother to peer into a scrying bowl if you already know Father isn't about to let you wed?" Arabella dropped onto the cushioned seat in the window embrasure, a frown still marring her lovely face.

"Isn't about to let either of us wed," Gelis amended, grabbing her sister's arm and pulling her to her feet. "He shall claim we are both too young even when we are withered and gray! Which is why we must use Devorgilla's magic. If the scrying bowl shows us the faces of our future husbands, we shall have the surety that there will *be* husbands for us. I will go mad without that certainty."

You already are mad, Gelis thought she heard her sister grumble. But when she shot a glance at her, Arabella wore her usual look of eternal composure.

An expression that could needle Gelis beyond patience.

Choosing to ignore it, she tightened her grip on Arabella's arm and dragged her toward the door. "Come," she urged, triumph already surging through her, "there is no one in the bailey just now. If we hurry, we can test our fortune before anyone notices."

"We will see naught but the bottom of the bowl," Arabella decided as they made their way belowstairs and out into the empty courtyard and an emptiness so stifling its heavy quiet threatened to dampen Gelis's confidence. Brilliant autumn sunshine slanted across the cobbles, and nothing stirred. The whole of the vast enclosure loomed silent, the thick curtain walls seeming to watch them, looking on in stern disapproval of their frivolous pursuit.

Gelis paused and took a deep breath. She also lifted her chin and straightened her shoulders. Better to feign bravura than give Arabella the satisfaction of sensing her unease. So she glanced about as unobtrusively as she could, trying to dispel the day's oddness.

But the morn *was* odd.

And unnaturally still.

No sounds reached them from the nearby stables. No birdsong rose from the rowan trees beside the chapel, and not a one of their father's dogs darted underfoot as they were wont to do, eager as they were for scraps of food or simply a quick scratch behind the ears. Even Loch Duich lay silent, with nary a whisper of lapping water coming from the other side of the isle-girt castle's stout walling.

The water in the scrying bowl glimmered, its silvery surface beckoning, restoring Gelis's faith as she knelt to peer into its depths.

"See? There is nothing there," Arabella announced,

dropping down beside her. "No future husbands' faces and not even a ripple from the wind," she added, poking a finger into the bowl and stirring the surface.

"No-o-o!" Gelis swatted at her sister's hand. "We mustn't touch the water!" she cried, horror washing over her. "Doing so will spoil the magic."

"There wasn't any magic," Arabella scoffed, drying her fingers on a fold of her skirts. "You saw yourself that the bowl showed nothing."

"It was glowing silver," Gelis insisted, frustration beating through her. " 'Twas the light of the full moon, caught there and waiting for us."

Arabella pushed to her feet. "The only thing waiting for us is the stitchery work Mother wishes us to do this morn."

"The embroidery she wishes *you* to help her with," Gelis snipped, tipping the moon-infused water onto the cobbles. "I ply my needle with clumsier fingers than Mother, as well she knows."

"She will be expecting you all the same."

Gelis clutched the empty scrying bowl to her breast, holding fast as if it still shimmered with magic. The face of her one true love, a man she just knew would be as much a legend as her father.

Bold, hot-eyed, and passionate.

Arrogant and proud.

And above all, he'd be hers and no one else's.

"Let us be gone," Arabella prodded. "We mustn't keep Mother waiting."

Gelis splayed her fingers across the bottom of the bowl. It felt warm to the touch. "You go. She won't miss me. Nor would she want me ruining her pillow coverings," she said, distracted. Faith, she could almost feel her gallant's presence. A need and yearning that matched her own. "I'll help her with some other task. Later."

Arabella narrowed her eyes on the bowl. "If you persist in meddling with such foolery, she will be very annoyed."

"Mother is never annoyed." Gelis pinned the older girl's back with a peeved stare as she left Gelis to stride purposefully across the cobbles, making for the keep and hours of stitching drudgery.

"Nor will I be meddling in anything," she added, blinking against the heat pricking her eyes when the bowl went cold and slipped from her fingers. "The magic is gone."

But the day was still bright, the light of the sun and the sweetness of the air too inviting for her to give in to the constriction in her throat. Across the loch, the wooded folds of Kintail's great hills burned red with bracken, their fiery beauty quickening her pulse and soothing her.

She loved those ancient hills with their immense stands of Caledonian pine, rolling moors, and dark, weathered rocks. Even if she wouldn't venture that far, preferring to remain on Eilean Creag's castle island, she could still slip through the postern gate and walk along the shore.

And if her eyes misted with unshed tears, the wind off the loch would dry them. Not that she'd let any spill to begin with. O-o-oh, no. She was, after all, a MacKenzie, and would be until her last breath. No matter whom she married.

And she *would* marry.

Even if the notion put a sour taste in her father's mouth.

Swallowing against the persistent heat in her own throat, she glanced over her shoulder, assured that no one was watching, then let herself out the gate.

It was colder on the lochside of the curtain walls, the wind stronger than she'd realized. Indeed, she'd gone but a few paces before the gusts tore her hair from its pins and whipped long, curling strands of it across her face. Wild, unruly strands as fiery red as the bracken dressing her beloved hills, and every bit as unmanageable — unlike Arabella's sleek midnight tresses, which ever remained in place.

"*She* would look perfectly coiffed in a snowstorm," Gelis muttered, drawing her cloak tighter as she marched across the shingle.

Marching was good.

She wasn't of a mood to amble. And she certainly didn't feel like gliding along gracefully, as was her sister's style. Truth be told, if her frustration didn't soon disappear, she might even do some stomping. Great sloshing steps straight through the shallows of the loch, heedless of sea wrack and rocks, needing only to put her disappointment behind her.

It scarce mattered if she looked a fool.

No one could see her.

Only the lone raven circling high above her.

A magnificent creature, his blue-black wings glistening in the sun as he rode the wind currents, sovereign in his lofty domain, impervious to her woes. Or, she decided, after observing him for a few moments, perhaps not so unaffected after all, for unless she was mistaken, he'd spotted her.

She could feel his sharp stare.

Even sense a slight angling of his head as he swooped lower, coming ever closer, keen interest in each powerful wing beat. Challenge and conquest in his deep, throaty cries as, suddenly, he dove straight at her, his great wings folded, his piercing eyes fixed unerringly on hers.

Gelis screamed and ducked, shielding her head with her arms, but to no avail. Flying low and fast, the raven was already upon her. His harsh cry rang in her ears as his wings opened to enfold her, their midnight span blotting the sky and stealing the sun, plunging her into darkness.

"Mercy!" She fell to her knees, the swirling blackness so complete she feared she'd gone blind.

"Ach, *dia*!" she cried, the bird's calls now a loud roaring in her ears. The icy wetness of the rock-strewn shore seeped into her skirts, dampening them, the slippery-smooth stones shifting beneath her.

Nae, the whole world was shifting, tilting and spinning around her as the raven embraced her, holding tight, his silken, feathery warmth a strange intimacy in the madness that had seized her.

Gelis shivered, her entire body trembling, her breath coming in quick, shallow gasps. Mother of mercy, the raven's wings were squeezing her, his fierce grip and the pressing darkness cutting off her air, making her dizzy.

But then his grasp loosened, his great wings releasing her so swiftly she nearly choked on the first icy gulp of air to rush back into her lungs. She tried to push to her feet, but her legs shook too badly and her chill-numbed fingers slid helplessly across the slick, seaweed-draped stones.

Worse, she still couldn't see!

Impenetrable blackness surrounded her.

That, and the unnatural stillness she'd noted earlier in the bailey.

It crept over her now, icing her skin and raising gooseflesh, silencing everything but the thunder of her own blood in her ears, the wild hammering of her heart.

Her well-loved hills were vanished, Loch Duich but a distant memory, the hard, wet coldness of its narrow shore barely discernible against the all-consuming darkness. The raven was gone, too, though his breath-stealing magnificence still gripped her.

She hadn't even seen him speed away.

Couldn't see ... anything.

Terror pounding through her, she bit her lip, biting down until the metallic taste of blood filled her mouth. Then, her legs still too wobbly to sustain the effort, she tried to rise again.

"*Please*," she begged, the nightmare of blindness a white-hot clamp around her heart. "I don't want—"

She broke off, losing her balance as she lurched to her feet, her gaze latching on to a dim lightening of the shadows, a slim band of shimmering silver opening ever so slowly to reveal the towering silhouette of a plaid-draped, sword-hung man, his sleek, blue-black hair just brushing his shoulders, a golden, runic-carved torque about his neck. A powerfully built stranger with a striking air of familiarity, for even without seeing him clearly, Gelis knew he was watching her with the same intensity as the raven.

An unblinking, penetrating stare that went right through her, lancing all resistance.

Claiming her soul.

"You!" she gasped, her voice a hoarse rasp. Someone else's, not hers. She pressed her hands to her breasts, staring back at him, her eyes widening as she sank once more to the ground. "You are the raven."

The bright silver edging him flared in affirmation, and

he stepped closer, the gap in the darkness opening just enough to show her his glory. And he *was* glorious, a man of mythic beauty, looking as if he could stride through any number of the legends of the Gael. Dark, pure Celt, and irresistibly seductive, it almost hurt to gaze on him, so great was his effect on her. He was a Highland warrior ripped straight from her dreams, and Gelis knew he'd be terrifying in the rage of battle and insatiable in the heat of his passion.

She also knew he wanted her.

Or, better said, *needed* her.

And in ways that went far beyond the deep sensual burning she could sense rippling all through his powerful body. His eyes made him vulnerable. Dark as the raven's and just as compelling, they'd locked fast with hers, something inside them beseeching her, imploring her to help him.

Letting her see the shadows blackening his soul.

Then, just as he drew so near that Gelis thrust out a shaking hand to touch him, he vanished, disappearing as if he'd never been.

Leaving her alone on the surf-washed little strand, the high peaks of Kintail and the shining waters of Loch Duich the only witnesses to all that had transpired.

"Oh-dear-saints," Gelis breathed, lowering herself onto a damp-chilled boulder. Scarce aware of what she was doing, she dashed her tangled hair from her brow and turned her face into the stinging blast of the wind, letting its chill cool her burning cheeks, the hot tears now spilling free.

Tears she wasn't about to check, regardless of her proud name.

The blood-and-iron strength of her indomitable lineage. A heritage that apparently held much more than she'd ever suspected.

More than she or anyone in her family would ever have guessed.

Still trembling, she tipped back her head to stare up at the brilliance of the blue autumn sky. To be sure, the raven was nowhere to be seen, and the day, nearing noontide now, stretched all around her as lovely as every other late October day in the heart of Kintail.

But this day had turned into a day like no other.

And she now knew two things she hadn't known upon rising.

Her heart full of wonder, she accepted the truth. She was a *taibhsear* like her mother, inheriting more than Linnet MacKenzie's flame-colored tresses, but also her *taibhsearachd*.

The gift of second sight.

A talent that had slumbered until this startling morn, only to swoop down upon her with a vengeance, making itself known and revealing the face of her beloved.

Her future husband and one true love.

There could be no doubt, she decided, getting slowly to her feet and shaking out her skirts, adjusting her cloak against the still-racing wind.

"I was wrong," she whispered, thinking of the scrying bowl as she turned back toward Eilean Creag and the postern gate. The magic hadn't disappeared.

It'd only gone silent.

Waiting to return in a most wondrous manner.

A totally unexpected manner, she owned, slipping back into the now-bustling bailey. She possessed her mother's gift, and knowing how accurate such magic was, she need only bide her time until her raven came to claim her.

Then true bliss would be hers.

Of that she was certain.

About the same time, but in one of Eilean Creag Castle's uppermost tower chambers, Duncan MacKenzie, the redoubtable Black Stag of Kintail, stood at an unshuttered window, hands fisted at his sides, the twitch at his left eye threatening to madden him. Scowling as only he could, he clenched his jaw so tightly he wondered he didn't crack his teeth.

He did feel the weight of his years. They bore down on him as ne'er before.

Their burden and his outrage.

His scowl deepened and he glared at the sparkling waters of Loch Duich, the fair hills of his cherished Kintail, and the eye-gouging clarity of the cloudless autumn sky. The lofty cliffs and headlands on the far side of the loch earned his especial disfavor. Too impassive was their stare, too uncaring, the soaring rock that should have been weeping.

He wouldn't weep either. As one of the Highlands' fiercest and most powerful chieftains, such a weakness fell beneath his dignity.

But he was mightily grieved.

"Saints, Maria, and Joseph," he swore, curling his fingers around his sword hilt, then releasing it as quickly. His trusty brand wouldn't help him in this pass. Truth be told, he dare not even consider the like. He did allow himself another glower at the wild mountain territory he called his own, great and boundless hills that had the gall to appear at such peace, so calm and untroubled.

He could scarce breathe for vexation.

Never in all his days had he felt so cornered, so well and truly trapped.

He blew out an angry breath and shoved a hand through his hair. That such a day should taunt him with its beauty only tossed fat onto the fire. The afternoon ought to be hung with shadows, a chill wind gusting round the curve of the tower, rattling shutters and bringing the stinging bite of rain. Or, better yet, the relentless pelting of icy-needled sleet.

Och, aye, such weather would suit him better.

Instead, the sun shone with a brightness that rivaled the finest summer day and fired his frustration to a nigh unbearable pitch. Wheeling around, he ignored the rolled parchment lying so brazenly on a magnificently carved oaken table, the missive's broken wax seals as damning as the words inked within, and fixed his wrath on the one person who should have warned him.

"You!" he fumed, his tone peremptory despite his great respect for his lovely lady wife, a woman as desirable now as she had been the day he first glimpsed her, but also the seventh daughter of a seventh daughter and, as such, blessed—or cursed—with the second sight.

She should have seen this coming.

"Why did you say nothing of this?" he demanded, striding across the chamber and snatching up the dread parchment. He waved the thing at her, his displeasure rolling off him to fill the tapestry-lined solar. "I willna believe you didna know. Not something of this import."

To his wife's credit, she didn't retreat in the face of his anger. As always, his beloved Linnet simply remained where she stood, her hands clasped before her, her gaze steady and unwavering, her chin lifted with just the wee shiver of stubbornness he secretly admired.

"You of all souls ought know that I cannot control what my *taibhsearachd* wishes me to see," she said, stepping forward to take the parchment from his hand and return it to the table. "Had I known, I would have told you. As is"— she paused to push her heavy, flame-colored braid over her shoulder—"I cannot understand the force of your reaction. There have been many other offers, and you've ne'er been pleased, but you've always brushed them aside. Ne'er have I seen you take to your solar in such a ferment."

"A *ferment*?" Turning to the table, Duncan poured himself a hefty portion of good and strong *uisge beatha*, tossing down the fiery Highland spirits in one throat-burning swig. "Fermenting doesn't begin to describe it," he avowed, slamming down the cup, then dragging his sleeve across his mouth. "Not in a thousand lifetimes."

To his horror, his wife's eyes filled with pity. Clearly misunderstanding the reason for his ire, she quickly took on her *Saint Linnet* demeanor, clucking and cooing as she reached to adjust his plaid and smooth his shoulder-length, wind-tangled hair.

Sleek, gleaming black hair shot through with only a few streaks of silver, a matter of great satisfaction to him. Not that he'd e'er admit his pleasure in retaining his youthful good looks. Or his tall, well-muscled form, his undisputed prowess and continued ability to best any and all comers, regardless of age, boasts, or strength. His pride in still turning female heads, at times even earning a few oohs and ahhs at his feats in the lists.

Och, nae, he wouldn't admit that such things pleased him.

Far from it, he set his jaw and folded his arms against his wife's coddling.

"If you find the thought of Gelis's marrying so unpalatable, why not offer Arabella?" Linnet smiled encouragingly. "She is the eldest, after all."

Duncan snorted. "You read the missive. 'Tis Gelis they want, and no other. Word of her high-spiritedness clearly reached them and"—he closed his eyes for a moment—"they'll know, too, of Arabella's calm. Seemly or no, it must be Gelis. Her fiery blood has blazed like a beacon and caught the devil's own eye!"

Drawing a tight breath, he glared at her. "And now I am to lose one daughter and offend the other!"

"Arabella will understand. And you must stop tying yourself in knots." She fussed at his plaid again, the damnable sympathy in her eyes worsening the twitch in his.

"For the love of Saint Columba, let it be," he growled. "I willna have your pity."

"You have my love," she returned, deftly unfolding his arms and entwining her fingers in his. "And my constant adoration. Though we have two daughters grown and well of an age to marry, my desire for you has ne'er lessened and shall ne'er lessen." She leaned close and kissed his cheek, the heathery scent of her hair swirling around him, almost letting him forget his turmoil. Then she stepped back and angled her head, the measuring look in her eyes breaking the spell. "Your age will not increase simply because Gelis becomes some man's wife. She will still be your daughter and you shall e'er be—"

"Think you I am so riled because of *age*?" His brows shooting upward, Duncan stared at her, uncomfortably aware of the heat flashing up the back of his neck. "My age, and even Gelis's own, has little to do with it!"

"Indeed?" drawled a deep Sassunach voice from the shadows. "Then why do you feel a need to remind us? The saints know you've made such a claim every time a new suitor has come to call."

His day now wholly ruined, Duncan clamped his mouth shut and spun around to face the speaker. He was a tall, scar-faced knight who leaned against the far wall, arms and legs casually crossed, sword at his hip, and such an air of imperturbability about him that Duncan was certain that the heat flaming the back of his neck would soon shoot out his ears as steam.

"*This* is a different suitor." Duncan's head began to throb.

An annoyance that worsened when the other man pushed away from the wall and appropriated a chair, lowering himself into it with a studied grace that was particularly annoying.

Especially since the chair was Duncan's own.

Crossing the room in three angry strides, Duncan jammed his hands on his hips and stared down at his long-time friend. The only soul who could dare show such insolence and live to tell the tale.

"What are you doing here?" Duncan took a step closer. "Have the southern boundaries of my territories gone so quiet that you can leave Balkenzie for the sole pleasure of coming here to plague me?"

Sir Marmaduke Strongbow leaned back in the chair, steepled fingers slowly tapping his chin. A champion knight and staunch supporter of the House MacKenzie, he affected as offended a look as his battle-scarred face allowed.

"You wound me," he said, stretching his long legs

toward the fire. "Balkenzie is ever held safe for you. And when I have business elsewhere, my sweet lady wife is better at keepering than most men. As well you know."

The Black Stag hurrumphed.

Sir Marmaduke pinned him with a stare.

"I will not contest Lady Caterine's many talents," Duncan conceded, restraining himself with effort. "Even so, you have yet to tell me why you e'er seem to lurk about at the worst possible moments?"

Perchance to help you becalm yourself?

Duncan blinked, certain he'd heard the lout mutter such nonsense under his fool English breath. But his friend and good-brother was merely studying his knuckles, the ghost of a smile playing around his lips.

A smile that indicated he'd soon spew some sage wisdom that Duncan knew he didn't want to hear.

"We've journeyed a long road together, and it grieves me to say this," the other began, proving it. "But mayhap you should be concerned about age if your memory serves you so poorly. I am here to collect your promised winter provender for Devorgilla. Caterine and I set sail for Doon within a sennight and you'd offered—"

"I ken what I offered!" Duncan began pacing, furious he'd forgotten. "Not that she needs aught. I'd wager my sword that old woman can spin porridge from moonglow and ale from sunshadows on the hills."

Certain of it, he paused by one of the arched windows, his gaze stretching across Loch Duich's glittering blue waters and beyond, seeking a certain little-visited corner of Kintail.

The only tainted corner of his lands.

His back to the room, he swallowed hard, not wanting

to admit the dread spreading through him, tightening his chest and robbing him of breath. Only when he knew nary a sign of it would show on his face did he turn around, immediately scowling upon seeing his wife presenting the Sassunach with a platter of oatcakes and cheese.

Just as she'd plied the courier from *that place* with good ale and a hot meal, even promising him a soft heather pallet before the hall's fire.

Ne'er guessing the damnation the man had brought them.

His mood more sour than ever, Duncan folded his arms. "Mayhap I should venture along when you set sail for Doon," he said, ignoring his wife's head-shaking in favor of throwing a dark look at his friend. "Perhaps the *cailleach* can toss together some toads' warts and newts' eyes, chant a few spelling words, and rid me of my troubles?"

His wife ceased her head-shaking at once. "Oh, Duncan, you are making your troubles," she said, setting down the tray of oatcakes and cheese.

"It scarce matters whether I am or not. Or if I traveled to Doon." Tipping back his head, Duncan stared up at the heavy-beamed ceiling, then at his wife. "I doubt even the great Devorgilla can undo the past."

Linnet's eyes widened. "The past?"

Duncan nodded. "So I have said. My own and that of Clan MacRuari."

"The offer for Gelis came from the MacRuaris," Sir Marmaduke observed, pushing to his feet. "The courier feasting on meat pies and stewed eels in the hall is one of that ilk. I heard the name before I came abovestairs."

Duncan frowned at him. "Be that as it may, this is one time when you are not privy to my affairs. Take heed before you speak that name so easily."

" 'Tis a name I've never heard before." The Sassunach slanted a glance at Linnet, but she only shrugged, her face echoing his puzzlement.

"I knew naught of them either," she said, her gaze lighting on the rolled parchment. "Not until their chieftain's man rode through our gates this morn."

"Very few know of them." Duncan took to pacing again, not surprised when two of his oldest hounds struggled to their feet to trail after him. Named Telve and Troddan for two ancient broch towers in nearby Glenelg, the beasts always knew when his moods were at their darkest. "From what I hear, the clan wishes it that way and"—he paused to shove a hand through his hair—"for certes, they are best avoided."

Sir Marmaduke snorted. "I see no reason for your concern, my friend. If you find the MacRuaris so unsavory, send their man on his way. As you've done with all the others."

Duncan sighed, his world contracting to a small, spinning place of misery.

Slowing his pace to match his dogs' stiff-legged gaits, he slid a look at his lifelong friend and the woman he loved even more than life, no longer caring if they could see into his soul, recognize the fears simmering there.

The saints knew he had good reason for them.

"I told you," he began, directing his words at the Sassunach, "this suitor is different. He is a man like no other. The last man I would see married to either of my girls. And"—Duncan pressed his fingers to his temples—"he is the one man I cannot refuse."

Linnet gasped.

Sir Marmaduke had the audacity to remain unmoved. His gaze flashed to Duncan's great sword, the jeweled dirk thrust beneath his belt. "Since when have you lacked the courage to decline an unwelcome marriage bid for one of your daughters?"

"They call him the Raven," Duncan said as if his friend hadn't spoken. "Ronan MacRuari is his given name. He is the scion of a dark clan, his house the most blighted in all the land."

Duncan paused, clearing his throat before his tongue refused to form the words. "I ought say *my* land, as they live hidden away in a bleak and empty corner of Kintail. Castle Dare is their home. A place I haven't visited in many a year. No man wishing to see the next day's sunrise would willingly set foot there."

"They are that evil?" Linnet sank onto a chair.

"They are that cursed," Duncan amended, knowing the distinction made little difference. "Tradition claims they had a sorcerer ancestor in their distant past. Maldred the Dire. An archdruid of such great wickedness his legacy has marked them, bringing doom and grief to the clan all down the centuries."

"Dear saints." Linnet clapped a hand to her breast.

Sir Marmaduke frowned, already reaching for his sword. "You must refuse this offer by any means. I will postpone the journey to Doon." He stepped forward, patting his blade. "My sword arm is yours, as always."

"Your sword arm is the last thing I'd want unleashed on the MacRuaris," Duncan said, touched by his friend's loyalty but well aware that he couldn't make use of it. "Such recourse is closed to me."

"I do not understand."

"You would if I'd spoken plainer words."

"Then speak them," his wife urged. "Please, I pray you."

His heart heavy, Duncan went back to the table, helping himself this time to a cup of tepid ale. The drink's staleness suited him. He picked up the rolled parchment, only to let it drop again as if it'd been an adder and bit him. "The offer for Gelis did not come from the Raven but from the man's grandfather, the MacRuari chieftain. He is the man I cannot refuse, not his grandson and heir."

"Why can you not refuse him?" His wife came into his arms, holding him tightly. "Surely you can?"

"Nae, I cannot," Duncan spoke true. "My honor forbids it."

"Your honor?" Linnet pulled back to stare at him. "How can you speak of such a thing with your daughter's life at stake?"

"Because," Duncan told her, the truth breaking him, "without the valor of old MacRuari, I would not have a daughter. Not Gelis. Not Arabella. Nor even you. Valdar MacRuari saved my life when I was a lad. I owe him that long-standing debt and now he is wishing to claim it."

"Oh." The color left Linnet's face. "Now I see."

And Duncan saw that she did.

Honor was everything to a MacKenzie. Even death was preferable to forsaking it.

"Indeed, I see as well." Sir Marmaduke sighed. "You have no choice."

"Such is the way of it," Duncan agreed, wishing it were otherwise. "As soon as arrangements can be made, Gelis must wed the Raven. God help the man if aught befalls her."

Chapter Two

❧

Gelis paused just inside the crowded bailey, her hand still on the latch of the postern gate. Chaos reigned, and she didn't need her newly discovered ability as a *taibhsear* to recognize that the turmoil was anything but the usual bustle and stir known to fill Eilean Creag's vast, cobbled courtyard. Not that the pandemonium ruffled her. Ever one to find a certain excitement in disorder, she put back her shoulders and ran her still-frozen fingers through her hair, not surprised to note that nary a pin remained.

The image of the raven remained as well, the memory of his dark good looks and spellbinding intensity making her heart pound and her blood quicken. Thinking, too, of the fierceness of his embrace, she leaned down to swipe at the wet sand and bits of seaweed clinging to the lower half of her cloak, not at all bothered that her efforts made so little difference.

She had more important matters on her mind than caring if anyone glanced askance at her.

As for her ruined clothes, she'd apologize to the laundresses and see that they received a few ells of fine woolen cloth for their trouble, if she could make her way to where they worked at a wooden trough across the bailey — a next to impossible undertaking, considering the throng of kinsmen and servants.

She bit her lip and glanced round. Some of the garrison men tried to look busy though clearly doing nothing, while others gathered in tight, noisy circles, their raised voices and agitation outdone only by the barking of the castle dogs. With the exception of her father's favorite old hounds, Telve and Troddan, every four-legged beast at Eilean Creag raced frantically about, scattering chickens, annoying horses, and lending to the general air of madness and mayhem.

Something was seriously wrong.

Determined to get to the bottom of it, she started forward, only taking a few steps before Arabella squeezed through the crush in front of her. Blocking the way, she reached out and gripped Gelis's arm.

"I knew you'd gone to the foreshore." Arabella's nose wrinkled at the sight of her mussed and dampened clothes. "You picked a fine day to go running about looking like a drowned fishwife."

"And you look like a prune with your face all screwed up." Gelis snatched back her arm. "It *is* a fine day. You won't believe what—"

"'Tis you who won't believe what Father has to say to you. He—"

"You told him about the scrying bowl." Gelis could feel her face coloring. "Instead of helping Mother stitch pillow coverings, you ran off to make trouble for me."

"Och, 'tis trouble for you, to be sure, but not of my making." Arabella grabbed her elbow again and started pulling her forward, toward the keep. "A courier arrived while you were out splashing along the lochside. He brought an offer for you and Father has agreed. He—"

"A marriage offer? For me, and not you?" Gelis stopped, shaking her head. "And Father agreed? Ach, I do not believe it."

"Right enough 'tis for you. And, nae, I dinna mind. Not at all. Truth is, I would not want such a furor on my shoulders!" Arabella looked at her. "Why do you think everyone is in the bailey? They're hiding from Father's fury."

She jumped aside when one of the castle dogs shot past, chasing two goats. "See? Even the dogs have left the keep, except for poor Telve and Troddan. And they're both cowering in a corner of Father's solar, looking frightened and with their tails between their legs."

"I don't understand." Gelis swiped at an escaping curl. "You said he agreed."

"He did. But that doesn't mean he's happy about it."

Gelis was too stunned to think straight. "That doesn't make sense. He's never greeted such offers with gladness. He wouldn't accept one that makes him so angry everyone in the castle runs outside to get away from him."

"Well he has." Arabella flicked at a speck of lint on her sleeve. "I heard him arguing with Uncle Marmaduke. He said something about his honor pushing him against a wall."

"I see." Gelis considered. "Whoever made the offer has Father by his danglers."

"Gelis!" Her sister looked scandalized. "If you speak

so crudely, no man will take you. Not even if he's a two-headed ogre or if Father presents you on a silver-gilt platter."

Gelis started to laugh, but closed her mouth when a cloud sailed across the autumn-blue sky, its passage darkening the cobbles and making her shiver. The raven's shadow was following her. She could feel him with her, sense his great wings beating the air. Glancing up, she saw only the cloud, but another chill rippled down her back. Whether she could see him now or not, her heart knew he was there. In his raven-form, he spiraled over the bailey, hovering first, then swooping near, almost as close as he'd been on the strand. Then he pinioned away, leaving only the bustling, sun-washed courtyard.

Her breath caught and a distinct tingle of anticipation fluttered low in her belly.

Exhilarating, and . . . delicious.

A surge of triumph filled her and she pressed a hand to her breast. He *was* her intended, she was sure of it. Either the marriage bid came from him or he was letting her know it would come to naught.

A man as powerful as the raven wouldn't let her be given to someone else.

On impulse, she seized her sister's arms, squeezing tight. "Whoever has offered for me won't be a two-headed ogre. I am certain of it. He will be the perfect husband for me. You will see."

"How I wish it for you!" Arabella shook free and dusted her gown. "But perfect husbands don't usually hail from obscure, dark-doomed clans. I heard Father say the man—"

"Pah!" This time Gelis did laugh. "As a man who's been

called a devil all his life, he ought not waste his breath railing over others."

"He sounded genuinely worried."

"Well, he needn't be, because I am not."

Arabella frowned. "You were born tempting fate. I just hope it doesn't whip around and bite you this time."

"It won't." Gelis reached out and tweaked Arabella's cheek. "I have *seen* my fate. That's why I'm not afraid."

The words spoken, she hitched up her skirts and wheeled around, dashing up the keep steps before her sister could reply.

Those few souls still in the hall started when she tore past them. Jaws dropping and heads swiveling, they stared after her as she raced along the hall's center aisle, making for the corner stair that led up to her father's solar.

A comfortable, tapestry-hung room where she would not only reveal her astonishing new talent, but also hear the most monumental news of her life.

Or so she imagined until she reached the tower's uppermost landing and burst into the solar, expecting to find her father prowling about, his eyes flashing and his fists clenched as he visited a litany of curses upon the head of her suitor. Instead, heavy silence greeted her, and it took her a moment to spy her father slouched in a chair near the hearth fire.

Gelis skidded to a breathless halt, some of her bravura leaving her.

Duncan MacKenzie wasn't a slouching kind of man.

Nor was he one who accepted defeat.

Yet that's exactly how he looked at the moment. Weary, numbed, and utterly defeated.

He leaped to his feet the instant he saw her, his usual

fierce mien snapping into place as if it'd been there all along. "By all the saints, lass, where have you been?" He came forward, gripping her firmly by the shoulders. "If I didn't know you better, I'd think you'd taken a swim in Loch Duich."

"Be gentle with her." Her mother stepped out of the shadows on the other side of the hearth. "Something has clearly upset her. Your bluster and scowls will only make things worse."

"That one doesn't know the meaning of gentle," Sir Marmaduke drawled from where he leaned against a table across the room. Her father's best friend and Gelis's uncle through marriage to her mother's sister, Caterine, he slid a pointed glance in Linnet's direction. "Perhaps you, my lady, should be the one to tell her."

Her mother looked uncomfortable, her eyes filling with sympathy.

A bad sign if ever there was one.

"None of you have to tell me anything." Gelis slipped from her father's grasp and unfastened her cloak, tossing it onto a bench near the door. "I already know," she blurted before her mother could try to explain. "At least, I think I do. Something happened down on the lochside. I had a vision and—"

"A vision?" Her mother's eyes widened. "What are you saying?"

"Just what you think." Gelis tossed back her hair, excitement making her heart pound. "I have your *taibh-searachd*. Who would've guessed, as there's been no sign of it until now, but it came over me when I was walking on the shore. At first I was terrified because everything went black and I thought I was going blind. But it was a vision, just like yours."

She paused, trying to ignore that her father's left-eye twitch was starting up. "It happened quickly. I'd been watching this raven, circling above the loch, and suddenly he flew right at me, wrapping his wings—"

"Good God!" Her father's brows nearly hit the ceiling. *"A raven?"* He threw a glance at her mother and Sir Marmaduke. "Are you certain? Sure you didn't fall asleep on the strand and dream this?"

"Gelis? Asleep on the strand?" Sir Marmaduke shook his head in mock confusion. "For all the years I've known her, getting her to sleep at all has been a trial." He gave her father a sage, all-knowing stare. "You'd best heed her words, my friend. They do give the matter an interesting twist."

"An interesting twist." Duncan flashed him a glare. "No one asked your vaunted opinion, Sassunach. *I* say she was dreaming. Or she imagined it."

"Stop it, both of you." Linnet stepped between them. She spoke calmly, her composure recovered. "Twists and turns in life usually happen for a reason."

Duncan snorted. "If there is a reason, it canna be a good one."

Linnet's gaze lit on a rolled parchment on the floor rushes beside his vacated chair. "For good or ill, we have yet to judge. That there is a connection, I've no doubt."

"Is this the missive with my marriage offer?" Gelis snatched the scroll off the floor, almost dropping it when the smooth parchment snapped around her fingers, seeming to grip her hand. "I—*oooh!*" She jerked, the dangling wax seal brushing against her wrist, its touch sending flickers of heat across her flesh.

Just enough to let her know that the scroll did indeed have something to do with the raven.

She doubted anyone else could infuse a mere piece of parchment and a bit of melted wax with so much power.

The notion made her tingle, and in places and ways wholly inappropriate for the circumstances.

Well aware that her cheeks were flaming, she set the parchment on the table, then smoothed her palms on the damp folds of her skirts. Even then, the prickling little tingles remained, tiny licks of flame streaking up her arms and spilling clear down to her toes.

"So you do know," her mother was saying, watching her intently. "Did you speak with the MacRuari courier in the hall, then?"

"No, Arabella told me." Gelis shivered, the strange prickles reminding her of how she'd felt when her future love-mate stepped through the shimmering gap in her vision's mist, no longer a raven, but the most dashing, compelling man she'd ever seen. She looked at her mother, her father, and her uncle, wondering if they could hear the thunder of her heart.

Sense her excitement.

"So he's a MacRuari." She made the words a statement. "I've never heard of them."

"Would that you needn't now." Her father started pacing, his hands clenched in white-knuckled fists. "I would give anything to prevent this union, lass. Anything I own."

"But not your honor."

He shot a look at her, a hard glitter in his eyes that she'd seen only when he'd been about to go warring. "There will be safeguards, ne'er you worry. I may be honor-bound to accept this offer, but once I have agreed, I am freed of my obligation." He paused, his expression not even softening when Telve shuffled over and leaned against his legs. "Thereafter, if even a shade of harm comes to you, I will see the Raven and Clan MacRuari wiped off the face of the Highlands."

"*The Raven?*" Gelis almost forgot to breathe. "The man who offered for me is called the Raven?"

Her father jerked a nod.

"The man you are to wed, yes," her mother clarified. "His given name is Ronan MacRuari. The *offer* came from his grandfather, Valdar, the MacRuari chieftain. Your father's connection to this man is the reason he can't object to the marriage. You'll understand once he's explained."

But rather than enlightening her, his jaw went tighter and his mouth compressed into a firm, hard line.

"You must tell her, my friend." Crossing the room, Sir Marmaduke offered him a brimming cup of *uisge beatha*. "She deserves to know."

Duncan snatched the cup and dashed the fiery Highland spirits onto the floor rushes. Slamming the empty cup onto the table, he glowered at his friend. "How would you tell one of your daughters she's to wed the scion of such a blighted clan? A family so scourged 'tis said the sun even fears to shine into their glen?"

Sir Marmaduke stared right back at him. "'Tis simple. I would start at the beginning."

"'*Tis simple*." Duncan's eyes flashed. "Were that so, think you I would be so wroth? Telling the tale from the beginning or starting with the arrival of the offer makes nary a difference. The chance of harm is the same."

"You're fashing yourself for naught. I won't be harmed." Gelis was sure of it. "Whatever darkness surrounds his clan, the Raven won't let anything happen to me. I know that from the vision I had on the lochside. Ronan Mac-Ruari isn't a fiend. He's a man whose soul is aching. He needs me. And he wants me. He'll treat me—"

"He'll treat you with all the chivalry and respect a man owes his lady wife." Duncan started pacing again. "I ne'er said he's a fiend. And his grandfather, Valdar, has more honor and heart than any man I've ever known. Excepting one." He tossed a look across the room to where Sir Marmaduke once again lounged against the table. "Be that as it may, there are unspeakable dangers at Castle Dare. The MacRuaris are not fiends. What they are is cursed."

"Then they need someone to *un*curse them." Gelis plucked a drying strand of seaweed off her skirts, twirling it around her fingers. "I have reason to believe that someone is me."

Duncan scowled at her. "Dinna make light of dark deeds that stretch back to a time when these hills were young. For centuries, every MacRuari—or those close to them—who thought he could rise above the curse fell to a tragic end. And if he survived, his remaining days were so plagued with horror that he wished he had died."

"I see." Gelis tossed the bit of seaweed into the hearth fire. "That does rather change things."

Duncan cocked a brow, looking skeptical.

Her mother appeared relieved. "If you desire, I'm sure we can find a way to decline the offer," she said, glancing at her husband. "Old ties or nae."

"That's not what I meant." Dropping into her father's hearthside chair, Gelis settled herself, making ready for a long, comfortable sit. "I am not afraid of the MacRuari curse and I certainly do want to marry the Raven."

Linnet's brow furrowed. "But you just said—"

"I meant that, hearing all this, I can't just ride off to wed the man as I was fully prepared to do." Leaning back in the chair, she smiled. "What I meant was that I now need to learn everything I can about the clan and their curse before I meet the Raven. Only then can I help him."

"Help him?" Her father looked as if the two words tasted of ash.

"So I have said." Gelis smiled. "And I can only do that if you tell me the tale. All of it and from the beginning, just as Uncle Marmaduke suggested."

As she waited for her father to begin, she strove not to appear smug. But it was hard. Difficult, too, to smother the laugh bubbling in her throat. Gelis MacKenzie, the Devil's own daughter, afraid of ancient curses and dark glens. Hah!

Truth was, she was anything but afraid.

She was eager.

Days later and many leagues distant, in a dark and still corner of Kintail, Ronan—the Raven—MacRuari lit the wall torches in his bedchamber, his mood worsening when the additional light failed to banish the room's shadows. A good score of fine wax candles burned as well, as did a particularly fat hearth log, its crackling, well-doing flames only underscoring the futility of such measures.

At least here at Castle Dare.

His family's home since time uncounted and a place so blighted that even a candle flame burned inward, keeping its light and warmth to itself and letting the castle residents shiver in the gloom.

A plague and botheration so vexing he burned to tear down the entire stronghold, stone by accursed stone. The saints knew, the reasons for doing so were beyond counting. Unfortunately, so were the circumstances that made him banish the thought as quickly as it'd come.

Clenching his fists, he closed his mind to the blackness and glowered at the thick gray mist floating past the windows. Impenetrable and cloying, each billowing drift filled the tall, unshuttered arches, curling, fingerlike tendrils seeping over the stone ledges and into the room, penetrating just enough to annoy him.

Ronan set his jaw, his entire body tensing. Once, in younger years, he'd whipped out his sword with a flourish and leaped forward, lashing at the window-mist only to watch the cold, damp tendrils slither away over the sills like a swarm of writhing, translucent snakes.

Now he knew better.

All the massed steel in the Highlands couldn't stand against such unholiness.

He bit back a curse, refusing to let the darkness win, even if a stony-faced mien was a notably hollow triumph. Unclenching his fists, he ran a hand through his hair, not surprised to catch the smell of rain in the air. Elsewhere in Kintail, he was sure, good folk were enjoying a fine autumn afternoon, a notion that squeezed his heart and caused a tight, pulsing knot to form in his gut.

He, too, would revel in standing on some mighty headland beneath a blue, cloudless sky, the wind fresh and brisk around him. Or, equally tempting, riding hard and fast along the edge of a sea loch, free of cares and curses, sun-blinded by the light glinting off the rippled water.

Light he meant to bring back to Castle Dare. If the sun had ever even touched its oppressive walls.

Which he sorely doubted.

What he didn't doubt was his ability to break the curse.

His face still grim-set, he cast a glance at the iron-banded coffer across the room. It was time to put his plan into motion. But before he could stride over to the chest, the dust-covered receptacle of his traveling clothes, the door to his bedchamber flew open and his grandfather burst in, a wine-bearing wraith of a serving wench close on his heels.

"Ho, lad! I bring good tidings." A big burly man, fierce-looking for all his shaggy, gray-shot hair, he swept past Ronan, his great plaid swinging about his knees, his long two-handed sword clanking against his side. He made straight for the windows, the mist-snakes retreating at his approach. "Pah! Do you see? Even they know when to cede defeat."

Ronan resisted the urge to arch a brow. Seldom were the times the dread malaise didn't withdraw when Valdar MacRuari entered a room.

Loved by his clan or nae, the old chieftain's fearsomeness could chase the shadows off the moon.

"Well?" he boomed, proving it.

"Man or mist, 'tis a wise soul who recognizes the time to depart." Ronan watched the last finger of mist slip over the window ledge. "I, too, have news—"

"Naught so joyous as mine." His grandfather swelled his chest, then turned a bushy-browed look on the large-eyed serving lass hovering at his elbow. "If Anice will stir herself to pour our wine, we'll drink to your good fortune."

Ronan frowned.

The girl stood with her gaze on the windows, her hands shaking so badly, blood-red wine sloshed over the rim of the wine jug, staining her skirts.

Daughter of one of the cattle herders, she'd swoon

of fright if she weren't soon returned to her parents' cot-house. It was a humble dwelling of turf, stones, and thatch on the outermost edges of MacRuari lands and far away enough to be spared the worst of Castle Dare's shadows.

Taking the ewer from her, Ronan dismissed her with a nod. The instant she scurried from the room, he poured two measures of the potent wine and handed a cup to his grandfather. "Joyous will be that slip of a lassie when you tell her we no longer need her services." His gaze steady on his grandfather, he took a sip of wine. "Even more joyous will be calling her back when I return. If everything goes to plan."

"When you return?" Valdar's brows flew upward. "My eternal soul, laddie, you canna be leaving. Not with your new bride set to arrive on the morrow."

Ronan almost choked on his wine. "My new *what*?"

"Your new bride!" Valdar thundered, narrowing his most piercing stare on Ronan. "The maid you should've been wed to all along. I've fetched her for you."

"Then you shall have to unfetch her."

"I think not." Valdar's stare went stubborn. "You need her."

Ronan scowled at him. "I needed Matilda. She is the one who should be at my side, still. Cecilia met sorrow and doom as my second wife. I'll no' have another."

His grandfather snorted. Adjusting his sword's wide, finely tooled shoulder-belt, he took a deep breath, clearly readying for a sparring match. "You'd barely grown a beard when you wed Matilda. She was comely, aye. A right fetching lassie. But she lacked the steel and wit for life at Dare. Your passion for her would've dimmed had she lived more than a few days beyond your wedding."

A muscle twitched in Ronan's jaw. "She should have lived and would have, had she not wed me. Cecilia—"

"Cecilia was a frail wee sparrow." Valdar thrust out his chin, daring him to deny it. "There be some who say she is better off at peace than suffering the fevers that gripped her each winter."

Ronan's scowl deepened. "She died in childbed, no' of a fever."

"As do many women in these Highlands every day, God rest their sainted souls."

"Cecilia was one too many."

Going to the fire, Ronan tossed two rich black peat bricks onto the flames. Thinking, *speaking* about his two late wives cut off his breath and squeezed his innards as if a giant hand had suddenly reached up from hell to clamp a great white-hot fist around him.

"Showing me your back won't change a thing." His grandfather's voice rose with all his lung power. "You, Castle Dare, and all within these walls need you wedded to a suitable bride. Only then will the darkness ebb."

"Say you?" Ronan turned around, his temples throbbing so fiercely he wondered his head didn't split in twain. "I say—again—I'll no' take a third wife." Ignoring Valdar's spluttering, he crossed the room and threw back the lid to his strongbox. "I've thought of my own way to rid Dare of its maladies."

"Bah!" Valdar frowned at the travel gear in the opened coffer. "By hieing yourself off on some fool journey?"

"Nae, good sir, you err." His own scowl equally daunting, Ronan lifted a folded cloak from the coffer and placed it on the bed. "'Tis no fool's journey, but a purposeful one. Since my father's passing, Maldred the Dire's curse has centered on me. I mean to—"

A sound very like thunder rumbled in Valdar's chest. "Maldred ne'er cursed Dare. He—"

Ronan snorted. "The man was an archdruid and a sorcerer. His wickedness and dark deeds have marked and overshadowed every MacRuari since his day. It scarce matters if he spoke the curse or nae, the result is the same."

"Which is why you must wed a fiery, handsome lass with enough spirit and vigor to banish Maldred's influence." His grandfather snatched the cloak off the bed and tossed it back into the strongbox. "Such a bride will bring light back to Dare, lessening Maldred's hold. If you come to love her, the shadows will fade. I am certain of it. Even the blackest powers can be conquered by love."

"Spare me such nonsense." Ronan retrieved his travel cloak and returned it to the bed. "I *have* loved. I loved Matilda passionately, as well you know. And dinna tell me there hasn't been love at Dare since Maldred's day." He flashed a look at Valdar. "I may be cursed, but I'm no dimwit."

"To be sure there's been love." His grandfather bristled. "I cared deeply for your grandmother, and your father loved your mother. But not enough to challenge Dare's darkness. Arranged marriages rarely bring the kind of passion that sets the heather ablaze."

"Yet you believe a third such union for me will burn so hotly?" Ronan took an extra sword belt from his strongbox and began rolling it into a tight coil. "Do you not hear the contradiction in your own words?"

Valdar's eyes lit with a conspiratorial glint. "My informants claim your new bride's fire would scorch the sun."

"I do not have a new bride. Nor will I accept one." Ronan set a wineskin on the bedcovers, next to his coiled belt. "Further, rumor has it that where I am going, there are women keen enough to rock the hills should I feel such a need."

His grandfather considered him. "And where might that be?"

"Santiago de Compostela. Once I've knelt at the shrine of Saint James and collected my scallop-shell badge, I am certain Maldred will plague us no more. Even he would recognize the power of such a token." The truth of it flashed down Ronan's spine. "Tangible proof I made the journey and prayed for our family's redemption. No shrine badge is holier than Saint James's scallop. The dark forces here will recoil—"

"Och, is that so?" Valdar wriggled his eyebrows. "I say you're blethering nonsense. 'Tis the MacKenzie lass's fire you need. Naught else!"

Ronan flipped back his plaid and folded his arms. "Should I wish a desirable woman's *heat*, the return journey through Spain and France will provide ample opportunity."

"Begad!" Valdar wagged a finger. "You needn't travel clear across the world to rid us o' Maldred. I'm a-telling you, your new bride shines so bright, her mere presence will send his darkness packing. I know it here." He paused, pounding a fist against his heart. "Gelis MacKenzie—"

"*MacKenzie*?" Ronan stared at him, his own heart stopping. "Are you mad? The Black Stag has left us in peace all these years. He'd not leave one stone or blade of grass unblackened if you even thought to bring a Mac-Kenzie woman to Dare."

"Not just any MacKenzie woman. Your new bride is the Black Stag's own daughter."

Pressing fingers to his temples, Ronan shook his head. "You ken, I'd gladly cross swords with Duncan MacKenzie. Any man. But the Black Stag can raise an army a hundredfold greater than ours. Inciting his wrath would mean Dare's end. I'll not—" he broke off, only now grasping his grandfather's words.

Staring at him now, at his self-satisfied grin, he was certain his aching head would explode. "*The Black Stag's daughter?*"

Valdar nodded. "None other, aye. Lady Gelis is his youngest."

Ronan felt the walls close in on him, the floor whip and buckle beneath his feet. "You *are* mad. I've ne'er heard a more fool scheme. Or a more trouble-fraught one."

"No trouble at all." Valdar made a dismissive gesture. "Duncan MacKenzie agreed to the match the very day my courier went to him."

"I find that hard to believe." Ronan spoke the words through tight lips.

"Only because there are things, circumstances, you're unaware of." His grandfather lifted a hand, pretending to study his knuckles. "The Black Stag owes me a long-standing debt. His youngest daughter shall repay it."

"By marrying me?"

Valdar looked up sharply, his expression triumphant. "So you will have her?"

"I will not." Ronan folded his arms. The Black Stag's daughter was the last female he'd even lay a finger on. "Never in a thousand years."

The triumph faded from Valdar's eyes. "You'll shame our house if you refuse."

"The shame will be yours, no one else's."

"I *am* Dare. As you will be when my chieftainship passes to you."

Ronan sighed. The thought of his fierce and proud grandsire losing face pricked him more than any of the old man's blustering arguments. Crossing to the table, he poured himself more wine, this time tossing down the cup's contents in one quick swig.

Turning back to his grandfather, he quelled the urge to grab his travel gear and be gone. Duty and his genuine love for Valdar held him in place.

Not that he intended to wed Duncan MacKenzie's daughter.

He did, however, wish to decline as tactfully as possible.

Frowning, he reached to set down the wine cup when, for one startling moment, the image of a striking, well-made young woman flashed across his mind. High-colored, with a wild tumble of curling, red-gold hair spilling around her shoulders and great, sparkling eyes, she stared right at him from a narrow, shingled strand. Comely despite her disarray, or perhaps even more so because of it, she stood with one hand pressed to her breast as the tide swirled around her ankles, dampening her skirts and molding them to her legs.

Shapely legs, he noted, before his angle of the unexpected image changed and he saw her from a great distance, almost as if he were looking down on her from the clouds.

Ronan blinked and the startling image was gone.

Shaken, he cleared his throat. "I think you'd best tell me what kind of long-standing debt the Black Stag owes you," he said, forcing his attention back to his grandfather before he noticed anything amiss. "Why would Duncan MacKenzie entrust his daughter's life to a MacRuari?"

"Because," Valdar returned, looking triumphant again, "he has me to thank for his own."

"You?" Ronan's jaw slipped.

"Aye, that's the way of it." Valdar tugged on his beard, his eyes going wistful until he caught himself and brushed a tad too energetically at his plaid. "You willna ken, but your father and the Black Stag were braw friends as laddies. Back then, I almost believed in Maldred's most curious legacy, the immortality said to haunt some members of our clan." He stopped fussing at his plaid and looked at Ronan, the over-brightness of his eyes the only sign the story agitated him. "I even thought I might be such a one. Blessed or cursed, it didn't matter. I saw myself as invincible."

"Go on." Ronan leaned a hip against the table edge, folded his arms.

"Young Duncan was a frequent visitor at Dare. His father was a wise man and felt the lad should know all of Kintail, even its darkest corners. That the lad bravely set foot in Glen Dare endeared him to us all and your da and the Black Stag were soon inseparable, almost like brothers."

Ronan couldn't believe it. "My father and Duncan MacKenzie?"

His grandfather nodded. "So I said and so it was. At the time, I kept a galley at Eilean Creag. A gift of the MacDonalds, it was one of the finest galleys in all the Hebrides. So fine, your father and young Duncan pestered me always to take them a-journeying in it." He blinked, swiped a hand across his whiskery cheek. "'Twas a glorious summer day when we set sail. All blue skies and strong winds, nary a cloud on the horizon. Until we neared the Isle of Scarba, near Jura—"

"Jura?" Ronan's brows arched. "You sailed that far south?"

"I told you, the lads wanted to go journeying." His grandfather looked peeved suddenly, older than his years. "I was taking them to Doon, to visit the MacLeans."

"But you never made it, did you?" A strange prickling started at the back of Ronan's neck, warning him. "Something happened and you saved the Black Stag's life."

His grandfather moved to the windows and stood staring out at the mist and rain, his hands clasped tightly behind him. "A storm blacker than I'd e'er seen blew in off the sea, turning day to night faster than you can blink. Huge, standing waves carried us off course, hurtling us way too close to the great Corryvreckan whirlpool."

He turned then, his eyes haunted. "The galley didna founder, but in the wild tossing, young Duncan was swept over the side. Close as we were to the Corryvreckan, he would've been sucked down into the sea had I not sailed to the edge of the whirlpool and plucked him from the water."

Ronan stared at him, finally understanding his grandfather's hold over Duncan MacKenzie. "Now I see. The Black Stag is indeed indebted to you. For your bravery and valor when other men might have—"

"That had naught to do with it." Valdar brushed at his plaid again, looking embarrassed. "I was a young fool, trusting in the dark luck of Maldred's legacy and certain no ill would touch me."

"Yet now, in claiming the debt, you'd risk ill befalling an innocent maiden?" Ronan regretted the words as soon as they left his tongue. He lifted a hand, took a step forward. "Grandfather, forgive me. I know you mean well—"

"Nae, I know well." His eyes blazing, Valdar came forward, grasping Ronan's hands with his own. "I am no longer young and foolish. I'm well aware of Maldred's shadows. The dangers. You must believe, I would ne'er have offered for Gelis MacKenzie did I not believe she'd be safe here."

Ronan pulled free and began pacing. "I'll still not have her. 'Tis impossible."

Valdar hurried after him, grabbing his arm. "You must. She is your salvation. She's Dare's salvation, as you are hers."

Ronan's stomach clenched. "I am no woman's salvation," he said, and the girl on the strand flashed once more across his mind. "Only her doom."

"You must at least think about it." His grandfather squeezed his arm. "You have till the morrow."

The words spoken, Valdar strode from the room, leaving Ronan to stare after him, his gaze boring into the murk beyond his opened bedchamber door until his eyes burned and his throat tightened with silent rage.

He couldn't, wouldn't marry Gelis MacKenzie.

Slamming down the lid of his coffer, he sank onto his bed and drew a long, frustrated breath. His grandfather's tidings had been anything but joyous.

The imminent arrival of the Black Stag's daughter wasn't a reason for celebration.

It was a disaster.

Perhaps the worst to befall Dare in centuries.

Chapter Three

✤

Not long after noontide the next day, Ronan descended the tightly winding stair to Castle Dare's great hall, only to stop halfway down, blessed inspiration hitting him like a fist in the gut. Overwhelmed by the simplicity of the solution, he leaned back against the stair tower's cold stone wall and released the breath he hadn't realized he'd been holding.

The infernal aching in his head left him as well. Praise be the saints. Swiftly and nigh completely, the fierce pounding receded, almost as if he hadn't spent the entire night tossing and turning.

Seeking answers that seemed impossible.

A way to appease his grandfather, keep peace with the all-powerful Duncan MacKenzie, not shame the man's daughter, and, above all, not endanger her.

"Your bride approaches, sir. The MacKenzies have been sighted!" Hector, one of the kitchen laddies, burst around the curve of the stair, his freckled face flushed with excitement. "A great party of them. Word is, they're just now riding through the glen."

"Are they now?" Ronan's mouth twitched in what he'd meant to be a frown before he caught himself. Nary a single visitor had entered Glen Dare in all of Hector's years. The boy deserved his pink-cheeked enthusiasm.

Not wanting to spoil it for him, Ronan forced a smile. "Why don't you take yourself off to the kitchens and tell Cook I said to give you sugared almonds for Lady Gelis. When she arrives, you may present them to her."

"Aye, sir." Hector bobbed his head, his grin spreading ear to ear.

"And, Hector"—Ronan reached to tousle the boy's head—"be sure to have Cook give you a portion as well. And a custard pastie."

Hector's eyes widened, his face glowing brighter than a candle flame. "I will do, sir, and...thank you!"

Then he was gone, hurrying away on his skinny, nimble legs. Ronan stared after him, more aware than was good for him that the lad's smile was the first real one he'd seen at Dare in longer than he could remember. That Gelis MacKenzie's arrival should be the cause of such an event, inadvertently or not, pinched a place too close to his heart for comfort.

Not that it mattered.

Now that he knew what he had to do, it made no difference how many MacRuaris might fall under her spell.

Frowning all the same, he took the remaining stairs two at a time, not surprised to find the hall filled to its smoke-blackened rafters. His grandfather's men crowded everywhere, talking among themselves, quaffing ale, and, he was sure, speculating. As were a few men he'd swear he'd ne'er seen before. Herders from the looks of them, quiet-living souls who preferred the boulder-strewn slopes on the edges of MacRuari lands to the cloying mists of its verdant glen.

Almost envying them, Ronan glanced deeper into the hall, letting his ears adjust to the din. A great babble that shook the walls, with all trestle benches occupied and those celebrants who hadn't found a seat cramming the aisles or jostling for space in the corners. Chaos reigned, but as soon as he stepped through the door arch, silence fell and all eyes turned his way.

Their stares stabbed him, the curiosity on their faces reminding him of how recently he'd sworn ne'er to take a third wife.

"The Black Stag's own daughter?" A man standing in the light cast by a wall torch thrust out a hand, touching his sleeve. "Is it true?"

Acknowledging the speaker with a nod, Ronan strode past him, making straight for his tall-backed oaken chair on the dais. His grandfather was already there, enthroned in a similar chair, waiting.

Ronan bit back a curse.

He, too, waited.

His heart pounded in slow, rhythmic beat. And with each step he took toward the high table, the heavy, rune-carved torque about his neck grew tighter. Its gold seemed to heat until it was all he could do not to glance down just to be certain some dark magic hadn't transformed the bit of ancient Norse frippery into a flaming, viselike ring.

Reaching the dais, he willed away the sensation, schooling his features into a mask of indifference as he clapped a hand on his grandfather's shoulder in greeting before claiming his own seat.

For the moment, all was well.

And if none of the craning-necked long-noses gawping at him from the trestle tables called for a bedding ceremony, all would remain so.

He hoped.

An innocent woman's life depended on it.

A goodly distance away, but closer to Dare than most wise folk would wish to tread, Sir Marmaduke Strongbow reined in his steed. His face grim-set, he raised a hand. As he was staunch friend to Clan MacKenzie and respected by all, the men riding behind him followed suit, halting their mounts until nothing moved in the deeply forested glen except the thick swaths of mist curling about the trees.

Mostly great Caledonian pines and firs, save the fringe of birches along the nearby burnside, they were scarce visible, their glistening trunks little more than dark smudges hidden by fog.

The kind of fog that curled a man's toes and lifted hairs he didn't know he had.

Sir Marmaduke shuddered, then drew his sword and laid it across his knees.

"We're being watched." He slid a look at Duncan, his voice low. "I've felt it since—"

"Mayhap since those two riders galloped away from yon heather ridge?" Duncan glanced over his shoulder, his gaze snapping to a steep, boulder-studded rise. "They were MacRuari scouts, belike. Valdar wouldn't be the man he is if he hadn't posted men to watch for us. He'll want his hall readied for our arrival."

Sir Marmaduke shook his head. "We aren't being observed by men. 'Tis something else. A sense of—"

"O-ho! Something else, you say." Duncan glowered at him. "Now you see why I'm not pleased about my daughter coming here. Why I've brought along half my garrison as her escort and refused to let Linnet and Arabella accompany us."

Shoving a hand through his hair, he glanced at the scudding clouds. Low and steely-gray, they sped past, almost as if they couldn't wait to reach the next glen. "For once you have the right of it, English. Glen Dare is filled with *things-that-aren't-men*. Peer hard at any clump of heather or outcrop and you'll see them."

Sir Marmaduke adjusted his grip on his sword. "I vow I can do without the pleasure."

Listening to them, Gelis allowed herself a none-too-discreet roll of her eyes. "If anything otherworldly dwells here, then they are moor fairies and rock sprites. I would like to see them."

"So speaks a maid whose life was spent within the shelter of Eilean Creag's walls." Her father narrowed his eyes on the enclosing mist, his scowl deepening. "Would that you were still there. Fairies and sprites are the last creatures you'll find on this tainted ground."

"Have a care, my friend." Sir Marmaduke pinned him with a warning stare. "You'll frighten her."

"I will, eh?" Duncan spluttered. "A naked army of your hump-backed, cloven-hoofed landsmen wouldn't scare her."

"And you should be glad of it!" Gelis flicked the end of her braid at him. "You love me best because I am fearless."

"Humph." Duncan shifted in his saddle. "You would be well served to have a bit of your sister's prudence."

Gelis laughed. "Arabella has enough *prudence* for us both. A lifetime's worth and then some!"

"Even so," Sir Marmaduke put in, "a touch of caution wouldn't hurt you. I wouldn't have believed it, but this glen truly is darker than it should be. Do not forget what we've told you; one word and we'll come for you. Faster than you can blink."

"Such a help-cry won't be necessary." Gelis smiled, excitement already beating through her. "I like it here. No harm will come to me, as I've explained."

Duncan mumbled beneath his breath.

Gelis straightened her back and looked about, seeing not the gloom, but the fine red glow of the autumnal bracken and the sparkle of pink-and-white quartz in the scattered, mist-dampened boulders. The swift, clear-watered burn flowing beside the deer track they followed.

Heartened by the beauty around her, the *peace*, she lifted her chin.

"Wild places have always called to me." She locked stares with her father, knowing he couldn't deny it. "You and Uncle Marmaduke don't understand power of place. Were Glen Dare as blighted as you claim, the burn would be fouled and sluggish, those deep, rocky pools dark and stagnant."

Beaming confidence, she waved a hand in the burn's direction. As if smiling back at her, its bright waters tinkled and splashed, the sound delighting her ears. Just as the large raven spiraling above quickened her pulse and made her heart skitter.

Several times now, she'd seen him, catching glimpses

each time the clouds and mist parted. Once, he was off to their right, gliding silently past the higher rock-faces. Now, he merely circled, watching her.

Waiting.

Eager to welcome her to his strange and wonderful home and letting her know he wanted her here.

It was him Sir Marmaduke was sensing.

Sure of it, Gelis flashed her most dazzling smile, hoping the raven would see. "I do not believe there is danger here. Though there is an ancient aura about the place. A magical air I've never felt anywhere else."

Her father snorted. "An ancient aura styled by Maldred the Dire." He grabbed her pony's reins, drawing her close. "The magic he practiced was dark, lass. Blacker than the bottom of the coldest, deepest Highland loch. Dinna be fooled by girlish fancies."

"I am not a girl." Gelis raised a challenging brow. "I'm a woman full grown."

Though she did have *fancies.*

Bold and exciting expectations she wasn't about to share with her father.

Dreams and desires so deliciously wicked, they'd scandalize her sister but caused her own belly to flutter and her secret place to burn and tingle in anticipation.

Any man who called this wild and dark glen his home would be wild and dark in other ways, too. And she couldn't wait to discover every one of them.

But when they rode through the pend of Castle Dare's gatehouse less than an hour later, pulling up in the cold, mist-swept bailey, some of her bravura slipped.

The tongue-waggers hadn't lied.

Castle Dare *was* a gloomy rickle o' stanes.

Menacing, too, with unusually high curtain walls and soaring machicolated towers. Gelis shivered, her nape prickling when she caught her first glimpse of the great square keep. Its dark bulk frowned down on them, the thick walling relieved only by the narrowest arrow-slits. Silent, weapon-hung men-at-arms clustered everywhere, their gazes assessing, their steel gleaming in the smoking torchlight.

Like scores of unfriendly eyes, the cross-shaped arrow-slits seemed to assess her as well, their blank stares making her shiver again. She reached to pull her cloak higher against her throat, but the instant her fingers brushed against her breasts, she lowered her hand. Putting back her shoulders, she ignored her uneasiness and moistened her lips, wanting to look her best when the Raven strode out to meet her.

Not for nothing had she chosen her most flattering gown, a rich emerald-green affair, its dipping front piece made even lower by her own clever hand. Richly banded by an exquisite gold border, the bodice displayed the swell of her breasts in all their abundance, including a very deliberate glimpse of the top rims of her nipples.

She meant to whet the Raven's appetite, not hide her charms beneath the folds of a heavy woolen cloak.

Even if Castle Dare's forbidding countenance did send a few chills down her spine. Lucky for her, she'd been weaned on dark looks and scowls.

Glancing at her father, she wasn't at all surprised to see him still looking as sour as if he'd bitten into something bitter.

"You could at least frown less fiercely." She smiled brightly just to annoy him.

"Be glad I am only frowning." He looked at her, his expression darkening even more. Dismounting near the keep stairs, he tossed his reins to a stable lad. "The Raven should have been on the steps to greet you."

Gelis gave a light shrug. "He'll be here anon." She made the words a statement, swinging down onto the bailey's wet cobbles before her father could contradict her.

Only the raven dared, staring down at her from his perch on a high turret, the piercing focus of his beady, black eyes leaving no question of his interest in her.

His intensity and need.

Then he vanished, his sleek black form swallowed by a swirl of mist.

Her heart thumping, Gelis hitched up her skirts and started forward, mounting the stone steps to the keep with a bold swiftness that carried her halfway up the stairs before the heavy, iron-studded door swung open and a huge, thickset man of years appeared, a wash of yellow torchlight spilling out from behind him.

"Ho! The MacKenzies — at last!" he boomed, planting his hands on his hips as he stood looking at them.

Strong-featured and with a shock of thick, gray-streaked hair and an equally wild-looking beard, he filled the arched doorway, his plaid thrown back to reveal a great, two-handed sword hanging at his side from a wide, elaborately tooled shoulder-belt.

"A fine e'en to you, my friends," he added, his bearded face splitting in a grin. "Welcome to Dare. Lady Gelis" — he stepped aside, almost losing his balance as several large, shaggy-coated dogs shot past him, bounding down the steps to greet her, their plumed tails wagging — "you are even more sparkling than the prattle-mongers claim."

"She is a maid beyond price." Duncan placed a possessive hand on her elbow. "Only my honor brings her here, Valdar. As well you know. She knows it, too."

The older man raised a brow. "Ahhh...so you told her of Corryvreckan?"

Duncan nodded. "She needed to know. Why I consented as well as what dangers lurk here. She also knows I view my debt as repaid by agreeing to this union." Escorting her up the remaining steps, he paused on the landing, standing almost nose to nose with his old friend. "Know that, and be wary. If any harm comes to her, I will wreak a more terrible vengeance on you than even Maldred could have conjured."

"Father!" Gelis could feel her face flaming. "You swore you wouldn't—"

"Your father has your best interests at heart." Sir Marmaduke joined them on the landing, his usually benign expression as grim as her father's. "There were unholy things in that glen, and leaving you here, in the midst of such terrors, is beyond—"

"Pah-phooey! The only terrors here are the looks on your two faces." Gelis glared at them, aware that her own eyes were blazing, but uncaring. "Father gave his word—"

"Whate'er I said ceased to matter when we rode into Glen Dare." Ignoring her, he kept his gaze on Valdar. "The place is passing strange, MacRuari. More so than I remember. I have half a mind to return to Eilean Creag now, without even entering your hall, and my daughter with me. Honor be damned."

"But you will not." Valdar curled his hands around his belt and looked him up and down. "Not as I know you."

"Perhaps he should take her back to the safety of his own keep." A deep voice spoke from the shadows and Gelis's Raven appeared, the whirling mist cloaking him in a swirl of silvery-gray. "She is fair and well-dowered. Many are the men who would take her, and gladly." He paused. "Good men whose homes aren't plagued by darkness."

Gelis's heart slammed against her ribs.

Her mouth went dry.

Every bright and airy word of greeting she'd practiced fled her mind and she could only stare, wide-eyed and speechless. His voice spooled through her, honeyed and rich, and although he spoke from the shadows, she'd almost bet his gaze was sliding over her. She could feel its heat scorching her. Hot and appraising, it stole like a slow-moving caress over her breasts and then down to her hips.

She took a few deep breaths, but something inside her kept winding tighter, each whirling twist warming her more, making her entire body tingle.

"I'm thinking Dare is too dark for her." Her father's voice sounded distant.

Gelis blinked, then frowned at him. "Nae, it isn't."

Dare was perfect and the Raven exceeded her wildest dreams. His voice alone sent silken heat spilling through her and she could scarce breathe standing so close to him. Already she could feel his touch and imagine his kisses, hear him murmuring love words in her ear.

"Humph." Her father grunted. "You dinna know what's good for you."

"Och, but I do." She kept her attention fixed on the Raven.

Tall and splendid, he stepped forward then, his piercing gaze now on Duncan. "Kintail, I would sooner you slay me here, where I stand, than that I should bring harm to your daughter." Flicking a look at Gelis, he whipped out his sword and tossed it into the air, catching it at midblade before offering it, hilt-first, to Duncan. "I, too, have honor, sir. I will not see it compromised."

"No-o-o!" Gelis flung herself between them, her arms spread wide. She stared at her father, the hot blaze in his eyes chilling her. "Don't you dare touch that blade!" she cried, backing up until the sword's jeweled pommel stone jabbed into her back. "I'm no longer your daughter if you do."

"You are more my daughter than you know." The fury fading from his face, Duncan shoved a hand through his hair.

Then he smiled.

A tight, uncomfortable sort of smile, but a smile all the same.

Gelis held her ground, not yet ready to cede.

Duncan looked out over the mist-hung bailey, then back at her. "Well met, lass, but rein in your temper. I gave the MacRuaris my word and willna retract it." Reaching around her suddenly, he seized the sword's blade, returning it in like fashion. "Sheath your brand, Raven, and be glad I have such a high-spirited daughter. For two bits, I would've run you through."

"The devil you would have." Valdar looked pleased, his eyes twinkling. "Never in a thousand years."

Duncan glared at him. "I've been called a devil, and worse. With reason, as you ken."

The older man threw back his head and laughed. "So

you would have spilled blood on my doorstep? Ruining the feast I've arranged for you? By glory, laddie, I'll not believe it." Still laughing, he slung an arm around Duncan, steering him through the door arch, into the well-lit hall. "Now you see why I wanted your girl. She has your fire and passion and, I hope, a good dose of her mother's compassion."

Duncan snorted at that and then the two men were gone, disappearing into the throng inside the great hall, Sir Marmaduke and the other men in their party with them. All lured by the tempting aromas of roasting meat and wood fires, the chance to rest weary bones and quaff well-filled cups of ale and wine.

The Raven didn't budge.

His dark eyes narrowed on her, her world seeming to narrow even more, the whole of it closing in on her until nothing remained but the cold, damp stone of the landing and the fierceness of his stare.

Gelis's heart pounded, her breath coming hard and fast after the spectacle she'd made of herself. Not that she wouldn't do it again if need be.

She would.

Especially if her boldness earned the Raven's favor. Something she had yet to notice.

"Do not think I would have done that for just anyone." She searched his face, not missing the muscle working in his jaw. "My father's sword arm is faster than the wind, his wrath greater than thunder."

The Raven arched a brow, annoyingly unimpressed.

Unnervingly silent.

Towering over her, he looked down at her with the same unswerving intensity as the raven on the turret. Torchlight glinted off his golden neck torque and sleek black hair, but his face was hard as stone, his eyes unwelcoming.

"I thought you wanted this match," she blurted, angling her chin.

"Me?" He sounded skeptical. "Lady Gelis, I was wed twice before. My second wife, God rest her soul, is barely cold in her grave, our stillborn son with her. Is it so difficult to think I am not desirous of a third marriage?"

"I am not afraid of childbearing." Gelis stood back and patted her hips, proud of her generous curves. Certain she'd guessed the reason for his discomfiture. "You needn't concern yourself for me. Why, Devorgilla, the great wise woman of Doon, once told me I have the perfect form for birthing. She assured me I would have many fine and strong sons."

"And I hope you do." He folded his arms and looked at her, his expression giving the impression that he hoped she'd bear those sons to a different man.

Displeasure and a cold, black anger poured off him, stealing inside her like thousands of tiny, ice-coated fingers, each one squeezing her heart.

Crushing her dreams.

Hoping she was mistaken, perhaps overtired from the journey, or that he was simply upset by her father's rudeness, she brushed at her cloak, causing its closure to open. The Raven's sharp intake of breath upon seeing the bared swell of her breasts encouraged her and she drew a deep breath, deliberately enhancing his view.

But rather than the appreciation she'd expected, his eyes grew more shielded, the set of his jaw looking tight enough to crack.

Confused, she hitched up her bodice, covering the top

rims of her nipples. Unfortunately, the movement made her breasts jiggle, which only served to deepen his scowl.

The wind freshened, too — a damp, gusting chill bringing the scent of rain while low, scudding clouds proved a fitting backdrop for cold miens and clipped words.

For the Raven's frosty indifference.

"I do not understand." She kept her chin lifted, met his gaze full on. "Your courier said—"

"My grandfather's man, not mine."

"Yet you did not hinder us in coming here." A surge of triumph swelled inside her. Now she had him. "You could have sent your own messenger, telling us you had no interest in our union."

"And dash the hopes of an old man? Causing you shame in the by-going?" He shook his head. "I think not, my lady. As I told your sire, I, too, have my honor."

"You have an odd way of showing it." She flicked a raindrop off her cloak. "Even your grandfather greeted me gladly."

"My grandfather is always glad-hearted in the company of women. He is overfond of them."

"And you are not?"

Rather than answer her, his mouth tightened into a straight hard line.

"That, you do quite well." Gelis eyed him hotly. "If there were a Highland prize-giving for frowning, I vow you would win it."

His dark eyes glinting, he gave her a look that would have made a lesser female's belly quiver. "That should not astonish you. If you would know the truth of it, it's been forever since I've smiled."

A sudden gust of wind caught his plaid then, lifting its

edge and riffling his hair, making him appear as untamed as the night around them. Gelis's breath caught in her throat. He truly was magnificent.

She swallowed, furious that he so affected her. That each time the torchlight fell across his face, he seemed to grow more handsome.

Dark, fierce, and dangerously dashing.

Even his scent had its way with her. A heady blend of leather, plaid, and wild, wide-open moorland, full of wind and rain, the scent was so like she'd imagined it would be that her pulse leaped and her throat began to burn, filling with a painful thickness she refused to acknowledge.

He was her raven and he should need and desire her as much as she wanted him. After all, it was he who'd come to her. Not the other way around, though she had sought him with old Devorgilla's scrying bowl. Remembering the day, she shivered. And when he finally stepped before her, barely a breath separated them.

"Come, let us go inside." His expression softened for a moment. "You are cold and it's beginning to rain."

"Aye, so it is." Gelis lifted her face, letting the light drizzle mist her cheeks. "I do not run from the weathers or angry, frowning men!"

He arched a brow. "Even so, I will not see you catch a chill."

She blinked, too stubborn to dash the raindrops from her eyelashes. "You fash yourself over a chill, yet would plunge me into embarrassment in the hall by announcing there will be no wedding."

He touched her face, using the backs of his fingers to smooth away the moisture. Despite her annoyance, a flash of excitement whipped through her.

"I did not say that." His fingers stilled, barely hovering above her cheek, so tantalizingly close, spirals of warm, silky pleasure spun through her, a sweet deliciousness settling low in her belly.

"Then what did you say?" She looked at him, wondering if he knew how thrilling she found his touch. That his mere fingertips were making her tremble and burn in wicked places. "Please tell me, for I cannot make sense of your words."

"That, too, should not surprise you. It hasn't been my custom to converse with fetching young females. Not many are bold enough to set foot in Glen Dare."

"Foolish chits."

"Many would say otherwise."

Gelis started to argue, but he touched his fingers to her lips, silencing her. "Did you not know that those who peek beneath rocks often see what they wish they hadn't?" He lowered his hand. "Our betrothal ceremony will take place shortly. In the great hall, this very e'en, just as you expected."

"And our wedding?" Gelis was persistent. "Your courier said it should take place at the soonest."

"My grandfather's man," he reminded her. "Nevertheless, I've a plan that will satisfy everyone." He tucked her hand into his arm and led her toward the door arch. "My grandfather and your father will not lose face, both keeping their honor, while you will come to no harm. Dare's darkness will be spared you."

Gelis bristled. "And you? You mention everyone else." She glanced at him as they entered the crowded hall. "Are you the only one who won't be satisfied?"

"I, fair lady, shall be best served of all." Ronan steeled

himself against the twisted truth, not mentioning that it was his conscience alone that would profit.

She lifted a brow. "You don't—"

"We're expected at the high table." He guided her through the crush, ignoring how her eyes had widened when he'd interrupted her.

If his plan was to succeed, he'd have to be far more rude than cutting her off midsentence.

A prospect that made a tight coil of anger pulse in his gut as he pushed a way through the boisterous kinsmen carousing in the hall's wide center aisle.

"Why are these men in such high spirits and the ones in the bailey so grim-faced and silent?" She tugged on his arm; started dragging her feet. "The men outside—"

"Are on duty, my lady."

"But tonight—"

"Is no different from any other. Not for the men guarding these walls." He looked at her, willing her not to press him. "I require them armed and prepared at all times. As you saw, they know it well."

She glanced back toward the door. "Surely on such an occasion—"

"There are no exceptions." Ronan tried to keep the bitterness out of his voice. "Not at Dare."

Color rose in her face. "But...oooh!"

A clansman stumbled into her, his ale-flushed face shining even brighter as he bowed near double in apology before lurching away to join his fellow revelers.

Men clearly enjoying the reprieve in Dare's usual evenings of silence and gloom.

Only the MacKenzie guardsmen sat quiet, their solemn ranks lining four trestle tables against the far wall.

Paying no heed to the rich food and drink laid out before them, they kept their eyes on their lady. Eyes shaded with disapproval when, just before the dais steps, she stopped to shrug out of her traveling cloak.

Ronan's own eyes narrowed. "That was unwise."

She smiled.

A flashing, triumphant smile that proved her to be a woman of even greater spirit than he'd already surmised. Disturbed by the discovery, Ronan's mood darkened with his worst temper since he'd learned of her imminent arrival and the reason for her coming.

As if she sensed her power over him, she preened, turning just enough so the glow of the torches spilled full across her display.

Ronan sucked in a breath, anything but unaffected.

"I see you know your worth, lady." He winced at the harsh words, but he could feel his body stirring in hot response, tensing and tightening in ways that were dangerous.

Bold as day, she held his gaze. Her eyes, an unusual shade close to fire-lit amber, shimmered, their depths shone with pure female willfulness and something he could only call amusement.

"I know your worth as well, Raven." She stepped close, so near her breath warmed his cheek and her breasts teased his plaid. "We will be good together. The hills will sing in approval, you will see." She tilted her head, her tone full of challenge. "I will not allow it to be any other way."

A muscle in Ronan's jaw leaped. "I want only what is meet for you," he said, taking her cloak.

That, at least, was God's holy truth.

And the reason her shining-eyed eagerness pierced him like a white-hot blade.

Feeling as trapped as if such a blade pinned him to the rush-strewn floor, he thrust the mantle into the arms of a passing servant. He scowled at the man's back, tamping down the urge to hasten after him, retrieve the cloak, and then swirl the thing around her shoulders again. Hiding the creamy expanse of her breasts and the well-defined curve of her hips, the glittering gold chain that circled her waist twice and then dipped low, ending in a great green bauble that rested *just there*, gleaming and winking at him from a place he had no business admiring.

Not if he wished his plan to work. Biting back a curse, he tore his gaze away and clenched his fists.

He could not, would not, fall prey to her charms.

Green bauble bouncing at her woman's mound or nae.

Her smile deepened, revealing a dimple. "The chain was a gift from Evelina of Doon, a friend of Devorgilla's," she said, looking pleased that the stone had caught his eye.

And not a bit surprised.

Ronan frowned, determining never to let his gaze light on the bauble again.

Not that she needed such wickedly placed gemstones to draw a man's attention.

He'd noted her sparkle, as his grandfather called it, outside, in the mist and shadows. Here in the great hall, under the blaze of the torches, she was dazzling.

Possessed of such fire and light that Dare's infernally cold-flamed torches sparked and flared with heat. Even the candles of a nearby standing candelabrum danced in her wake, those flames, too, giving off a burst of warmth he could feel from several feet away.

Unfortunately, he could also feel other stares.

Already seated at the top of the high table, Valdar lairded it in style, lifting his wine cup in repeated toasts and looking more jovial than Ronan had ever seen him.

The Black Stag sat as if carved of stone, his expression leaving no doubt that he, too, had seen him eyeing the green bauble.

"He didn't know I have it." Gelis lifted the chain, twirling a length of it around one finger. "He wouldn't have approved. I wanted it because Evelina swore it would bewitch a man."

"Indeed." Ronan could scarce push the word off his tongue.

"You do not like it?" She let the chain drop. "Evelina—"

"Whoever the woman is, she should ne'er have given you such a thing." He looked at her, careful to keep his gaze above her neck. " 'Tis a siren's toy."

"I know." Gelis laughed.

Ronan frowned. "Do you see the man in the shadows behind the high table? The gaunt one with flowing white hair and a raven painted on his robe?" He indicated the ancient, not surprised to find his stare on them. "That man is Torcaill, and he's here to bless our union. I do not care to keep him waiting."

"Neither do I," she quipped, her dimple flashing. "I am pleased to see you so eager!"

Ronan made a noncommittal humph and offered her his arm. It was the best he could do without telling her that what he was, was eager to be gone from her. A fool could see she'd take great glee in unraveling his plan.

Proving it, she refused his arm and set her hands on her hips. "Your friend Torcaill is holding a binding cord."

She turned to watch the ancient approach the high table, the long golden cord dangling from his hands. "Why does he need the like?"

"Because he will use it to bind our hands when he—"

"You wish him to handfast us?" She stared at him, eyes wide. "I thought—"

"We never spoke of a handfasting!" Valdar slammed down his wine cup. "'Tis a true betrothal ceremony we need." He leaped to his feet, his eyes blazing like a Norse thunder god. "A betrothal this e'en, with a wedding soon to follow."

"We ne'er spoke of aught." Ronan met his glare, for once allowing his greater size and strength to work to his advantage. "Torcaill will perform a handfasting, as I summoned him to do." He turned to the Black Stag, his voice firm. "A handfasting is as binding as a betrothal or wedding. As honorable. I chose it because of the circumstances at Dare. If, after a year and a day—"

"Pah!" Gelis waved a dismissive hand. "I will not feel any different months from now than I do this day. We do not need a trial marriage."

"I deem it sensible." Her father leaned forward, entirely agreeable. "I will leave here with a lighter heart, knowing this day's deed can be so easily undone."

"Not so!" Gelis lifted her chin. "A handfasted couple is as married as any other once certain intimacies are accomplished." She smiled again. "After that, no one can unsay the pact."

Her father's expression darkened.

A bit farther down the high table, her scar-faced uncle took a slow sip of wine. "That being so, you have no cause to reject such a ceremony."

"Then so be it." She gave a light shrug, her gaze on the druid's golden cord. "I am not worried."

Ronan braced himself, his own worries multiplying with Torcaill's swishy-robed preparations. "Aye, so it shall be done," he agreed.

Already the ancient stood before them, his gnarled fingers wrapping the silken cord around their joined hands, his incantations binding them with words even more constricting than his sacred golden rope.

Drawing a tight breath, Ronan glanced at the raftered ceiling, wishing the graybeard had words that would make the rest unfold with equal ease.

Unfortunately, something told him there wasn't enough druidic magic in the world to help him.

He was wholly on his own.

Left to his own devices to convince Gelis MacKenzie she wanted nothing to do with him.

Chapter Four

❖

For you, my lady. Sugared almonds." A pink-cheeked boy with bright red hair placed the sweets on the high table, carefully setting them next to the trencher Gelis shared with the Raven. "My lord thought you might like them."

"I am fond of sweets." Gelis reached for one, her words causing the boy's flush to deepen. "Thank you."

Beside her, Ronan stiffened. "Sugared almonds are Cook's favored fare, offered to all Dare's guests."

"Say you?" She had her doubts about that, but flashed her best smile all the same.

Seeming not to notice, her newly handfasted husband applied himself to the roasted meat on the trencher.

Not about to let him spoil the moment, she picked up the bowl of nuts and held it out to the boy. "Why don't you take a handful for yourself?"

"Och, I have my own." His small chest puffing, he produced a grubby leather pouch, opening it to reveal a portion of the sticky treats. "Lord Ronan wanted me to have them."

"Ah, is that so?" She slid a glance at him, pitching her voice for his ears alone. "You already mentioned how infrequently guests honor Dare, but I am pleased to see that you are fond of children."

"Hector is a good lad." He set down his cup without looking at her. "He tends Dare's dogs and helps with the chickens."

"I will soon have more duties." The boy's face lit with importance. "The lord has promised me a *sgian dubh* when he next leaves the glen. Once I have it, I shall join the night patrol. They've chosen me to train because I have sharp eyes."

"And if you had a fine dirk now?" Gelis spoke to the lad, but turned a questioning look on the Raven. "I might have the perfect *sgian dubh* for you."

Hector's eyes rounded. "You do?"

"If she does, you may have it." Ronan gave approval, his face hard-set though his words were kind.

Gelis winked at him. "I have gifts for you, too." She leaned close, making sure her breasts brushed his sleeve. "If you would but have them!"

In answer, his jaw tightened.

He said nothing.

A few seats away, Valdar slapped the table. "A spirited gel, what did I say?"

Next to him, Duncan hrumphed. "I vow this hall will soon be ringing with her liveliness." Leaning around his host, he aimed a pointed glance at her. "Mind your outbursts, lass, or you might find yourself back home before a year and a day rolls around."

"Dare is my home now." Gelis returned his stare, her chin lifted. "I shall not be returning to Eilean Creag save to visit."

This time it was the Raven who hrumped.

His grandfather hooted.

Encouraged by the old man's mirth, Gelis edged closer to Ronan, near enough so that he couldn't help but catch her precious attar of roses scent. Triumph hers, she watched his nose quiver. Sadly, the rest of him remained as rigid as if he were made of granite.

She forced a smile, undaunted.

Seduction was her game.

And she meant to win.

"Dare was as good as your home—once!" Valdar's booming voice sounded again as he reached to clink his wine cup against Duncan's. "You would be wise to remember those days and have done with your fomenting. It serves naught. The deed is done, by all the Powers!"

"'Tis still a hard matter." Duncan swung around to cast a dark look at Sir Marmaduke. "Even if some have forgotten their own ill ease none so long ago."

"There are times we must be satisfied with what the fates give us." Sir Marmaduke lifted the wine flagon and refilled his cup. "In especial, once a deed is done."

The Black Stag's brows snapped together.

Sir Marmaduke merely sipped his wine.

"He but speaks the truth, Father." Gelis wriggled the fingers of her left hand, proud of her new ring's sparkle. "'Tis too late for objections."

Valdar slapped the table again. "So I said, just!"

Tight-lipped, Duncan held his peace.

Glad for it, Gelis turned back to Hector. The lad still

hovered at her elbow, so she flipped aside her golden waist-chain and its bauble, revealing a delicate *sgian dubh* at her hip. It was a child's dagger, and its beautifully worked horn handle gleamed in the torchlight.

"This is a special dirk," she said, handing it to the boy. "My brother Robbie gave it to me when I was about your age. Our father fashioned it for him, and I've kept it as a talisman. It will serve you well."

"O-o-o-h, it shall! I thank you." Hector curled his fingers around the dirk's sheath. "Wait until the lads in the kitchens see this."

"You misremember, lass." Duncan spoke up as soon as the boy darted away with his prize. "'Twas your uncle Kenneth who gave Robbie that wee blade," he reminded her. "He made it in the good years, before he turned—"

"Now is not the time to speak of that one." Sir Marmaduke placed a hand on his arm. "Be glad Gelis has an admirer in the lad. His merriment will prove a greater talisman than any child's miniature dagger."

The Black Stag shook his arm free. "She shouldn't have need of a talisman! By all the saints, I shall be glad when—"

"It will gladden you even more, Kintail, to hear that she has no need of such a token." Ronan set down his eating knife. "No harm shall touch her."

Gelis put aside her own knife. The way he'd said "no harm shall touch her" made her chest tighten and the tops of her ears burn.

Something told her he meant he wouldn't touch her.

Not harm, but him.

His hands, and in all the ways she'd dreamed of being caressed by a husband.

Caressed and loved.

Her heart thumping, she lowered her lashes, eyeing him as surreptitiously as possible. Unfortunately, the truth of her suspicion stood etched all over him. Never had she seen a man so determined not to notice her.

Not wanting to believe it, she shifted in her chair, deliberately pressing her knee against his thigh, a ploy that made him jerk away faster than if she'd jabbed him with a white-hot fire poker.

She frowned and withdrew her knee, opting for another tactic.

"Perhaps you should try the sugared almonds." She nudged the bowl in his direction. "Their sweetness might improve your mood."

His expression darkened. "There is naught under the heavens capable of such a feat, my lady. Not sugared almonds. Nor one so fair as you."

"So you find me appealing?"

"You would take any man's breath." He looked at her, his gaze piercing. "As well you know."

"You do not look very breathless." She had the boldness to jut her chin at him, her amber eyes glittering with irritation.

His own annoyance riding him, Ronan ignored her pique. The uncomfortable way her very presence made him suspect that one wee slip in his dealings with her might see the course of his life changing.

And in ways he couldn't control.

His grandfather's jollity as he jested with her father proved equally bitter. Valdar's every hooted laugh and eye twinkle twisted his innards, as did the hope brightening the faces of Dare's guardsmen, the bursts of good cheer rising from the trestle tables.

Such gaiety wouldn't last.

One glance at the tightly closed hall windows proved it. Already, threads of mist slipped in through the shutter slats. Long, slithering tendrils hushed along the hall's outermost tables, dousing candles and causing the hanging crusie lamps to splutter and extinguish.

As did Ronan's brief and mad hope of seizing his unexpected fortune and risking another chance at love.

So he did what he could, reaching for a rib of fire-roasted beef, then drawing back his hand to pull his earlobe instead. At once, a stir and racket ensued at the next table as Torcaill the druid pushed to his feet.

"I, Torcaill of Ancient Fame, do bless the Raven and his lady!" His strong voice rising, he lifted his walking stick, shaking it heavenward. "May they prosper in the name and glory of the Old Ones!"

Cheers rose and the mist wraiths withdrew, disappearing back through the closed shutters whence they'd come.

Torcaill made one last flourish with his *slachdan druidheachd*, the great druidic wand seeming to shimmer and glow as he lowered it.

He looked round, the spread-winged raven decorating his robe gleaming in the torchlight. "I wish you a fair night—one and all!"

Valdar half-rose from his chair. "Ho, Torcaill!" he yelled when the druid turned and strode away. "The night is no' yet by with. You must bless the bridal bed."

"All has been said." Torcaill paused, one hand clutching his staff, the other pressed against his berobed hip. "My bones are aching and I seek my own bed. Your grandson and his lady have my fullest sanction and the goodwill of the Ancients. 'Tis enough."

"Word is you dinna even have a bed!" Valdar hooted, slamming down his wine cup. "Or did I have bog cotton in my ears all the times you've sworn you canna be bothered by sleep?"

"I will see he reaches his cottage safely." Ronan stood. "The mist is thick this night. I'd no' want him to stumble ere he reaches his door."

Then, before the stunned faces at the high table could sway him, he strode from the dais, leaving kith and kin to think what they might.

If he'd planned rightly, Lady Gelis wouldn't be so eager to press her knee against him again.

Her knee, or any other part of her delectable, rose-scented self.

Much as he'd regret it.

"She's one of the chosen, I tell you." Torcaill stepped from the dark of the trees almost as soon as Ronan let himself out a little-used gate in the castle's outer walling. "The brilliance of her nigh blinded me."

Ronan suppressed the urge to snort. "She is a bright one, aye." He looked at the druid, almost adding that the great green bauble glittering at the vee of her thighs all night had near blinded him.

That, and other things.

Not to mention the effect of the top crests of her nipples. Pert and crinkly crescents of a fine rosy hue, they'd peeked above her bodice each time she deigned to draw a particularly deep breath.

Which, he'd observed, she'd done far too often.

He frowned, his jaw and other places tightening.

Even now, in the chill dark of the wood, he could see the creamy fullness of her breasts, the sweet press of her nipples against the edge of her low-dipping gown.

He also remembered the silky huskiness of her laugh and the way she seemed fond of sliding a slow finger up and down the hilt of her eating knife.

"You err, my friend." He reached to flick a fallen leaf off the druid's cloak. "Lady Gelis is earthy, not chosen."

Earthy in ways that weren't good for a man.

He was sure of it.

A sense of doom circling round him, he bit back a groan and shoved a hand through his hair, so distracted he wasn't sure if he'd blurted out his woes or kept them to himself.

Not that it mattered.

Torcaill of Ancient Fame, as all addressed the white-maned wizard, wasn't a man to hide secrets from.

"She has the third eye." He gripped Ronan's arm, squeezing. "I saw its light shining like a lodestar. She—"

"The sight?" Ronan couldn't help his surprise. "That canna be. My grandfather knows her as well as if she'd grown up beneath his over-long nose. He would have told me if she was a *taibhsear*."

Torcaill made a dismissive gesture. "I *do* have the third eye, and I've never known it to lie."

Ronan released a breath, too aware of that truth to argue.

"You still mean to follow your plan." Torcaill looked at him, his eyes seeing all.

"I have no choice."

"There are always choices."

"And you no longer approve of mine."

"I did not expect her to be gifted." The druid pulled on his long white beard, his gaze thoughtful. "She has great power, that one. Even the cold flames of Dare's torches responded to her. Did you not feel their bursts of warmth?"

"I felt Lady Gelis's heat and naught else!"

Ronan scowled. The old wizard's ability to loosen his tongue was almost as vexing as his own inability to ignore his bride's charms.

Her siren charms, the saints preserve him.

Gelis MacKenzie was the meaning of seduction.

It scarce mattered whether she had a third, fourth, or even a fifth eye.

She affected him.

He swallowed a curse. His head was beginning to hurt and a hot throbbing ache between his shoulders threatened to drive him mad.

"She needs your protection." Torcaill's voice didn't hold a jot of sympathy. "Her gift—"

"Hell's bells!" Ronan glared at him. "Why do you think I began this mummery if not to keep her safe?"

"You mishear me, lad." Looking annoyingly sage, the druid raised a hand, one gnarled finger aimed at a sliver of mist snaking across the ground toward their feet. When the mist wraith rose and curled back into the trees, disappearing behind the moss-grown trunks, the old man lowered his arm.

"Your bride," he continued, "needs to be safeguarded from more than shadows and yon creeping menace."

"Say you?" Ronan wrenched out his sword and thrust its business end into the dark, peaty ground. "I say such menaces ought to beware."

He'd no sooner spoken the words before the pounding between his shoulders worsened. The night now thoroughly ruined, he tightened his grip on his blade's hilt. Somewhere a high-pitched wailing broke the silence. Choosing to ignore it, he deliberately let his sword slide deeper into the soft, leaf-covered earth.

His earth, as some souls might need to be reminded.

He also glowered.

Just for the sheer pleasure of it. And as fiercely as any riled Highlander can.

At once, the weird keening faded. Even the nearby mist shrouds quivered, then withdrew. Whether from his fury or his blade, each billowing curtain slid away, finally settling over a tumbled gathering of ancient burial mounds and standing stones. The resting place of Clan MacRuari's hoariest forebears and the tainted ground whence such thick fog often came.

Giving the crumbled relics one final glare, he knew a moment of triumph when the mist disappeared into the ground, leaving only the light haze of the moon. The wind dropped as well, though he'd swear the air went colder.

Either way, he'd made his point.

Or so he thought until he turned back to Torcaill and saw a look on the old man's face that he hoped wasn't pity.

"Your blade and your scowls will not aid the lass," the druid warned, shaking his head. "Not when they realize the prize beneath your roof."

"They?" Ronan tossed another glance at the ancient burial ground. "Why do I think you don't mean the mist wraiths? Or the moldering bones of my ancestors."

"Because I do not." Torcaill followed his stare, his

long white hair blowing in a wind Ronan didn't feel. "You ken who I mean. I've seen it in your eyes. Just as I know their return is why you wished to journey to Santiago de Compostela."

Ronan yanked his sword out of the earth, cleaned its tip with an edge of his plaid, then jammed the thing back into its sheath.

He looked at the druid. "Is there aught you do not know?"

"I know all that I am meant to know."

Ronan folded his arms. "Might that include the whereabouts of that which my enemies seek?"

"The Raven Stone?" The druid looked at him as if he could scarce believe his ears. "Think you I would not have destroyed it years ago if I did? Rendering the stone worthless is the only way to break the curse and stop the Holders of the Stone from returning."

"They have not been here since I was a lad." Ronan frowned, remembering. "Valdar banished them. The battle near broke him, as you'll recall. And now—"

"And now"—Torcaill tapped him on the chest with his walking stick—"you must fight them. Soon, they will show themselves. They will hide behind their mist and shadows only so long. Then they will seek your lady, believing her gift can be used to lead them to the stone."

"A curse on the wretched stone. If I had it, I would smite it in two, proving its worthlessness."

The druid said nothing.

"'Twas Maldred's own wickedness that cursed the MacRuaris," Ronan argued. "Not his foul stone. The Holders are fools to desire it."

"Be that as it may, it is a treasure that is theirs by right, as well you know," Torcaill said, looking unhappy all the same.

"To be sure, I know." A chill passed through Ronan, even as the back of his neck flamed.

Every clansman of his name knew that Maldred the Dire was said to have stolen the Raven Stone from the Holders, thus acquiring his great powers, along with the eternal enmity of the magical stone's true holders.

The dark souls believed to have originally trapped a living raven within the stone's hollowed center, forever granting the stone's holders all the power and wisdom of that ancient and sacred bird.

Ronan frowned.

His gut twisted and he drew his sword again, needing its weight in his hand.

Lady Gelis in the clutches of the Holders was unthinkable.

If the fabled band of wizards even existed.

Maldred the Dire's bitterest foes, legend claimed they'd vowed to sweep into Glen Dare again and again, their warrior descendants wreaking havoc and vengeance all down the centuries until the Raven Stone was returned to them.

Fireside ramblings Ronan had never truly believed.

Even when, in tender years, he'd hid from their rampages, taking shelter in Dare's kitchens behind his grandfather's pile of wine casks as the red-eyed devils scoured the glen, searching for the Raven Stone.

A horror he'd later decided had only been a vengeance raid by a long-forgotten enemy clan.

An excuse he'd had to set aside some days ago, having thrown open his bedchamber window shutters only to see a shadowy figure peering up at him from the edge of the woods beyond the curtain walls.

Dark-robed, cowled, and with eyes like two red-glowing coals, scorching hatred had burned in the Holder's stare.

A fiery-eyed glare that melted the window's iron hinges.

Ronan set his jaw, his gaze once again on the silent burial ground and the deep ring of pines sheltering the time-worn stones. Autumn-dead bracken choked whatever paths had once wound between the ancient cairns and monoliths. Maldred's desecrated grave slab lay broken, its two halves covered with lichen and a drift of fallen leaves.

Nothing stirred.

But when the moon slid behind the clouds, plunging the wood into darkness, he couldn't help but shudder.

He looked at the druid, a man he called friend and had trusted since birth, as had his father and grandfather before him. Many more MacRuari chieftains as well, if one could believe the clan tongue-waggers.

"Tell me, Torcaill," he began, not mincing words. "The Holders are men, are they not?"

There was only a slight hesitation. "They are men, aye."

Ronan nodded, satisfied.

"Then they will ne'er leave this glen alive." He tightened his grip on his sword hilt, the smooth leather banding warm beneath his fingers. "Every last one of them can join Maldred in yon tainted ground. Let them battle each other as they should have done centuries ago."

"Think you it will be so simple?" Torcaill's deep voice

echoed in the stillness. "There is your bride to consider. She changes all."

"She changes naught." Ronan firmly disagreed. "She returns to Eilean Creag on the morrow. Her father wishes to leave at first light. Lady Gelis shall accompany him."

Torcaill lifted a brow. "That is how you mean to safeguard her?"

"Sending her away is the only way to ensure her safety."

"Letting her ride out with her father would invite the destruction of the entire party." The druid looked at him, his expression earnest. "Can you live with such a tragedy, should it come to pass?"

"The Black Stag is a mighty warrior. His scar-faced friend, the Sassunach, is equally capable. They can see her safe and swiftly from this blighted glen." Ronan paused, reasoning. "I will ride with them. Take along a score of Dare's best men. Not that Kintail would require us. He is feared in all the land. Beyond our borders as well, if you'd believe the songs sung of him."

Torcaill remained unimpressed. "Such lays are not sung by those who melt steel."

"The Holders will not yet have noticed her." Ronan drew a breath, willing it so. "She can be gone before they know she was even here."

"They knew she was here the moment her retinue crossed into MacRuari territory."

"We can still get her away. By stealth, if need be."

Torcaill shook his head. "They would see you."

Ronan snorted. "Let them. Think you I fear the miscreants?" He glared at the older man, willing him to see his strength. "I have cleaved grown men in twain, fought off a score of axe-wielding half-Celt, half-Norse Islesmen and sent them running back to their Hebrides before they could cry Thor or Cuchulainn. A MacRuari ne'er runs—"

"Bah!" The druid waved a hand. "You have never faced such as these," he warned, his eyes gleaming in the darkness. "Their power is so great they could charm your beasts into throwing the lot of you, even make them trample you with their flailing hooves."

"The devil roaring!" Ronan blew out a breath, not at all liking his options.

"There is a way."

"And you will be knowing it, for a wager!"

Torcaill flicked at his robes. "I but offer counsel, as I have ever done."

Ronan waited. "Well?"

"It would be well if you were to keep a cool head and sharp wits."

"Be that your advice?" Heat flashed through Ronan. "Have you e'er known a MacRuari whose wits weren't sharp? My own are honed enough, I say you — as is my sword."

"None doubt it. But you will be distracted." Torcaill glanced at the enclosing wall of great Caledonian pines, his brow knitting when several mist tendrils slithered into view.

Turning toward them, he raised his hand, but the mist snakes shimmied and quivered, quickly receding into a thicket of whin and broom before he could point his finger at them.

Ronan cleared his throat.

The druid smoothed a fold of his cloak.

"Whether you would hear it or nae," he said, "Lady Gelis poses problems you must—"

"I know what I must do about her," Ronan snapped, wishing he did.

That annoying tinge of pity on his face again, the druid sighed. "Any man's head would be turned by Lady Gelis. His blood stirred and heated. You must not let her cloud your thinking."

"She will no' be here long enough to do the like." Ronan remained firm. "After what you've told me this e'en, I am determined to see her gone. Safely so, and no matter what it costs me."

Torcaill's expression turned to one of disappointment. "Have you not heard a word I've said?"

"Och, to be sure and I have." Ronan blew out a breath. He'd heard every word as clearly as if the wizard had branded them into his flesh.

He just didn't like them.

"Then heed me well"—Torcaill strode after him when he started to pace—"you must keep the lass safe within Dare's walls."

Ronan whirled on him. "Within the walls, you say? What makes you think the Holders won't breach them? If they are so all-powerful, they might just blow down our gates with a puff of their sulfuric breath!"

"You ought not jest—"

"I would rather jest than believe the like." Ronan put a hand to the back of his neck, certain it would soon catch fire. "I told you, I have ne'er fully believed the tales about Maldred and his foes and am no' sure I wish to now."

He started pacing again, then spun back around as quickly. "No, I *know* I do not want to believe in them."

Even if he had seen a strange red-eyed figure lurking at the wood's edge.

Odd souls were known to roam the Highlands at times.

He'd just happened to catch sight of one.

As for the melted shutter hinges, he was sure there was a good explanation.

"Whether you believe or not matters little," the druid declared, further fouling his mood. "You have the choice of keeping your bride safe behind Dare's walls or sending her to her doom."

Ronan frowned at him. "Keeping her from *doom* is and has been my greatest concern."

Torcaill looked pleased.

With more than a little style and dash, he raised his staff, thrusting it into a thin shaft of moonlight.

"I might be the last druid to wear the badge of the Raven," he announced, "but I still have enough power to serve you and your lady."

She is not and ne'er shall be my lady, Ronan almost roared. But the old man's eyes were shining and his sometimes bowed shoulders had gone remarkably straight.

When the entire length of his *slachdan druidheachd* suddenly made a loud popping sound, then crackled and shone with a bright silvery-blue light and he began chanting a warding spell, his voice rising with pride on every word, Ronan knew who'd won this particular battle.

Even if it pained him to hear an incantation meant to protect his marriage bed.

He had no intention of sharing his bedchamber with Lady Gelis.

Pallet materials for a cozy night's bedding already awaited him in a quiet niche off the great hall.

He'd taken due precautions.

So he folded his arms and watched the druid's display. He even forced a nod of appreciation. Above all, he refrained from telling Torcaill that his best efforts would be in vain.

Maldred's curse and the Holders weren't the greatest dangers to his bride.

He was.

And no wizard's spell would protect her from him.

Chapter Five

✤

Gelis knew something was amiss.

The surety of it intensified with every step she took up Castle Dare's winding stair tower—no, the glowering keep's cold and dismal stair tower, chill, and with only the feeble light of a few hissing, sputtering rush torches to pierce the gloom. Not that the murkiness bothered her.

She had plans for remedying Dare's dreariness.

Indeed, she secretly welcomed the darkness, hoping she'd be rewarded when she dispelled it.

At the very least appreciated.

Unfortunately, the soul she so wished to please hadn't shown himself since he'd disappeared in the wake of his druid friend, claiming he'd see the ancient safely to his bed.

Gelis huffed and almost tripped on the hem of her skirts.

It was *her* bed that ought to be on Ronan MacRuari's mind this night.

Not a graybeard's.

However gallant the thought.

Hitching up her cumbersome swish-swishing gown, she quickened her steps. She also bit back another snort. Chivalry hadn't sent the Raven hastening from the feasting table. He'd removed himself from her presence. And she had a fairly good notion that he had no intention of redressing the slight.

She tightened her lips. The shame of such a notion pulsed through her from the tops of her burning ears clear down to all ten of her tingling toes.

That was what plagued her.

Not his keep's unsavory stair tower.

Nor that the men sitting around the high table had fallen into such a loud and windy discussion about the demands and intricacies of effective lairding that no one noticed when she pushed to her feet and walked away.

Not to hide and lick her wounds.

O-o-oh, no.

She simply needed time alone to decide her next move.

Thinking about seduction wasn't easy with a good score of flapping male tongues blethering on about disciplining errant clansmen or what to do when a trusted friend and ally suddenly lifted a few prize cattle.

Or the virtues of expanding one's lands by conquest and inheritance, followed by a heated discourse on the fine art of Highland feuding.

Or whose bard sang the sweetest harp songs.

Gelis straightened her back.

Harp songs, indeed. She had more pressing matters weighing on her.

Meaning to sort them, she tugged on the sleeve of the

large-eyed serving lass leading her up the stairs. The girl halted at once, her slight form jerking as if a two-headed water horse had seized her.

Gelis blinked, certain she'd never seen such a fearful creature.

"Anice," she began, wishing her own agitation wasn't pressing her to ask what she burned to know. "Are you certain the Raven wished me taken to his chamber?"

"His explicit orders, aye." The girl bobbed her head. "I readied the room myself and Hector carried up an extra basket of peats for the fire."

But when Anice led her from the stair tower's top landing a few moments later, taking her to the Raven's oak-planked door, more cold and darkness greeted them.

The bedchamber, though vast and quite imposing, proved decidedly *un*readied.

Of extra peat bricks, naught was to be seen. Nor even a stick of wood, or the merest twig, or even a bundle of dried bracken. Indeed, the hearthstone appeared swept bare with only a thin scatter of ash indicating a fire had ever burned there at all.

Gelis peered into the dimness, the insult making her face grow hot. The shutters were thrown wide, letting chill damp air pour inside, while the moon's luminance shone cold on the room's terrible disarray.

"Saints o' mercy!" Anice stood frozen, one hand on the door handle, the other clapped to her throat. "The room was in perfect order. I swear it."

Shaking her head, she stared at the clothes strewn across the floor, the mussed and tangled bedding. "We'd even brought up a bath," she said, throwing a panicked look at Gelis. "Victuals and wine. Refreshments—"

"Never you mind," Gelis halted her babble, sweeping into the room before the girl had a chance to swoon. "Someone"—and she was certain she knew who—"clearly forgot to secure the shutters, and the wind has done the damage."

"Och, nae, I dinna think so." The girl looked doubtful. "The wind—"

"Wind is naught but just that." Gelis glanced at the sideways rain blowing past the windows. "Cold, gusting, and at the moment, quite wet."

Anice bit her lip, unconvinced.

"I'll own it was an unusually discerning wind," Gelis allowed. She stepped deeper into the room, a dark suspicion making her cheeks flame even hotter.

Her chest tightened with annoyance, but she held her tongue, not willing to say more until she was certain.

Though, truth be told, she already was.

The *wind* had been more than discriminating.

It'd been revealing.

Her own coffers and travel bags remained untouched. Her carefully selected bridal accoutrements stared at her from across the room, the lot of her treasures stacked in a quiet and inoffensive pile in a corner.

The chaos was masculine.

An untidy swath of rumpled tunics and plaids, the messy jumble made all the more damning for the bulging money purse and wine skin peeking up from its midst. A handsome black travel cloak flung haphazardly across a bearskin rug on the floor banished any lingering doubts, as did the gleaming mail hauberk, sword belt, and brand tossed into a glittery silver heap near the door.

The Lord Raven had been packing for a journey.

An effort he'd abandoned in great haste.

Like as not, the very moment he'd heard her and Anice ascending the tower stairs.

Gelis almost blurted one of her father's choice epithets, but caught herself. She did put her hands on her hips. "That table by the window" — she glanced at Anice — "is that where you placed the repast?"

Looking miserable, the girl nodded.

"Just there, my lady." Her gaze went to the heavy oaken table. "And a right feast it was. A fine joint of roasted mutton, spiced salmon pasties, jellied eggs, and even a platter of Cook's fresh-baked honey cakes. Heaped high, those were, and sprinkled with ginger."

"A feast, indeed," Gelis agreed, unable to deny it.

That the girl spoke the truth stood out all over her.

Puzzled, Gelis picked her way across the clothes-cluttered room to the empty table. Not so much as a crumb marred the dark gleam of its scrubbed, age-blackened surface.

There *was* a lingering aroma of roasted mutton.

Faint, but definitely there.

Gelis sniffed the air, now catching a delicate hint of ginger as well.

"Could it be," she began, turning back to Anice, "that the castle dogs snatched the food?"

She'd seen the great furry beasts when she'd first arrived and they'd rushed down the keep steps to greet her. Her father favored similar dogs, and they'd been known to devour greater spreads of victuals than Anice had described. True masters at the art of food-snatching, they could wolf down the offerings of a well-laden table and be gone before even the most watchful soul took note.

But Anice was shaking her head.

"Och, nae, it wouldn't have been the dogs." She looked sure of it. "They ne'er set foot in this room. Nary a one. They're afeart—"

"Perhaps of the room's master?" Gelis lifted one brow. "No one could blame them for that," she quipped, unable to check herself this time. "I have scarce happened across a more stony-faced, cold-hearted man."

"Do not think too ill of him, my lady." The girl took a few steps into the room. "To be sure, he gave you a poor welcome, but he had his reasons."

"No doubt," Gelis agreed, trailing a finger along the smooth edge of the table. "A man twice married always has reasons. Either to seek a new wife or to avoid one."

Unbidden, the Raven's own words about his previous marriages rang in her ears. As terse as when he'd said them, they haunted her now.

Likewise, the shuttered expression that had crossed his face when he'd uttered them.

Is it so difficult to think I am not desirous of a third marriage?

Gelis straightened, putting back her shoulders before thoughts of his former wives could sour her mood. Already, she could imagine blissful evenings in this bedchamber. Candlelit coziness and leisurely repasts enjoyed at this very table where she stood. Endless hours of raw and heated pleasure in the massive four-poster bed across the room.

Perhaps a tumble across one of the three great bear-skin rugs gracing the bedchamber floor.

Lusty tumbles, all naked limbs and hot, breath-stealing kisses and sighs.

Sinuous, carnal pleasures of the sort she'd likely never experience.

Not with a man determined to shun her.

A situation she refused to accept, she decided, furious at the direction her thoughts were taking.

She'd come abovestairs to plan a seduction. Not to stalk about a cold and messy bedchamber, pricked by needless jealousy over two faceless, dead-in-their-graves females who deserved only prayers and pity.

"Dinna look so downcast, my lady." Anice took a few more steps into the room.

Overbold steps for a maid so timid.

Proving it, she laced her fingers before her, twining them so tightly together that her knuckles gleamed white against the room's shadow.

"The Raven's not himself of late." She lifted her voice, not looking at Gelis, but at the tall window arches, the rainy night beyond. Her gaze lingered there a few moments before she glanced over her shoulder at the door.

"His coldness has naught to do with you," she finished. "His heart is good, I say you. Once you know him better, you will see—"

"I have seen more than you know." Gelis flicked a speck of lint from her sleeve. "Truth is, I've seen enough to know him better than he knows himself."

The girl's eyes rounded and she looked about to say something, but before she could, a gusting wind swept in through the opened shutters. A chill burst of rain splattered across the tabletop, the icy spray stinging Gelis's cheeks and dampening her gown.

"These shutters ought to be secured," she said, leaning across the table to reach for them, her fingers closing around the cold iron of the latches in the very moment the shutters disappeared.

"A-ieeee!" She jumped back, one hand to her breast as the wind's roar became a high-pitched buzzing in her ears and the tall window arch lengthened and widened, growing ever larger until the black, rainy night surrounded her.

From somewhere distant she heard a keening cry, a low moan that could have been her own. She slumped against the edge of the table, or something hard and solid, the cold iron of the shutter hinges shifting beneath her fingers, changing into the icy-wet, limpet-crusted rock of the great sea stones scattered along Eilean Creag's lochside strand.

Heart pounding, she tightened her grip on the rock, her fingers slipping on the sleek wetness of sea-tangle. The buzzing in her ears grew deafening, then stopped, plunging her into silence as the blackness began to shimmer and ripple, slowly lightening to misty, luminous silver.

A glimmering and transparent curtain through which she caught glimpses of Eilean Creag's stout curtain walls and postern gate, the shining waters of Loch Duich, and her beloved peaks of Kintail rising beyond.

He was there, too.

High above the loch, his great wings beating the air as he spiraled on the wind, his black eyes staring down at her. She lost her footing in the slippery rock pool, falling to her knees even as the raven vanished from the sky and her own words flew back to her.

I've seen enough to know him...

And then she did see him.

A raven no more, he strode out of a parting in the mist,

his gleaming blue-black hair lifting in the wind, the glint of his sword and the bright golden torque about his neck commanding her attention.

I have seen… The words persisted, a repetitive hammering in her ears.

He crossed the strand with purposeful strides until he loomed above her, a man of fierce passion and heated blood, his dark eyes blazing.

Leaning down, he seized her arm, pulling her roughly to her feet. "You have seen what I wish you to see and you know naught of me."

Gelis swayed, her senses whirling. "I—"

"Be glad it is so!" He jerked her hard against him, kissing her. A hot, demanding kiss as swift as it was savage, for he broke away as quickly, his grip on her shoulders the only thing that kept her standing.

His breath harsh, he looked at her, his gaze more piercing than ever. "Pray God you ne'er meet the truth."

And then he was gone, Eilean Creag's little strand and the rippled waters of Loch Duich with him.

Only the slippery cold wetness of the sea rocks remained. Hard and solid beneath her clutching fingers as the mist receded and the sea stones finally vanished as well. Their chill, seaweed-strewn surface no more than icy-wet shutter latches; the empty, rain-splattered table in front of Ronan MacRuari's bedchamber window.

"O-o-oh, mercy me!" Anice's voice banished the last shimmers of the vision. "You've gone so pale," she cried, clutching Gelis's arm. "Are you ailing? Shall I fetch the hen wife? The Raven—"

"No bother. I am well enough." Gelis drew herself up, her fingers still clenched around the shutter latches. "Only weary from the day. The long journey here and now this room," she improvised, grasping for an explanation.

One that sounded halfway believable and wouldn't reveal how very much she *did* need Ronan.

How much he needed her.

More sure of that need than ever, she kept her grip on the shutters. She looked out at the night, almost impenetrably dark with low, racing clouds. Beyond the castle walls, the dark Scots pines guarding Glen Dare were hidden in the deeper gloom, but the wild gusting wind was gone and only a fine rain was falling. The kind of soft misty rain all Highlanders knew and loved. Blessing its comfort and familiarity, she leaned closer to the window arch and breathed deep of the chill night air.

Her heart began to thump heavily and her throat thickened. Glen Dare *was* beautiful, its reputation as being blighted an unfair misconception she knew she could set to rights.

Almost feeling Castle Dare's walls beseeching her to do so, she let her gaze wander, not seeing the stronghold's forbidding gloom but imagining its heart calling to her.

Showing her the proud and great place it could be.

Across the bailey, quite a few men still patrolled the battlements, their tall, weapon-hung forms looming into view then disappearing again each time they passed one of the wall-walk's torches.

Far below, mist swirled and eddied across the cobbled courtyard. There, too, guardsmen could be seen. Most stood gathered near the torchlit entrance to the gatehouse's tunnel-like pend while others moved along the perimeters of the walling, clearly keeping a watchful eye on the silent byres and outbuildings.

Gelis shivered, her romanticizing forgotten. Her Mac-Kenzie blood quickened, making her scan the battlements with an even sharper eye.

Watchmen were everywhere, those she'd first noticed and others who stood silent in the shadows, almost blending with the darkness.

She frowned. Her father didn't send so many men on night patrol unless they were under serious threat of a siege.

She started to say so, but just then glanced beneath the tower window and all thought of sieges and night guardsmen vanished.

"Well then!" Her lips twitched and she leaned farther out the window. "There is the truth of the *wind* and the missing repast."

Anice looked at her as if she'd sprouted horns. "The truth of the wind?"

Nae, the truth of a certain raven-haired, flashing-eyed devil who tossed feast goods out the window, Gelis almost blurted. Instead she reached for the younger girl's elbow, pulling her to her side.

"There," she announced, waiting for the girl to peer down into the bailey. "See for yourself."

"By Glory!" Anice sprang back from the window. "The mist must've—"

"The mist is as innocent as the wind." Gelis shoved a damp curl off her forehead. "I'll be the last to rumple my nose at Highland magic, but I've yet to hear of mist or wind that would pitch perfectly good victuals out of a tower window."

Only someone bent on ruining a wedding night would dare.

A *handfasted* wedding night.

From some wild-hearted corner of her soul, Gelis was seized by an overwhelming urge to laugh. But if she did, she doubted she'd be able to stop, and she didn't want to frighten Anice. So she dashed yet another loose curl off her face and pretended to eye the mess below.

And it was a mess.

If she wasn't mistaken, she'd also spied the splintered staves of a bathing tub.

Not to mention the remains of a small but sumptuous feast. Carefully prepared delicacies splattered across the wet-glistening cobbles. Two smashed wine ewers. She narrowed her eyes, squinting to see through the thick swaths of mist curling around the tower. Her efforts rewarded, she caught a glimpse of two jewel-encrusted wine chalices.

Treasures now scratched and dented beyond repair.

Drawing another deep breath of the damp night air, she lifted her chin, the chalices forgotten.

Her bond with the Raven was a treasure, too.

A far greater treasure; and she wasn't going to see it sundered.

No matter how often he might ravage her sleeping quarters or how many times he chose to send an evening repast sailing out the window.

She wouldn't be intimidated.

And she wasn't going anywhere.

About the same time, but in a well-hidden niche just off the great hall's darkest corner, Ronan lay on his back on a thin pallet of heather and bracken. A lumpy, somewhat damp-smelling pallet, its dubious comforts made all the more unpalatable by his conviction that something small and four-footed moved about within his bedding's meager stuffing.

Even so, wrapped snug in his plaid and with the entrance to his hidey-hole concealed in deep shadow, he should've felt cozy enough to seize at least a few short hours of sleep.

A much-needed respite from his cares, however brief.

Instead, he found himself scowling up at the niche's smoke-blackened ceiling.

Naught had gone as he'd planned.

Torcaill's dire words rolled around in his head, robbing him of his night's rest, while a persistent pinch in his gut warned that it'd been purest folly to order a sumptuous bridal feast carried to his bedchamber.

No good would come of his nonappearance at such an intimate table. He rubbed a hand down over his face, drew a long breath, and released it slowly. Trying to explain why he'd absented himself, both from the repast and from his dazzling bride's bed, struck him as being as unwise as it was unpleasant.

His scowl deepened. He'd rather walk naked through a thorny bramble patch.

He'd suffer the same and worse if he could spare himself the occasional bursts of his grandfather's laughter. Late though it was, Valdar's gleeful hoots and guffaws still rang out from the opposite end of the hall.

Duncan MacKenzie's voice reached him as well, deep and congenial, though the words were indistinct. Not that he needed to hear them to guess that now that the two old friends apparently conversed alone, the Black Stag's animosity had lessened.

Few were the men who could resist Valdar's gregarious charm.

Fewer still the men able to resist Lady Gelis.

Ronan folded his arms beneath his head, his gaze fixed on a crack in the ceiling. He needed to sleep. He would not, could not, spend the night's remaining hours lying here thinking about her. Closing his mind, he concentrated on the cold wind racing past the hidey-hole's narrow slit window. Turned his ears to the steady patter of rain against the keep wall, the granite cobbles of the bailey.

The sounds lulled him, bringing sleep nearer.

He turned on his side, weary now. His eyes drifted shut, but more than slumber sought him.

Something strange was happening.

Along with sleep, unaccustomed warmth stole into the musty little niche where he'd spread his pallet. A sensation that seemed to intensify each time his grandfather gave another bark of laughter.

The warmth of bright spring days when broom and whin cloaked the hills in a mantle of gold and the Highland air was softer, sweeter than the finest wine.

Days the like of which hadn't graced Glen Dare since his earliest childhood and were best forgotten.

Even if he'd swear he could feel that warmth now.

Smell the wild Scottish roses growing in such profusion on his mother's trellised arbor, her own personal challenge to the demons of Castle Dare: a tiny but well-tended garden nestled against a far wall of the bailey.

A boyhood refuge gone the way of all other bright and good things at Dare.

Nothing remained of his mother's pride but a woody

tangle of thorny root-stumps and a fallen jumble of moss-grown stones.

The memory—and the strange sensation of warmth—woke him and he flipped onto his other side. The wind seemed to have gusted in through the window slit, its icy passage stinging his eyes.

He set his jaw, glowering once more at the ceiling crack. Truth was, he intended to do so until all such mummery left his thoughts.

He had no business thinking about spring days alive with birdsong or a brief span of years when Dare's hall was no stranger to soft chuckles and smiles.

Nor his grandfather's agony when his current jollity turned again to tears.

Such ponderings served naught.

But he *could* feel the warmth.

And the scent of roses filled his senses on every indrawn breath.

Even more strange, the ceiling crack was suddenly gone and *she* filled his vision.

A dream, he knew, but she was there all the same.

His high-spirited bride, standing on a narrow shingled strand with what looked to be an imposing curtain wall looming behind her. All ardent woman and desirability, she watched him, her flame-colored hair bright in the autumn sunshine, her magnificent breasts and shapely hips more than apparent.

Sparkling as the glittering loch waters at her feet, she beckoned, her allure pulling him deeper into sleep. Somewhere inside him something twisted and cracked, freeing him of his usual caution.

Need, want, and an inexplicable urgency swept him.

Then, his entire body tightened and he found himself standing only a hand's breadth in front of her.

He drew a harsh, rapid breath, then seized her by the arms and pulled her tight against him for a hard, demanding kiss. A devouring, all-slaking, open-mouthed kiss full of tangling tongues and hot sighs.

The kind of kiss he'd been burning to give her ever since he'd seen her march so boldly up Dare's steps, her wicked green bauble bouncing against the vee between her thighs.

Some lucid part of him wondered if her gift allowed her to invade his sleep, but his dream-self didn't care why she was there, tempting him.

Only that she was.

Groaning, he jerked her even harder against his chest, his fingers tightening on her arms as he plunged his tongue ever deeper into her mouth. His heart thundered, his need near bursting as she swirled her own tongue seductively over his.

Heat swept him, her attar of roses scent enfolding him, bewitching him.

He thrust a hand into the silken mass of her hair, twining his fingers in the bright, glossy curls. Soft, nubby curls with a surprisingly familiar feel.

A feel that was just a wee bit worn, not nearly as soft as he'd thought, and decidedly woolly.

His eyes snapped open.

The illusion, dream, or whate'er it'd been spiraled away. An odd lurching disappointment shot through him and he pushed up on his elbows to glare at the bunched plaid clutched so tightly in his hand.

His own plaid, still wrapped snug around him save

that he'd managed to pull it up over his chin. Its edge tickled his nose, the seductive scent of roses wafting up from each woolen fold, reminding him how often she'd leaned over-close at the high table.

How many times she'd endeavored to brush her breasts against his arm, her attar of roses perfume nigh undoing him.

His brows snapped together. "By all the living saints!" he cursed, lifting up just enough to fling the rose-reeking tartan into a corner.

When he tried to roll onto his side and found he couldn't, he made another discovery.

The delicious warmth he'd been imagining hadn't been imagined at all.

He *was* engulfed in warmth.

But not because his entirely too tempting, bauble-wearing bride returned his dream-kisses with such heated fervor. Nor thanks to the unexpected coziness of the muffled converse he'd caught from the dais end of the hall, his grandfather's occasional bark of jolly laughter.

He was warm—overly warm—because his favorite hound, Buckie, was sprawled across his lower legs!

As if the great scruffy beast sensed Ronan's ire, he opened one eye, giving him a long, steady look before shutting it again and continuing with his snores.

Ronan swallowed a curse. The dog wasn't just warming him. His entire lower body beginning somewhere about midthigh tingled and burned as if the devil and his minions were jabbing him with red-hot fire needles.

He might not rid himself of the sensation for days.

It was that bad.

And ordering Buckie to move wasn't an option.

The old cur was lame in his back legs and deserved his rest even more than Ronan. Nor would he budge if Ronan did glower and scold him. Unlike the other castle dogs, Buckie was wholly impervious to his dark moods.

Far from slinking away whenever *that look* came onto Ronan's face, Buckie would simply shuffle over and lick his hand.

Something he'd done ever since Ronan had found him tied to a tree on the edges of Glen Dare, thin, half-starving, and covered in welts. Ronan had doubted the then-young dog would survive the night.

But he'd thrived, and to this day, Ronan could hardly take a step without Buckie trailing along at his heels.

Nor, it would seem, would he find undisturbed sleep this night.

Sighing, he lay back again, determined to try.

But he'd no sooner closed his eyes and drifted into the sweet bliss of a deep, dreamless sleep when the sound of hastening footfalls woke him.

That, and the renewed surge of red-hot fire tingles in his legs when Buckie stirred and pushed slowly to his feet.

Trying again not to curse, Ronan once more opened his eyes, this time staring up into the smoking, hissing flames of a handheld rush light.

A few sparks dropped onto his chest and he brushed at them, frowning.

Now he knew what had disturbed Buckie.

He blinked. Then he raised a hand to wave away the smoke from in front of his eyes, half wondering if he'd wakened in the fires of hell.

Before he could decide, the rush light moved and he

saw Anice, the large-eyed slip of a serving lass, peering down at him. Her throat worked convulsively and her thin little face looked white as the moon.

"O-o-oh, sir!" she cried. "You must come at once! They've ravaged your bedchamber and—"

"What?" Ronan blinked again, the last dredges of sleep making it hard to think. "They who?"

The girl shook her head so rapidly that one of her thin black braids slipped from its pins. "I'm sure I dinna care to know," she wailed, and then Ronan *did* know.

He leaped from the pallet. "Lady Gelis," he demanded, snatching up his plaid. "Is she harmed?"

"Nae, sir, she's fussing about the fine victuals having been tossed out the window."

At the niche's opening, Buckie dropped onto his haunches and whined.

Ronan's eyes widened. "The repast I ordered? It was tossed out the window?"

Anice looked down at the rush light in her hand, unable to meet his eye. "Aye, that's the way of it, my lord. The lady thinks it was you what did it."

The Raven's stomach clenched, an icy dread streaking down his spine.

Whipping around, he dashed from the little niche to sprint across the darkened hall, making for the stair tower. He raced up the winding stairs, taking them two at a time and not even bothering to curse when, almost at the top, a misstep caused him to slam his bare toes full into one of the unyielding stone steps.

Pain shot up his leg and made his eyes water, but he didn't even scowl.

There'd be time enough for that later.

He hadn't expected the Holders to move so quickly.

Nor, he realized, hearing Buckie clumping up the stairs behind him, would he have believed how much Lady Gelis's safety meant to him.

Somehow, somewhere in the brief span of time since she'd first flashed him her brilliant smile and he'd dreamed of kissing her on some narrow strip of shingled shore, she'd become more than a well-born lass he wished to keep from harm.

She'd become important to him.

And that was a greater danger than the Holders and all their unholy mist wraiths combined.

A greater danger indeed.

And one he wasn't at all sure he could conquer.

He just knew that he must.

Chapter Six

✦

Prepared for the worst, Ronan burst into his bedchamber only to come to a skittering, undignified halt. Far from requiring rescue, Lady Gelis knelt calmly on the bearskin rug in front of the hearthstone, her delectably rounded bottom bobbing in the air as she jabbed an iron poker at a tidy pile of just-beginning-to-smolder peat bricks.

Ronan's eyes widened. He stared at her, well aware his jaw was slipping. His breath lodged in his throat, making it difficult to think. Worst of all, her flame-bright hair caught the fire glow and his fingers itched to touch the gleaming strands.

A man could lose himself in such silky, glistening tresses.

Lose himself and much more.

He frowned.

Praise the saints she hadn't yet undressed.

Even so, it took all his strength to tear his gaze from her jigging buttocks.

When he could, his pent-up breath left him in a great, gusty rush.

"What goes on here?" He strode forward, his stare pinned on the iron poker in her hand. "Who—"

"We both know who is responsible." Cool as spring rain, she set aside the fire poker and stood. "One glance was all I needed"—she made a sweeping gesture, turning—"though I vow anyone would have guessed upon seeing..."

She froze, her extended arm poised in midair. "Mercy!" she gasped, her eyes widening. "You're naked!"

"Bah. I—" Ronan started to deny it, but clamped his mouth shut instead.

He *was* naked.

He firmed his jaw and squared his shoulders, opting for a show of dignity. With each breath, he became more aware of the heavy plaid still clutched in his hand, the dry bits of rushes and herbage tickling the bare soles of his feet.

Lady Gelis was staring at him.

He could neither move nor speak.

Great folds of tartan dangled from his fingers to pool on the floor. Rather than throw the plaid around him, he'd simply snatched it up and run, so great had been his urgency to reach her side and ensure her safety.

Now he looked the fool.

"You forgot to don your plaid," she said, quite unnecessarily.

"Nae," Ronan lied, "I did not wish to waste time with such trivialities in my haste to see what was amiss here."

Her eyes twinkled. "There is naught amiss here that cannot be easily rectified."

Something in her tone warned him.

Against his better judgment, he glanced down, his worst dread confirmed.

Her jigging buttocks had affected him more than he'd realized.

Heat shot up the back of his neck. His vitals caught flame. After all, it wasn't every day such a desirable female stood staring at his man piece.

Nor could he recall having ever seen a more amused-looking female.

Or one who looked quite so triumphant.

Ronan cleared his throat, pride not letting him sling on his plaid too hastily. "Fair lady, you'd be hard-pressed to find a Heilander who doesn't sleep naked as the good God made him." He held her gaze as he spoke, forcing himself to use slow and careful movements as he covered himself.

The plaid finally in place, he dusted his hands, blessed composure his once again. "Anice woke me," he began, doing fine until he perceived a certain canine stare boring into him from the door.

Buckie lay sprawled across the threshold, his shaggy head resting on his paws, his milky eyes keener than Ronan had seen them in years.

Definitely unblinking, and perhaps even a wee bit accusatory.

Ronan let out a long breath. "Anice and my dog, Buckie, woke me," he started again, the correction earning him an appreciative tail swish. "Anice said the victuals I'd sent up for you went missing and that—"

"So you admit they were meant for me?" Gelis pretended to examine her fingernails. She had him now. "Not for the two of us?"

"I hardly see how that matters." He brushed at his plaid, looking more trapped than if she'd pinned him in a corner with a twelve-foot lance.

"It matters to me."

He lowered his brows, but said nothing.

Gelis felt her lips quirk.

"You needn't glower so," she said, allowing the quirk to flash into her brightest smile.

If anything, his mien darkened.

"I am not wroth with you. Even if I am not accustomed to discovering my evening repast has been tossed out the window." She gave a light shrug, willing her smile to blaze. "Truth be told, I am quite content."

The Raven humphed.

"That, sweet lass, I find hard to believe." He looked at her, his brows arcing. "'Tis impossible for you to be at ease. Here, in this place"—he planted his fists on his hips—"and with me."

She gave a soft laugh. "Nae, especially with you," she declared, her breath catching.

Her heart leaped, some wild devil inside her making her close the distance between them and poke a finger into his proud, plaid-draped chest.

"Truth is, I welcome challenges," she announced, jabbing her finger harder on each word. "I wouldn't be my father's daughter if I didn't. So-o-o"—she lifted a fold of his tartan, ran her thumb over its soft warmth—"I'll start by asking where you were going?"

"There are *challenges* here that would daunt even your redoubtable sire." He narrowed his eyes at her, deftly ignoring her question. "Were the window shutters bolted or opened when Anice brought you up here?"

"They were flung wide, the wet wind gusting into the room."

"And you shut them?"

"I did."

From the door, his dog shifted and resettled his bulk with a grunt.

The Raven shot him an irritated look. "The shutters," he continued when the beast stopped his scuffling, "did you notice anything unusual when you closed them?"

"You mean besides the whirling mist, denser than any I've ever seen, and my smashed feasting goods spread across the cobbles?"

"I mean . . . *anything.*"

"Perhaps the staves of what appeared to be a broken bathing tub?"

"The bathing tub as well?" His brows lowered. "You are certain?"

Rather than answer him, Gelis lifted her chin and fixed him with her best so-you'd-doubt-me stare. A look that she'd learned at her father's knee and that would have made a man of lesser mettle tremble in his boots.

The Raven remained unperturbed.

"You have peat ash on your face," he said, reaching to brush his thumb across her cheek.

A grave mistake, for as soon as he touched her, her attar of roses scent wafted up to befuddle him. He swallowed hard, tried not to breathe until he'd wiped away the smudge.

But the scent was too seductive.

He bit back a groan, the heady fragrance thrusting him right back into his dreams until he could feel her melting against him, lush, warm, and pliant. As if they still kissed, he could feel her lips parting beneath his and the hot silken glide of her tongue over and around his.

The scorching heat that had whipped through him, burning away his defenses until all that mattered was the wild frenzy of their passion.

As in the dream, he could hear the soft lapping of the wavelets on the shingled strand and feel the afternoon breeze lifting his hair. The sweet warmth of spring sunshine, and a blaze of desire such as he'd never known.

Not even with his long-dead first wife, Matilda.

Horrified, he jerked his hand from Gelis's cheek and wheeled away from her. His gaze fell at once on the great four-poster bed across the room, his anguish complete when he spied the piles of his folded clothes mounded on the bed's luxuriant furred coverings.

His grand black cloak and his opened, half-packed leather travel bag.

Rose attar perfume and lusty dreams forgotten, he spun back around, not at all surprised to find his bride standing with her hands braced against her hips, her amber eyes alight with challenge.

"Your money purse and wine skin are there." She flicked a hand toward the shadows behind the door.

Glancing that way, he saw more of his gear gathered in a neat little pile. His hauberk had been laid carefully over a chair, the mail shirt's silvery links gleaming softly in the candlelight, while his extra sword and sword belt rested on the floor, half-hidden in deeper shadow.

He refused to goggle.

And under no circumstance would he acknowledge the cold, hard knot beginning to pulse between his shoulders.

He did clench his hands.

With the exception of the wispy more-an-annoyance-than-a-threat mist wraiths that were wont to slither across window ledges and sometimes probe into the great hall, slinking along the tops of the trestle tables, none of the unholiness associated with Maldred the Dire's curse had ever dared to actually penetrate Castle Dare's walls.

Until now, he owned, the certainty of it tightening his chest.

"Those clothes and gear are my travel goods." He looked at her, some foolishly optimistic corner of his soul hoping she'd put his suspicions to rest, proving him wrong. "They were locked in my strongbox, my extra sword hidden beneath the bed."

"So Anice said when we found them strewn about the room." She held his gaze, her words taking his hope. "She also said that only you have a key to your strongbox."

A truth that made the matter all the more damning.

Not about to tell her so, he folded his arms. "And if I do?"

"Then you were in here before I came abovestairs," she informed him, sliding a glance at Buckie, who now occupied the entire threshold.

The dog's fluting snores indicated he slept, but a single eye, cracked no more than a sliver, followed Ronan's every move. One somewhat tatty-looking ear was lifted as well, craftily poised to catch every word.

Ronan's mouth twisted.

Gelis was watching him just as carefully, and he didn't doubt her ears were equally sharp.

"So you do not deny it?" She narrowed her eyes. "You were in here."

Ronan made a dismissive gesture, not trusting himself to speak.

He *had* been in the room earlier.

But only long enough to ensure that all her comforts were met. A fire laid, the bedding freshened, and his carefully planned feast-for-one spread upon the table.

An insult he'd hoped would see her riding away with her father at the morrow's first light.

A fool plan he now regretted, wishing he could simply tell her the whole fell truth. But even voicing such darkness could be dangerous, his thoughts too easily led down paths he didn't dare to tread.

"Well?" She raised a single red-gold brow. "At least admit that you were packing for a journey."

"Have a care..." He let the warning trail off, knowing it was too late.

The j-word had been spoken.

And Buckie had heard, as a glance at the door proved. Already, the old dog's other eye had popped open and his tail was thumping against the floor.

Ronan ignored him.

Lady Gelis flashed the beast a smile.

"Do not encourage him." Ronan frowned. It wouldn't do for Buckie to become attached to her. Or look forward to excursions he could no longer enjoy. "His hips are bad, so his days of adventure are over. His legs don't always support him and he falls. Buckie ne'er leaves the keep."

"Indeed?" She gave him a look that could've been interpreted as implying that Buckie's plight was his fault and had nothing to do with the beast's wobbly back legs.

Fighting the ridiculous urge to defend himself, Ronan wondered how everything had slid out of his control. He'd come abovestairs to see what had happened, possibly to defend Lady Gelis against whoe'er or whate'er had ravaged the bedchamber. Instead, he'd found her tending the hearth fire and the room already put to rights.

Worse, she asked questions he didn't care to answer and shot him looks that made him feel like a gangling, beardless laddie who'd just been caught with his hand down a kitchen lassie's bodice.

As if she knew it, she smiled at him.

Not a warm, adoring kind of smile as she'd given Buckie, but a *smug* one.

"Talking about your dog and that-which-you-don't-wish-mentioned-in-his-presence doesn't change that I know you were preparing for one." Her words explained the smugness.

Walking briskly to the bed, she picked up one of his folded tunics and placed it with a touch too much care in his opened travel bag.

"Eilean Creag is a busy place," she mused, reaching for another tunic. "There are comings and goings through all seasons. Some men wish my father's advice or to trade with him, while others plead aid or offer an alliance. The stream of visitors never ends."

She dropped the second tunic into the leather bag. "Do not think I am some light-minded creature unable to recognize a man's I-daren't-say-the-word kind of gear. Or" — she looked at him meaningfully — "when someone is in haste and must rush away before a task is completed."

Ronan's brows snapped together. "A MacRuari ne'er leaves any task unfinished. Nor do we run from aught."

He stepped closer to the bed — to her — a flash of pride whipping through him.

Glen Dare and his family might be blighted and cursed, but he loved both fiercely.

Nor was it for naught that each newly born MacRuari babe was fed a spoonful of clan earth as his first nourishment. As Torcaill had sung earlier, during the feasting, the tradition sealed the child's lifelong bond to his home glen.

Such as it was.

It remained theirs.

And there wasn't a MacRuari living, dead, or yet to be born who'd deny its pull. From the clan's dimmest beginnings, their ties to Glen Dare were unbreakable; their love of the dark woods, bog and moor, and the steep, mist-hung hills, deep and abiding.

Sacred.

As was their honor, something that seemed to weigh more heavily on him the longer he dallied in his new bride's fetching, rose-scented presence.

He shut his eyes, drew a tight breath.

Then, knowing he shouldn't, but unable not to, he seized her by the shoulders. "Hear me, lass, and I will tell you of Glen Dare's MacRuaris."

"Ooh, aye?" Her voice was a purr, soft and honeyed. "Mayhap there are things I could tell you!"

Ronan blanked his emotions, more than sure that she could tell him things.

Certain, as well, that he did not wish to hear them.

He let his gaze bore into hers, willing her to understand. "Anything a MacRuari does is done with deliberation and purpose, and always for the good of the clan." He tightened his grip on her, hoping to strengthen the truth of his words. "You err if you believe otherwise."

"Say you?" Her eyes sparked. "We both know there isn't a Highland chieftain in all these hills who wouldn't claim the same. I am more keen to hear why it is Mac-Ruari custom for their men to shun their brides."

"Nae, that is no' the way of—" Ronan broke off, guilt sweeping him.

He was shunning her, albeit for her own good.

"'Tis true I stayed away of a purpose this e'en," he admitted, frustration and remorse crowding him, making him speak as true as he deemed wise.

"Even so"—he strove for his most persuasive tone—"I had naught to do with the shambles you found upon entering this chamber."

Naught save having wished her gone.

A departure he'd still greet with gladness.

But a regret that made him release her as quickly as if she'd turned into a writhing, two-headed viper, eager to sink venomous fangs into him.

He choked back a bark of bitter laughter.

He was the carrier of poison.

He paused.

The room's increasing cold circled up his legs and higher, snaking ever tighter around his chest until he could scarce breathe.

"I suspect," he began, using a strength born of long practice, "that your arrival has stirred whate'er of Maldred's malignancy yet lingers."

Lady Gelis waved an airy hand.

"'Tis common knowledge there's a touch of darkness in every clan and glen in all broad Scotland," she returned, leaning close again. "The sweetest glade gives way to the blackest peat bogs and some of our bonniest lochs are said to be the haunts of the most ferocious water horses and bulls."

She drew a great breath, making her breasts swell. "Even my own fair Kintail is no stranger to ill-wishing and the evil eye! Many are the tales—would you care to hear some of them?"

Ronan sidestepped her, taking up a stance beside the hearth fire.

"Glen Dare's darkness is different, my lady."

She swung in his direction. "Perhaps not when viewed from another angle. My father says Robert Bruce once told him that any trap can be sprung—any ambush averted—if a man uses his wits and the land to best advantage."

Ronan's brows drew together.

She had him there. He wasn't about to argue with the wisdom of Scotland's greatest king.

Even so, he'd spoken the truth.

Leastways as much of Dare's sad truths as he wished to share with her.

Unfortunately, she looked anything but satisfied.

She looked ready to clamp her fist around his heart and squeeze hard until he revealed all his secrets.

Her every curve beckoned and enticed. The sweet tilt of her lips, plump and reddened, begged for kisses. And one of her braids was coming undone, leaving a welter of rippling, unruly red-gold curls to spill over her breasts, so tantalizingly displayed above her gown's deep-dipping bodice.

Ronan's jaw locked and his hands clenched at his sides.

His deepest self ached for her, filling him with a need that bordered on feral. He swallowed hard, his entire body tense and his heart thundering. Hot blood roared in his ears, blotting even the fierce howl of the wind.

Ne'er had he seen a more desirable female.

And ne'er had he wanted one less.

Even if the shunning of her would haunt him all his days.

So the lad wanted her.

There could be no denying it.

A dark-cloaked figure standing outside Dare's walls gave a great, gusty sigh, well pleased he'd lingered long enough to enjoy the fruits of his labor.

It hadn't been easy for one of his years to work a spell powerful enough to send not only feasting goods but an entire, brimming bathing tub sailing out a tower window.

The task had cost him greatly.

But he'd managed, and his immense satisfaction even stirred the midnight boughs of Glen Dare's dark pines and silent alders. The proud hills, so loved by Clan MacRuari, pretended not to hear, turning disapproving ears to the gloating wind.

And in the empty trough of the moon-washed glen, the late-night waters of the burn swirled and frothed, roiling with a cold deeper and more biting than the ancients e'er intended.

Ancients so old, their names had long been lost.

Save a venerable, persistent few.

He was one such, and he stepped out of the cloaking mist now, drawing as near to Castle Dare's walls as was prudent. He hadn't reached his sage and hoary age by

being foolish. His earlier feat had taxed him, the powerful
jolt of Maldred's saining spells still strong after so many
centuries.

More debilitating than he or any of his followers would
have believed, the pain sat deep in his bones, slowing his
gait and dulling his senses.

Tiring eyes already red and burning from exertion.

Not that it mattered.

The buffoons and drolls who called Dare their own
would soon pay for their vices. Naught but soot and ash
would be left to them, their sojourn with the treasure of
others ended by their own unwitting hand.

The figure almost smiled.

At long last the MacRuaris possessed a prize they'd
fight to keep.

The old man, because his heart was soft. And the
younger, their only true threat, because he desired the girl.

If that one lost his heart as well, the possibilities for
leverage were endless.

He need only bide his time.

This time the figure did smile.

Reveling in it, he lifted a bony long-fingered hand and
adjusted the cowl of his robes. The night was chill and
wet, the racing wind not good for one of his indeterminate
years. And despite his many powers, he'd yet to master a
spell against the elements.

Though that, too, would soon be possible.

As would...anything.

Once the Raven Stone was his again.

For the now, he angled his head to peer through
the gloom until his gaze found the dark bulk of Dare's
tower. As arrogant as the race, it soared high above the

castle's machicolated walls. Mist—in great part, his mist—curled around its impassive stones while the craftily narrow windows were shuttered and black against the night.

All, that was, but one.

It, too, was tightly closed, but faint yellow light gleamed through the shutter slats.

Focusing on those narrow slivers of soft, flickering light, the figure felt his heart begin to thud with anticipation. He breathed deep, his sharp sense of smell letting him catch a whiff of attar of roses even here.

That, and the stronger musk of man.

Clearly, they were still together.

More than pleased by the implication, the figure didn't even blink when a wind gust snatched his hood from his fingers and blew his long, white-maned hair across his face, the whipping strands stinging his eyes.

He'd enjoyed too many successes this night to pay heed to such a little nuisance. So he shoved back his streaming hair, smoothed his robes, and turned away from Dare's walls, eager to seek his bed.

He had a feeling his dreams would be most pleasing.

The doom of the MacRuaris was assured.

It was only a matter of time.

Chapter Seven

❧

Ronan stood by the hearthside, adjusting the fall of his plaid as surreptitiously as possible. His mind was a careful blank and his expression as stony as he could make it. Both talents he'd been honing for years. Unfortunately, he was less skilled in tempering his more lustful urges.

But a man's plaid was good for many things.

The voluminous folds perfect for hiding any unwanted problems that might arise.

Determined to avoid such a problem, he squared his shoulders and drew a long breath. In the time he'd needed to steel himself against Lady Gelis's charms, he'd come to a very important decision.

When the sad day arrived that Valdar was no more and Ronan took his place at the head of the clan, his first chieftainly act would be to forbid the wearing of low-bodiced gowns within Dare's walls.

A decree against full bosoms—in particular, those

with fetching nipples—would be even more pleasing, if impossible to enforce.

He almost smiled at the notion all the same.

Leastways until Lady Gelis took another dangerously deep breath and her decidedly pert and rose-hued nipples threatened to pop into view.

Ronan scowled at the prospect.

His plaid stirred.

Lady Gelis's breasts swelled even more.

"So-o-o . . ." She picked up her glittering green temptress bauble and fingered the thing as she eyed him. "Are you saying I now have two MacRuari men who wish me gone?"

Ronan blinked. She'd distracted him with all her deep breathing and bauble fingering.

"Two MacRuaris?" He wasn't following her. "Wishing you gone?"

She nodded. "You, by your own admission"—she flung out an arm to indicate the room—"and if I am to understand your suspicions about who was behind the ravaging of this chamber, your archdruid forebear. Mordred the Dire, may the saints rest his soul."

"Maldred." The bedside night candle hissed and guttered on the utterance. "Such was his name and I'd be surprised if you could find a saint—any saint—who'd deign to bless the dastard."

"Then I say he is to be pitied, not reviled."

Ronan's jaw slipped. "*Pitied?*"

Her head bobbed again. "Och, for sure, and I'd say so."

Entirely certain, she tilted her head, well aware that the golden light of a well-burning brace of candles was playing advantageously on her fiery tresses.

When the Raven's mouth tightened, she knew he'd noticed.

Pleased, she let her eyes twinkle.

She also looked at him, wondering when he'd notice that his oh-so-carefully-donned plaid was slipping down his shoulder. And what a fine shoulder it was. Broad, well-muscled, and gleaming in the firelight, its manly allure made it all too difficult to concentrate on some hoary MacRuari ancestor and his centuries-old curse.

Even so, she wanted to try.

"In the great hall this e'en, your druid sang that Mac-Ruari bairns are fed a spoonful of clan earth, sealing their love for kith and kin, the home glen," she began, watching him carefully. "Is it true?"

"So true as the morrow, aye."

"Can it be Maldred did not receive one?"

"For certes he was given such a token. Not heeding the practice would have seen the banishment, or worse, of the hen wife who helped birth him." He scowled, and the plaid dipped a bit lower, this time revealing an equally fine bit of hard, naked chest.

Something inside Gelis squeezed. Everything in her world seemed to sharpen and then recede until she saw only the fire-gilded expanse of the Raven's bare, beckoning skin. Looking at it set off a tingling flurry of warm, delicious flutters deep in her belly.

There, truth be told, and lower.

She shivered.

Her mouth went bone dry.

He was frowning at her, clearly mistaking the reason for her silence. The flush, she knew, was spreading across her breasts and inching slowly up her throat, soon to flame her cheeks a bright, glowing red.

She took a strengthening breath, forcing her mind off his chest and back to his maligned ancestor. "Could it be that bairns in Maldred's day were not yet given such spoonfuls of earth?"

He shook his head. "The ceremony is a clan bonding ritual older than the ringtailed lout himself."

"And it works?"

"You have already heard that it does." He yanked up his plaid, his scowl going even blacker.

Almost as black as the whirls of decidedly masculine chest hair she'd caught a fleeting glimpse of before he'd jerked his plaid back in place.

That accomplished, he pushed away from the table and began to pace. "The clan earth runs in our blood," he said, slanting a glance at her. "A MacRuari would be skinned, spitted, and roasted before he'd leave these lands."

"Then" — Gelis laid on her most triumphant tone — "it follows that a MacRuari wouldn't sunder them either. Not the glen or its people."

Ronan stopped in his tracks.

He almost choked.

"Maldred the Dire was no ordinary clansman. He cannot be measured against the rest of us. His legacy —"

"His legacy is a broken grave slab."

Every muscle in Ronan's body tensed and his mouth compressed into a hard, firm line.

Across the room, bright amber eyes flashed hotly.

Ignoring their heat, he picked up the fire poker and jabbed at the peats.

"Once, my lady, when I was too young to know better,

I tried to do something about Maldred's cracked grave slab." He kept his attention on the softly glowing peats. "Spurred by clan pride and a boy's innocence, I marched into the overgrown burial ground, determined to wedge the two pieces of weathered stone back together again."

"But you couldn't." She spoke the obvious.

"Nae, but that is no' the purpose of my tale."

He glanced over his shoulder at her, not surprised to see her jaw set stubbornly again.

"See you, I needed only three bold strides on that weedy, tainted ground before my right foot plunged knee-deep into a rabbit hole. The thing was hidden beneath a clump of tussocky deer grass." His fingers tightened around the fire poker. "I broke my ankle that day. The injury kept me from accompanying my father on a long-anticipated journey to Inverness."

He paused, remembering. "There were some amongst the clan elders who felt I'd been punished for daring to try to repair Maldred's gravestone. My own concern was more with losing out on the adventure of a foray into a bustling township. To a wee laddie who'd ne'er yet left this glen, it was a bitter disappointment."

Even more damning, when the break did not heal well, he was left with a painful limp that took him nearly a year of steely willpower and hard training to banish.

That, of course, he kept to himself.

And that, to this day, the ankle plagued him if he forgot himself and stepped wrongly. Almost feeling its dull throbbing now, he propped the fire poker against the hearth and turned to frown at his bride.

"Be it a broken tomb or a proud stronghold such as your father's Eilean Creag, men make their legacies," he said, blotting his mind to his wretched ankle. "Most times, they reap what they deserve."

"Say you?" Lady Gelis's eyes glittered all the brighter.

Indeed, were she a less prickly female, he might even suspect his tale had made her a bit misty-eyed.

Dewy-eyed for the lad he'd been.

Not the man he was.

A distinction that only worsened his mood.

Buckie chose that moment to prudently push himself to his feet and shuffle away, disappearing into the shadows of the fusty-smelling corridor.

Ronan scowled.

Would that he might escape so easily.

Behind him, one of the peat bricks popped with an uncharacteristically loud crackle. A shower of fiery, orange-red sparks puffed into the air, several of them finding the backs of his naked calves.

"Eee-ow!" He jerked, twisting to swat at his legs and almost losing his plaid in the process. He grabbed at the downward-slipping folds, certain he heard a burst of feminine laughter.

Hearty laughter, with no attempt made to stifle it.

But when he straightened, Lady Gelis was simply watching him.

The soft, doe-eyed look was gone. In its place, her lifted-chin, set-jawed look was fixed steadily on him.

"If your clan talespinners speak true, and as your own tale implies," she declared, twirling her bauble chain, "your ancestor sleeps in an untended tomb in a forgotten burial ground overrun with nettles and bracken."

Ronan's jaw tightened. "His grave is hardly forgotten, my lady."

It was a scar on the land.

"But it *is* neglected." She strode forward, not stopping until they stood nearly toe to toe. "As is the half-ruinous stone crest above the keep door. I saw it when we arrived, recognizing its age."

Ronan's fingers froze on his half-refastened plaid-knot. He'd forgotten the crest.

Ancient, cracked, and moldering, the thing was barely recognizable as a one-time heraldic shield. Wind, rain, and cold, along with the sheer weight of the ages, had blurred its details, leaving only worn and crumbled stone.

A forever remembrance of the destruction and ruin Maldred had wreaked upon the clan.

Upon him.

Him, and all those he'd foolishly allowed a place in his heart.

"Was the crest Maldred's?" Lady Gelis was peering up at him, her fingers doing a deft job of finishing his plaid knot. "It looks old enough to have been his."

Ronan expelled a slow breath. "Aye, it was his. He built this tower. Leastways the oldest parts of it. If clan tradition may be believed, he chose this site because an earlier pagan sacrificial circle once stood here."

"Indeed?" She patted the plaid knot, her fingertips just brushing his shoulder.

Ronan nodded, relief flooding him when she lowered her hands.

"Some clan elders believe the crest is carved on one of those ancient stones," he said, still feeling her warmth on his skin. "If their suspicions are true, the sacrilege may have been what originally brought Maldred into conflict with the Old Ones, earning their eternal wrath and damnation."

"Eternal damning is harsh."

"Misusing a sacred stone—for whate'er purpose—is an affront to the ancients. Only one as brazen as Maldred would have dared seize such a relic for a crest stone. I'm surprised you even noticed the thing." He looked at her, making certain his face showed no emotion. "Not many do."

"Perhaps they do not look clearly."

"And you do?"

She tilted her chin. "I see much, aye."

Ronan arched a brow.

An odd prickling at his nape warned that she meant more than his ancestor's age-pitted heraldic shield.

"There are things here you might prefer not to see, my lady. Glen Dare folk are cautious. They prefer not to stick their hands in wasps' nests."

"Wasps' nests?"

"So I said, aye."

He wasn't at all surprised when her expression went even more stubborn.

"Most hereabouts wouldn't cast an eye on Maldred's crest if their lives depended on it. Not even if you threatened to thrash their naked flesh with a switch made of thorny wood and stinging nettles."

"Be that as it may, I still find it a great sorrow to hear an ancestral grave likened to a...a wasp's nest." Her eyes still sparking, she leaned close.

So near that her breasts—and the infernal bauble and its slinky, double-looped chain—pressed into him. Her rose scent assailed him as well, the heady fragrance addling his wits and wearing down every last one of the shields he'd thrown up against her.

Clearly bent on bedeviling him, she remained where she stood, not budging an inch.

"There are things we must discuss, *Raven*." Her eyes gleamed and a swirl of rose-scented warmth seemed to slide around him, almost a caress. "Matters of great import that have naught to do with Maldred the Dire or the state this room was in when I came up here."

Ronan drew a breath, tried hard not to move.

Speech was out of the question.

His most damnable *bits* were reacting to her.

Mere stirrings, praise the saints, but if she kept taunting him, a full-fledged river of heat would soon pour into his loins and then he'd be hard-pressed to resist her.

Seemingly oblivious — or perhaps not — she lifted a hand to his face. "Look," she urged, "see what I can show you."

"Show me?"

She nodded. "You know my mother has the *taibhsear-achd*? I —"

"You have the same gift." He made the words a statement. "Torcaill said you did."

"He spoke true," she admitted, her chin lifting. "And sometimes, if a *taibhsear* touches someone, that person can see what the seer does."

Ronan swallowed, quite certain he didn't wish to peer into any such image.

Not now, not on the morrow, and not even next year.

Perhaps never.

But already she was pinning him with her gaze and resting her palm against his cheek. Her fingers slid down to touch his mouth, lingering there as the room suddenly darkened around them and he lost sight of her, seeing instead Maldred's blight of a crest stone.

"By glory!" He stared, but the thing was truly there, hovering before him.

No longer cracked and crumbling, the stone shimmered with a brilliance that hurt his eyes. The sculpted raven, its proud outline barely visible on the stone as he knew it, looked almost alive. Glistening feathers seemed to ripple in a distant wind, and two curving horns that he'd ne'er before seen appeared to rise from the bird's head.

But before he could focus on this wonder, she took her hand from his face and the fleeting image faded, disappearing as if it'd never been.

Ronan blinked.

He put his own hands to his head, pressed his fingers against his temples.

"I canna believe you did that." He looked at her. "How—"

She gave a light shrug. "I do not understand how or why such a wonder is possible. My mother warned me that it is so. 'Tis a marvel to be accepted, not questioned."

"I should like to speak of it!"

She smiled, her eyes glittering with some wild, inner fire that put two spots of red on her cheeks. "Och, aye, we need to discuss many things"—she glanced at her hand, then back at him—"though I vow Maldred wishes—"

"That cloven-footed he-goat is naught but moldering bones. He is beyond wishes."

"Has he told you so?"

"Nae. And I have no desire to ask him."

"Perhaps you should."

Ronan felt his brows shooting heavenward.

The notion of asking his long-dead ancestor anything was too preposterous to contemplate. Catching a glimpse into Lady Gelis's vision was one thing. Conversing with his forebears—especially Maldred—was something entirely different, and he wanted naught to do with the like.

Resuming his pacing—and at a clip that would keep even a fleet-footed MacKenzie damsel at bay—he shoved a hand through his hair and strove to find the best words to explain things to her.

"Be glad he is naught but bone and bad memories." He tossed her a glance as he marched past the windows. "His wishes, if you knew them, would—"

"All souls have wishes." She looked more peeved than enlightened. "Hopes and dreams never leave us, even when our bones are no more."

"Humph."

"'Tis true." She'd moved to stand by the hearth, her chin still stubbornly set and her arms folded. "If you call yourself a Highlander, you must know it."

Ronan bit back another snort.

He was more Highland than she knew. Frowning again, he increased his step, not about to tell her. Such things didn't need proving. Nor did he care to reveal that he'd seen more than his share of every string she harped on.

Hopes and dreams enough to fill a score of lifetimes. And bones—bones of loved ones—in such number he could scarce count.

"Do you think Maldred's heart didn't quicken to the same things you hold dear?" she persisted, proving she wished to torture him.

Bending, she snatched up a plump black peat brick from the creel by the hearthside and waved it in his direction. "The reek of peat smoke or the scent of heather, the howl of a winter wind and the crash of waves upon the shore, mist on the braes or a Highland moon sailing through wind-torn clouds."

She tossed the peat onto the fire and dusted her hands. "All those things filled his days just as they do yours. Enduring, beautiful things capable of squeezing the hearts of the most hardened amongst us. Such are the things that bind Highlanders to those that have gone before. Not our great dignity and pride, but our deep love of these hills. Maldred surely felt it, too."

"I am sure he felt a great many things." It was the best Ronan could do.

His head was beginning to pound.

"And"—she drew a breath, clearly not finished—"without doubt, he had wishes. Perhaps one of them was to be remembered more kindly."

Ronan smothered a word he'd not utter in front of a lady.

"You would think otherwise if you knew more about him. Greed and an unquenchable thirst for power were his only concerns." A gust of wind rattled the window shutters. "He believed he was immortal. Truth is, he was a malevolent old sorcerer who—"

One of the shutters came loose and cracked loudly against the wall.

Ronan went long-strided across the room and secured the banging shutter.

A task he executed too hastily, for when he yanked on the rain-soaked shutter, slamming it into place, the wretched thing pinched two of his fingers.

Gritting his teeth, he resisted the urge to howl in pain.

"Leave Maldred in the remote past where he belongs," he said as soon as he trusted himself to speak. "He is undeserving of your sympathy and"—his gaze lit on his leather bag, the neatly folded piles of his journeying gear lining the great four-poster bed—"if you would hear the truth of it, I was packing for a journey. But days—"

"A long one and far from here—judging by what I have seen." Disappointment flickered in Lady Gelis's eyes. "I knew it was true."

Ronan started toward her, one hand raised in denial. "'Tis no' what you think, lass. I packed—and unpacked—days ago. My travel goods were returned to yon strongbox long ere you arrived."

Doubt creased her brow. "But—"

"I cannot explain why my gear was strewn about the bedchamber." He grasped her upper arms. "I can only swear that I had no hand in it. And"—he drew a breath, not liking how the brightness in her eyes was making his chest hurt—"I will get to the bottom of it and ensure the like doesn't happen again."

He glanced at the empty table. "None of it."

"I believe you. Nor am I frightened here." She looked down at his hands holding her, then back up at him. "I also know you wouldn't intentionally hurt me."

Ronan released her at once and turned aside before she could see him wince.

The odd ache in his chest grew hotter, tighter.

She should be frightened.

Very frightened.

Instead, she slipped around him, her attar of roses scent floating about her like a fragrant cloud, her damnable green bauble glittering in the soft glow of the hearth fire.

Ronan reached to curl his hands around his sword belt, only to remember he wasn't wearing one.

He frowned, folding his arms instead.

She smoothed her skirts. Then, putting her hands on her hips, she placed herself just so that she effectively blocked his way to the door.

"Well?" She angled her head.

"We have naught else to speak of this e'en," he said, knowing it wasn't the answer she'd wanted. He knew, too, that the words would cut deeper than any sword.

But if he stayed any longer, he'd regret more than her mere presence.

Wishing it were not so, he turned to leave. "I'll order the house guard to patrol the corridor outside your door. Your night rest will not be disturbed."

"Wait."

The word fell between them, an iron weight around his ankle.

"I will not have any night's rest unless you tell me where you meant to go."

Ronan frowned.

She flicked a glance at his travel gear. "I am a curious woman."

An iron yoke seemed to settle onto Ronan's shoulders, joining the shackle at his foot.

He cleared his throat, risked one answer-seeking glance at the ceiling.

But the age-blackened rafters remained mute.

"It is the least you owe me." Lady Gelis was looking at him, her eyes intent. "If you have a lady love and were perchance setting off to be with her, then I would understand much."

"A lady love?" Ronan almost laughed.

She nodded.

"Nae, for truth, lass, you err."

"A woman is behind most things a man does." Her tone dared him to deny it. "A woman or land gain and wealth."

This time he did laugh.

If such a rusty-sounding grunt could pass for laughter.

"Ah, well," he owned, "you might just have the right of it. A woman was behind my travel plans, though no' for the reason you suspect."

One red-gold brow lifted, her amber eyes all attention. "Oh?"

"Aye." He spoke true. "Leastways in that the death of my second wife spurred my decision. It was after her passing that I began to consider making the journey to Santiago de Compostela in Spain, shrine of Saint James. I'd finally decided to go the day Valdar told me about you."

"You wanted to go on a pilgrimage?"

"To kneel at the shrine and collect my scallop badge, aye."

"I have seen such men. My mother is known for welcoming them. She offers a fresh pallet for the night and a warm meal to those who pass through Kintail. But you..." The words tailed away on a tinge of skepticism. "You do not have the look of such a man."

"Be that as it may, I was committed to going." He started toward the door.

She followed. "Why?"

Ronan hesitated, ran a hand through his hair. "I thought — hoped — that if —"

"Ahhh, now I understand." Something that sounded like pity shaded her voice. "You believed such a pilgrimage would ease your grief." Her eyes went all soft again. "How you must have loved your wife to suffer her loss so deeply. An arduous journey to the ends of the world..."

Ronan stiffened, the words piercing him.

He did not deserve her sympathy.

"There are few things a man will not do when his heart makes the demand."

"I am sorry. I wish—"

He raised a hand, staying her when she moved to step closer. "You have had a tedious journey yourself. Rest now and we shall talk on the morrow."

Just not about the late Lady Cecilia.

Looking as if she meant to do exactly that, Lady Gelis drew a breath to speak, but Ronan turned and left the bed-chamber before she could.

He closed the door behind him, striding no more than six paces down the dimly lit passage before pausing beneath a high-set arrow slit. Chill night air streamed through the narrow opening and he leaned his back against the wall, lifting his face to the welcoming draught.

Feeling worn and empty, he flattened his hands against the cold damp of the tower stones, seeking strength from their solidity.

Lady Gelis's words still rang in his ears.

His head throbbed with the way she'd looked at him, her unwanted compassion echoing even here in the shadows of the corridor.

For a maid so gifted as a *taibhsear*, her perception had failed her sorely where his late wife was concerned.

He hadn't loved Lady Cecilia.

Not even a shred.

His hands clenched against the wall. Try as he had, theirs was a match forged in hell, and he'd despised her almost from the first.

Even more damning, he'd killed her.

Chapter Eight

❧

Two things became immediately clear to Gelis when she wakened early the next morning.

First, and most disturbing, she was alone.

Her bed—nae, the Raven's massive oaken four-poster— nearly swallowed her whole. She eyed the broad expanse of sumptuous coverings and furred throws, not missing that they were barely rumpled. And of the sea of goose down pillows massed along the elaborately carved headboard, hardly a one proved disturbed.

Only the pillow she herself had slept on.

Her late-night hopes that the Raven might return during the small hours, slipping silently into the bed to ravish her, had been for naught.

She pushed herself up on her elbows, puffed a tiny goose feather off her cheek.

Then she frowned.

What should have been the most glorious morning of

her life was remarkable only in that she'd wakened without Arabella's snores ringing in the day.

Not that her oh-so-perfect sister had e'er believed that she made such ghastly nocturnal music!

Gelis knew.

She also knew she needed to make haste.

Clear and clean morning air was streaming in through the still-closed shutters. And the dim gray light just beginning to dispel the room's shadows indicated she'd slept longer than had been wise.

Her second realization wouldn't suffer fuzzy, sleep-addled wits.

Seducing Ronan MacRuari wasn't going to be a walk through the heather.

She'd need more than bouncing green love-baubles and scandalously dipping bodices.

Fortunately, she had a plan.

And she was more than ready to set it in motion.

Heart thumping, she scrambled down from the great bed's high mattress and hurried across the rushes to a little oaken table in the far corner.

Naked, but too excited to mind the chill that was raising gooseflesh on her skin, she eyed the grooming goods set neatly before her.

Someone, likely the large-eyed girl, Anice, must've slipped into the chamber only a short while ago and had obviously taken great care to please.

The provided amenities were no less fine than those she was accustomed to at Eilean Creag. A large bowl, a drying cloth, and a ewer of fresh bathing water awaited her morning pleasure. Best of all, a small earthen jar of her own rose-scented soap had been placed on the table as well, and she dipped her fingers into it quickly, eager to rush through her ablutions and be on her way.

Already, she could hear a great bustle stirring in the bailey below. Trumpet blasts, men's shouts, and the clank of armor filled her ears. The snorts and whinnies of restless, hoof-stamping horses reached her as well, that great ringing clatter a sure sign that her father and his guardsmen were readying for imminent departure.

At the thought, her breath snagged and she clapped a hand to her throat. An awful tightness spread through her chest, and for one wild, crazy moment, scenes from her life as she'd known it up till now flashed before her.

Not *taibhs*, images called forth from her gift, these images were ripped from her heart.

She closed her eyes, the memories so clear she could almost reach out and touch them.

Her father, with his oh-so-commanding presence, almost larger than life, always plaid-wrapped and sporting his sword, would remain her forever hero. Her mother, *Saint Linnet* to all who knew and loved her, beautiful still, and the most caring soul she knew.

Even Arabella, so prim, serene, and—at times—so vastly annoying. Telve and Troddan, too. Her father's enormous, impossibly shaggy, and best-loved dogs, always begging ear fondles and treats. Eilean Creag itself whirled across her mind's eye, her beloved home filling her vision until her eyes burned and blurred.

"Pah-phooey!" She blinked furiously, swiping at her cheek before she did something unthinkable.

MacKenzies didn't cry.

And she wasn't about to spoil that long-held tradition.

Ignoring the stinging heat making it so difficult to see,

she hurried to her nearest coffer of raiments and flung open its lid. She grabbed the first gown she closed her fingers on, then dashed about the room, snatching up a few other necessities she'd let carelessly fall to the floor as she'd undressed the night before.

"*Cuidich' N' Righ!*" The MacKenzie battle cry split the morning. "*Save the king!*"

Gelis started.

Her fingers froze on the gown she'd been wriggling into, its finely wrought folds of bright blue and gold gathered in bunches about her hips.

"*Cuidich' N' Righ!*" Her father's powerful voice sounded again, this time quickly followed by the enthusiastic echoes of his men.

Even Sir Marmaduke's English-tinged roar.

Panic rising, she yanked up her gown, thrusting her arms into the sleeves.

The war cry was all she'd needed to hear.

MacKenzies only used the slogan in battle or when on the verge of an important leavetaking.

Nae, she corrected herself, in the very moment of such a farewell.

"O-o-oh, wait!" She dashed about, searching for her shoes. "You canna leave yet!"

Thrusting her fingers through her tangled, unbound hair, she concentrated, willing herself to remember where she'd pitched her wretched footgear.

But the answer didn't come.

And her bluidy *cuarans* were nowhere to be seen.

"Hell's bells and damnation!" She whirled in a circle, scanning the floor rushes, the great bearskin rugs scattered here and there.

Desperate, she dropped to her knees and peered beneath the bed, seeing naught but a welter of dust balls and smelly, matted rushes.

"Arrgghhhh! So be it!" Frustration welling, she leaped to her feet and ran from the room.

Any who looked askance at her because her hair tumbled loose to her hips and no shoes adorned her feet could, well...they could just take a flying leap into the nearest and most ripe dung pit!

A particularly vile and stinky one.

There were, after all, more important things in life than perfectly dressed hair and...shoes!

Feeling better already, she sprinted along the dimly lit passageway and tore down the winding turnpike stair, not stopping until she raced through the darkened great hall and burst onto the keep's outer stair.

A thin drizzle of rain greeted her.

That and utter chaos.

Crowded and torchlit, the bailey swarmed. Stable lads dashed hither and thither and MacRuari guardsmen lined the battlements, their steel glinting and their expressions somber. Her father's men were already mounted, the whole illustrious lot of them gathered near the entrance to the gatehouse pend, banners snapping and spirits high.

Everywhere, dogs barked and chickens squawked. A loose boar, escaped from his pen, ran underfoot, his zig-zag path across the cobbles increasing the madness. His curling tusks gleamed in the morning light while his squeals and grunts only made the castle dogs bark all the louder.

Most damning of all was the great ear-splitting screech of Dare's iron-spiked portcullis clanking upward, the creak of wood as the heavy, double-hinged gates swung wide.

"No-o-o!" She bounded down the steps, her heart's wild hammering a great roar in her ears until she saw her father—and *him*—sitting their mounts a bit to the side of the gatehouse, apart from the general hubbub.

Her father looked carved of stone. Braw and impossibly well-favored for a man of his years, the rigid set of his jaw and the way he held his shoulders would have sent her fleeing in the opposite direction did she not know what a loving heart beat beneath his fierce exterior.

Would that she could say the same for the Raven!

Looking equally tense, his bold stare blazed right at her, its ferocity almost burning her. Unblinking, he watched her, his dark eyes narrowed and his silky blue-black hair lifting in the breeze. His golden torque gleamed at his neck and he wore his great black travel cloak, the one she'd found tossed across a bearskin rug.

Garbed thusly, he reminded her so much of the raven of her visions that she almost stumbled on the stairs.

Chills rippled down her back and her senses sharpened. Her pulse leaped and her skin began to tingle, awareness of him singeing her.

A man should not be allowed to be so compelling!

So blatantly ... sensual.

His stare intensified and he seemed to grow larger, the bailey around him to dim and recede.

The air between them crackled, almost as if charged by trapped lightning. But then her uncle Marmaduke rode into view, his arrival shattering the spell.

He drew up beside her father and the Raven. Holding his sword a mite too casually, at least to the eyes of those who didn't know him, he watched the goings-on carefully, his scarred face revealing naught of his true emotions.

Save for a flicker of concern when he spied her tangled, unbound tresses; her bare feet flying over the slippery wet stone of the stairs.

Gelis's heart squeezed.

Once again scenes of home seized her.

She hitched her skirts, hastening down the last few steps much faster than she should have, caring only to reach her loved ones before it was too late.

Torcaill the druid was there, too.

Well mounted and looking proud, the ancient jabbed a tall walking stick into the air. His voice rose above the pandemonium, calling out blessings as the contingent of MacKenzie warriors spurred their beasts, surging as one through Dare's yawning gates.

Her father turned in his saddle to watch them go, his own great warhorse beginning to sidle and fret, clearly eager to be gone.

"Wait!" Gelis careened across the cobbles, dodging dogs and leaping over chickens. "You cannot go until—"

"Ho, daughter! I'm no' going anywhere—no' yet." Her father swung down from his steed as she drew near, striding forward to sweep her into his arms. "No' before I'm assured that you"—he threw a glance over his shoulder, his dark eyes narrowing suspiciously on the Raven—"passed a *satisfactory* night!"

Resplendent in his gleaming black mail and hung about with more steel than was surely necessary, he set her from him. "I'd hear the truth, lass." His gaze bored deep. "'Tis no' too late for you to return with us. Your uncle and I—"

"Ho, indeed!" Valdar's bearlike figure stepped out of the shadows. "I told you fine that all went well with them." He hooked his hands around his sword belt, looking pleased. "I saw the lad racing up the stairs to join her late last night—saw him with my own two eyes."

Sir Marmaduke lifted a brow, his doubt only increasing the old man's mirth.

Valdar wriggled his own brows in Sir Marmaduke's general direction. He hooted heartily, his great barrel-bellied girth jigging with merriment.

"Och, suffering saints save me!" he burst out, eyes dancing. "I saw it all, I did."

"You have a crafty tongue in that head of yours, Mac-Ruari." The Black Stag eyed him, clearly rankled. "Many sets of feet tramped up those stairs last night. That two of those feet belonged to your grandson means naught."

Gelis felt her face warm.

The Raven was still watching her, his gaze sharp.

"Means naught, eh?" Valdar rocked back on his heels. "Mayhap not that he ran up the stairs, I'll agree. 'Twas *how* he was running up them that makes the difference!"

His point made—leastways to him—he looked round as if awaiting accolades.

"Och, aye, Kintail," he announced, "hills rocked and the moon wept when that boy reached his bonnie bride's door last night!"

The heat staining Gelis's cheeks slid around to scald the back of her neck.

Her father's brows snapped together.

"Have done with such gabble, MacRuari." His tone was thunderous. "You're no' making sense. Dinna make me call you a blethering old fool."

Valdar laughed and slapped his thigh.

"Fool I may be," he boomed, his bearded face splitting into a grin, "but I'm man enough to ken that a young stirk doesn't go tearing up stairs nekkid unless he—"

"*Naked?*" Duncan MacKenzie roared with all his lung power. His hand flew to his sword hilt. "Saints, Maria, and Joseph! I'd have expected more of—"

"Caution, my friend." Sir Marmaduke's voice cut in. "They are handfasted—good as wed."

The Black Stag scowled, fixing his long-time friend with his most formidable stare.

"Hell's afire!" He flung back his plaid, his eyes blazing. "Why I have a brain in my head when I have you to constantly remind me of things that canna be changed, is beyond me! Besides, running naked up stairs, and on his way to greet a lady, is just—"

"He was naked save his plaid." Gelis raised her own voice. She just omitted that he'd held the plaid in his hand. "Valdar must not have gotten a good look at him. The stair tower isn't well lit."

Her father mumbled, cursing under his breath at no one in particular.

Valdar rubbed his hands together, beaming still. "A spirited gell, did I no' say so already?"

Ignoring him, Gelis gripped her father's arm. "Now who is being a *blethering old fool*?"

She leaned close, her voice low. "Or would you claim it isn't custom for men of these hills to go bare-bottomed beneath their plaids? Especially when within their own good walls and heading to their own bedchamber."

The Black Stag looked down at her, his mouth clamped tightly shut.

"And" — she lifted on her toes, speaking into his ear — "he had every right to enter that bedchamber — as well you know!"

"I'd know what riled you so greatly, you'd come hallooing down here with your hair undone and no shoes on your feet." He jammed his hands on his hips, took in her dishevelment. "If he —"

"He had naught to do with my appearance this morn — you did." Gelis tossed her head, flipping her hair over one shoulder. "I heard our clan battle cry and thought you were leaving —"

"Havers, lass." He grabbed her, pulling her against him for a swift embrace. "You should ken I'd ne'er have left without seeing you. I knew you'd be down —"

"But the war cry — I heard it."

"To be sure, you did." He released her, his expression lighter.

Almost as if he was going to laugh.

But he caught himself, lowering his voice instead, "I only bellowed the war cry to put the fear o' God in this pack of cloven-footed MacRuaris!"

Gelis stared at him, not knowing whether she should laugh or scold him.

"You never change, do you?" She spoke the words lightly, knowing her love for him shone in her eyes.

"My girl." His voice was rough, deep, and only for her. "Have a care with yourself, you hear?"

She nodded.

He said nothing else.

A muscle jerked beneath his left eye and she touched the place with her fingers, pressing gently until it stilled. A common trait shared by many MacKenzie males, the twitch made her breath seize, the sight of it reminding her of kith and kin she might not see again for many days.

Her beloved Loch Duich and the great hills guarding its shores; a land dressed in clouds, mist, and heather.

But Dare was her home now, so she swallowed against the lump in her throat, squared her shoulders, and prepared to bend the truth one more time.

"My night was good," she lied, lifting her voice so everyone present could not fail to hear her. "There is no reason for you to leave in anger or in doubt of my happiness."

"She speaks true, Kintail." The Raven appeared beside her. "Her night was a peaceful one."

No longer mounted, he looked between her father and his druid. That one, too, had dismounted and now hovered at the Raven's elbow. The ancient's long flowing mane glowed white in the bailey's torchlight, and he clutched his tall walking stick in a gnarled fist.

Her father glowered at them. "Then see you that all her nights are that, just!"

"I shall." The Raven took her father's hand in both of his, the gesture seeming to startle the older man. "I desire naught more than to know her well."

"Harrumph!" Valdar whacked his thigh again. "'Tis more to desire than—"

"And I suggest we be on our way," a deep voice interrupted him.

Sir Marmaduke again.

Mindful of her father as always, he'd surely recognized the telltale brightness beginning to show in the Black Stag's eyes, and no doubt, too, the way he'd started blinking more than was usual. For all his scowls and bluster, no one was worse at suffering farewells.

Proving it, he arched a contrary brow. "We'll leave when I am ready."

"'Tis best to be away anon." The Raven lost no time in siding with her uncle. "The mist through the glen will be at its lightest if we ride now," he said, casting a glance at the hovering druid. "If we dally —"

"Since when did a bit o' mist hinder a Heilander?" The Black Stag drew himself up, adjusting his plaid with a great flourish. "But I'll no' stand about saying soppy good-byes like a woman!"

The words spoken, he reached for Gelis, crushing her so hard against him she feared he'd cracked her ribs. But he released her as quickly, his misty eyes explaining the lack of a verbal farewell. Then he whipped around, vaulting up into his saddle before she could even catch her breath.

"We're off!" he shouted, already kicking his heels into his mount's sides, sending the beast racing for the yawning gatehouse pend. "*Cuidich N' Righ!*"

Gelis pressed a hand to her mouth, her throat too thick to call out to him.

Not that he would have heard her.

The Black Stag was already gone, the echoing thunder of his horse's hooves all that was left of him.

"He'll be fine." Her uncle slung an arm around her, pulling her close. "See that you are. It would break your father if aught happened to you."

"Nothing will."

Nothing except happiness, she added in silence, willing it so.

He gave her a quick nod. Something in his eyes made her think he'd heard the unspoken words. But before she could decide, he, too, was striding away.

Swinging up on his horse with no less style than her father, he whipped out his sword, raising it high. "*Cuidich N' Righ!*" he yelled, charging after her father, his cry loud in the mist-hung morning.

"Save the king," Gelis returned, her voice catching.

She blinked hard and swiped a hand beneath her eyes, somehow unable to see her uncle's receding back as he rode away. Drifting wet mist dampened her cheeks, stinging her eyes and spoiling her view.

"They are good men. My sorrow, lady, that the parting is difficult for you."

Gelis started, whirled around.

He was at her side again.

Magnificent in his black cloak, he towered over her, his midnight gaze much too intense and his proximity more than disturbing.

Gelis swallowed, any words she might have said lodging firmly in her throat.

So greatly did he affect her.

Something flickered in his eyes then, and he lifted a hand, bringing it almost to her cheek as if to dash away the dampness she was trying to so hard to ignore.

But before his fingers touched her, he lowered his hand, turning away so swiftly she wondered if he'd even reached for her at all.

Indeed, she blinked and found herself alone.

From somewhere, she heard the hollow clatter of hooves on cobbles, the sound moving away from her and into the mist and dark beyond Dare's walls.

Even Valdar was nowhere to be seen, though she couldn't blame him for seeking the comforts of his hall on such a chill, damp morn.

Not now that all the excitement was over.

But then, as she turned to make her own way back into the keep, she did spy another soul remaining.

Buckie.

And the sight of him caused her heart to wrench.

The dog sat in the lee of the gatehouse wall, staring fixedly into the shadows of the tunnel-like pend. His head was lowered, his ears hanging, and his great plumed tail flat and unmoving against the wet cobbles.

"Buckie!" Gelis called to him, but his only response was a single twitch of one tatty-looking ear.

"Come, old boy," she tried again, crossing over to him. She stroked his head, laid on her most coaxing tone. "I'll give you a fine meat-bone to chew beside the fire."

He looked up at her then, his milky eyes sad.

"Och, Buckie, please..."

But the dog refused to budge. With a pitiful groan, he returned his attention to the empty gatehouse pend, once more ignoring her.

"You love him that much, eh, Buckie?" Gelis bit her lip, shoved a mist-dampened curl off her brow.

She also blinked hard, fighting another ridiculous attack of the stinging heat that seemed wont to jab at the backs of her eyes this morn.

"As you will then, laddie, I'll leave you be." She gave the dog one last head-and-ears fondle, then turned and strode resolutely across the bailey.

Gathering up her skirts and lifting her chin—just in case anyone was watching her—she mounted the keep stairs, ascending them with a studied grace that would surely have impressed her sister.

She spared a glance at Maldred's heraldic shield as

she neared the landing, but in the gray morning light, the stone's ancient engravings appeared even more worn and age-smoothed than before.

Squinting up at the thing, she could barely make out the lines of the raven's sculpted wings.

No matter.

She reached for the hall door's heavy iron latch, letting herself into the warmth and firelit coziness of the great hall. The day was young, and it was time to see to the first stages of her seduction plan.

But first she needed to find her shoes, do something with her hair, and then make a quick visit to the kitchens.

If the fates were on her side, Ronan MacRuari would learn the mettle of a MacKenzie woman.

And that she—Gelis MacKenzie—wasn't one to accept defeat quietly.

As Gaelic winds blow, strong and fey, about the time Gelis hurried up Castle Dare's winding turnpike stair, her mind busy with her *plan*, another soul bustled about a tiny, thick-walled cottage on the Hebridean isle of Doon.

That sweet isle, little more than a deep-blue smudge against silver-misted skies, was a different world. A nigh-mythical place that—to most—proved difficult to reach due to the isle's high black cliffs and the treacheries of its surrounding waters.

The black skerries with teeth sharp as a razor's edge and rip tides capable of claiming the most stout, well-manned sailing vessel.

Truth be told, those who were granted access to Doon's golden-sanded shores had only the good graces of Devorgilla to thank.

Bent, grizzled, and slow of gait, but with twinkling

blue eyes that defied her age, the far-famed wise woman of Doon was selective in whom she called friend.

Likewise, she made a formidable foe.

And she it was, Devorgilla of Doon, who unwittingly or otherwise, now mirrored Gelis's circular ascent up Dare's winding stair tower.

Even if the crone's circuitous path only took her round and round the tidy, peat-smoke-smelling confines of her cozy, low-ceilinged home.

As a good, nae, as the most revered *cailleach* in all the Highlands and the Isles, she wasn't just hobbling round her central hearth fire.

O-o-oh, nae.

She was scuttling along *deiseil*, circling her fine smoldering peat fire in a sunwise direction. She chuckled to herself as she went, taking care to croon to the little red dog fox trotting along in her wake.

The wee fox, Somerled by name, knew better than any that the crone's mind was just as busy that morn as was Lady Gelis's in distant Glen Dare.

Devorgilla pressed a hand against her hip and glanced at him as she passed her cottage's two deep-set windows, her wizened face wreathing in a smile when the sharp-eyed fox swished his thick, white-tipped tail.

Her faithful companion and helpmate for some years now, he understood her well.

She winked at him, pleased when he flicked his tail once more.

"Ach, laddie, we have much to celebrate this morn, eh?"

Without halting her shuffling black-booted feet, she snatched a twist of dried meat from a small wooden bowl on her table and tossed the tidbit to the little fox.

She cackled with glee when he leaped in the air, catching the treat before it fell to the flag stoned floor.

"*Guid,*" she gushed, watching him fall into place behind her again, prancing along as if he hadn't just performed such a bold and dashing maneuver.

She, too, felt nimble just now.

Power sizzled through her bones and lightened her heart. And though she wouldn't own it—the Old Ones frowned on those who boasted—she was almost sure even her finger- and toenails tingled with magic.

So she continued on her way, mumbling blessings and indulging in a wee bit of humble if well-deserved self-praise.

'Twas well enough earned.

If she dared say so herself.

Her third rounding of the cottage's central hearth fire completed, she paused. She raised her hands, palms upward, her gaze following her black-sleeved arms but seeing much more than her ceiling's blackened, herb-hung rafters.

Then, when her palms began to warm and pulse with the Old Ones' benevolence, she lowered her arms. Well satisfied, she turned her attention to the steaming cauldron hanging on its great iron hook above the pungent, earthy-sweet smolder of the peats.

Unable to help herself, another gleeful cackle—or two—rose in her throat.

She didn't even attempt to stifle them.

Even though her excitement and bustling was clearly a great botheration to Mab, the tricolored cat curled in the exact middle of Devorgilla's sleeping pallet and pretending disdainfully that it was just another ordinary Doon morn.

Not that any day on that cliff-girt, sea-bound isle could be called the like.

Devorgilla wagged a finger as if to emphasize the point.

Her wee fox lifted a paw in absolute agreement.

"We showed those *mist wraiths*, eh, Somerled?"

The fox's golden eyes glittered.

"Banished them with a mere wriggle of my fingers, we did!"

Chortling still, the crone demonstrated. Her bright eyes full of merriment, she thrust her hand into the cauldron's steam and twitched her fingers, causing the drifts of steam to shift and waver.

"Mist wraiths—fie!" She withdrew her hand. "Let them try to rise again. Perhaps next time I shall tie them all in knots!"

She nodded to herself, very much liking the idea, but set the possibility aside for the moment.

Other chores and duties beckoned.

Stooping to the side, she plunged her hands into a large wicker creel, retrieving a handful of plump, waiting-to-be-smoked herring.

A gift from Sir Marmaduke Strongbow and his lady wife, Caterine, but originally from Glenelg's joy woman, Gunna of the Glen, the prized fish needed to be hung one by one to a taut-stretched drying rope she'd affixed across the modest breadth of her cottage.

With a practiced eye, Devorgilla set about her task, making sure the choicest specimens were placed just above her e'er-burning peat fire.

Herring thus cured would be carefully guarded. Each one stashed away as delicacies of great worth, only produced when guests of particularly high standing came to call.

"Noble folk the like of the Black Stag's daughter and her raven," she announced, slanting a proud glance at Somerled as she fastened another fine and weighty herring to the string above her fire. "They'll no doubt wish to thank me, sail to Doon bearing gifts and oblations..."

She let the words tail off, preferring to glory in how easily she'd banished the mist snakes.

How one stern look and a mere wriggle of her knotty-knuckled fingers had sent the foul slithering creatures scurrying back to the hell whence they'd come.

"O-o-oh, aye, Somerled," she skirled, snatching up another fat and glistening herring to hang in the cloud of steam gathering above her cauldron, "the flow of the tides and the currents aren't strong enough to hinder Devorgilla of Doon's powers!"

"Fool woman!"

The powerful voice came from within the cauldron steam.

"Gaaaaa!" Devorgilla jumped.

The fish went flying from her fingers.

"Cease meddling with matters beyond your ken!" A towering dark-robed figure glowered at her from the swirling vapor.

Glaring fiercely, he scowled down his long nose, his white-maned hair whipping in an unseen wind as he raised an arm and shook a great, silver-glowing staff.

Devorgilla lurched backward, toppling the herring creel.

Somewhere behind her, Mab hissed and Somerled barked.

The figure waved his staff more vigorously. A shower of blindingly brilliant silver-blue sparks and spangles sprayed everywhere, lighting the cottage as if it were noontide on a bright midsummer's day.

"Be warned, woman!" The figure's eyes fixed on her, penetrating. "Try such foolery again and I'll do more than just frighten you!"

"Frighten me? Devorgilla of Doon?" Some sliver of her earlier pride made her shake out her black skirts. She jutted a somewhat bristly chin. "Be that the style of you, then? Preying on old, helpless women?"

Somerled bumped her leg, lending support.

For a moment, the figure looked almost nonplussed.

But then his frown returned and he aimed his staff at the spilled herring. Speaking a spell darker and more ancient than any of her own, he touched the end of the walking stick to the toppled creel, turning it and the precious fish into a charred clump of smoking black goo.

Somerled's brush shot straight upward, his snarl protective.

Devorgilla placed a black-booted toe over her little friend's paw, staying him before he did anything foolish.

"Aye." She bobbed her grizzled head, her eye on the interloper. "Preying on helpless old women...and spoiling their stores!"

The figure leaned close, his white head and his ancient, robe-draped shoulders looming out of the cauldron's mist. "I see no helpless female but a *foolish* one! Be glad I came to counsel you before your ill-placed interference causes more harm than good!"

He turned a meaningful look on the ruined herrings.

"There are those who would do the like to you! And those you hold dear."

Straightening, he jabbed his staff at the charred creel once more, this time restoring the basket and the herring to their former condition.

"Heed me if you are wise!" He looked at her, his gaze fierce. "Leave any reckonings to those more able."

Devorgilla huffed.

Putting back her admittedly thin shoulders, she started to argue, but already he was fading. The cauldron's steam whistled and swirled, closing around him, blotting him from view.

"Stay away from Dare..."

The words came as if from a great distance.

They echoed around the tidy little cottage until that warning dwindled, too, leaving Devorgilla and Somerled alone once more.

Mab—Devorgilla was sure of it—would be somewhere far out on the moors by now.

Safe, and seeking a comfortable bed.

"But we shall not be scared off, eh, Somerled?" She leaned down to pat the fox's head, alarmed to see that her hand was trembling.

"Come, come, my little friend," she cooed, hefting the creel of herrings onto her hip and hobbling toward the door. "We have much yet to do."

Above all, she needed to wash the herring—and the creel—with water from her special sacred well. Whether the basket and the fish looked fully *unspelled* made no difference whatsoever.

The figure had wielded some hoary magic with his spark-spitting staff, and she wasn't one for taking chances.

Nor would she do any further finger wriggling.

Instead, she opened her door and stepped out into the chill morning. Not quite sunrise, a fine silver-blue haze shimmered across the glade surrounding her cottage.

Unfortunately, the eerie luminosity reminded her of their *visitor*, and she shivered, not liking him or his warnings.

"*Counsel*, he called it," she scolded, shifting the creel to her other hip. "Counsel-schmounsel, I say!"

Trotting along at her side, the little fox slanted a glance up at her, all hearty agreement.

"And," she added, encouraged, "there's no reason we canna use some other means to help our charges, eh?"

She paused halfway across the glade and set down the creel, just to rest her back. The thing was heavy and, truth was, she was getting too old for such onerous chores as lugging full baskets of herring to her well and back.

Devil-blast the long-nosed, white-maned buzzard who'd made such a trek necessary!

"Call me a *foolish woman*, indeed!" Pressing both hands against the small of her back, she stretched. She rotated her shoulders and rolled her neck, her angry gaze on the early morning sky.

A few stars still glimmered, distant and frosty, while a crescent moon yet hung above the tops of the alders and birches ringing her circular glade. And far below Doon's cliffs, out across the still-dark waters of the Hebridean Sea, the tides were running fast and pale gray light was just beginning to edge the clouds.

Not that she cared—now—if the sun ne'er broke the horizon this morn.

She had more important things to do.

"Ach, Somerled." She snatched up the herring creel with a deal more vigor than before. "Now I know what must be done."

The little fox cocked his head, eyes bright.

Waiting.

Eager as ever to do her bidding.

Pleased, and with a decidedly light spring in her step, Devorgilla led the way to her special well, her wee help-mate matching her hurrying strides.

And just before they reached the well, Devorgilla cackled again.

Their magic-staff-swinging visitor, all piercing eyes and wild-tossing, white-maned hair, had done more than he'd ever intended.

Far from simply *warning* her, he'd shown her what she'd overlooked till now.

And she intended to take full advantage.

Whether it pleased the old goat or not.

Chapter Nine

❖

Gelis stood in the middle of Castle Dare's great kitchens, her hands fisted at her hips, unwilling to believe that her *plan* would shatter on the will of one stiff-necked, nae-saying ox of a man who called himself Dare's master cook.

To her way of looking at it—at the moment, anyway—he appeared as unbending as the thick stone columns supporting the kitchens' high-vaulted ceiling.

He certainly seemed to have his mind set on vexing her.

With one notable exception, rarely had she seen a man so utterly unmoved by her best dimpled smile and kindest morning greetings.

Nor did he seem overly appreciative of her rose attar perfume. Not that the delicate scent was noticeable against the stronger kitchen smells of roasting meat, simmering stews, and onions.

So many onions!

The great pile of them made her eyes burn, and she stepped farther away from the table where two young boys busied themselves chopping the odoriferous bulbs.

Unfortunately, the sharp bite of *onion air* wasn't so easily avoided.

Not if she wished to enlist the cook's aid.

Doing so required suffering the kitchens, pungent as the great groin-vaulted area was.

She bit her lip and tried not to breathe too deeply. She also stifled the urge to tap her foot.

Showing annoyance would get her nowhere.

So she eyed the cook carefully, focusing all her thoughts on winning his favor.

Affectionately dubbed Hugh MacHugh, or so she'd heard, the double name reflected his extraordinary size.

And he *was* incredibly large.

Ranging head and shoulders above most men and making up nearly as much in breadth and girth, his great bulk dwarfed even the vastness of the huge, arched roasting hearth looming behind him.

Gelis kept her chin lifted all the same.

Hugh MacHugh would have a chink somewhere.

Most men did.

And those who didn't weren't worth the bother.

So she narrowed her eyes and kept her perusal appraising.

There had to be something that would get her past his head-shakings and lock-jawed denials.

Not nearly as old as she would have expected, Hugh MacHugh appeared genial enough otherwise.

Clear blue eyes, twinkling and bright, watched her from beneath a high forehead, smooth if a bit wary.

Autumn-bronze hair graced his brow, if the carefully combed strands were a bit wispy. And he sported round apple-red cheeks and a curling copper beard, obviously his pride.

He was pulling on that beard now.

Yanking on the glossy rose-red curls as he wagged his head, tsk-tsking her every request.

"Nae, it canna be done, my lady." He folded massive, well-muscled arms across his chest. "In all my days, I have ne'er gone against Lord Raven's wishes."

He looked at her, his red-bearded chin outthrust.

Gelis took a step closer to him. The reek of onions and simmering beef pottage swirled around her, as did the pungent smell of fresh fish packed in barrels of seaweed and brine.

"But you have the goods here," she wheedled, lifting a hand to count the delicacies on her fingers. "They've not yet been returned to the larder."

Hugh MacHugh grunted.

His arms remained firmly crossed.

"See you for yourself"—Gelis pointed to the heavy oaken worktable forming the centerpiece of the kitchens— "is that not the selfsame joint of roasted mutton, platters of which were sent to my room yestere'en?"

A crimp appeared in the cook's fine, high brow.

"The scent still lingered in the air." Gelis twitched her nose, demonstrably. "'Twas the same roasted mutton I can smell now."

She flicked a glance at the savory evidence. "Ah-h-h, yes," she observed, letting her nose quiver again. "I am quite sure of it. The seasonings, see you..."

The crimp in the cook's brow became a crease.

Gelis waved a hand, silencing him when he opened his mouth to protest.

"And there, on the trestle table by the far wall"—she whirled in that direction—"are those not the spiced salmon pasties prepared to tempt the Raven's palate?"

Hugh MacHugh's tight-drawn lips said that they were.

"Or there…" She trailed off, thrusting out an arm to indicate a bowl of jellied eggs and a linen-draped platter that she suspected held Hugh's own prized honey cakes, the tasty delicacies dusted with ginger.

She lifted a brow. "Are those not leftover goods? Victuals now destined for the castle dogs?"

The cook shuffled his feet, unable to meet her eye.

Sensing victory, she went to the table and lifted the edge of one of the cloth-draped bowls.

"Ah-h-h…" She nodded thoughtfully. "More than enough for your lord's hounds and any empty-bellied beggars who might come calling at the postern gates!"

To her surprise—or not—Hugh MacHugh began to flush.

He looked down, nudging a surprisingly small foot against a crack in the kitchen's stone-flagged floor.

"I, too, would have relished such a feast." Gelis pressed her luck. "I know you ken I was robbed of such enjoyment—as was your lord."

The cook's head snapped up, his pink-tinged flush turning scarlet.

"I told you, my lady—"

"The Raven's wishes, I know." Gelis picked up a stew ladle, pretending to examine it. "Tell me," she ventured, setting the thing back down, "has he expressly forbidden me to explore my new home?"

"With surety, nae." Hugh pulled a length of cloth from beneath his belt and dabbed at his glistening brow. "He only ordered that you are not to leave the keep unescorted."

"And I shall not." Gelis pounced. "A score of your lord's best guardsmen shall accompany me," she improvised, wondering if she'd dare ride out alone at all after making such a false claim.

" 'Tis true," a feminine voice spoke from the door to the wine cellar.

Anice.

She stepped into the kitchens, a clutch of willow bands in her work-roughened hands, her large-eyed gaze on the cook.

"The Raven's men await her now—this moment," she said, and Gelis hoped only she heard the tremor in the girl's lie. "They're gathered outside the gatehouse."

Hugh scratched his ear, clearly undecided.

In the corner, Hector pushed up off the stool where he'd been sorting peas. Quiet until now, he came forward, his chest puffed and his new *sgian dubh* peeking up from the top of his left boot.

He paused beside a pile of empty wicker baskets and coiled ropes. "I heard the Raven say so myself," he declared, not batting an eye. "The lady may go where she pleases."

"Ha." Hugh MacHugh wasn't fooled.

Indeed, he was a great towering pillar of suspicion.

But something in his aspect altered.

A trace of indecision—or *softening*—as his gaze flitted between Anice and the lad.

Most especially when he looked at the girl.

Striding over to her, he snatched the willow bands and tossed them into a corner.

"I dinna believe a word either of you are blethering," he said, somehow not quite managing to sound very fierce.

"And I told you to leave be with the wine barrels. One of the lads could have repaired the hoops." He grabbed her hands, turning them palm upward. "'Tis no' work for a lass."

Anice flushed.

Gelis almost laughed.

So that was the way the cat jumped!

Proving it, the scowling-faced giant dragged Anice across the room, stopping in front of a long wooden rack on the wall. Hung with every manner of cook pots, long-handled ladles, and scummers, it also held an assortment of mortars, and pestles, trivets and measuring weights, and a few round earthen jars.

"Here!" He snatched one of the jars and, removing its rag stopper, thrust in his fingers to withdraw a smelly, greasy-looking unguent.

This he smeared onto Anice's palms before taking her elbow and guiding her to a little three-legged stool next to the pile of ropes and wicker baskets.

"Stay there until your hands absorb the selfheal cream." He straightened, wiping his own hands on the cloth tucked beneath his belt. "You can use the time to remember that I have a nose for smelling lies. That's aimed at you, too, laddie," he added, flashing a glance at Hector. "I'll no' have the like in my kitchens. No' for any reason."

That last, Gelis was sure, was meant for her.

Feeling duly chastised, she cleared her throat.

"You mustn't blame them. They but meant to champion

me. They'll both know I'd hoped my *surprise* would help me gain the Raven's favor." She lifted her chin. "I do not yet have it, you see."

She spoke plain, giving Hugh MacHugh the honesty he'd demanded.

Unable to let her only friends here — save Valdar and Buckie — take the brunt of his burst of temper.

However *un*fierce it truly was.

Already, some of the agitation had left his face. In its place, his earlier look of indecision returned, making him appear almost boyish, save for his full red-gold beard.

Pulling on that beard again, he eyed her. "So you desire the Raven's favor, eh? Now you've given me something to chew on, my lady."

The words spoken, he began pacing, stroking his beard all the while.

Silent, he strode to and fro between the stinky little *onion table*, his larger oaken worktable, and the great double-arched roasting hearth.

"I'll do your bidding, lady." He paused at last, drawing up beside Anice and dropping a hand onto her shoulder. "In great part because I ken Anice would ne'er have told such a whopping falsehood unless she truly believed you have the heart to ride out—"

"Och, she does!" Anice bobbed her head. "You should have seen her when we entered the bedchamber and—"

"Be that as it may, she will ride out under full escort—as she said." Hugh MacHugh was adamant.

"But..." Gelis hedged, ashamed to admit her deceit. "There isn't an escort waiting for me. Not yet anyway. I'd meant to gather one..."

That was true enough.

Though she'd feared they'd say her nae.

The cook looked at her, his blue eyes sharp. "They shall accompany you, never fear."

Gelis smoothed her hands on her skirts. "They might not be pleased—"

"Leave it to me." He smiled then and patted his considerable girth. "I'm no man o' letters with a silvered tongue. Nor a great lord like your sire, commanding men with the flip of a finger. But"—his eyes twinkled—"there isn't a man in the garrison who wouldn't do my bidding for a double portion of viands or a plump sack of my honey cakes!"

"Then you'll help me?" Gelis could scarce believe it. "With everything?"

Hugh MacHugh nodded, his red beard gleaming.

"O-o-oh! Thank you!" Gelis threw her arms around him, hugging him fiercely, uncaring that he smelled of onions and fish brine.

And when she pulled back, she somehow wasn't surprised to see a bit of dampness misting his eyes before he quickly knuckled it away.

Hugh MacHugh, master cook and curly-bearded giant, was a romantic.

Who would've thought it?

A good portent, to be sure.

Willing it so, she whirled, grabbing first Anice, and then young Hector, embracing them as well. But her high spirits plummeted when she turned to leave and nearly tripped over Buckie.

He lay sprawled on the stone-flagged floor, the deep shadow cast by the teetering pile of empty wicker baskets making it almost impossible to see him.

But she saw him now and the sight made her heart wince.

If anything, the dog looked even more dejected than he had in the bailey.

"Awwww, Buckie..." She dropped to her knees beside him. "I didn't know you were there," she crooned, fondling his ears, stroking a hand down his shaggy back.

His tail swished across the stone floor, but when he twisted round to peer at her, his eyes were still sad.

Defeated.

Gelis frowned. "Now, Buckie. You know he'll be back."

The dog blinked.

Then, with a bit of an effort, he struggled to his feet and stood looking at her.

His tail swished again.

When his gaze slid to the door and he shook himself, his eyes turning hopeful, Gelis knew she had a problem.

Remembering her promise, she rubbed the dog's bony shoulders.

"A fine meat-bone for you, h'mmm?" She did her best to make the bribe sound tempting. "I am sure Hugh can spare one."

Hugh MacHugh grunted.

Gelis pretended not to hear.

Instead, she pushed to her feet, prepared to insist. "He can have a stew bone, anything with meat on it. Or perhaps the mutton..." She stopped, her gaze snapping to the pile of empty creels.

Hector was perched on one of the upturned baskets, his feet resting on a tight-wound coil of heather rope.

Gelis frowned again.

Something—indefinable and niggling—flickered at

the edge of her mind. She lifted a hand, began tapping her forefinger against her chin.

And as she tapped, her gaze lit on Anice. The girl still sat on the little three-legged stool, her selfheal-smeared hands resting on her lap.

Hands damaged repairing the hooping on Castle Dare's wine barrels.

Gelis's finger stilled in midtap.

She spun around, searching a shadowy corner across the kitchen. The willow bands Anice had carried up from the wine cellar lay there still, innocent and . . . beckoning.

Stirring memories.

Gelis stared at them, an idea forming.

Her heart began to thump.

As if he sensed her excitement, Buckie barked. His eyes began to brighten and his tail swishes became rapid, full-fledged wags.

Watching him, Gelis had to struggle against raising a balled fist and shouting *Cuidich N' Righ!*

She wasn't as successful in stifling a little bounce of joy.

Or the laughter she couldn't seem to quell.

It bubbled forth, uncontained.

"Lady—" Anice stood, reached out a goop-smeared hand. "Are you well?"

Gelis dashed a hand across her cheek. "I am fine, never fear," she managed, the words garbled by her mirth. "Indeed, I am feeling better by the moment."

Then, not caring that Hugh MacHugh, Anice, and even Hector were gawping at her as if she'd run mad, she crossed the room to seize one of the willow bands and wave it before her like a prize.

"I will need this, too," she announced, beaming at the slack-jawed cook. "To go along with a meat-bone and—"

Hugh ran a hand over his head. "You want the willow band? To go with a dog bone?"

"Aye, and"—Gelis nodded, her mouth twitching—"a coil of rope and—" She broke off, knowing she was going about this the wrong way.

So she set down the length of willow and smiled.

"Tell me, Hugh MacHugh," she began, "have you ever heard the saying that a man must fight for what he wants in life?"

Hugh MacHugh gave her a look of astonishment, but finally nodded.

"Then you'll understand that women must do the same," she expanded.

When he only stared at her, owl-eyed, she snatched up the willow band, brandishing it like a sword.

"I am about to ride into battle. And this"—she laughed as she wielded the bobbing willow—"is going to help me win."

"God go with you and keep you." Ronan stared after the departing company of MacKenzies.

Riding as one, they moved fast. Tight-knit, banners flying, and shouting their slogan, the fore riders in their ranks were already cresting the next ridge.

Ronan watched them, his every sense alert.

Mounted no less nobly and drawn up high atop his own vantage point, he felt a great surge of relief. By long custom, he shot a glance over his shoulder, but saw naught amiss. Even so, his horse shifted and tossed its head, the low clouds and scudding mist making him nervous.

He patted the beast's neck, spoke a few soothing words.

And still the MacKenzies rode on.

Scores of powerful hoofbeats tossed up clumps of sod and thundered on the chill morning air, the clank of armor and the creak of leather drowning out the soft soughing of the Highland wind.

The saining words Torcaill murmured so quietly.

Ancient blessings so old their meanings were indecipherable to anyone who hadn't lived them.

Ronan slid a glance at the druid, noting that his staff gleamed bright silver against the drifting mist.

Indeed, the thing pulsed and glowed in rhythm with the rise and fall of the graybeard's incantations.

Safeguarding spells that seemed to be working, however much the words sounded like gibberish.

Ronan frowned.

Grateful as he was for the druid's support, it galled him that such measures were necessary.

That Glen Dare wasn't as...others.

His heart began to hammer in his ears and he let out a long breath, almost a sigh.

He kept his gaze pinned on the riders, his shoulders tense until the valiant array spurred up the braeside to gather on the hill's summit.

And not just any summit.

Steep, heather-covered and scored with rock-strewn corries, the rise marked the end of Dare's influence and the beginning of the Black Stag's own territory.

Not surprisingly, the skies were brighter there. Indeed, as he looked on, pale sun broke through the clouds, the slanting rays streaming down to glint brightly off so much massed steel and valor.

The Black Stag was easily recognizable. Ever a man apart, he sat his horse proudly, black mail gleaming and his dark hair whipping in the wind. Nearby one of his men held the MacKenzie banner aloft, silken furls snapping.

"The saints hold that one dear." Glad for it, Ronan kept his back straight, in respect.

Beside him, Torcaill lifted his *slachdan druidheachd* in silent salute.

As if Kintail knew, he raised a hand.

For one long and disconcerting moment, Ronan was sure he could feel the older man's stare boring into him. But then the Black Stag turned, signaling to his trumpeter.

At once, the man sounded retreat.

The sharp blast, shrill and ululant, echoed off the hills even as the standard bearer wheeled his steed in Ronan's direction, briefly dipping the great wind-tossed banner.

That last gesture of farewell completed, Duncan Mac-Kenzie thrust up his arm once more. His great steed reared, powerful forelegs cleaving the air before MacKenzie wrenched him around and went charging after his men.

Then they were gone, the whole glittering lot of them disappearing over the ridge.

Ronan stared at the empty air where the Black Stag had been but a moment before. "The devil himself couldn't make such a flourish."

Torcaill shrugged and lowered his staff. "There are many who call him a devil."

Ronan humphed.

"That race is famed for their hot blood and flair." Torcaill carefully slid his walking stick into a sheath tied to his saddle. "Even so, their leave-taking wouldn't have been such a triumph had *she* been with them."

Ronan tensed again.

The words could have been a pail of cold water dashed in his face.

Twisting in his saddle, he glared at the druid. "Say you."

"You know it, too." The ancient's eyes narrowed, looking deep. "Even if she might have left the glen unscathed, naught would have changed. She belongs here, with you."

Ronan snorted.

He slashed the air with a denying hand.

If Gelis MacKenzie belonged in Glen Dare—with him—the fates were more than unkind.

They were cruel.

Wishing it were otherwise, he closed his eyes.

When he opened them again, he was prepared for the druid's penetrating stare.

"Tell me again what you said earlier, Torcaill of Ancient Fame," he pressed.

He flicked at a fold of his plaid, waiting. He kept his expression neutral.

His mind as blank as was possible.

"I would hear the words once more."

Torcaill wagged his white-maned head. "You disappoint me, my son."

"Humor me...please."

"It is possible I have already told you more than I ought."

Ronan edged his horse a few steps nearer to the druid's. He leaned close. "Then there can be no harm in repeating what I have already heard."

Torcaill drew a long breath. "When she touched

you . . . you said she placed her hand on your face, brought her fingers to your lips?"

Ronan nodded.

Then he straightened, flipped his plaid over one shoulder. Why the druid found it necessary to be so explicit was beyond his ken.

It also made his face burn, much to his annoyance.

So he frowned. "That isn't the part I mean—as well you know!"

"Ahhh . . ." Torcaill's long white beard stirred in the wind. "Have you so soon forgotten what I told you about the significance of that touching?"

Ronan did his best not to give the druid a withering look.

He'd forgotten naught.

Would that he had!

"I see you do remember." Torcaill looked at him down his overlong nose.

Ronan returned the stare.

The other's certainty was grating on his nerves.

Even so, he *had* to know.

"The maid spoke true. And her ability to show you what her gift lets her see says much about her power," the druid continued, clearly intending to needle him. "Only those most blessed can lay hands on a *nontaibhsear* and grant them such glimpses."

"The image could have come from my own youth." Ronan squared his shoulders, warming to the idea. "Maldred's crest was not always as worn and indistinguishable as it is now. When I was a lad, it was—"

"Anything but 'shimmering with a brilliance that hurt the eyes,'" Torcaill quoted him, looking superior. "Even then the stone's carvings were showing their age. Nae, nae, laddie, 'twas a look into a more distant time she was giving you, for whate'er reason."

"And you do not know that reason?"

The druid shifted in his saddle, his gaze—his suddenly wary gaze—sliding to a tangle of whin and broom a bit farther down the pine-clad knoll.

"Well?" Ronan didn't hide his impatience.

Turning back around, Torcaill peered at him from beneath down-drawn brows. "Like as not, the maid has no idea her power is so great."

"That is no' what I asked you."

"Mayhap not, but I have told you all I may."

It was all Ronan could do not to grind his teeth. He did stiffen, and not in a way that was pleasurable.

Torcaill eyed him placidly, his hair and beard lifting in the wind. "It is not for me to question why the Old Ones let her show you what she did. I can only tell you that they will have had their reasons."

"Think you I do not know that?" Ronan glowered.

The druid only arched a brow.

Ronan felt his restraint waning.

"If the Wise Ones had reason to send me a *taibhsear* as a bride, perhaps it would serve their purpose better if I were made aware—"

"You will know what you must when the time arises for you to know it."

As I have told you before.

Ronan was sure he heard the unspoken accusation.

He choked back a snort.

His head was beginning to ache, so he did what he could, turning his darkest look on the heavens, the gray, lowering clouds scurrying past so swiftly. Pinning his stare on a particularly dark and thundery-looking cloud, he enjoyed his scowl.

There were satisfactions to be had in such small victories.

He didn't dare aim such a glare at Torcaill.

Much as he'd like to!

He was about to give in to the temptation when a great gust of sleety wind whipped his hair across his eyes.

A splatter of icy raindrops stung across his face.

"Saints o' mercy!" he groused, biting back a stronger curse as he swiped a hand across his brow.

Then he strove for patience.

Becoming riled would only serve to tighten the druid's lips even more.

That much he knew.

Noting how clamped those lips already were, he tried to search the ancient's face for answers.

But that, too, proved impossible.

Torcaill's attention was already elsewhere. Once again, he was eyeing the thick growth of whin and broom crowding the lower braeside.

Ronan immediately saw why.

Something moved there.

Something unseen and…heavy.

He could hear it moving through the underbrush, its lumbering passage lifting the hairs on his nape. For a moment, he thought he caught a flicker of gray against the yellow of the whin and broom. But then the thing was gone, leaving nothing more ominous on the hill than the rustle of leaves stirred by wind.

"I'll be away now," Torcaill said, sounding distracted.

Ronan flashed a glance at him, the large gray *something* forgotten.

Especially when the druid slid a hand into the folds of his robes, then fumbled about until he withdrew a particular leather pouch. Age-stained, lumpy, and secured with an equally ancient-looking leather tie, the pouch boded ill.

Quite unperturbed, Torcaill hung the thing from his saddlebow.

Ronan rested a hand on his own saddlebow and leaned forward. "Did you not say you'd accompany me back to Dare?"

"I have thought better of it." Torcaill smoothed his robes, taking care—it seemed—not to look again in the direction of the whins and broom. "Perhaps I shall ride along the outer edges of the glen. Do a bit of circuiting. There can be no harm in refreshing my saining sites."

Ronan felt his impatience returning. "Tilting, weather-pitted stones that have marked our bounds since before the first dew e'er wet Highland grass! Think you that mumbling a few words o'er their moss-grown faces will change aught?"

"That remains to be seen."

"So be it." Ronan nodded.

There was nothing else to say.

The druid's straight back and the proud set of his gaunt shoulders tied Ronan's tongue. Already he'd been more disrespectful than he would have wished.

But so much plagued him of late . . .

"I've refilled my pouch," Torcaill was saying. He patted the pouch's bulging sides, his hand then staying there, reverently. "Sacred ash gathered from the last Lammas fire and a few small fagots of rowan for burning, and a goodly supply of old bits of iron."

"Then we of Dare shall sleep at ease this night!" Ronan put as much conviction into the words as he could, well aware that the druid meant to scatter his saining goods around the glen's ancient boundary markers.

Mumble his spelling words, and wave his lit fagots in the air as he circled the stones.

Looking at Ronan now, his eyes gleamed.

"There's enough should you wish me to ride past Creag na Gaoith," he offered, patting the leather bag again. "Lammas ash is powerful. I could—"

"Nae." Ronan shook his head, the gesture final.

Bitter.

He should never have encouraged the old fool.

And the last thing he wanted was the ancient—or anyone—going near Creag na Gaoith.

Rock of the Wind was a black place. A mass of towering broken crags rising high above one of Dare's bonniest corners, half of the once-proud rock bastion now lay tumbled and moss-grown at its foot. The great fallen stones spilled into the sweet little lochan there, the sight a damning and permanent reminder of what lay beneath.

"She needs to be let go."

Ronan almost choked.

He did blink, the druid's words piercing him. "She has been gone . . . for years."

Words so true, guilt shamed him to the core. Thinking of the rockslide that killed his first wife Matilda wasn't why the dread name of the place sent such a flood of chills streaking through him.

It'd been the reminder of the cause of that tragedy.

He couldn't allow the like to happen again.

Especially not to *her*.

His gut twisting at the thought, he shoved back his hair and set his jaw. "I'll no' have you or anyone poking around Creag na Gaoith." He spoke the sentiment aloud this time. "No good would come of it."

Torcaill drew himself up. "Perhaps you should ride by there. Lay your ghosts."

Ronan scowled at him.

He didn't have any bogles.

But a short while later as he somehow found himself riding ever nearer to that once beloved spot, he couldn't deny that *something* lurked in the bracken and heather hemming his path. Thick birches and bramble bushes grew there, too, almost impenetrable—just as he remembered—until the trees gave way to the peaceful little lochan, so hidden it didn't even bear a name.

Whatever he'd spotted up ahead, large, gray, and moving slow, didn't have a name either.

Saints forbid he encounter the beast.

His mood was too foul to cross swords with some bespelled creature sent by the Holders to torment him.

Ronan shuddered.

He pulled his travel cloak tighter about him, glancing from right to left as he rode, conscious now of every squishy, sucking clip-clop his horse's hooves made on the damp carpet of fallen autumn leaves.

Then he heard it again.

A rustle of leaves as he'd caught back on the knoll. This time accompanied by the unmistakable snuffling and sniffing of a large animal. Its panting breaths as it moved stealthily through the undergrowth.

Ronan's heart started beating slow and hard.

He drew his sword, holding it ready.

Then he rounded a great cluster of Scots pine and rowans and jerked his steed to such a jarring halt he nearly cut himself in the thigh.

A dog sat in the middle of the path.

"Blazing heather!" Ronan's brows shot upward; his jaw dropped.

He swung down from his saddle, starting forward in disbelief.

But there could be no mistake.

The great tongue-lolling, tail-wagging beast sitting before him wasn't some mysterious denizen from hell.

It was Buckie.

Chapter Ten

❧

"By all the Powers!" Ronan stared at his dog, eyes wide. Disbelief and amazement buzzed in his head. "What mummery is this?"

A familiar bark tried to explain.

But Ronan only shook his head and ran an agitated hand through his hair.

The beast *couldn't* be here.

Yet there he sat, head cocked and eyes bright. His bony haunches rested almost smack in the middle of a slimy red-green patch of sphagnum moss and his swish-swishing tail was more than a little mud-grimed, as were his legs.

Sticky bits of bracken clung to his shaggy, gray-tufted coat.

He smelled abominably.

Ronan hadn't seen the dog look happier in years.

But he'd kill the miscreant who had set him loose.

Fury tightened his chest. His golden torque seemed to

squeeze his neck, making it difficult to breathe. He started forward, hands clenched at his sides, the dog's obvious joy at being out only flaming his anger.

After this, Buckie's confinement to the keep would prove even more difficult than before.

And that was a crime beyond payment.

Ronan's mood darkened and he stepped wrongly, his foot sliding on the slick dead leaves matting the narrow little deer track.

"God's curse!" he roared, his arms flailing before he righted himself.

When he did, he scowled all the blacker, tried not to be moved by Buckie's panting, tongue-lolling excitement.

Whether the foray pleased the old dog or not, he could have done irreparable damage to his hips.

Creag na Gaoith was a goodly distance from Dare Castle. The terrain between was rough and challenging. A man riding a sure-footed, stout-hearted garron required all his skill and several hours to reach the Rock of the Wind and its little boulder-rimmed lochan.

That Buckie had made it so far was nothing less than a wonder.

And—as Ronan had already decided—the sure death of whoe'er proved responsible.

Spurts of anger shooting all through him, he bent to scoop Buckie into his arms. If need be—and it appeared such was the case—he'd hold the aged dog clamped across his lap for the ride back to Dare.

It was then that he caught the scent of cookfires.

The mouthwatering aroma of choice sides of beef roasting slowly on carefully tended spits.

A faint tinge of Norse ale, and if his senses weren't lying, a distinct whiff of fiery Highland *uisge beatha*.

Water-of-life, and every Highlander's cure-all, the much-prized spirits had naught to do in this benighted place, the devil's own playing ground.

Ronan frowned.

From behind, his horse nudged him in the shoulder.

Buckie barked and wriggled from his arms...then bolted off down the path before Ronan could seize him.

If anyone was of a mind to call the dog's loping, loose-limbed, hinky-hipped trot a bolt.

He had other worries.

Vikings had settled in the glen!

The evidence was clearly visible...winking at him through the trees: a great and colorful sailcloth awning— the marauding Norsemen's favored *tent*—curving proudly near the jumble of outcropping rock at the head of Creag na Gaoith's nameless little lochan.

Boldly striped in red, blue, and gold, the shelter appeared open on one side, revealing—if he wasn't mistaken—a crude wood-planked floor within.

A well-laden trestle table and a bench piled high with cushions.

"By all that's holy!" He blinked.

Then he shook his head, knuckled his eyes.

The Viking tent didn't go away.

Far from it, Buckie suddenly appeared from around one of the supporting poles. Capering like a hinky-hipped puppy, he put his nose to the ground, sniffing at a securely fastened tie-rope before bounding over to a well-doing cookfire close to the lochan's edge.

The cook fire he'd smelled...complete with a haunch of spit-roasted beef.

Dare beef, like as not.

Determined to find out, he wheeled about and swung up into his saddle. He whipped out his blade, raising it high. But before he could spur his horse and thunder into the clearing, *she* stepped into his path.

"My husband—I greet you!" She beamed up at him, all light and laughter, her amber eyes dancing. "I dare say you took your time in getting here."

Ronan nearly choked.

Worse, he could hardly breathe.

Full of vigor and feminine spirit, she peered up at him. "I'd begun to despair that you'd come."

"You, my lady, look anything but despairing."

"So I would hope!" She hitched up her skirts and twirled. "Though I am not exactly dressed for a feasting-in-the-wild, having left Dare in such haste this morn," she announced, laughing.

"A feasting?" Ronan could scarce get out the words.

Her smile dimpled.

"Our nuptial celebrations," she emphasized, pointing to the striped sailcloth awning. "Meats, libations, and more await your pleasure."

My pleasure would be knowing you safe within Dare's walls.

The words jammed in his throat.

His fool arm appeared stuck as well, frozen in place above his head, his fingers clasped tight around his leather-wrapped sword hilt, the long steely blade shining in the wood's dim lighting.

He winced, wishing he could sink beneath the nearest bog pool.

She rattled on, clearly unaware of his discomfort. "Every succulent delicacy that was tossed out our bed-chamber window is on yon table," she enthused, looking more fetching than ought to be allowed. "I went to the kitchens and secured the untouched remains from your cook."

Ronan looked at her, his surprise complete. "The meal I'd ordered for—"

"For me, aye, but now for us both to enjoy! We have"— she lifted a hand, began ticking off viands—"thick slices of cold roasted mutton, the very same spiced salmon patties and jellied eggs, and even Hugh MacHugh's ginger-dusted honey cakes."

Ronan's brows arched.

"And not just that." She flicked another glance at the well-spread table board. "There are additional savories as well."

It was all Ronan could do to keep from telling her that *she* was the savory.

Blessedly, speech failed him.

She flashed a dimpled smile. "Hugh MacHugh was generous."

Ronan could only goggle.

She was beyond all, a vision against the cold gray of the wood, the dark trunks of the great Scots pines crowding the little path.

Behind her, mist and cloud swirled across the jagged face of Creag na Gaoith, but—as if to bedevil him—a single shaft of sunlight slanted through the trees, the golden light falling directly across her, gilding her.

Not that she needed any such embellishment.

Prominent and well-made, her breasts swelled above a tighter-fitting, lower-dipping bodice than he'd yet seen her wear, and her flaming hair had loosened from its braid to hang about her shoulders.

Not even attempting to tame her wild tresses or right the front of her gown, she held his gaze. Her eyes smoldered, their gold-flecked depths proud and full of challenge.

The top rims of her nipples were plainly visible.

Ronan swallowed.

His jaw went so slack he doubted he'd e'er be able to firm it again.

Another, more self-minded part of him twitched and jerked.

No danger of slackness there.

Indeed, if he ran any harder, the wretched thing might just snap in two.

Ignoring it, he finally managed to lower his arm and shove his fool sword back into its sheath. He dismounted and made a bit of a show brushing at his travel cloak, flicking its folds into place.

Ne'er had he felt more like a bumbling, witless bravo.

It was unthinkable that he had nearly gone charging through the underbrush, brandishing his sword and yelling for *Vikings* to come out of their hidey holes and fight like men.

The near shame of it coursed through him.

He gritted his teeth and drew a tight breath. He would not redden in front of her.

Nor would he let her see how deeply she affected him.

Unfortunately, from the look she was giving him, he suspected she knew fine.

"Of course, you were startled." She came closer, her red-gold curls swinging about her hips. The scent of roses swirled around him. "It was my intention to surprise you."

His nose quivered, her perfume almost overwhelming his senses.

"To be sure, and you did, just! Surprise me." He eyed her sharply, scarce able to think straight. "But did you no' consider Buckie—"

She brushed aside his concern and took his arm, her grip firm. "Buckie is in fine fettle. He's enjoyed the day and still is."

Ronan harrumphed.

"His pleasure in the day will circle round to bite him when he wakens on the morrow and canna stand." He looked down at her, ignoring how right her hand felt on his arm. "I'm sure you meant no ill, but allowing such an aged beast to run all the way from Dare to—"

She laughed, a pleasing, flirtatious sound, bright and lively, that warmed the chill air. Truth be told, her laughter could have even warmed *him* if the reason for it weren't so objectionable.

Ronan frowned.

For sure, he'd judged her wrongly if she found humor in poor Buckie's plight.

"You mistake—I see it all o'er you." She slanted a mischievous glance at him as she tugged him forward, leading him through the trees to the clearing with its dark-watered lochan and her garish Viking tent. "Buckie's presence here is another of my surprises. He didn't walk a step of the way. He rode, and in great style!"

Ronan stopped short. "*He rode?*"

Another ripple of laughter and a sharper tug on his arm was all the answer she gave.

Until she marched right through the slithering mist snakes beginning to wind here and there across the leafy ground and pulled him into the clearing.

"There! See for yourself how Buckie got here." She pointed triumphantly at an empty wicker creel.

Large, hung about with ropes and what looked to be the willow banding used to hoop his grandfather's wine barrels, the large basket was clearly an onion creel.

The thing sat beside the lochan's boulder-strewn shore, its telltale reek carried on the wind.

Ronan stared.

A suspicion—something—snapped tight somewhere deep in his chest.

He swallowed hard.

Then he blinked, unaccustomed heat pricking his eyes when he spotted one of Dare's horses chomping grass not far from the creel.

Someone had placed the beast's saddle on a nearby boulder and it was at the saddle that Ronan now stared. A rope dangled from the high-armed cantle at the back of the saddle, the rope's purpose squeezing Ronan's heart.

His gaze flicked to the onion creel then back to the saddle, not that he could really see it now, blurry as his vision had gone.

He cleared his throat, squaring his shoulders before he risked turning back to *her*.

"Dinna tell me you rigged a carrying basket for Buckie?"

"I did!" She smiled. "Hugh MacHugh and Hector helped

me. We put Buckie in the basket at Dare and his feet didn't touch the ground until he got here."

She blinked herself then and swiped a hand across her cheek. "I vow he enjoyed the ride!"

"And where did you get such an idea?" Ronan could still scarce believe it.

"From Jamie Macpherson," she returned, the answer making no sense at all. "James the Small of Baldreagan, though his real style is James of the Heather."

"I ne'er heard tell of him." Ronan tried not to sound annoyed.

Truth was, the very way she'd said the man's numerous by-names perturbed him.

"Jamie has an old dog, Cuillin," she twittered on, her eyes sparkling. "He crafted a riding basket for him, and when my father saw it, he had similar carriers made for his own aged hounds, Telve and Troddan."

She tossed her hair over her shoulder, as if that explained everything. "The dogs accompany Father every-where, though he didn't bring them along to Dare."

Ronan almost snorted.

The Black Stag would have known why he left his beloved canines at home.

Would that he'd been so careful with his daughter.

"Jamie would have brought his dog here with him," she declared, her lips curving in another dazzling smile. "He ne'er takes a step without Cuillin at his side."

Ronan humphed.

The admiration he heard in his lady's voice annoyed him greatly.

His golden neck torque squeezed him tighter than e'er before.

Dog lover or nay, he was certain he didn't like this Jamie Macpherson.

"I am sure I've heard of other such *dog-creels*," he lied, something deep and ridiculous pricked inside him, forcing him to undermine the other man's brilliance.

"Indeed, I may have seen three or more such devices in Inverness," he embellished, feeling the fool but unable to halt his tongue. "And perhaps another on Skye, last time I visited Aidan MacDonald of Wrath. That one, too, is well keen on his hounds."

Lady Gelis's brows lifted, her gaze teasing.

Teasing, taunting, and all-seeing enough to send his own brows dipping into a deep, down-drawn scowl.

"You needn't be jealous of Jamie." She laughed the words, her merriment making him frown all the more. "He was one of my father's favorite squires. He's newly married and happily settled at Baldreagan, his home. He would love Buckie."

As if he knew he was being discussed, that long-eared brute trundled over to them. Looking quite pleased with himself, he eyed them, his bright gaze going from one to the other, his tail wagging furiously.

Then he was off again, hinking away to trot along the lochan's shore, eagerly sniffing every rock and clump of heather he passed.

Jamie Macpherson faded from Ronan's mind.

He looked back at his bride, shamed that—for a space, anyway—he'd thought her capable of allowing harm to come to the old dog.

He ran a hand through his hair, shamed, too, that his feelings for her would suddenly swell so fiercely in this of all places.

He bit down on the inside of his mouth, shamed even more that he wasn't awash with guilt.

Far from it, very different emotions were whipping through him. Even when he slid a cautious glance across the lochan to where the worst jumble of stones hugged the foot of Creag na Gaoith.

No ghosts lingered there.

Only nothingness stared back at him.

The hollow whistling of the wind, the rattle of tree branches, his own thundering heartbeat, and—he still couldn't believe it—Buckie's excited snuffling.

"Well?" *She* was standing before him, poking his chest with a finger. "What do you think?"

"Lady, I am...overwhelmed." He winced, hoping only he heard the thickness in his voice. "Truth is, I dinna know what to say."

"Then say you are pleased." She stepped back, attar of roses in her wake. "And"—her smile went wicked—"that you will not be wroth with your cook for helping me."

"Nae—by Saint Columba's knees! I am anything but displeased with you and I will go easy with Hugh—I promise you." But his gaze went to her Viking tent, the sight of it sobering him.

The tent could so easily have belonged to some broken half-Norse Islesman, wandering the hills and aching for trouble.

Or worse...a trap laid by the Holders.

Ronan glanced at the sky, certain the clouds were darkening, their roiling mass closing in on Creag na Gaoith, their fast-moving shadows blotting the sun.

He looked back at her, wondering how she could *glow* in such a benighted place.

"You are wroth." She folded her arms. "I can feel it rolling off you."

"Nae." Ronan pulled a hand down over his chin. "I am just…"

"You are—"

"Ach, lass! I would know what filled your mind with such folderol!" He jammed his hands on his hips, the dangers she'd faced taking his breath. "Such folly could have been the end of you! Traipsing alone through Glen Dare, a milky-eyed, nigh-toothless dog as your sole protection—"

She laughed again, her gaze flitting to the great awning of her Norsemen's tent.

"I rode out with more guards than e'er accompanied me on a day's outing from Eilean Creag," she tossed back at him, her chin lifting. "You just haven't seen them because I ordered them to leave me be, to stay within guarding distance, but well out of sight."

"Dare guardsmen are here?" Ronan glanced round, seeing no sign of them.

"They are…everywhere."

Ronan almost laughed.

Seldom had he heard a better description of his grandfather's garrison.

And of a sudden, he could feel them, too.

Not their eyes, they were too well-trained for such an intrusion. But their presence came to him now, a wall of massed strength and vigilance, waiting and watching as always.

Only he had been caught off guard.

His senses fooled by creeping shadows moving through the whin and broom, a brightly colored swatch of striped sailcloth, and the curling blue drift of wood-and-peat smoke rising on the cold morning air.

"They set the fire for you." He made the words a statement. "Built yon Viking tent—"

"So you know it's a Norseman's shelter?"

"Save us—to be sure, I know."

"But—"

"Sakes, lass."

He stood straighter, all the pride of the hills behind him. "Any Heilander who's sailed the Hebridean seaboard would recognize such sail-screens."

He rocked back on his heels, pleased with his knowledge. "I saw the sailcloth tents in my youth when my father took me on a journey through the Western Isles. 'Twas a sight I ne'er forgot, the colorful encampments of the Islesmen, those who still clung to Nordic ways."

"I am pleased you know of them." She tossed her head and smiled again. "When I heard that Glen Dare has more mist than other glens, I thought such a shelter might serve us well. My sister and I have used them on our travels and ne'er has a drop of rain spoiled our night's sleep."

Ronan's gut tightened.

Rain and wind were the least of Glen Dare's nuisances.

"I have more Viking gifts for you," she said before he could tell her.

Spinning around, she dashed for the shelter, hair swinging and hips swaying. "A fine Nordic armlet of heavy gold, inlaid with gemstones," she called over her shoulder, "brought back from Orkney by my cousin Kenneth."

Reaching the awning, she ducked beneath its flap, disappearing into the shadows only to reappear a moment later, a gleaming gold armpiece clutched in her hand.

"This, too, hails from Orkney." She hurried back to him, brandishing the thing as she came. "My father gave it to me years ago and I've been saving it for you."

"For me?" Ronan blinked, at first not comprehending.

By the time he did, it was too late.

A mist wraith had wound itself around one of the tent's tie-ropes. Inching ever higher, it was already quite near to the tent flap, its whole quivering, transparent length very close to where Lady Gelis stood, eyes shining.

Oblivious, she held out the Nordic armlet, offering the gift to him.

"Hell's afire!" He grabbed her and shoved her to the side, away from the tent, the force of his push sending her to her knees.

"*Aaaagghhh!*" Her shoulder slammed into one of the angled support poles and the golden armpiece went sailing.

She toppled sideways, landing with a gasped *whoosh* on the peaty, grass-tufted ground. Her bodice split wide and her breasts spilled free, jigging wildly as she scrambled to her feet.

Ronan flinched, her cry lancing him.

He flung himself between her and the infested tie-rope. Already reaching for his sword, he had the blade half-drawn before he realized the mist snake was gone.

The day had turned light and breezy, the cloud shadows swiftly moving away.

Nothing stirred but the rushing of the wind and a tiny gray wagtail flitting past to light jauntily on a red-berried rowan branch.

Slanting rays of cold autumn sun fell across the Viking tent, picking out its bright colors and making the glassy, peaty-dark surface of the lochan glitter as if it'd been scattered with jet and diamonds.

Somewhere a raven gave its harsh call.

Buckie hoppled around in a circle, howling and barking like a dog possessed.

And Ronan had ne'er felt a greater fool.

"Mother of God, lass, forgive me." He whirled around, his arms spread wide. "Ne'er would I hurt you, no' e'er. I'd sooner cut my own flesh—"

"I am well." The tremble in her voice belied her words. "No ill has befallen me—or will!"

She dusted her skirts and made no move to tuck her breasts back inside her torn bodice.

Buckie padded up to her, pressed his great bulk against her soiled skirts.

Ronan let his arms drop. "I will see you safely to Eilean Creag." The words formed before he could stop them. "Anywhere, so long as you are afforded safety."

"Pah!" She cut the air with a hand. "I am where I wish to be."

Ronan scoffed. "You live on dreams, methinks!"

He scowled at her.

She bent to retrieve the fallen armlet, her breasts still swinging.

Straightening, she let her eyes speak the words her lips held close. "I know you would not hurt me," she did say, watching him. "Nor am I frightened by whate'er menace caused you to push me."

"Sweet lass, I am the menace—"

"Nae, you are my raven."

Ronan's gut clenched at her innocence. "You err, lass. I am—"

"I believe you know what you are." She lifted her chin. "To me and, aye, what I am to you!"

"Lass—"

"Even so," she cut him off again, "there are things about me that you need to know."

On the words, she set the armpiece on the rough-planked table and whipped up her skirts, revealing a *sgian dubh* strapped to her thigh.

"The wee blade I gave Hector was not my only one." She looked at him, her color high. "Ne'er think I walk about unprotected! Much as I cherish our legends and tradition, I am not some large-eyed, song-trilling milkmaid born on the hill who trusts in naught more than charms and saining rituals to keep her safe."

Reaching for the deadly blade, she withdrew the dagger a few telling inches from its fine leather sheath. The brightly gleaming steel shone wickedly narrow, its razor-sharp edge clearly honed to kill.

Ronan narrowed his eyes on the weapon, glad for something besides her naked, still-jigging breasts to focus on.

"My mother—a master at knife-throwing—gave me this dirk." She kept her chin raised, her eyes glinting as bright as the sun on the lochan.

"She learned the craft from her brothers," she hurried on, caressing the richly tooled sheath as she spoke.

"And you learned well." Ronan was sure of it.

She nodded, clearly proud. "Mother *taught* me well. She also ne'er let me forget that her skill once saved her life."

She paused then, her fingers stilling on the dirk's sheath.

Ronan felt a sharp pulling in his loins, wondered if

she knew how much the play of her fingers on that long leather sheath was rousing him.

As was every other part of her!

He bit back a groan, his blood heating. Ne'er had he seen a more tempting creature.

Her breasts gleamed in the day's soft light.

Her nipples puckered in the chill air. Hued the exact shade of dusky-rose he'd imagined; he could scarce bear looking upon them.

Nor, saints preserve him, could he resist.

Heedless, she flicked a clinging twig from her skirts and tossed back her tangled, flame-bright hair. "Like Mother, I, too, would ne'er hesitate to use my talents to safeguard myself or those I hold dear!"

Ronan grunted.

He believed every word she said, but the wind was freshening. Light gusts tugged at her up-hitched skirts, lifting the edges and giving him brief, tantalizing glimpses of her red-curled femininity.

And the sight—so unwittingly revealed—was nigh unmanning him.

Quickly, before he did something they'd both regret, he reached and yanked down her skirts. Not wanting to risk helping her adjust her bodice and thus, inevitably, touch her flesh, he shrugged off his great travel cloak and swirled it around her shoulders.

"You will catch a chill if you dinna cover yourself." The excuse sounded ridiculous even to him.

She lifted a brow.

Her lips quirked then curved into another of her dazzling smiles.

"My health is as stout as yon Highland garrons." She

glanced at the two horses, quietly grazing side by side near Buckie's onion creel. "I ne'er take a chill."

As if to prove it, she lifted her hands and removed his cloak, slipping out of it quickly before his warmth and his scent bewitched her so thoroughly she couldn't ever bear to be parted from it.

Already, her heart was skittering and it was all she could do not to clutch the thing against her breasts, branding his heat and the clean, manly essence of him into her skin.

Instead, she folded the cloak carefully and placed it on the trestle table's cushioned bench.

Then she drew a breath, opting for honesty. "I know you covered me so you wouldn't have to see my breasts."

To his credit, he didn't deny it.

He did, however, look more miserable than she'd yet seen him.

"Lass—"

"Dinna say it." She looked down, tied her bodice laces as best she could with fingers she pretended weren't trembling. "I have eyes, see you?"

Her task complete, she brushed the grass and dirt off her skirts. She needed to busy herself lest she burst into tears—or great gales of laughter—at the futility of her gown-fastening efforts.

Retied, her already-dipping bodice once again covered her, but only just.

Her breasts strained against the ripped cloth, the generous swells barely contained. And, much to her horror, her right nipple was poking through a jagged little tear she'd somehow overlooked in her haste to redo the laces.

Indeed, she looked more scandalously naked than before!

A truth plainly evidenced by the Raven's tight, hard-set expression as he struggled not to glance any lower than her carefully lifted chin.

"You have much more than eyes, sweetness. I would that you didn't." He took a step closer; his voice came rough, husky. "And you shouldn't have —"

"What I shouldn't, husband mine, is allow you to keep telling me you are a menace." She snatched a jug from the table, sloshed a measure of wine into a cup, and thrust it into his hands. "Drink," she urged, drawing herself up, "perhaps Valdar's fine Gascon wine will loosen your tongue."

Pray that ne'er happens, she was sure he said beneath his breath.

She shoved a curl off her forehead, her heart thumping. "I know our union was meant to be. You know that I have visions and I have seen you in them!"

He stared at her, wine cup poised at his lips, his face an unreadable mask. But a muscle jerked in his jaw, its sudden appearance giving him away.

He knew.

She was sure of it.

"You know this, I am thinking!" She tossed back her hair. "Know that you've come to me as a raven and as . . . yourself! That you reach for me, dragging me against you and kissing me. So why" — she jammed her hands on her hips, her voice rising — "when we are together, myself nigh unclothed, do you look on me with such coldness? Why —"

"Och, lass, you err." He shook his head, his eyes

darkening. "It has naught to do with you. 'Tis me, only me, I swear to you. Ne'er have I—"

"Do I have the breasts of a crone?" She tore at her bodice ties, yanked her gown open. "Am I so undesirable that you—"

"Nae!" He threw the wine cup to the ground. "Ne'er you even think it!"

"But—"

A sound, deep, masculine, and elemental came from somewhere and then she was in his arms, crushed hard against him, held even more tightly than in the visions.

"Lass, lass! You are more desirable than any woman I have e'er known." He drew back to look at her. "E'er, I say, do you hear me? Ne'er have I been more tempted!"

"But—" The ground seemed to tilt beneath her feet and a blast of chill wind stole her protest.

She bit her lip, her heart thundering wildly. His gaze pierced her, dark and feral.

Heat blazed between them, alive and crackling, a sizzling rush of *need* so fierce her knees buckled and she would've plunged to the ground if not for his iron-bound grip on her.

"If you desire me, then make me yours!" She saw the *want* glinting in his eyes and it spurred her on, making her bold. "I am your wife. Do not shun me!"

She thrust her fingers into his hair, twining them in the thick raven strands as she pressed into him, aching, burning for his kiss.

But rather than oblige her, he stiffened, already pulling away from her.

"No-o-o!" She clung to him, holding tight. "I won't let you do this—"

"I have already done the unthinkable." He tore free of her grasp, agitation shimmering off him. "And, aye, you deserve the truth, though I'd give anything to have spared you."

"Then speak true." She put back her shoulders and stood tall. "See that a MacKenzie does not melt in the rain—or crumple upon hearing words she'd rather not!"

"Ach, lass." He blew out a breath. "Let me tell you this much," he began, starting to pace. "Torcaill told me how powerful your gift is. He sensed it and, aye, deep inside, I was no' surprised, as I have had...dreams."

He rammed a hand through his hair, glanced at her. "'Twas just as you say. Me, holding and kissing you, needing you more than the air I breathe."

"Then why do you reject me?" She came after him hot-foot, chin raised and breasts bouncing. "There can be no reason. Especially if you know—"

"There are scores of reasons!" He whirled to face her, the weight of Creag na Gaoith pressing on him. "Do you see yon scarred and broken crag?"

He flung out an arm, indicating the dread heights, the mass of rubble at its foot. "Tell me, lass, if you are blessed with the *taibhsearachd*, why did you choose such a maligned place for your feasting-in-the-wild?"

She blinked. "Why not this place?"

Her confusion hit him full-on, a white-hot knife twisting in his heart.

She glanced at the lochan, its shining water clear and bright in the cold afternoon sun. "I'd ridden for hours and saw nowhere more pleasing."

"And so it was...once."

"Once?"

Ronan nodded, finally seeing Creag na Gaoith's bogle peering at him from amidst the fallen stones.

A pale, almost-too-faint-to-see image, his first wife, Matilda, stood there, delicate as a spring bloom. But watching him all the same, her flaxen-blond hair unmoving in the wind, her sky-blue eyes calm, trusting as always.

Ronan blinked and she was gone.

But his guilt—and his dread—remained.

"My first wife died there," he said, speaking quickly before prudence stayed his tongue. "We came here often and were walking there, on the other side of the lochan, when a sudden rockslide took her life. We'd only been wed a few days."

"Dear saints!" The color drained from his new bride's face. "I am sorry. How horrible it must have been for you."

"It was, and the guilt haunts me still."

"Guilt?" Her voice was shocked. "You couldn't have prevented a rockslide."

"Say you?" He reached to finger one of her glossy curls, needing her vibrancy, the light and warmth that seemed to glow from within her.

"To be sure I say it!" she charged, a flush staining her cheeks. "How could you have—"

"Perhaps"—he released the curl—"because in that very moment, as we strolled along beneath Creag na Gaoith, I thought to myself that I loved her so desperately I would 'move mountains to please her.'"

"What?" Her eyes widened. "Don't tell me you blame yourself because of a thought?"

"That is the way of it, aye," Ronan confirmed, the truth sending bile to his throat. "I am cursed, see you. My thoughts sometimes take on frightening shape and form,

the darker — or more irresponsible — ones causing irreparable damage if I do not marshal them quickly enough."

"I do not believe that." She frowned at him, her chin
more stubborn than ever. "And even if it were true, I know
that —"

"It is true, I assure you. There are many —" he broke
off, his eye caught by a movement at the edge of the
clearing.

Something large and grayish-white crashed through
the heather, its massive head lowered and its great curving horns the most deadly he'd ever seen.

"A bull!" Gelis clapped a hand to her throat and stood
frozen.

"That's more than a bull!" Ronan lunged and grabbed
her, once again shoving her aside. "Hold Buckie!"

And then the unholy creature charged, bursting from
the trees with a terrifying bellow, the thunder of its hooves
blistering the air, its earth-shaking speed leaving no time
for finesse.

And totally ruining what could have been a moment of
revelation.

Spinning round, Ronan seized one of the Viking tent's
support poles. He ripped it from the ground and ran forward into the bull's path, couching the pole like a lance.

Behind him, Gelis screamed.

He ran on.

And then his world split, breaking apart on the bull's
outraged roar as it hurtled toward him, head low and horns
weaving, a murderous glint in the creature's eyes.

Eyes red as fire.

Chapter Eleven

✦

Gelis! Tip the table and get behind it!" Ronan yelled with all his lung power, raising his voice above the ever-louder drumming of hooves. "Do it now—with Buckie!"

Somewhere the two garrons screamed, their plunging, whinnying fear blending with Buckie's frantic barking and the wild fury of Ronan's own blood in his ears.

Then the ground shook and the great Scots pines edging the clearing careened sideways, their tall, dark trunks colliding with the sky.

Ronan dropped to his knees, aiming the sharp-ended tent pole like a long pike. He braced himself, waiting. Hoping the bull wouldn't change his course.

Praying he had the strength to withstand the crash.

Then, quick as winking, the beast tossed its thick, shaggy neck and swung about, thundering ever nearer, but not toward the sharp end of the pole.

Now he charged from the side, hurtling straight for the

middle of the pole and at a speed that left Ronan no time
to reposition himself.

Crrraaaaack!

The impact snapped the tent pole like a twig. Unscathed,
the bull thundered past, his horntip missing Ronan's hip by
a hair's breadth. The beast flung himself around at once,
his powerful hindquarters clipping Ronan's shoulder and
knocking him to the ground.

He slammed onto the splintered pole shaft, white-hot
pain shooting through him. Cursing, he rolled to the side
and leaped to his feet, gaining his balance only moments
before the bull charged anew, hurtling straight for him.

Heart in his throat, he vaulted over a patch of heather
as the bull barreled near, the beast's hot, snorting breath
blasting him as it shot past and circled around.

This time the animal paused.

It was the break Ronan needed.

With a great screech of steel, he whipped out his
sword, already slashing and stabbing. He swung the blade
in a lightning-quick windmilling arc, ready and waiting
for the bull's next charge.

Head low and swinging from side to side, the beast
kept its distance. Bellowing furiously, it pawed the earth
again and again, its powerful right hoof cleaving a deep
black scar in the mossy, peaty ground.

Then the great, unholy head lifted and swung in
another direction, the beady red eyes fixing on the toppled trestle table and the striped welter of the collapsed
tenting.

Fiery eyes focusing, the creature shook itself. Then he
shot forward with a tremendous burst of speed, tearing
across the clearing even as Ronan raced to cut him off.

"No-o-o!" he roared, waving his sword above his head, flailing his other arm like a madman, anything to distract the bull.

Draw him away from Gelis and Buckie.

"To me! To me!" he yelled, almost upon the beast. "Wheel about, you—"

"Cuidich N' Righ!"

The cry merged with his own just as he took a wild, slashing swipe at the bull's rolling, muscle-bunched back. A bright, silvery *streak* arced beneath his down-swinging blade, deflecting the blow as the eye-blinding flash whizzed past the bull's ears, barely grazing him, before plunging hilt-deep into the ground at the animal's feet.

His bride's *sgian dubh*.

And not a third the length of his sword, yet the bull nearly upended itself trying to stop its hurtling momentum before crossing the dirk's steel.

With a great unearthly cry, the beast tossed up its hind legs and jerked about, its forelegs scoring the earth in the fast, furious turn. Still bellowing, it took off, pounding away toward the heather whence it'd come.

In a blink, even the thunderous drumming of its hooves faded.

The bull was gone.

Panting, Ronan threw his sword onto the grass and bent over, his hands braced on his thighs. Sweat stung his eyes, near blinding him, and every muscle in his body burned. Screaming pain pulsed in his side where he'd slammed into the shattered tent pole, a heated agony so fierce he suspected he might have cracked a rib.

Not that he cared.

Lady Gelis's dirk raging up from the rich black earth was the most beautiful sight he'd ever seen.

Just as Buckie's barking set his heart to soaring.

Both meant they were alive and unharmed.

Relief coursing through him, he straightened. Then he dragged his forearm across his brow before stooping again to retrieve his sword and the *sgian dubh*.

"Did I not tell you MacKenzies are bold?"

Gelis's voice, ringing.

Ronan almost dropped both weapons.

He whirled around.

She stood before him, all high color and heaving breasts, her eyes bright and her wild, flame-red hair tangled and wind-tossed.

"Though," she observed, speaking as lightly as if they stood before a cheery hearth fire, "it would seem our nuptial feast has been ruined again."

Once more he felt the ground tilt beneath his feet, albeit for a very different reason.

He looked at her, now certain she could bring any man to his knees.

"Had my dirk not nicked your sword, we would have had him!" she declared, her dimples winking.

"Sweet thunder of heaven, lass! That bull could have had you — *wanted* you!" He jammed his blade into its scabbard, shoved her *sgian dubh* beneath his own low-slung sword belt. "Praise God you weren't injured!"

He seized her, yanking her so swiftly in his arms that he lifted her off her feet.

"You are not, are you?"

"Nae." She shook her head. "I am . . . well! Not even a bit shaken."

"You could have been killed." The very thought chilled him. "Seldom have I seen such an aggressive bull, attacking for no good cause or reason. No' even in the wilds of Ettrick Forest, that bull-infested morass in the south."

"There we agree." A slight catch in her voice revealed her to be more shaken than she let on.

She'd slung her cloak around her shoulders and pulled it closer now, her fingers trembling a bit as she readjusted its clasp.

"I, too, doubt such a beast roams distant Ettrick!" she emphasized, her magnificent breasts clearly outlined beneath the drape of her mantle. "And, it was you, not I, who stood the gravest danger." She paused, her amber eyes narrowing. "You are not hurt?"

He snorted.

His entire right side was on fire and every indrawn breath was a torture, but he'd sooner lop off his hand than admit it.

Most humiliating of all, judging by the flaming ache in his left foot, he suspected the bull had tromped on his toes in one of his thunderous passes.

"I saw how hard you fell onto the tent pole," she said, making it worse. "Are you sure—"

"'Twas nothing," he lied, grateful his voice wasn't a wheeze. "I am much more concerned with you."

"Then all is . . . good!"

"Humph." He sounded less than convinced.

Gelis lifted her chin. "You should be concerned with me," she said, putting her best MacKenzie challenge into the words. "I am your wife, was *meant* to be your wife. Truth be told"—she met his gaze boldly—"no pair has ever been better suited."

Silence.

Unperturbed, she poked a finger in his chest. "You know it in your heart."

"I know I should have seen you away from this place the moment you stepped out of yon trees." He flashed a glance toward the tall Scots pines. "That I didn't—"

She pressed her fingers against his lips. "Perhaps the Old Ones drew us here?" She angled her head, watching him. "They have a way of kenning us better than we know ourselves. We fought the bull together. Perhaps that shared triumph was a lesson?"

"Be that as it may, you will no' come here again."

He released her then, stepping back to study her face, his own pale in the cold autumn light. Dark shadows were just beginning to shade the skin beneath his eyes and deep lines bracketed his mouth.

His gaze dropped to Buckie. The dog stood pressed against her, his hips a bit wobbly but his ears still perked and his hackles raised. Clearly, he had no intention of taking himself elsewhere.

Not that he could with one of the Viking tent's tie-ropes looped around his neck in a makeshift collar, the other end held securely in her hand.

"You see," she said, following his gaze, "we were safe all along. And"—she reached to take his hand, twining their fingers—"if the bull *had* charged us, you would have slain him first. That I know."

Ronan harrumphed again, wishing he were as certain.

Nor did he know how they were going to make it back to Dare, especially with Buckie.

The two garrons were gone.

"We are no' safe even now." He pulled his hand from

her grasp, turning aside to stare off in the direction the beast had taken. "He could return any moment."

"Not that bull."

She sounded sure of it.

Ronan eyed her, something about her tone lifting the fine hairs on his nape. "What do you mean no' *that bull?*"

Had she, too, noted the creature's odd red-glowing eyes? Guessed—as he had—that the creature was bespelled?

If so, she ought to ken they were safe from him nowhere.

To be sure not here in a scarce-to-be-defended clearing with no place to hide or run should the thing have a change of heart and come thundering back again.

Instead, a hard-riding group of Dare's best guardsmen came spurring into the clearing, the two missing garrons led behind them. They drew up fast, stout warriors all; each man a faithful stalwart, tough, seasoned, and well-hung with bristling steel.

"Ho! Ronan!" The first called, lifting a hand in greeting. "What goes on here?" He rode forward, his sharp gaze noting the collapsed Viking tent. "We heard Buckie barking and then your two mounts came crashing through the trees."

Ronan took a deep breath, dignity not letting him show his relief at their arrival.

He'd forgotten their hidden presence.

More than evident now, they swung round into a shielding semicircle, upright and alert, their hands ready to draw swords at a single eye-blink if need be.

And clearly unaware of what had transpired.

"You did not see him, then?" Ronan turned back to Sorley, the eldest and most able guardsman.

"See who?" Sorley's plaid rippled in the wind. "Torcaill?"

"Nae." Ronan made a dismissive gesture. "That one is far from here...sprinkling Lammas ash and iron chips round our boundary markers."

The druid forgotten, Ronan kept his gaze on the straight-backed, proud-featured veteran. "Tell me true," he pressed, "did you no' catch a glimpse of a great wild-eyed bull, gray-white and massive? The beast went charging off in the very direction whence you came."

Sorley shook his bearded head. "We only saw yon two garrons."

"And a wee dog fox," another guardsman put in. "Strange creature, that. Creeping through a thick patch o' bracken, he was. Then, soon as he saw us, he hopped up onto an old holly stump and raised a paw as we rode past, almost as if he were saluting our progress."

"Weird eyes, he had," another added, edging his horse near. "Deep orange, and...knowing."

Sorley snorted. "Shrewd-eyed foxes!" he scoffed. "I saw no such a creature or a bull!"

"The fox *was* a weird one," a third voice chimed, "though I missed the bull for sure."

Gelis eyed the men with interest, her cloak clutched tight against her breasts.

Ronan dismissed the comments with a deft flick of his hand.

"Good men of Dare, hear me." He glanced round, his deep voice strong, lifting. "It scarce matters whether you spied a strange-eyed fox or the bull. Only that we quit this place anon and see my lady wife safely returned to the keep."

If any present felt a need to lift a brow upon hearing him refer to Gelis as his *lady wife*, they were too well-trained to show it.

Only the lady herself dared a reaction, her eyes flying wide.

But she caught herself as quickly, her glance turning artful.

"Might I hope that you intend to make me thus?" She leaned close, her voice pitched for his ears alone. "Could that be the reason you desire such haste?"

"I desire haste because I would know you away from this place," Ronan flashed back at her, his voice equally low.

"We shall see." Her lips curved in a smile that was pure female triumph.

Off to the side, several guardsmen coughed.

One cleared his throat.

Ronan frowned.

Like it or nae, the temptation of her words was sliding through him. Warm and honey-sweet, they slipped ever lower to curl around his vitals, squeezing and rousing.

A tight, pulling hunger, hot and urgent, that only served to blacken his scowl.

And, saints preserve him, made him consider doing just what she suggested!

Feeling like a great gowk, for he was sure the notion stood emblazoned on his forehead, he allowed himself a hearty bit of his own coughing and throat clearing.

Let his men crane their necks and gawp at him. Doing so would serve them naught.

Making sure of it, he put back his shoulders and stood tall.

"You, Tam," he called, pointing at the youngest guardsman, "ride hot-foot back to Dare and see that Hugh MacHugh sends a hot bath to my chamber—and readies another in the kitchens for Buckie!"

The young man jerked a nod, then yanked his mount around and was gone, cantering away across the heather.

Satisfied, Ronan turned to the next-youngest guardsmen, a pox-marked valiant whose spotted face would not have been so notable if he wasn't cursed to have a missing front tooth as well.

His visage, quite passing until he smiled, didn't at all match his by-name, Dragon.

But he was proud—and particularly good with animals.

"You, lad!" Ronan couldn't bring himself to call out the ludicrous name. "Take yon onion creel and fasten it to my saddle's cantle, then heft Buckie into the thing and stand watch o'er him until I am ready to ride."

Dragon bobbed his head. "As you will," he acquiesced, already dismounting and hastening toward Buckie's empty carrier basket.

"The rest of you"—he ignored the attar of roses wafting past his nose and made a great sweeping gesture, taking in the lot of the remaining guardsmen—"gather up Lady Gelis's *shelter* with all speed. As soon as you have, we ride."

"And yon toppled feasting goods?" Sorley dismounted, his gaze snapping to the tipped-over trestle table.

The fine viands scattered across the grass—up to and including the spit-roasted side of beef, the aroma of which had so tempted Ronan but a short while before.

It, too, lay ruined.

The perfectly done beef knocked clean off its spit and trampled into the ground.

Ronan eyed the chaos, his mind already elsewhere.

"Leave the food." He spoke the order crisply and reached to swing Gelis into her saddle. "If yon bull returns, he's welcome to it all. Perhaps with a full belly, he'll be less inclined to sink his horns where they don't belong!"

Not that he believed it.

What he suspected was that he could search the width and breadth of the land and would ne'er see the benighted creature again.

Praise all the saints.

About the same time, but back at Dare Castle, a tall, cloaked figure hovered outside the gatehouse. He clutched his robes tighter against the biting wind, resentful that Maldred the Dire's ancient warding spells still held such power. The strength of it pulsed and vibrated everywhere. Like bile, it rose all around him, poisoning the air and even rippling beneath his feet, creeping up from the ground to seep through the soles of his boots.

The figure's brows drew together in a frown.

As a Holder—and one vested with more skill than most of his kind—he should stand above his foe's craft.

Yet the foulness of the place was nigh suffocating him.

Indeed, it was all he could do to keep his back erect and his shoulders straight. The sooner he put distance between himself and the stronghold's proud, spell-soaked walls, the better.

But he'd be damned—again—if he'd lower himself by hastening away.

Not after such a splendid victory.

So he remained where he was, a few painful paces outside the worst of Maldred's influence, and watched the castle guards close the massive double gates.

They, too, had been so easily fooled.

The figure's lips twitched and he had to struggle against the urge to rub his hands together in satisfaction.

It wouldn't do if such a gesture was seen.

But he'd never dreamed it would be so easy.

Best of all, the old chieftain had proved to be an even greater buffoon than his witless garrison. They'd at least challenged him upon his arrival. Valdar, however, had welcomed him to his table, gustily offering meat and libations, the warmth of his fire. Not once doubting the tale his visitor spun so cleverly.

Never guessing that he was seeing what he *expected* to see and not a carefully spun guise.

The figure relaxed his grip on his cloak, pride warming him more.

Then, at last, the gatehouse's heavy portcullis creaked downward, clanking loudly into place.

The figure released a relieved breath and turned away.

Gaining strength with each step that carried him farther from those dreaded, hated walls, he shoved back his hood. Now, finally, he could revel in the chill wind tugging at his robes and whipping his long white hair and beard against his ancient face.

Now, the cold no longer touched him.

Not as it would have many lifetimes ago.

Better yet, the darkness of the wood was just ahead.

Wispy fingers of mist swirled there, almost luminous in the fast descent of the gloaming. A few more steps and the shadows would engulf him, erasing his presence until he chose to show himself again.

Much as the purpose of that next meeting galled him.

Not that it mattered.

He had no choice, after all.

And whether the Raven acted on his warning or nae, the outcome would remain the same.

Entirely in his favor.

Pleased—if such a one as he could ever truly be so—the figure stepped into the trees.

And as soon as he did, night began to fall on Dare.

Chapter Twelve

❧

Ronan held back a curse as his little cavalcade jingled through the scudding mist. He stared into the gloom, his jaw locked and his entire body wound tight as a bowstring. He shifted in his saddle, so stiff he might have been hewn of graven stone.

Had he truly praised the saints not so long ago?

Well earned as such paeans might have been, he was now of an entirely different mind.

Several hours and many cold and drizzly miles after the bull attack, he felt more like challenging than praising long-dead holy men. Truth be told, at the moment, he was more than capable of calling out anyone.

Friend, foe, and, aye, even those of otherworldly nature.

A black wind was whistling past his ears, each icy, indrawn breath burned his lungs, and his fingers felt frozen on the reins. Squaring his shoulders, he sat up straighter, refusing to grimace.

That small victory he would claim, difficult as it was.

Every inch of him flamed with pain, especially his ribs, though the day's bitter chill had taken care of his throbbing toes.

Blessedly, he could no longer feel them.

Would that the rest of him wasn't proving so susceptible to every jarring, jolting bit of the long journey home.

Even his head throbbed, the annoying pounding in odd rhythm with his garron's endless, clip-clopping hoofbeats.

As for his ribs, he'd known they were cracked not long after leaving Creag na Gaoith, when he'd halted to shrug off his travel cloak, twist around, and sling the mantle's voluminous warmth over Buckie's onion creel.

The *twisting round* left no doubt, that one simple movement sending a white-hot fire-vise to clamp around his chest. Fierce and scalding, the pain stabbed him, stopping his heart and cutting off his breath.

Only his pride — and his lady riding beside him — kept him from crying out.

Just as pride and her presence wouldn't let him show his disappointment now on noting how dismal Dare looked silhouetted against the bleakness of what promised to be a particularly black wet night.

Thick, billowy mist poured down the braes, and the deep green tops of the pines near the curtain walls were already sinking from view. High above, an early moon broke through the clouds, silvering the rolling spread of the moors and the long slopes of rock and heather.

But then the moon vanished, slipping from sight and leaving Dare's gatehouse to loom before them.

Night-darkened and formidable, the machicolated walls stood out against the blackness of the trees, the double towers' gloomy face making the brief autumn sun of Creag na Gaoith seem a distant memory.

A muscle began to twitch in his jaw.

This was Dare at its worst.

But the gates creaked open at their approach, dutiful as always. And the heavy iron-tipped portcullis rattled noisily upward as the little party cantered near.

Ready as ever to greet any guests, Dare beckoned with bright lanterns and torches lighting the way through the long, tunnel-like entrance. Still more brands smoked and sputtered in niches set into the bailey's walling. But rather than seeming welcoming, the hissing flames only threw eerie orange haloes into the darkening twilight.

Wild flickering circles of mist-hazed light that looked too much like staring, piercing eyes of red.

Ronan shuddered and then ducked as one of the flaring pitch-pine torches popped as he rode past, the wretched thing sending a spray of sparks and ash right at him.

He bit back a curse.

Then he allowed himself the scowl he'd been trying so hard to squelch.

A frown he surely deserved, for his head pounded and his patience had long since flown. Even more vexing, despite his ills, he couldn't banish the image of Gelis's fingers sliding up and down the sheath of her thigh-dagger.

Or the sweet triangle of lush red-gold curls he'd glimpsed so briefly when she'd whipped up her skirts to show him the *sgian dubh*.

He slid a glance at her, not at all surprised to see that the day's turn in weather scarce affected her.

She sat her steed as if she'd been born on the beast's own back. A true daughter of a thousand chieftains, she held herself erect and kept her shoulders straight, her chin proudly lifted. Indeed, she rode along as easily as if the summer sun shone bright above them and the blue roll of the hills weren't blurred by mist and the fast-encroaching darkness.

Even so, the day's cold and wind had touched her. Her cloak and skirts were damp, the woolen folds clinging to every lush curve and swell of her voluptuous body. Even more telling of her nature, Ronan was sure, her braid had come undone, again. Wholly loosened, her flame-bright hair tumbled in a welter of riotous curls over her shoulders to her hips.

Eyeing those curls now, he swallowed, certain he'd ne'er seen a more fetching sight.

Every line and curve of her stirred him, her very dishevelment taking his breath, and in ways that pained him far worse than any cracked rib or crushed toes.

But now wasn't the time to heed such an ache.

Already they were riding into Dare's thronged bailey and mist swirled everywhere. Snaking tendrils curled rapidly over the damp, wet-gleaming cobbles, and great, billowing sheets of it blew across the open spaces.

The tower stood dark and silent, its narrow slit-windows and arrow loops showing scant light while its massive bulk proved nearly obscured beneath the fuzzy-white drifts rolling in off the moors.

A quick glance showed that Maldred's hoary crest glared down on the bailey from its place of honor above the keep's oaken, iron-studded door. But, surprisingly, the ancient stone looked more like an ordinary clump of hill-granite than Ronan had ever seen it.

Of the bold horned raven of the vision his lady had shown him there was nary a trace.

Indeed, the stone's engravings had so deteriorated that it was no longer recognizable as a heraldic shield.

But before he could wonder o'er the matter, Sorley, Tam, and the Dragon pushed through the tumult, eager to see to his wishes and help him and his lady dismount.

The Dragon lavished his usual care on Buckie, lifting the now-tail-wagging dog from his onion creel.

"See he is bathed properly and combed," Ronan said, turning aside even as the pock-faced, gap-toothed guardsmen strode away with the dog. "Then have Hugh MacHugh give him as many meat-bones as he desires."

A wind-muffled *as you wish* drifted back to him, but he scarce heard.

Nor did he do more than nod his thanks when Sorley handed him the Nordic armlet Gelis had gifted him with just before the bull appeared.

At the moment he had greater matters on his mind than bejeweled armpieces.

His lady had somehow slipped through the ring of guardsmen and was tripping up the outer keep stairs, already nearing the landing.

But it wasn't her light step or her remarkable speed that sent him bolting up the steps after her.

Not even the tempting bounce of her shining, loose-swinging hair.

Nor the promise of her seductive siren's bauble, bouncing just-so betwixt her thighs, its glittering green gemstone an allure powerful enough to turn the most resolute abstainer's best piece into granite.

Nor was it the way she seemed to glow from within.

An irresistible beacon to a man so long without a woman's warmth and loving.

Och, nae, it was nary a one of such disasters.

It was the horrible red stain soiling one side of her uphitched skirts.

Ronan stared, at first not comprehending.

Then something inside him ripped.

The world turned as red as the spreading stain and his pain vanished.

At his elbow, young Tam was just lifting his travel cloak from Buckie's onion creel, and a laundress stood by, her hands outstretched to take it.

Ronan almost plowed them down in his haste to reach the keep stairs.

"Suffering saints!" He pounded up the steep stone steps, catching Gelis just as she set her hand on the door's great iron latch. "Hold, lass! Dinna you move!"

Gelis started at the loud words.

She swung around to face him, about to ask what was amiss, but he was on her in a wink. Eyes blazing and hair whipping in the wind, he swept her into his arms and kicked open the hall door.

"Someone fetch the hen wife!" he yelled, racing through the crowded, smoke-hazed hall. "My lady is injured!"

He crashed into a trestle table, near overturning it before sprinting on, knocking aside startled, wide-eyed kinsmen.

"Bring bandaging and have MacHugh send up his self-heal unguent!" he roared, bursting into the dimness of the stair tower.

"Put me down!" Gelis wriggled in his arms as he bounded up the curving steps, taking them two, sometimes three at a time. "You'll kill us both!"

"Hush, lass." He clapped a hand over her mouth, pressing her head against his shoulder. "You'll weary yourself if you speak."

"Pah-phooey!" She squirmed, her protest muffled. "You are the one who was hurt, not me."

"Say you?" He gained the top landing, streaked down the darkened passage. "'Tis you who are bleeding, no' I," he flashed, slamming open his bedchamber door.

He ran across the room, barely avoiding a collision with the steaming bathing tub some fool had placed in the middle of the room instead of before the hearth fire.

Then, chest heaving, he lowered her to the bed with a gentleness that belied his wild flight across the great hall and up the turnpike stair.

"Your skirts are bloodied," he panted, stepping back now, a glossy spill of raven hair falling across his brow. Shoving it aside, he looked at her, the dread in his eyes squelching her denial.

She blinked. "My skirts?"

"Aye, yours." He swiped at his hair again. "To be sure, and they're no' mine!"

His dark brows lowering, he leaned close and snatched up a fistful of her damp, red-stained gown. He shook the reddened folds at her.

Gelis pushed up on her elbows, eyeing her ruined skirts. "I am not hurt—not badly," she insisted, only now feeling the slight sting on her thigh.

The faint but steady throbbing and the telltale trickle of warmth.

"I must've cut myself when I withdrew my *sgian dubh*." There could be no other explanation. "'Tis nothing, I say you. I've done so before and—"

"You are bleeding worse than a Martinmas goose!"

"But unlike that unfortunate creature, I shall live to see the morrow."

The Raven's expression said he doubted it.

He dropped her skirts and strode to the table. Grabbing a ewer, he half-poured, half-sloshed water into a basin. His hands were shaking.

Even in the room's dimness, she could tell.

Especially when he snatched a small drying cloth off a chair back and his hand passed in front of the light cast by a candelabrum.

A thought—horrible and damning—popped into her mind.

Her brows shot upward and she stared at him, her fingers digging into her bloodied skirts.

"You do not think *you* caused me to cut myself?"

"It would not be the first time."

"*Dia!*" She slashed the air with her free hand. "I have never heard aught more foolhardy!"

With an oath that would have done her father proud, she yanked up her gown, flipping it back to expose her legs. "See you, Raven—look here," she cried, thrusting her right leg at him. "'Tis a wee scratch, naught more, and was done by my own clumsy hand!"

"How it happened scarce matters." He set the basin on the night table, plunged the linen into its depths. "Only that it doesn't again."

"It won't." She fumbled to unlatch the buckle of her dagger's thigh-belt, tossing the thing to the floor. "I'm not often so clumsy—" she broke off, her mouth twitching. "With my *sgian dubh*, anyway."

He humphed.

" 'Tis true." Sheer stubbornness made her emphasize the point.

He turned a skeptical face her way.

Keeping her own expression confident, she looked on as he wrung out the cloth. His hands still shook. She swallowed, striving to find a way to reassure him.

But he'd clenched his jaw and when he stepped up to the bed, his gaze fixed on the tiny scrape on her thigh, she would've sworn his eyes darkened.

Indeed, they almost smoldered.

"S-surely" — she jerked when he touched the dripping, icy cloth to her leg and began wiping at the dried streaks of blood — "surely, you do not believe you have the Droch Shùil?"

"The evil eye?" He dabbed carefully at her inner thigh. "With surety, nae, though I've heard enough tales of those who have but to glance at something they admire and blight it — much to their distress!"

"Then why —"

"Because what plagues me is far worse," he spoke over her objection.

His eyes still on her leg, he reached to dampen the cloth again.

"I believe your *nick* was a warning." He missed the basin rim by a good hand's breadth. "I can't risk daring Providence much farther."

Gelis watched as he corrected his mistake, this time finding the bowl.

And still his gaze hadn't left her thigh.

Not even as he wrung out the cloth.

"Providence brought us together, as I've tried to tell you," she argued, not objecting when he lifted her knee, bending her leg a bit to better dab at the thin runnels of blood striping her calf.

"And"—she leaned forward—"if you've any doubt, I can assure you it was my own haste in drawing my dagger that caused me to nick myself. It had to do with the bull, not you."

"The bull?" He looked up.

She nodded. "Did you not see his red eyes and ears?"

His fingers stilled on her calf. So she *had* known. "I saw his fiery eyes"—he kept his answer neutral—"but his ears looked grayish-white to me."

"Ah well..." She leaned back against the pillows and stared up at the bed's dark, heavily carved canopy. "Then I guessed rightly. He was indeed a creature of the *saoghal thall*."

"The Yonder World?"

"So I would say, aye." She plucked at a loose thread on one of the pillows. "Why else would I have seen his telltale red ears?"

Before he could answer, she rushed, "My *taibhsear-achd* let me see him more clearly than you did. Everyone knows enchanted creatures from the Nether Regions have red eyes and ears. Surely even you will not deny it?"

The Raven snorted and turned away to rinse the cloth again.

He did slide a glance at her. "And you know much of bespelled beasts?"

"I know enough." She broke the thread she'd been fretting at, twirled the length of it around her finger. "That is why my hand slipped when I pulled out my dagger."

"The charge of a bull is enough to unsteady anyone's

hand." The words spoken, he reached for her knee, this time dabbing gently behind it.

Gelis bit her lip.

His touch was doing more than cleaning the blood streaks from her legs. Every glide of his hands on her skin sent delicious tingling warmth shivering and spilling through her, a cascade of delight that rippled clear down to her toes and—she drew a shaky breath—spread *up* her legs as well.

Sweet titillating sensations, they spiraled across a certain very feminine part of her, each luscious new swirl of desire making her pulse and tingle with an almost unbearably delicious thrumming.

Almost as if he were touching her there.

Wishing he would, she squirmed on the bed. She imagined, no, she willed, his fingers to circle higher. To caress and stroke her, perhaps even to look at her *there*, peering as intently between her legs as he was now staring fixedly at her wee, meaningless cut.

After all, when Evelina of Doon had given her the golden bauble-chain, the one-time joy woman had sworn that if all else failed, she need only ensure he catch such an intimate glimpse of her.

If so, the older woman had vowed, he'd be unable to resist her.

Such was the nature of men.

Embarrassed by such a scandalous notion, however rousing, she drew a deep breath when he dipped and rinsed the cloth once more.

Then, summoning her boldest self, she deliberately eased her knee just a tiny bit farther to the side.

"My sister once saw such a creature," she blurted, hoping

to disguise her wickedness. "Deep in Glenelg, though it was an enchanted stag, not a bull."

"Say you?" He arched a brow, his attention still on her cut.

She nodded...and moved her leg just a teeny bit more.

A muscle jerked in his jaw and he straightened, tossing aside the bloodied cloth.

"And what did your sister do?" He was still looking down at her, his gaze now focused a little higher. "Was she—Arabella, I believe?—injured?"

"O-o-oh, nae." Gelis shook her head, excitement making her heart pound.

Soon she would have him.

She shivered, tossed her hair back over her shoulder. She was beginning to burn. Heat and tingles coiled through her, igniting her passion and making it hard to concentrate on anything but her wish that he'd seize her.

Grab her swiftly, and kiss her senseless, finally making her his own.

Instead, he angled his head and—she was sure of it—his gaze went a bit predatory.

She moistened her lips.

"Your sister was fortunate then," he said, his voice now as dark as his eyes. Heat and sensuality shimmered off him, warming and exciting her. "Perhaps the Old Ones do look after MacKenzie women."

"Arabella doesn't need their help. Nothing ever happens to her." She heard the huskiness in her voice and shivered. "She could walk through a blizzard and emerge without a hair out of place."

"And the bespelled stag?" The Raven cocked a brow again. "He left her be?"

"He just stood there, watching her." She could scarce speak.

He *was* looking at her.

She could feel the flames of his stare licking at her.

"Then he could no' have been all that formidable." His gaze grew even hotter, so intense she was beginning to sizzle.

For sure, *that part* of her was melting.

She moistened her lips again.

"Ah, but he was a fearsome beast," she chattered on, the heat between her legs making her wriggle. "Like our bull, he had eyes of fire and blood-red ears. To be sure, he would have attacked her, but Arabella recognized him for what he was and threw a silver coin at him."

"A silver coin?"

"Just that." She nodded. "We'd been to the market fair earlier that morning and she still had a small cache of coins with her."

"You weren't with her?"

"I hid away when it was time to leave the fair." She shifted on the bed, keenly aware of the dampness beginning to mist her inner thighs. "Some of the local chieftains were looking for young warriors of particular fighting strength. I wanted to watch their competitions."

"And your sister did not?"

"She was tired and only wanted to return to Eilean Creag," Gelis remembered, leaving out how Arabella had rolled her eyes when she'd suggested they stay longer to watch the strength trials. "She'd spent hours searching for colored thread and bone needles but couldn't find any to please her. That's why she still had coins later."

The Raven stepped closer. Something in his gaze made

her think he was scarce listening to her, only looking at her. He reached to smooth the hair from her cheek. His touch, when it came, was slow and deliberate, claiming.

It made her breath catch.

"I have heard of throwing silver coins at such beasts," he said, still holding one of her curls, rubbing the strands between his thumb and his fingers. "But I have ne'er met anyone who had tried the like."

"Such beasts always turn away from silver." She could hardly hear her own voice above the thundering of her heart. "Be it a silver-barbed arrow, a silvered dagger, or even just a simple coin."

She flicked a glance at her *sgian dubh*, still thrust beneath his sword-belt.

"See there"—she indicated the hilt—"silver inlays. That's why I threw it even though I knew I could never pierce a bull's hide, no matter how good my aim."

"But if you struck him or—"

"Or," she cut him off, "if my blade fell before him, I knew he'd turn and run. He would never have been able to cross it, not such a creature."

"Perhaps you should have tossed the blade in my path." He let go of her curl, stepping back as if it'd turned into a snake and bitten him. "You might have been better served."

Ronan regretted the words as soon as they leaped off his tongue. But his ribs were flaming again, the pain worse than ever. And he was quite certain the toes of his left foot had swollen to such a degree that he might never get his boot off.

"Forgive me, lass," he began, "but—" he broke off, a glitter of green atop a strongbox catching his eye.

The siren bauble.

At once, all knightly restraint left him.

He sucked in a great breath, more aware of the ache in his loins than any other. In three great strides, he crossed to the strongbox and snatched up the golden chain, waving it so that its sparkling gemstone swung before him.

"I am no eunuch, see you!" He dropped the thing betwixt her still-parted thighs. "I've only meant to protect you. Save you from the curse that plagues me. The blackness that claims any and everyone I've e'er cared for! But you . . ."

He thrust both hands in his hair and shut his eyes.

When he opened them, she stood before him, her siren's chain dangling from her hand. "You err, my lord," she said, so close her breasts brushed his chest. "I do not need saving. I am the woman meant to save you."

"Humph." He started to back away, but she leaned into him, the hot thrust of her nipples almost taking his breath. "By the Rood, lass, you dinna know what you're—"

"Och, but I do!"

Lifting up on her toes, she slung her chain around his neck, using the golden links to pull his head down to hers. Then her lips touched his and his heart stopped beating.

The world split, spinning away until nothing remained but her lushness against him, the silky-hot sweetness of her lips, and a heady, thought-numbing whirl of rose perfume.

"Ach, saints!" He whipped an arm around her, dragging her even closer. "I am lost . . ."

He thrust his free hand into her hair, twining his fingers in the cool, glossy curls. "Lost, I say you," he breathed against her lips, and then he could speak no more.

His heart thundering, he slanted his mouth over hers, kissing her fast, hard, and deep. Plundering and ravishing, he claimed her lips, at last giving in to the fire inside him. She clung to him, returning his kisses with equal heat, her tongue swirling around his, slipping and sliding, their breaths mingling, warm and honey-sweet.

He swept his hand down her back and around to her breasts, cupping and kneading them. His fingers circled and toyed with her nipples, each sweet tug and pinch making them draw ever tighter until his own *tightness* threatened to spill.

His need almost desperate, he broke the kiss.

"Nae, don't stop." She clutched at him, smothering his face with tiny kisses, licks, and nips, murmuring words that should have made him blush.

Instead, they hardened him even more.

"Ach, God!" He grasped her by the shoulders, setting her from him, some still-coherent part of him pleased to see that her own breath was coming as fast and shallow as his. Pleased, too, to see the telltale flush of arousal staining her magnificent breasts.

His heart knocking wildly, he plucked her dagger from his belt and threw it aside. Not taking his eyes off her, he reached to undo the heavy clasp of his sword-belt.

He needed, wanted, to be naked with her.

He had to make her his. Dare, Maldred, and all the world's curses be damned.

It was time.

The knocking in his chest grew louder, a thunderous hammering in his blood, his ears.

"Sweet lass, I—"

"I heard tell the lass had been injured." A ringing female voice came from the doorway.

Auld Meg, Dare's hen wife.

Ronan spun around, his unbuckled sword-belt flying from his hands.

Behind him, Gelis gasped and an overloud metallic *clink-clinkety-clink* revealed that she'd dropped her bauble-chain as well.

Auld Meg's gaze snapped to both, lingering especially on the glittering golden links.

The great green gemstone, winking wickedly from the innocent floor rushes.

"It would seem I was misinformed." She shifted the basket of healing goods clutched against her hip.

"It would seem you have forgotten to knock!" Ronan jammed his hands on his hips and glared at her.

"And I say you have bog cotton in your ears." Auld Meg huffed, all bristling indignation. "I've been pounding my knuckles raw a-waiting for your by-leave, thinking your lady in peril all the while."

"I erred."

"So I see." She glowered back at him.

Still standing in the open threshold, her stout frame silhouetted against the light from a wall torch, she looked nearly as broad as she was tall, especially when she mimicked him by bracing a pudgy hand against her own more than generous hips.

"Be that as it may," she began, eyeing him shrewdly, "if the lady has no need of my sphagnum moss dressings, mayhap *you* can make use of my special goldenrod ointment!"

"Me?" Ronan lifted a brow, not at all surprised when

she marched into the room and plunked her healing basket onto the table.

"Aye, you," she announced, clucking as she plucked a fat earthen jar from the basket and thrust it into Gelis's hands. "And what I've brought is far better than Hugh MacHugh's selfheal ointment. 'Tis my own fine unguent of Saint-John's-wort, germander, speedwell, and goldenrod that you'll be needing, I'm thinking. Blended with butter and grease, it will soothe your cracked ribs before the next sun rises."

Ronan's brow furrowed. "My cracked ribs?"

Auld Meg waved a hand. "Dinna do me the insult o' doubting my own good eye. I can see what ails you, right enough! It's there in every step you take." Coming closer, she wagged a finger in his face. "The unguent will soothe your smashed toes as well."

Ronan humphed.

His lady spoke up at last. "I'll see to it," she said, clutching the little jar of ointment. "And I...thank you."

This time Auld Meg grunted.

But her eyes brightened, some of the sternness slipping from her face.

"You do that, lassie." She looked Gelis up and down, her voice taking on a confidential tone. "'Tis long past time the lad has a maid what kens how to handle him!"

"Dinna even think it," Ronan protested the moment the grizzle-headed old bat swept from the room, closing the door soundly behind her.

He snatched the fat little jar from his lady's hands and set it on the table.

Experience had taught him that the unguent's noxious smell clung to one's skin for days.

Sometimes even a whole fortnight.

Gelis frowned, her gaze on the jar. "But she did seem to know—"

Ronan snorted. "There is naught wrong with my ribs and, with surety, no' with my toes!"

"You are sure?"

"I am certain."

"Then prove it by kissing me again."

"Lass, I will kiss you until the hills blush." He yanked his tunic over his head, reaching for her before it hit the rushes. "Now, this night, the morrow's morn, and all the days thereafter."

The words spoken, he caught her to him, pulling her close against his naked chest. He captured her lips, kissing her deeply. He swept his tongue against hers, claiming and demanding, needing her all.

She leaned into him, their hot breath and the wild tangle of their tongues seeming to spur her on. His own desire breaking, he ran his hands down her back and over her hips, finally clutching and squeezing her buttocks, drawing her flush against him.

She sighed, her mouth opening wider beneath his. "Yes," she breathed, slinging her arms tightly around him, her hips beginning to rock and press against his.

Her full, heavy breasts were crushed to him, the shifting of her thighs against his a sweet torture beyond bearing. A great shudder raced through him and he tightened his arms around her, digging his fingers into the lush curves of her hips, the sweet, plump rounds of her luscious bottom.

Ne'er had he burned with a greater passion.

And ne'er had a mere tapping at the door made him more furious.

He jerked around to glare at the door. "Be gone, old woman! You can continue your meddling on the morrow."

"'Tis me, sir." Young Hector, his voice hesitant.

"Be gone with you, too, lad." Ronan ran a hand through his hair, almost panting. "I'll no' be disturbed now."

A pause.

But the kind that pulsed with someone's presence.

With surety, no light footfalls could be heard padding away from the door.

"'Tis your grandfather, my lord," the boy called. "He wishes to see you in his privy quarters."

Ronan sighed. "Now?"

"At once, sir," came the reply.

"Hells bells and damnation." Ronan strode across the room and yanked open the door. "Whate'er bothers him that he canna sleep on it?" he demanded, trying his best not to glower at the lad.

Hector swallowed, his cheeks flaming bright as his carroty hair. "He wants to speak to you about the man who was here earlier. He says—"

Ronan's eyes widened. "A visitor?"

Hector bobbed his bright head. "A courier, sir," he embellished, his chest swelling a bit. "From the Black Stag, he was, come not long before the gloaming and bringing a letter for you."

"Indeed?"

"So it was, aye," the boy confirmed. "I saw the man meself, sir."

"Did you now?" Ronan lifted a brow. "And you're sure he was a MacKenzie?"

Once more Hector nodded.

"Then run down to my grandfather and tell him I'll

be there forthwith," Ronan said, reaching to pat Hector's shoulder.

But when the boy turned and dashed away down the torchlit corridor, he frowned.

By gloaming every MacKenzie in Kintail save his bride would have been huddled round Eilean Creag's hearth fire gnawing well-roasted beef ribs and quaffing the finest of ales. Some, perhaps, with a plump, full-breasted laundress warming their laps.

Of that he was certain.

The visitor couldn't have been a MacKenzie.

Likewise, whoe'er the mysterious courier had been, Ronan was sure he was up to no good.

Chapter Thirteen

✦

"A MacKenzie, you say?"

Ronan stood in the middle of his grandfather's privy quarters, his hands fisted against his hips, and trying very hard to keep the annoyance out of his voice.

But it wasn't easy.

Someone—a *Holder*, saints preserve them—had guised himself as a MacKenzie for the sole purpose of confusing an old man. And if he could get his hands on the dastard, he'd gladly spend his last breath to make certain he ne'er tried the like again.

Ever.

"Aye, I said he was a MacKenzie." His grandfather remained stubborn. Oblivious to the truth. "Did you no' hear me the first time?"

Ronan pulled a hand down over his chin, seeking words that wouldn't alarm.

"Every last one of the Black Stag's men departed with

him," he finally reminded the older man. "You saw them go. I rode with them to the end of our glen."

"Be that as it may, one of them returned." Valdar leaned forward in his high-backed oaken chair. "A courier, he was," he insisted, his furred bed-robe straining over his girth. "Sure as I'm sitting here."

A courier from hell, Ronan almost blurted.

Instead, he choked back a snort, doing his best to disguise it as a cough.

Already the old man's face was flushed red and glistening, while the light from a spiked candle near his chair clearly showed tiny beads of perspiration beginning to mist his brow. Most worrisome of all, his eyes glittered dangerously and he couldn't seem to keep his left foot from thumping against the floor rushes.

Ronan didn't want to think about what might happen if his grandfather knew the missive's contents.

He could scarce stomach them himself.

A warning, Raven... meet me at the Tobar Ghorm on the morrow's noontide to learn who amongst your men would betray you. Do not be late and come alone... your own life and the lives of those you hold dearest hang on a thread. Ignore my summons at greatest peril.

Dungal Tarnach

Frowning, he rolled up the parchment and thrust it beneath his belt, not bearing its blackness in his hands. He could feel the inked poison affecting him, drying his throat and making the pain in his ribs throb and burn.

Still, he had to get to the bottom of it.

"The man was winded." Valdar stabbed the air with a finger, making his point. "He'd ridden hard and fast by the looks of him, said he only wished to deliver Kintail's letter and be on his way."

Ronan went to stand before the fire, stepping close to catch the warmth of the well-burning birch logs. "Mac-Kenzie didn't send him. He had nothing at all to do with it."

"So say you!" Valdar hooted.

"Aye, that is what I say."

Valdar shook his head.

"Split me! Kintail wanted to surprise us, is what he did." His beard jigged with conviction. "That'll be the way of it, I vow. The reason you didn't see his man circle round and ride back here."

Ronan folded his arms.

"I knew Kintail before you were born, know him as well as I knew your own da." Valdar half-rose from his great carved chair, but dropped down again almost immediately.

Almost as if his legs wouldn't hold his great bearlike body.

"Like as not he wishes to announce a lairdly feasting at Eilean Creag," he boomed, regardless. "Invite us all for a sennight's merrymaking to mark your nuptials! Or"—he hitched up his squirrel-lined robe and wriggled his brows—"perhaps he seeks a Dare man for his other daughter, the more quiet, older one."

Ronan said nothing.

Twice now, his grandfather had swiped an arm over his brow. And the damnable scroll—whatever its true purpose—was burning a hole in his side.

Soon, he, too, would have sweat streaming out of his pores.

He could feel it coming.

"And you," Valdar roared, displaying his powerful lungs to be unaffected, "you dinna even believe the man was a courier."

He leaned forward again, his big hands gripping the chair arms. "I see the doubt all o'er you."

Ronan glanced up at the hammer-beam ceiling and released a long, slow breath.

Then he strode across the tapestry-hung chamber and unlatched the nearest window shutters. He flung them wide despite the night's raw, wet wind.

"I didn't say the man wasn't a messenger." He stepped back from the blast of icy air. "Only that he wasn't a MacKenzie."

"Pshaw!" Valdar leaped to his feet, swaying crazily before sinking into his chair again.

"Think you I dinna have eyes that can see?" He wagged his head at Ronan. "I know a MacKenzie when I see one!" he jerked, blinking a time or two. "Tall the fellow was and built like a prize stirk, his hair as black as your own and that of the Black Stag hisself."

"Forget the Black Stag!"

Ronan crossed the room in three great strides. Leaning down, he braced both hands on his grandfather's chair arms and looked him hard in the eye.

Something ailed him, and the thought of the possible causes chilled Ronan's blood.

"Did this courier give you aught to drink?"

Valdar bristled.

He met Ronan's stare, belligerence all over him.

"Since when does a visitor bring his own ale to a Highland table?" he demanded, his bearded chin jutting.

"Our guest received Dare's finest meats, libation, and entertainment—as is fitting!"

Ronan leaned closer. "Did you leave the table at any time?"

"And did *you* fall into the cesspit?" Valdar wrinkled his nose, waved a hand between them. "You smell worse than a barrel o' rotten fish."

Ronan straightened. "'Tis Auld Meg's goldenrod unguent."

"That foul goo?" The old man's brows drew together. "I wouldn't allow that clapper-tongued she-goat to smear her bog slime on my big toe!"

"She didn't." Ronan flicked at his plaid, not about to admit that his toes were packed in the odious-reeking ointment.

"Lady Gelis did the honors." He saw no reason to deny it. "She insisted when Auld Meg decided I might have need of her unguent. My lady—"

"*Your lady!*" Valdar's eyes lit with mirth.

He shot to his feet again, this time standing tall.

"Ho, laddie! And she dipped her fingers in that stinking rot for you?" He stared at Ronan, his mouth twitching. "Did I no' tell you she was a fine piece o' womanhood? I vow she has greater stones than some men!"

Ronan's face heated.

He knew exactly what she had between her shapely thighs, and *stones* had naught to do with it.

Praise the saints!

And damn him for thinking of *that* part of her now. Already, he could feel a stir and a twitch below. Nae, it was more a sharp pulling, hot and insistent.

He frowned.

If only he hadn't called her his lady.

The thought alone roused him, and in ways that had little to do with the heated pulsing at his loins.

It had to do with his heart, which made it all the more frightening.

"She meant well," he began, hoping to correct the slip before his grandfather guessed the truth. "Auld Meg convinced her I'd bruised my ribs earlier, and mayhap I did. The like happens. Lady Gelis only—"

"You're under her spell, you are!" Valdar rocked back on his heels, all but choking on his laughter. "Ne'er did I think you'd fall so quickly," he roared, slapping his thigh. "You, who'd vowed to monk yourself."

Clearly no longer troubled by whatever had plagued him, he grabbed Ronan's sleeve and pulled him to a table near his bed. Set with a round of plump green cheese, honey bannocks, oatcakes and butter, it also held a small pewter flagon.

Still chuckling, he snatched up the flagon and sloshed a generous measure of *uisge beatha* into a cup.

"Seeing as your lady has befuddled your wits tonight, I'll tell you that *this* is all that ails me this e'en." He thrust the fiery Highland spirits into Ronan's hand. "I was in fine fettle o'er having an unexpected guest at my hearthside and drank a wee bit more than I should have. If I'm a bit wobbly on my feet, that's why."

He leaned close, raising his voice above the hard drumming of rain on the shutters. "You needn't fuss o'er me like an old woman. The courier didn't poison me. And even if he'd tried, I'm no bairn to be so easily cozened."

Ronan set down the cup untouched. "I didn't say—"

"You didna have to." Valdar tossed back his own

uisge beatha, slapping down the little cup with a loud *clack.* "I've known you since you were in swaddling. And"—he swiped the back of his hand across his mouth—"'twasn't Kintail's man who sought to cozen me. 'Tis you!"

Ronan blinked. "Me?"

"Aye, you." His grandfather put back his still-powerful shoulders. "Treating me like a feeble auld mannie!"

"I ne'er meant—"

"You mean to protect me, I know, but I dinna need the like." He waved a hand when Ronan started to protest again. "Ne'er did, if you'd hear the truth of it!"

Suddenly looking younger and more vital than he had in years, he whirled and plucked a great Norse battle-axe off the wall. Grinning broadly, he leaped into a fighting stance and made a few grand flourishes with the axe, then slapped the thing onto the table.

"Dinna ask how often that axe blade's run red with the blood of our foes," he said, not even panting. "I say you the times were...numberless!"

"Ach, Grandfather." Ronan clapped a hand on the older man's shoulder. He hadn't wanted to make him think he doubted his strength.

He'd feared the Holder had harmed him somehow.

Grateful that he hadn't, Ronan sought to reassure him. "Everyone at Dare knows of your valor. I only—"

"You want to shield me, I just said!" Swatting Ronan's hand away, he smoothed his bed-robe. "But you forget, I'm no' faint-heart. Think you I'd have sailed right to the edge of the Corryvreckan and plucked your lady's father from that boiling whirlpool if I were?"

But that was years ago.

Ronan kept the thought to himself.

Valdar's eyes sparked as if he'd heard all the same.

"A man doesn't lose his heart just because he might count a few gray hairs in his beard!" He thumped his chest in emphasis. "The spirit is the same, especially a Highlandman's spirit. We are the best of men!"

"No doubt"—Ronan looked from his grandfather's proud, bristly face to the open window—"and there are surely few who would argue the fact."

Valdar poked him in the ribs. "But?"

Ronan winced, just managing to swallow a yelp.

But his entire body tightened and he clenched his hands, his gaze still on the dark, wet night beyond the window. Somewhere out there, like as not quite close, lurked a Holder by the name of Dungal Tarnach.

Man of thunder.

A man of such power he clearly possessed the ability to make himself appear as a MacKenzie.

Or bespell Valdar into seeing him thus.

"A Highlander won't be coddled either," Valdar gusted on, stepping around to plant himself in front of Ronan. "And we dinna like things kept from us!"

Lunging, he flashed out a hand and plucked the rolled parchment from Ronan's belt. "Hah!" he cried, leaping back to wave the thing over his head like a trophy.

"Now we shall see what you were trying to keep from me!" He grinned, already unrolling the scroll. "I've a mind Kintail wishes to throw a feast in my honor."

He winked at Ronan, his eyes twinkling. "Now that'd be one secret-keeping I'd forgive you, laddie."

But when he stepped up to the table and held the scroll

close to the light of a candelabrum, the delight left Valdar's eyes.

"So I erred." His great shoulders dipped as he stared at the heavy black lines scrawled across the parchment.

"You didn't err. You were fooled...and by a master at deception. The Holder clearly guised himself as one of Kintail's men." Ronan put his hand on the older man's shoulder, pleased when they lifted again, squaring.

Even more pleased when Valdar's chest swelled and his face reddened with fury.

Rage was good.

He'd feared a different reaction.

"The lying jackal!" Valdar roared suddenly, crumpling the scroll in his fist. "So they've returned at last, the double-dyed ring-tailed dastards! And this time armed with belly wind and lies!"

"We do not know that." Ronan hated the admission, but it had to be made. "Too much is at stake not to take the warning seriously."

Valdar's brows shot upward. "Dinna tell me you mean to meet the bastard?"

"I see no choice." Ronan ran a hand through his hair, released a breath. "Not if my lady's life is in danger."

Something inside him twisted at the possibility she'd be harmed by someone at Dare.

The very notion jellied his knees.

"Then I'll go with you." Valdar swung away from him and snatched up his Viking axe. "'Tis overlong since Blood Drinker quenched his thirst!"

"Nae." Ronan took the axe from him and hung it back on the wall. "You and Blood Drinker will stay here—someone needs to look after Gelis."

And keep a sharp eye on everyone else.

He frowned. Those words, too, lodged in his throat, the meaning behind them too horrible to voice.

But Valdar had puffed up his chest and jammed his hands on his hips, once again looking much younger — and stronger — than his years.

"I will do as Dungal Tarnach proposes." Ronan spoke before he could change his mind. "I'll meet him at the Tobar Ghorm and I'll go there alone."

Valdar snorted.

"If you make it!" Striding back to the table, he poured himself another cup of *uisge beatha*, draining it in one quick gulp. "The loch surrounding the Blue Well's islet is vile. 'Tis known to be infested with nameless creatures, it is. Dark, terrible things much worse than water horses and water bulls. Things —"

Ronan cut him off with a hand wave. "Be that as it may, I can't risk not going."

Valdar harrumphed. "I still dinna like it."

"Neither do I," Ronan agreed.

But he'd like it even less if he ignored such an opportunity and ill befell his lady.

His lady and Valdar and even himself.

Since time immemorial — or, to be specific, since Valdar stole the Holders' Raven Stone — the turned druids had reviled Clan MacRuari, vowing their ruination unless the powerful stone was returned to them.

If they'd now won a MacRuari as an accomplice, no chances could be taken. Frowning, Ronan picked up the parchment and reread the boldly inked lines.

Even on a second reading, they galled.

"I'll ne'er believe it." Valdar snatched the scroll and

tossed it into the fire. "There isn't a man at Dare who'd turn coat on us."

"Mercy on the man's soul if there is." Ronan watched the parchment blacken and burn. "He'll no' live long enough to e'er change sides again."

But a short while later, as he paced Dare's rainswept battlements, needing the night's cold brittle air and icy wind to clear his mind, it wasn't the possibility of a betrayer that twisted him in knots.

It was wondering why a Holder would warn him.

Gelis dreamed of a man of spirit and hot blood.

Tall, well-favored, and with silky black hair just dusting his wide shoulders, he moved through the darkness of the small hours, naked save the gleam of his skin in the moonlight and the glint of gold banding his neck and circling one powerfully muscled arm.

Quiet as fate, he came to her, slipping into the bed and drawing her near. He tightened his arms around her, warming her with his heat and his strength. His arousal, hot, thick, and heavy, pressed against her hip, scorching her skin and making the lowest part of her belly clench with need.

That part of her melted, on fire and tingling.

She sighed, her own arms sliding around him, seeking his nearness. She ached for his touch, there where she needed him most and her womanhood pulsed and burned with desire.

As if he knew, his hand found her. His fingers skimmed over her maiden hair, drifting ever lower to gently caress the very center of her, cupping her fiercely.

"Och, lass, forgive me. I did no' want this." His voice,

dark, rich, and seductive, made her shiver. "But I canna resist you . . . am lost, as I've told you."

She cried out, reaching to clutch his shoulders and rocking her hips to increase the sweet pressure against his seeking, stroking fingers. But the drowsiness of sleep kept her gasps and sighs trapped inside her.

And hard as she tried, as was the way with dreams, her grasping hands and her aching hips refused to move.

He kissed her anyway, thrusting his hand into the loose spill of her hair and pulling her lips to his. Murmuring ancient Gaelic love words, he claimed her mouth in a hard, bruising kiss, deep and ravenous.

"Precious lass, let me touch you," he begged, the words hot silk against her lips. "There's no' a breath I take nor a beat of my heart that's no' steeped with wanting you."

"Ahhhh . . ." At last the dream let her move again and she arched into him. In reward, hot, tingling need rippled through her, drenching her.

She went liquid, her mouth opening wide beneath his. Her tongue swirled and thrust, seeking and tangling with his. Their hot breath mingled, each intimately shared gasp intoxicating her all the more.

Incredible pleasure whirled inside her, bright, sinuous flames that ignited her senses and curled her toes, making her wind and stretch on the cool richness of the bedsheets.

"Ahhhh," she cried again, this time letting her knees fall apart, opening herself to him.

"*Mo ghaoil*—my dear—you shouldn't have done that," he growled, lifting up on his elbows to stare down at her, every muscle-ripped inch of him poised above her, the bold look in his eyes making her even more hot, wet, and slippery.

He tightened his grip on her heat then, but released her as quickly. Still murmuring Gaelic love words, he smoothed his hands swiftly upward, seizing and kneading her breasts. Hot and strong, his fingers squeezed and plumped her flesh, the pleasure of it finally shattering the spell of her dream and letting her cry out her need.

"Yesss…Ronan!" She writhed against him, her fingers tangling in the coverlets and her thighs clamping around the plump feather pillow caught between them.

"Ronan…" She kicked the pillow aside and flung off the covers.

Flipping onto her stomach, she swept an arm across the cold and empty sheets.

Bedding icier than any she'd ever shared with her sister.

Impossible that a man had lain there with her.

With surety, not the Raven.

She'd only dreamed that he'd come to her.

Her own female need and desire had spun the wild, abandoned kind of passion she ached for so badly.

The heady, set-the-heather-ablaze kind of lovemaking she knew no man save Ronan could give her.

"No-o-o!" She dug her hands into the coverlets, her fingers gripping the richly embroidered sheets and the somewhat scratchy fur throws.

"Please." She choked on the word, a hot, scalding wetness tracking down her cheeks. "Come back—I need you…"

But only silence answered her.

That, and the hollow whistling of the cold night wind; the touches and voices that weren't there, reaching and whispering from the shadows.

"Ronan…" The name hung in the darkness, filling her soul even if her cry echoed back to her, hollow and unanswered.

Her heart pounding, she damned her dreams—for they only made her want him more—and rolled onto her side. A chill spread through her then, a coldness coming from deep in her soul. She reached for the cast-off covers, just closing her fingers on them when she saw him.

He stood across the darkened bedchamber, his tall form cloaked in shadow. Behind him, a few peat embers still glimmered on the hearthstone. The faint, orangey glow of the peat edged the wide set of his shoulders and the satiny spill of his sleek, raven hair.

No longer naked, he appeared swathed from head to toe in his great voluminous travel cloak, though she was sure the mantle would have needed laundering after shielding Buckie and his onion creel from the rain on the long journey back from Creag na Gaoith.

Shifting on the bed, she knuckled her eyes and then scrunched them to see him better. He stood unnaturally still, and although his face was cast in shadow, his eyes glinted darkly, and something about the way he was staring at her lifted the fine hairs on the back of her neck.

His neck, she saw with a start, was unadorned.

The fine golden torque he favored, nowhere to be seen.

Only the cowled folds of his robe's hood, gathered like a yoke of bunched, dark wool around his shoulders.

He lifted a hand and took a step forward, as if to gain her attention. But if he spoke, a sudden blast of howling wind stole the words. Again and again, the gusts battered the tower, rattling the shutters and filling the room with the cold, damp scent of rain and old wet stone.

Stone steeped in silence, its cold, lichened essence feeling almost pagan.

"Ach, *dia*," Gelis cried, her own words lost in the swelling, ear-piercing din.

Now a high-pitched, keening wail, the roar of the wind blotted everything but the wild buzzing in her head and the deafening thunder of her pulse.

The table and even her pile of strongboxes melted into the floor, quickly followed by the fine stone-carved hearth and its little clumps of glowing peat. Then the massive stone walls began to shake and weave, falling one by one into the darkness, their disappearance letting the deeper shadows swirl into the room.

"Gaaaaah!" She flung out an arm when one of those shadows rushed past her, the Raven's great four-poster bed vanishing in its wake.

She pitched forward, her bare feet and the flats of her hands hitting the floor rushes only to plunge right through them, her spiraling fall hurtling her into even greater, colder blackness.

"Gaaaaah!" she cried again, tumbling and spinning, her flailing arms grasping only air before she slammed hard onto something that felt distantly familiar, like the furred coverlets of her bed.

But the bed was no longer there.

Nothingness surrounded her.

A great dark void pressed in on her from all sides, cold and cloying, terrible in its emptiness.

Only *he* remained.

Her heart began a slow, hard thumping as she stared at him, dimly aware of the hand she'd clutched so fiercely to her breast and of the eerie quiet that now replaced the wild screaming winds of moments before.

Looking at ease in the chaos, her raven seemed oddly taller now.

His dark eyes glinted ever brighter, and he held out his arms, silently beseeching her as the darkness around him grew blacker.

Black as a tomb.

"*Ronan*—I pray you, stop. Don't do this…" But her voice sounded far away, as if she called to him from the bottom of a very deep well.

You're frightening me.

Those words, too, she held back, shamed by her fear.

Not that he could have heard her.

Already the blackness was consuming him. Dark and dense, it poured in, swirling first around his ankles and then whirling ever higher to slide around his knees and finally spread upward, circling his hips and all of him.

As if the shadows sought to bury him.

"No-o-o!" She clapped her hands to her cheeks, shaking her head. "Please stop."

Silence answered her, its deadness worse than hell's coldest wind.

She swallowed hard, her fingers digging into the swell of her bosom. She began to tremble, wanting to squeeze her eyes shut when the darkness reached his neck, but she couldn't look away.

Then only his eyes were visible.

Dark and piercing, they still glinted right at her, glowing as hotly as the hearth's reddish-orange peat embers she could no longer see.

But then she *was* staring at the peat embers.

The raven was gone.

And she was sprawled naked across his well-appointed bed.

Her bedchamber — nae, his — appeared as always.

No black winds tore at the wall hangings or rattled the soundly latched shutters. The table by the window and her own towering stack of hump-backed, iron-bound coffers stood exactly where they should.

Untouched, and certainly not *melted*.

Even the scattered bearskin rugs on the floor were undisturbed, without even a single stray bit of dried mead-owsweet or what-have-you marring their glossy pelts.

That alone was a clear indication that no unholy wind had swept through the room.

Even so, she drew the bedcovers to her chin.

She knew fine what she'd seen.

Even if she also knew someone else could have stood beside her and not noticed a thing amiss.

She knew better.

Something was sorely amiss.

And she had enough experience with such matters to guess exactly what it was.

"Saints, Maria, and Joseph!" Her father's favorite curse slipped from her lips and she fell back against the bedcushions, her entire body shaking.

Staring up at the richly carved bed ceiling, she clenched her fists and fought hard against slipping into the deceptive peace of slumber.

Two truths were bearing down on her and she could deny neither.

The first seized her each time she drew a new, lung-filling gulp of the cold, early morning air.

Ronan *had* spent at least a few hours in her bed.

The sheets and coverlets reeked of him, or, better said, of the rank-smelling goldenrod goo she'd spread across his ribs and smeared onto his toes.

The second truth ripped her heart and stole her breath, its horror splitting her soul.

The blackness she'd seen consuming Ronan could only mean his death. And the icy cold, stone-drenched emptiness had to have represented his tomb.

Gelis shuddered, hating the interpretation.

But try as she might, she couldn't find another explanation, much as the reality struck her like an iron-hard fist in the belly.

The Raven truly stood in mortal danger.

She'd just have to be sure she was ready when the blow came.

She'd be damned if her Raven's foes would defeat her.

And she'd face down the devil himself before she'd let them conquer him.

Enough was enough.

Chapter Fourteen

✦

Aye, that's what I said, just!" Valdar leaned back in his great carved laird's chair, his mailed shirt gleaming brightly beneath his plaid. "He rode out well before sunrise. And, nae, he didn't tell me his business."

He looked around the high table as if seeking agreement, seeming pleased when the kinsmen sitting there responded with assorted grunts and nods.

Even so, Gelis wasn't fooled.

She took a deep breath. "He told no one where he was going?"

Valdar snorted. "My grandson?"

Anice, just setting down a platter of buttered bannocks and cheese, flushed and hastened from the dais. She stopped only long enough to right an upturned trestle bench, then quickly disappeared into the bustling hall.

Several men at the high table cleared throats or scratched at their elbows.

Sorley and the other garrison guards did the same at a

nearby long table, each one studiously avoiding her gaze. Gelis frowned watching them. The men who'd readily helped her get Buckie and her Viking tent out to Creag na Gaoith now seemed far more interested in gobbling their oats and examining the floor rushes.

Some appeared to inspect their fingernails.

Ignoring them all, Gelis folded her arms. "I must speak with him, Valdar."

He's in danger.

She held back the words, not wanting to alarm the old chieftain.

Though, in truth, she was certain he knew.

"That one was e'er a man of his own mind," he blurted, sitting forward to snatch up his ale cup. "We'll not be a-seeing him until he comes hallooing back in through the gates. Like as not, sometime late this e'en."

Gelis pounced. "You know where he is."

Valdar wagged his bearded head. "I'm a-guessing, lass. No more."

"Then where do you *guess* he is?"

"Off to Kyleakin to see about acquiring malt for MacHugh's brewhouse, mayhap," he offered with a shrug. "Word is our stores are low. Or"—he winked broadly—"perhaps he's chasing down the peddler said to be journeying through your da's territories these days. Could be he wants to fetch a few fine gee-gaws and ribbons for you!"

Gelis didn't believe a word.

But Valdar held her eye, the image of graybearded innocence, save that he had donned a hauberk.

A precautionary measure if ever there was one.

Especially in light of the long, two-handed sword propped

just a bit too casually against his chair and the wicked-looking Norse battle-axe resting on the table.

Called Blood Drinker, or so she'd heard, the axe held pride of place next to a wooden bowl of slaked oats and a jug of watered-down morning ale.

Gelis narrowed her eyes. "His absence wouldn't have anything to do with all the steel in the hall, would it?"

"Steel?" He blinked, not quite managing to look surprised.

"Aye, steel." She made a sweeping gesture. "And I don't mean your men's eating knives."

Valdar coughed.

Grabbing his ale cup again, he helped himself to a healthy swig.

The other men at the table rushed to fuss at their plaids, clumsily trying to conceal the telltale glints and bulges of weapons peeking up from their boots or other sundry hiding places.

A quick glance into the crowded lower end of the hall showed that every MacRuari present was equally well armed. Gelis swallowed a curse, then scrunched her eyes to see better through the smoke-and-torch haze hanging above the long rows of tables. Her heart caught when she spotted at least two other Norse battle-axes propped against trestle benches.

She also spied young Hector perched in a window embrasure, Buckie sprawled at his feet. And—no great surprise—the boy's newly acquired *sgian dubh* wasn't tucked into a boot or beneath his belt, but proudly displayed atop one of the window seat cushions.

Most disturbing of all was the giant figure of Hugh MacHugh lurking near the hall's vaulted entry. Pacing to and fro in front of the massive oaken door, he held a sharp-bladed meat cleaver clutched in his hand.

Her stomach lurched at the sight.

Everyone knew a master cook had too many duties not to be busy at his kitchen fires.

Especially at this early hour of the day.

She frowned.

Then she puffed a curl off her brow and stepped closer to the high table. "Dare is readying for a siege." She didn't bother to make it a question. "I've lived through enough at Eilean Creag to tell."

"Dare is e'er prepared for trouble." Valdar dug his spoon into his bowl of slaked oats, stirring. "The *showing* you see this morn has more to do with you than any foe who might or might not be bearing down on our walls."

Her brows rose. "With me?"

"So I said."

"But that makes no sense."

Valdar stopped stirring his oats. "It did to my grandson." He glanced up, eyeing her. "That much I can tell you. Before he rode out, he ordered every man not on the walls to hie himself into the hall to guard you."

For one shining moment, a surge of pleasure wrapped round and filled Gelis, swelling her heart and warming her until she realized the true meaning of Valdar's declaration.

Her gaze flashed to the Blood Drinker. "So we *are* under siege?"

"Nae." He waved his spoon at her. "The Raven didn't want you following him again. He set his men to keep watch so you canna leave the hall."

Gelis blinked.

Then she looked from him to the well-filled tables of guardsmen and back to him. Whether or not the Raven cared enough about her to wish to prevent her from hastening after him — perhaps into danger — she still wasn't happy with Valdar's spoon-wielding explanation.

"What about all the weapons?" She put her hands on her hips. "We both know those swords and dirks aren't meant for use against me. So" — she summoned her most persuasive smile — "just who is to be the recipient of their sharp ends?"

"That I canna say, lass."

"Canna or willna?"

Valdar took renewed interest in oat stirring.

"I see." Gelis tilted her head, pretending to consider. "Then I shall just have to find someone else to question."

She glanced out over the torchlit hall, her eyes narrowed and searching, looking for the one soul she suspected might have answers.

It took less than a wink to find her.

She'd only needed to study the shadows darkening the hall's entry. There, where Hugh MacHugh paced in all his ruddy, rough-hewn glory. Great-eyed Anice hovered near the door, the adulation on her face undisguised now that she felt herself unobserved.

Gelis smiled. Her pulse quickened.

Leaving Valdar to his oats and his spoon, she turned away and hurried from the dais. She strode across the hall, secretly pleased when the Raven's hard-faced, steel-toting stalwarts made way for her, each man stepping back respectfully at her approach, clearing a path through their midst.

Soon, success would be hers.

A woman in love—and she was sure the timid serving lass had hung her heart on Dare's cook—would never refuse help to another woman suffering the same affliction.

Her own heart began to pound and her breath caught on the realization that she loved the Raven.

She shivered, a delicious swirl of warmth spilling through her. Truth was, she knew, she'd loved him ever since the morning she'd first glimpsed him in vision. She could still see him that way, striding so boldly toward her on Eilean Creag's little shingled strand.

Making her blood heat and all the woman inside her quiver with desire.

She'd die if aught happened to him.

Remembering his kisses—and the horrible blackness she'd seen enfold him in her most recent vision—she hastened her step, almost colliding with a kitchen laddie weaving his way across the hall with a platter of sausages and fresh-baked bannocks.

Somewhere a shutter cracked in the wind and someone slammed it shut, the noise overloud in her ears. Fearing the onset of another vision, she pressed a hand to her breast, relieved when the *buzzing* in her head proved no more than her own blood pounding in her temples.

Almost at the entry, she skirted several castle dogs squabbling over a bone. She deflected the interest of another when he trotted up to her, eager for ear rubs and back scratches. Then one of the iron-bracketed resin torches flared as she dashed past, the flames leaping upward, dancing wildly and sparking a plume of bright, hissing ash.

And finally she was there.

The hall's great iron-studded doors loomed but a few

paces before her. Hugh MacHugh still marched to and fro, his stride long and purposeful, the blade of his meat cleaver glinting in the torchlight.

But Anice was gone.

Disappointment swept her, but she tamped it down, hastening instead to insert herself in front of the cook, effectively blocking his path.

"My lady." He stopped at once. "A fine morn to you."

"Aye, and it would be if I knew where my husband has ridden off to." She leaned forward, so close she could almost smell his nervousness. "I don't suppose you can tell me?"

He shook his head. "Nae, I—"

She overrode him. "I already know...you canna say." She drew herself up, said a silent prayer of thanks that she wasn't some wee slip of a maid, easily blown away on the slightest puff of a breeze.

"But I do wish to have a word with Anice," she added. "Where is she?"

Hugh MacHugh swallowed. "Anice?"

"Herself, and no other." Gelis lifted her chin. "She was here just moments ago. I saw her standing there"—she pointed to where a little charcoal brazier hissed and glowed in a shadowy corner—"and watching you."

Hugh MacHugh's face reddened.

"I didn't see her, my lady," he said, shuffling his feet.

But his gaze flicked to the door.

"Ha! So she left the hall, did she?" Gelis darted around him, seizing the door latch. "Then I will just go after her. She couldn't have gone far."

To her surprise, the cook didn't argue with her.

Instead, he drew a hand over his thinning red hair and blew out a breath.

"She went to gather broody hen eggs," he admitted, his big hands working on the shaft of his meat cleaver.

"Then perhaps I shall...help her!" Gelis hitched up her skirts and tugged on the door latch.

Hugh MacHugh's hand closed around her wrist. "It willna do you any good to go out there, my lady."

"Ah, but I do disagree," she owned, jerking free.

She yanked open the door and scooted out onto the landing before he could try to stop her again.

But she saw at once that he had no need.

A tight phalanx of guardsmen lined the entire length of the keep's outer stair, their close-packed ranks grim-faced and silent.

And even if she'd consider nipping past them, their drawn and crossed swords blocked the way.

She was well and truly trapped.

Though she *would* catch Anice and speak to her later.

That knowledge — and her pride — lifting her spirits, she straightened her back and walked to the edge of the landing with all the dignity she could muster. She put her hands on the cold stone of the landing wall and leaned out into the chill morning wind, pretending to relish its briskness.

One, two obviously deep gulps of the brittle air — and perhaps an appreciative sigh or an artful head toss — should be enough to convince the guardsmen.

It wouldn't do to have them think their new lady had been about to gallop down the keep stair and streak across the bailey, looking for broody hens!

But when, after enough air gulping and head tosses,

she turned to go back inside, all thought of hen eggs, Anice, and even stony-faced guardsmen fled her mind.

Maldred the Dire's heraldic crest was gone.

Or rather, she couldn't see it.

Her jaw slipping, she stared up at the space above the hall door where the great hoary stone should have been. Either her eyes had suddenly gone as milky as old Buckie's or her *taibhsearachd* was playing some new trick on her.

Yet no weird buzzing filled her ears. And neither the landing nor the solid bulk of the keep walling appeared to fade or waver.

Everything looked and felt as it should — save for the missing crest stone.

Her heart thumping, she stepped closer, craning her neck to get a better look. In that moment, the sun broke through a cloud, its bright morning light silvering the tower wall like a polished mirror.

At once, she spotted the great stone slab that was once Maldred's, recognizing its distinctive shape set so prominently above the door.

But the sight sent chills down her spine and she had to clasp a hand to her mouth to keep from gasping.

The stone might still be there, but no one could ever call it Maldred's again.

Every last faded line of incising and carvings had been erased.

The stone stared down at her, its age-pitted bulk looking no different from the other squares of granite masoned so proudly into Dare's walls.

But the power of it stopped her heart.

That, and the distinct impression that the stone could

see her. Then the clouds closed over the sun again and the odd sensation vanished.

Gelis shivered and rubbed her arms.

Then she smiled.

Whatever force had smoothed the stone's surface, she knew in her heart it boded well.

Dare was on its way to healing.

She was absolutely certain of it.

Ronan was almost certain he'd made a grave error.

His little skiff, scarce more than a cockleshell, tossed and pitched in the cold, choppy waters of Loch Dubh. The small, black-watered loch vexed and bedeviled him, giving itself as dark as its benighted name.

Scowling, he set his jaw against the pain in his ribs when the skiff plunged into yet another deep trough, but struggle as he would, the tossing waves and icy, spray-filled air undid each hard-won ply of his carefully wielded oars.

A driving wet mist drove up the loch and low clouds raced across the surrounding hills. The gusting wind blew in his face, making it ever harder to reach the little islet standing out so blackly against the thick gray fog shrouding the fine, rolling sweeps of Dare's highest moorland.

But a dark-cloaked figure stood waiting on the islet's stone jetty, the man's penetrating stare piercing the whirling mist and keeping him on course.

Tall, white-maned, and wind-beaten, the berobed observer could only be Dungal Tarnach.

Or so Ronan hoped.

He tightened his grip on the oars, almost sure of it.

No one else save Valdar knew his true whereabouts.

And the power of the man shone bright against the islet's thickly wooded foreshore, his mere silhouette edged with a shifting orangey-red glow that lit the tall ash and scarlet-berried rowan trees behind him.

The glow brightened as Ronan drew near, the wind swinging round to buffet him from behind and send the little skiff racing across the foaming waves, directly toward the old stone pier and the slick, weed-hung rocks lining the strand.

"So you came—Raven." The man nodded in greeting, then held out a hand to aid him ashore when the skiff bumped against the jetty.

Ronan gripped the extended hand, pride not letting him refuse the courtesy. "I would hear what you have to say," he said simply, stepping up onto the pier. "I trust I will not have cause to regret meeting with you."

The Holder looked at him, his eyes like smoldering coals. "Come with me to the Tobar Ghorm and you can decide what you make of my tidings."

"There are tales told in my family of the Blue Well," Ronan said as they left the jetty to follow a narrow track through the trees. "The well was sacred to the Ancients. A place where folk no longer remembered gathered on certain days to drink the water and leave offerings in the hope of securing good fortune or curing ills. The Old Ones—"

"Still hold Tobar Ghorm as hallowed."

Ronan frowned. "Then I find it an odd trysting place for a Holder."

Dungal Tarnach turned to face him. "The well's sanctity is the reason I chose it," he said, the strange glow edging his robes gone now.

Even his eyes no longer glimmered eerily but appeared a faded light blue.

They'd left the trees and now stood in a small clearing overgrown with dead heather and thigh-high, autumn-red bracken. The Holder glanced at the Tobar Ghorm, his almost-ordinary gaze fixing on the barely discernible well in the center of the little glade.

Of very great antiquity indeed, little remained of the well save a tumble of toppled stones. Some were covered with early Celtic carvings, while others appeared simply moss-grown or riddled with lichen.

Even so, cloaked in soft mist as the clearing now was, it was all too easy to imagine ancient rites taking place there. Perhaps, too, that those so gifted might use the well's *Druidecht* to pass easily between this world and those beyond.

Ronan shuddered and drew his plaid closer about his shoulders. The Tobar Ghorm's pagan magic yet pulsed here, untouched by the centuries, its *life force* seizing him like a fist clenched around his soul.

Unthinkable that a turned druid would dare risk treading here.

Yet Dungal Tarnach stood proud, not a trace of shame or humility on his face.

He looked at Ronan then and for one brief moment a trace of sadness flickered in his eyes. "You think one such as I cannot hold a place such as this in high honor?"

"I did not say that." Ronan frowned, feeling oddly chastised.

"You did not have to."

"I—" Ronan bit off the words, not even sure what he meant to say.

He glanced up at the low black clouds racing so swiftly across the sky, wishing they could whisk him back to Dare. The Tobar Ghorm and its little islet were more than dark, bleak, and lonely.

The place was having a weird effect on him and he didn't like it.

Most especially he didn't care for the way — since stepping into the clearing and nearing the well — he couldn't help but notice the lines on the Holder's face or the bony thinness of his shoulders.

The slight hitch in his step when he walked, as if his hips pained him.

"Did you know, Raven," he said then, suddenly standing next to the well, "that even on a day as dark as this, the water of the well remains blue as sapphire?"

As if to prove it, he leaned over the fallen stones and peered down into the rubble. Straightening, he turned back to Ronan.

"You should look." He glanced at the well again, his robes lifting in the wind.

"I saw the water as a lad," Ronan admitted, remembering his awe at its brilliance.

And, too, how his young boy's heart had believed his father's tale that the dazzling blue was the eye color of a beautiful but tragic Celtic princess who'd drowned herself in the well when her sweetheart was killed in battle.

Preferring death to life without him, or worse, being forced to wed another, she'd rowed herself out to the little islet and taken solace in the only way she knew.

Ever since, or so legend claimed, she granted favors and healing to those visiting her well, taking especial care to help those unlucky in love, not wanting others to suffer the sorrow that had taken all joy and light from her life, ultimately causing her death.

Pushing the tale from his mind, Ronan strode across the clearing to join the Holder at the well. He did not attempt to peer through the jumble of stones and weeds to see the glittering water.

Instead, he folded his arms. "So-o-o, Dungal Tarnach," he began, "if you are indeed the man who penned a certain missive, I would hear the name of the traitor in my midst."

The Holder raised a brow. "You doubt my identity?"

"I would only be sure I hear the words from the man who brought such tidings." Ronan narrowed his eyes, taking in the Holder's simple robe and his flowing white hair and beard. "You do not look like any MacKenzie I ever saw. Or did you use *Druidecht* to bespell my grandfather?"

"Valdar MacRuari saw what he expected to see—as did all your men."

"Dare men are no fools." Ronan spoke with conviction. "They know men that are *others* roam our glen from time to time. They know to be wary."

"And they knew MacKenzies were still riding through your lands." His mouth quirking, the Holder lifted a hand, palm upward to the heavens.

In a blink, he was changed.

For one earth-tilting moment he stood before Ronan no longer looking aged beyond measure, but like a shadow image of the Black Stag. Or, at the least, like a man who shared that one's blood and name.

Then he lowered his hand and was himself again.

Tall, berobed, and gaunt, his white-maned head held proud despite the slight stoop to his shoulders.

"So you are Dungal Tarnach." Ronan refused to acknowledge the man's transformation talent.

All druids were skilled thus.

Even Torcaill, though they never discussed such things.

Ronan kept his eyes intent on this druid, now a Holder. "It matters little to me under which guise you cloak yourself. I would only hear who thinks to betray me."

"He means to do more than betray you." Dungal Tarnach held his gaze, his faded blue eyes equally earnest. "His plan is to taint your food and drink with poison. He will seek to kill you, your lady, your grandfather, and any others who might have the misfortune to sit at your high table when he chooses to make his move."

"And do you know why?" Ronan could scarce speak past the bile in his throat. "Dare men are known for their loyalty. I cannot think of a single one who would turn so viciously against his own clan."

The Holder shrugged. "Then perhaps you should consider the other thing Dare men are known for—they dwell on blighted ground. Outside this glen, your name rarely passes good folks' lips. They fear just thinking of you will touch them with your darkness."

Ronan grunted. "It is because of the like that our men are so true, so beholden to our own."

When the Holder only shrugged again, he flexed his jaw and struggled against clenching his hands. A horrible suspicion was beginning to unravel in his mind and he didn't want it to take shape.

Dungal Tarnach cleared his throat. "This man is weary of living as you do," he said, voicing Ronan's dread. "He is one who hopes to turn the minds of your other men once you are no more."

"Bah!" Ronan slashed the air with his hand. "The others would string him up on the nearest gibbet."

"Perhaps." The Holder fingered his beard, considering. "But he might meet with success, convincing them that without you, Dare's darkness can be lifted."

Ronan snorted.

Dungal Tarnach stepped closer, gripping Ronan's arm. "He has sought to treat with us—the Holders—vowing to throw open your gates and let us search Dare for the Raven Stone. In return, he asks that we help him eliminate any of your men who might resist him. Once that is done—"

"He means to live off our riches and expects you to take your Raven Stone and vanish from our bounds," Ronan finished for him, sure that was the way of it.

Not surprisingly, the Holder nodded.

And although he'd been so certain, the confirmation chilled Ronan's blood.

He paced away, then swung around before he'd gone three paces. "You haven't told me his name. Who is he?"

"I cannot speak his name." Dungal Tarnach lifted his hands, showing his palms. "Letting it touch my tongue would diminish my own power. I—and all my kind—have suffered enough each time we speak of your thieving forebear. I will not foul my breath on this man.

"But"—he raised an arm, pointing across the clearing—"I will show him to you."

Ronan followed the Holder's outstretched arm, his heart slamming against his ribs when he saw his foe standing at the edge of the narrow track to the jetty.

Encircled by a flickering bluish glow, he stared right back at Ronan, his eyes blank and unseeing.

His identity was unmistakable.

"Christ God!" Ronan cried, staring.

And then the image vanished, leaving only the glimmering blue haze against the trees.

When that, too, faded, Ronan whirled around to face the Holder.

"I canna believe it!" He ran a hand through his hair, vaguely noting that his fingers shook. "No' him. I'd have trusted him with my life—and have!"

"Men are turned by many things." The Holder looked down at the well again, his shoulders seeming to dip a bit. "Greed and wealth, always. Love and hate can be powerful motivators. Or, as with your ill-famed forebear, simply a raging thirst for power."

"I still canna believe it," Ronan repeated, shaking his head.

His stomach roiled and he felt sick inside, as if he'd been walking along a cliff edge and someone he trusted had just strode up to him and kicked him over the edge.

He started pacing again, then froze, a new thought stopping him in his tracks.

"Why did you tell me this?" He shot a glance at the Holder. "Would it not have served you better to keep silent?"

Dungal Tarnach was still peering down at the Blue Well. When he finally looked up, he sighed.

"Nae, it wouldn't have served me to keep this from you," he said, his voice sounding old, tired. "Nor would it have done us any good to have agreed to your man's terms—though he knows nothing yet of our refusal."

"Say you?"

The Holder nodded. "We deemed it wise to bide for

time, telling him we'd give him our answer on the next full of the moon."

"You wished to warn me first?" Ronan spoke the obvious.

Again, the Holder inclined his head.

"I do not understand," Ronan said, and he didn't.

To his surprise, Dungal Tarnach smiled. "Would that I could tell you my druidic honor obliged me to warn you of such treachery in your midst," he said, that odd almost-wistful note in his voice again.

"Alas," he continued, "it had naught to do with the three greatest precepts druids abide by. Do you know them?" He glanced at Ronan, one white brow arcing. "We train for twenty long years, enduring much hardship to hone and perfect our skills. But above all, we vow to honor the gods, to be ever manly, and to always speak true."

"And you are speaking the truth." Ronan knew it in his bones.

"To be sure." The Holder lifted his voice above the rising wind. "But not for those reasons. They would only have swayed me...many years ago."

"And now?"

"Now..." Dungal Tarnach looked away, his gaze seeming to search for an answer in the thickly clustered ash and rowan trees crowding the edge of the glade. "Now, I warned you because doing so serves our purposes as well."

Ronan almost choked.

His jaw did slip. "Warning me serves the Holders?"

Dungal Tarnach looked at him, his gaze no longer a harmless blue. "We seek only the return of what is ours. The Raven Stone, as you know," he said, the red glint in his eyes deepening on each word. "The stone was tainted when Maldred stole it from us. His thievery—taking the property of friends—greatly diminished the stone's power."

"Then why do you still want it?" Ronan felt a ridiculous surge of hope.

"Because even tainted, the stone is ours." The Holder stood straighter, seeming to grow in height and dimension. "It is of untold sanctity and significance to us. And its powers are still formidable."

"Then why didn't you jump when you were handed a chance to search for it within our walls?" Ronan puzzled. "You're no' making sense."

"Druids always make sense," the Holder corrected him. "Turned or nae, we ne'er waste a word. Had we agreed to such a treacherous plan as was offered to us, the stone's value would have decreased yet again. We must find the stone on our own terms, not accept it from the hands of a man whose heart is so blackened he'd spill the blood of his own to gain his wicked ends."

"I see." Ronan released a breath, understanding indeed. "So now that you've assured the stone won't lose further power, you mean to keep plaguing us?"

"We mean to continue our search—as we have done since time was."

"And if I tell you I have ne'er truly believed in the stone? Or that my father and grandfather and all those before them spent years looking for it, always to no avail?"

"Then I would tell you that their failure makes no difference. The stone does exist and we will get it back."

The words spoken, Dungal Tarnach stepped forward

and offered his hand. "I will also tell you I wish you well in dealing with your man."

Ronan took the Holder's hand, gripping tight. "And I...thank you for the warning."

"It will be the only one given. The next time we meet, there will be no niceties. But"—his eyes flickered blue for just a moment—"I was gladdened to meet you here today. You are a good man, Ronan MacRuari. In another life we might have been friends."

The words spoken, the Holder turned and walked away, quickly disappearing into the trees on the far side of the clearing, leaving Ronan alone.

His fury, though, erupted all around him, pressing close and cutting off his air.

"By all that's holy, I still canna believe it," he roared, spinning around to race through the underbrush.

Heart pounding, he charged down the narrow path to the jetty and leaped into the little skiff before he had time to disbelieve Dungal Tarnach's words.

In his heart, he knew he'd spoken true.

He could only hope he wasn't mistaken.

If so, he was about to kill an innocent man.

Chapter Fifteen

✦

Hours later, Gelis wrinkled her nose and wondered how much longer it would take for Anice to pay a visit to Dare's grandest luxury... a privy chamber reserved solely for women.

Set deep into the thickness of the stair tower's walling, the tiny room boasted a mosaic-tiled floor and not one but two air-spending window slits. A wicker basket near the *necessary* brimmed with a goodly supply of clean and fragrant sphagnum moss, while a small wooden corner shelf held a laver kept fresh with cold, scented water and a tiny jar of lavender soap, adding to the chamber's charm.

Not to mention the usual amenities.

The pride of Dare's womenfolk, the privy was rumored to have been designed by Valdar's mother, a woman of Norse descent who, by all recollections, lived before her time.

Thinking of her now, confined as Gelis was to her chosen hiding place, she was glad the Norsewoman set so much store on a lady's privacy and comfort.

It made her vigil pass with greater ease.

Even though, at the moment, her oversensitive nose twitched too much for her to appreciate the chamber's luxuries.

She only cared that no one had suspected her plan when she'd slipped from the hall, pleading an aching head.

She also said a prayer—including a nod to the Old Ones—that Anice would soon appear.

Her nose could not take much more of the little room's particular tang.

Well-appointed or nae.

But then the door creaked open and she lunged, clamping tight fingers around her quarry's arm and drawing her from the piquant-smelling little chamber right back out into the open of the stair tower landing.

"Lady!" Anice stared at her, eyes wide. "You near frightened the life out of me."

"I had to speak with you." Gelis kept her grip on the girl's elbow and pulled her deeper into the shadows. "I must know where the Raven went this morn and why every man is bristling with steel."

Anice flushed and bit her lip.

"You must tell me what you know," Gelis insisted. "My husband is in danger."

"Ahhhh, lady." Anice looked down, fussing at her skirts. "I know less than anyone. Would that I could help you—"

"But you can!" Gelis refused to give up. "You must know something. I saw it in your eyes when you fled the high table earlier. Come"—she let go of Anice's arm and glanced down the stairwell, making sure they were alone—"if you do not know where he is, tell me why you looked so frightened."

Anice drew a deep breath. "'Tis the Holders," she said, looking miserable. "Leastways I fear they are the reason he rode out so early, why the men have taken up extra arms."

"The Holders?" Gelis blinked.

Anice's head bobbed. "They were the original Holders of the Raven Stone and Maldred the Dire's bitterest foes," she began, twisting her hands. "Some say they still exist, or at least their descendants. They sweep into Glen Dare again and again, always searching for their stone, wanting it back."

"Pah-phooey!" Gelis puffed a curl off her brow. "If there are such men, I vow the Raven and his Dare men could make small work of them."

"Not the Holders, lady." Anice leaned close, her voice low. "They are not like other men. They are...shadowy and have glowing red eyes. 'Tis known that they can melt steel and iron, charm any beast, and that they practice all manner of other nefarious magic."

Gelis flicked her braid over her shoulder. "If such terrors exist, I am sure they can be defeated. I vow my own father has fought and bested worse enemies."

Anice looked unconvinced.

"So-o-o," Gelis considered, her mind already racing, "do the mist wraiths I've heard castle folk whispering about have anything to do with these men?"

"Aye, they do." Anice dropped her voice even lower. "The mist snakes are the Holders' minions. There have been many sightings of them in recent times. Even Hugh says—"

"Is Hugh MacHugh the reason you stay here?" Gelis angled her head. "The Raven once mentioned he'd offered to return you to your parents' home, but you declined. I know MacHugh is fond of you."

Anice's cheeks brightened. "He is a fine man," she admitted, her face turning even pinker. "But I stayed on because of you, my lady."

Gelis's brows lifted. "Because of me?"

"Aye." Anice began worrying her hands again. "I came here to work as lady's maid for the Raven's second wife, see you? The lady Cecilia."

She paused, glancing aside for a moment. "After her passing, I thought about leaving because the darkness here frightens me sometimes, but then I heard you were coming and knew I couldn't leave."

"Why not?" Gelis looked at her. "If you were unhappy, surely it would have been better to go?"

Anice's chin rose. "I thought you might need me. And I wanted to serve you."

"But you did not know me," Gelis puzzled. "That doesn't seem—"

"I knew your father," the girl said, completely surprising her. "He—"

"You met him before he brought me here?" Gelis could scarce believe it.

Anice nodded. "He helped me once and I never forgot it. I'd gone with my parents on a trip to town—to Inverness—and was so overwhelmed by the size of the market and the noise and all the people that I became separated from them."

"You were lost?" Gelis encouraged her.

"Horribly," Anice confirmed, "and so frightened, my lady."

"And my father helped you?"

"I...bumped into him." Anice tucked a strand of dark hair behind her ear, her blush returning. "I was crying and running through the market stalls and just plowed right into him. He caught me by the shoulders and asked me what was wrong and when I told him, he took me up on his horse and brought me safely to my parents' door."

Gelis blinked against a hot prickling at the backs of her eyes. "That sounds just like him," she said, smiling at the girl. "I am glad he was the man you bumped into."

"I am, too, my lady." Anice's own eyes shone a bit over-bright. "So you see why I stayed on when I heard you were to be the Raven's new wife."

Wife.

The word leaped at Gelis, biting hard and making her heart seize. Even worse—saints forgive her—the very thought of another woman having been the Raven's own jabbed hotly at all her softest and most vulnerable places.

Never before had the notion lanced her so.

But never either did anyone at Dare seem to speak of his two former ladies.

Only in hand-muffled mutterings she'd done her best not to hear.

She swallowed once, then twice, and even nipped the inside of her cheek trying to hold back the questions burning on her tongue. But then curiosity and the green-tinged stabs still pricking her overrode her willpower.

She tossed back her hair and drew a deep breath.

Nothing helped.

So she blurted, "You served the Raven's second wife, Lady...Cecilia?"

Anice looked surprised, but nodded. "Aye, I did. Even to her last day, God rest her soul."

"You were there at the birthing?" Gelis hated herself for asking, but her tongue seemed to have taken on a mind of its own. "When she ... died?"

"Aye." Anice's brow knit. "Auld Meg and I attended her. We couldn't do anything to help her. She —"

"The Raven must've been heartbroken." The words tasted like cold ash in her mouth.

Gelis frowned.

Shame scalded her, but the taste of bitter ash remained.

Now she'd surely damned herself.

"I know how much he loved his first wife," she rushed on anyway, unable to stop, "but can you tell me ... do you think he loved Lady Cecilia as much?"

"He didn't love her at all. No man would have —" Anice clapped a hand to her breast, her eyes wide. "O-o-oh, forgive me, lady, I shouldn't have said aught. But the words just popped out."

Gelis waved a hand, not trusting herself to speak.

Her heart split wide, relief flooding her.

Even though she was quite sure she was very wicked to be gladdened that the Raven hadn't been passionately in love with his second wife.

She knew from kitchen blether that the woman had been a frail flower. Tiny and dark-haired, and everything she wasn't. In truth, she'd feared her own well-rounded dips, curves, and *fillings* might not appeal to a man used to loving a woman the size of a sparrow.

She bit the corner of her lip.

Now she knew different.

Hope began to pump through her. Her blood surged. She'd been so certain the Raven deeply mourned Lady

Cecilia. That her ghost would always stand between them.

"Pray dinna be wroth with me, lady." Anice was peering at her, her eyes worried.

Gelis leaned back against the curve of the stair tower wall, her knees suddenly wobbly. "Nae, nae, I am not vexed," she said, feeling anything but.

She felt absolutely giddy.

"So the lady wasn't well-loved?" The question made her face heat, but she had to know. "The Raven never speaks of her."

"She wasn't very kindly. Not to any of us." Anice looked down at her hands, then back at Gelis. "I am not surprised the Raven doesn't speak of her. Not after the way she cursed him before she died. She —"

Whack!

The slamming of the hall door interrupted her, the sharp cracking noise echoing in the stair tower and even shaking the walls.

"Valdar!" The roar from the hall followed at once, thundering and furious. "Touch naught!"

"Sweet Jesu — the Raven!" Gelis hitched up her skirts and ran down the stairs, Anice quick on her heels.

Already, other voices were rising, loud and alarmed, the sudden din accompanied by the barking of dogs, shouts, and the sound of scraped-back benches and scuffling.

Panting, the two women burst from the stair tower into chaos. Everywhere men were jumping to their feet and the floor was strewn with crockery and cups from several upturned long tables. The castle dogs raced about in circles, getting underfoot and greatly lending to the ruckus, while near the stair-foot two cursing men stood half-naked, using their plaids to smother burning floor rushes.

Gelis veered out of their way, nearly falling headlong over a toppled candelabrum.

Anice *did* stumble into it, the hem of her skirt catching fire from the still-burning candles scattered in a ring around the thing's curving arms.

"Aggggh!" she wailed, freezing.

"Here!" Gelis yanked a linen off the nearest table and dropped to her knees to swat at the flames with the bunched cloth. " 'Tis out already — dinna fret."

Pushing to her feet, she grabbed Anice's arm, pulling her deeper into the throng, away from the candelabrum fire and the two men.

Busy slapping at the smoking rushes with their plaids, they had the flames nearly under control, and — more urgently — across the hall, the Raven still bellowed, his angry voice sharp against the tumult.

"Dear saints, what has — aaiieee!" Gelis leaped aside as four of the castle dogs sped past, nearly knocking her down.

Righting herself, she shoved back her hair and grabbed up her skirts to rush forward again, pushing and pressing through the tight-packed throng.

"Ronan!" she called, finally seeing him.

Just gaining the dais, he tore up the steps to that raised platform, the dark fury on his face closing her throat.

Ronan! She tried to cry out again, but her voice emerged as a rasp, her chest so tight she could hardly breathe.

Panting, she clasped a hand to her breast and looked on in horror as he raced across the dais, murder in his eye. Valdar and the others were already on their feet, but they sprang back from the table, shock on their faces as he whipped out his sword, raising it above his head.

For one horrible moment, Ronan held the brand high and stared down at the rich viands spread across the pristine white linen. A great platter of roasted stag haunch hadn't yet been touched, but the bread and ale clearly had.

As well, more than one cup held dredges of his grandfather's prized Gascon wine.

And someone—or perhaps all of them—had done great justice to Hugh MacHugh's excellent cheese pasties.

Ronan's heart twisted and a terrible fear ripped his innards.

Pray God he wasn't too late.

Then, with all the rage inside him, he brought down his sword, swiping the glittering blade the full length of the high table.

Food, wine-and-ale cups and ewers, *everything* flew to the floor with a deafening clatter, the crash plunging men into silence.

Spinning around, he raised his blade again, this time searching the packed hall. Some still-hoping part of him willed that he'd only just made a fool of himself and that when he met his supposed betrayer's eyes, he'd see only surprise and innocence.

But then he spotted the man.

And his entire stance was one of wariness.

His face blanched with guilt.

"Sorley!" Ronan jumped down from the dais, his sword flashing. "A reckoning!"

"You're mad!" The guards captain backed away, hands in the air. "Whatever you heard is untrue."

"What makes you think I've heard aught?" Ronan advanced, the other man's slip sealing his fate.

As if he knew, Sorley's own blade appeared in a quick-silver move. "Ooh, aye, your time has come, Raven," he snarled, vaulting over a bench, his sword already slashing.

Ronan met his arcing swipe, the two blades sliding together with an ear-piercing screech. "Aye, my time is nigh," he hissed, "but no' how you mean it!"

His muscles straining against the guardsman's strength, he drew on his own reserves and flung him back, lunging before the other could gain his balance.

But Sorley recovered as quickly, bringing up his sword and springing forward, their blades clashing again and again. Men pulled back benches and tables, forming a watchful ring around them. From the corner of his eye, Ronan saw Torcaill raise his *slachdan druidheachd* at the edge of the circle.

The long wand gleamed bright silvery-blue as the ancient raised his voice, chanting out his protection.

Sorley saw him, too, and laughed.

"Dare needs more than an old man's mumblings," he sneered, his blade stabbing. "Only your blood will cleanse it!"

Ronan grunted and fought off the other's furious slashes. The ringing of steel and his own blood roared in his ears, blotting out all else.

His ribs blazed with unbearable heat, the muscles in his arms and shoulders on fire. The pain in his left foot slowed him, making it ever more difficult to hold his own against the guardsman's attack.

Somewhere a woman screamed—Gelis?—and the terror in her cry gave him a burst of strength.

"*Cuidich N' Righ!*" he yelled her war slogan, his blade clanking and scraping against Sorley's.

With renewed zeal, he claimed the assault, yelling and slashing and driving the other back. They circled and feinted, then circled again, swords thrusting and clashing, their gazes locked and heated, both panting with exertion.

Sweat dripped into Ronan's eyes, stinging and blinding him, but he didn't dare blink. Instead, he leaped backward and then spun around, raising his blade high for a deadly, two-handed swing.

But Sorley whirled as well, a bright splash of red streaking around his middle even as Ronan's sword sank deep into his shoulder, sliding against bone.

Sorley's eyes bulged and his own blade fell from his hand. He clutched his stomach, the blood gushing there spilling over his hands and onto the rushes.

"A Highlander ne'er betrays his own," Ronan panted, sickened by the sight of his own steel plunged deep into a kinsman's breast.

He stared at his erstwhile friend, some detached part of his mind wondering why a shoulder cut bloomed so fatally red around the guardsman's waist.

And then Sorley toppled face-first onto the rushes and he saw.

Gelis's—nae, Hector's—*sgian dubh* raged hilt-deep from the guardsman's back.

The boy stood at the edge of the throng, staring round-eyed at the little blade's horn handle.

"He j-jumped onto it," he spluttered, shaking his head. "I was only holding it and h-he leaped backward and then whirled round. I didn't mean—"

"To be sure, and you didn't."

Gelis.

Her face pale, but her eyes shining, she was suddenly at the lad's side. She pulled him against her, stroking his hair and crooning. Shielding his eyes as Ronan did what he must, flipping his kinsman onto his back and then bracing his foot against the dead man's chest to free his blade.

He tossed the sword aside and dropped to his knees, reaching to shut Sorley's eyes, but before he could Gelis cried out and slumped to the rushes.

Ronan jumped back up, scooping her into his arms and clutching her against him, but she fell anyway, twirling and tumbling through icy darkness.

Down and down she fell, the loud buzzing in her ears blending with her scream and the distant sound of a man calling her name.

Then—as before—she slammed to a halt, this time landing on something hard and cold.

Stone, or tight-packed earth, it cradled rather than hurt her. But the darkness was suffocating. Impenetrable and cloying, it swirled around her like a great black shroud, pressing ever closer until she was sure her lungs would burst from lack of air.

Gelis.

The man called her name again, his voice deep and much louder now.

Then suddenly the blackness lightened and receded a bit, but she still found herself in a small, cramped place, airless and cold.

She shivered and drew up her knees, chilled by the spinning gray mist and the surety that this was a place forsaken and damned. Sculpted of stone and silent as the ages, its emptiness reached for her, clinging tight and grasping, as if she was its sole salvation.

Then *he* was there.

Kneeling as he'd been just before her fall, though—as before—his gold neck torque was missing, and his well-loved features seemed just a bit different—not quite those she knew so well, yet still achingly familiar.

The streaming raven hair was the same, thick, glossy, and skimming his shoulders, just as his eyes blazed with an inner heat, though she knew instinctively that the passion burning there was not for her.

This man wasn't the Raven.

And his needs, though passionate, were...others.

A burning desire that went deeper than this world, calling to her from a great, great distance even though he knelt on bended knee before her, his outstretched arms so close she could have grasped his hands.

If she could have moved her own.

But she could only stare, her heart thumping wildly, and the icy gray mist holding her firmly in place, not letting her move or even cry out.

He loomed closer then, kneeling directly before her, so close she could smell the cold, damp must of ancient earth and stone that clung to him.

Again, she shivered, his chill sweeping her, seeping deep into her bones.

His stare pierced her, seeming to search her soul as a large stone appeared in his hands. Gray, round, and absolutely ordinary, it nevertheless managed to glow and pulse, its heat singeing her.

"I beg you..." His voice rang in her ears.

No longer kneeling, he bent over her, his stone cradled

against his chest. "Free the raven," he pleaded, the words seeming to catapult her into the air, sending her spinning upward and away from him.

Free the raven...

She heard the plea again and again, the three words accompanying her as she spiraled ever higher until, at last, she began falling again, once more hurtling through darkness, but this time landing on something soft and warm.

Her eyes snapped open and *he* was still there.

He leaned over her, looming close, just as he had a moment before, but his stone was gone and the bright glint of gold shone at his neck.

They were no longer in the tight and musty confines of a cold stone-lined room. Now she lay secure in the enclosed silk-and-furred safety of her own dark oaken four-poster.

But her breath hitched and through the gap in the bed's brocaded curtains she spied at least a dozen fine wax candles flickering in iron wall brackets.

The Raven's bedchamber, she'd bet her life, though she searched the shadows, needing to be sure.

Familiar wall tapestries and her husband's own bearskin rugs greeted her, not to mention the untidy pile of her well-packed MacKenzie strongboxes.

On the far side of the room, a birch-and-peat fire blazed on the hearth and Buckie sprawled in its glow. At ease, though still wholly alert, he'd rested his head on his paws and was staring at the bed, his rheumy gaze unblinking.

Gelis's heart squeezed seeing him there, some memory she couldn't quite place making her eyes water and burn.

But the man bending over her and stroking her hair so lovingly was the true reason a tear spilled free to track down her cheek.

He *was* caressing her lovingly.

And the look in his eyes said everything.

"*Ronan.*" Her voice cracked on his name. "I thought you were going to die."

"And I feared you had!" He drew a great breath, his eyes dark. "Sakes, lass, but you scared me."

He shoved a hand through his hair then and glanced over his shoulder at Buckie, his own voice a bit huskier than usual. "You frightened us both."

His ears perking on the words, the old dog pushed to his feet and hinked across the room to join them, his hips swaying and his claws clicking wherever the floor rushes proved a bit thin.

"I've ne'er seen Buckie enter this room." Ronan looked down when the dog bumped against him.

He dropped a hand to rub Buckie's ears, but the dog took no heed. Pressing closer to the bed, the beast thrust his head past the curtaining to nudge Gelis's arm with his nose.

Ronan stepped aside when Buckie's tail began to swish enthusiastically.

Gelis smiled, certain the world was melting.

The Raven grunted and—she was sure—tried to appear unmoved.

"He hasn't left your side since you fell to the rushes in the hall," he said then, speaking above the popping of the fire's birch logs. "If you'd hear the right of it, he prowled back and forth in front of the bed until his legs wouldn't carry him anymore and then he went to rest before the fire."

"He...ach, fie on me!" Gelis lifted a hand to swipe the dampness from her face. "MacKenzies never cry!"

"Neither do MacRuaris, but you brought me close." He looked at her, his expression dark, almost desperate. "I—damnation, lass! Whate'er have you done to me!"

With a groan, he flung back the bed drapes and grabbed her by the shoulders, pulling her hard against him. He kissed her roughly, digging his fingers into her flesh and squeezing tight, holding fast as if he feared she'd slip from his arms any moment, disappearing into nothingness.

"Dinna e'er do that again." He drew back to breathe the words against her lips, his heart pounding so fast, she could feel its furious beat through his plaid.

She appeared to be naked.

Something she only now became aware of, with his arms tightening around her and the slightly scratchy wool of his plaid rubbing against her nipples.

They peaked and tingled and a distinct molten dampness touched her inner thighs, that part of her, too, reacting to his embrace. The way he kissed and nipped along her jawline, then dipped his head to nuzzle her neck.

"You undressed me." She shivered on the words.

"Sweet lass—I had to." He sat beside her on the bed and pulled her even closer, one hand now smoothing circles up and down her bared back. "For all I knew, there could have been more than one blackheart in the hall. I had to make certain you were unharmed."

"I am...well." She leaned into him, sure her heart would burst any moment.

"Was it your gift, then?" He kissed her brow, rubbed his face against her hair. "Just tell me that whate'er befell you wasn't something you ate or drank in the hall."

He looked at her, his gaze earnest. "That was Sorley's plan, see you. He—"

"It had naught to do with him." She closed her eyes, not wanting to think about the scene in the hall.

How frightened she'd been and, aye, how certain that Ronan was doomed.

After all, she'd seen his death foretold when her *taibh-searachd* had shown her the blackness slowly engulfing him.

Or so she'd believed.

Now she knew better.

And her relief watered her knees.

"It was my second sight, aye." She touched a finger to his golden neck torque. "One of several *taibhs* I've had in recent times. I thought they were all of you. Though"— she took a deep breath—"now I know they were not, leastways not the last two."

He sat back at once, his jaw hardening. "You have visions of other men?"

Gelis scooted away from him and scrambled off the bed, heedless of her nakedness.

In truth, she felt like whirling and jigging, so greatly did his jealousy thrill her.

But the soul who'd appeared to her deserved and needed her help.

Whirling and jigging could wait.

So she took another deep breath and tossed back her hair.

"Not *other men*," she said, setting her hands on her

hips. "But one who looked very much like you. I believe he was your forebear, Maldred the Dire."

The Raven shot to his feet. "That's no' possible. He's been dead since pagan times... since before these great hills were young."

He frowned. "Nae, it canna be. He—"

Gelis tilted her head. "Will you deny the kisses we've shared in the mists of my visions?"

She let her gaze slide down the front of him. "Our passion?"

"That's different." He shook his head, clearly caught off guard. "Aye, that was very, very... other."

"How so?" She stepped up to him, twined her fingers in his hair. "If you can hold and kiss me in such a place, why can't Maldred appear to me there as well?"

"Because I am alive."

"That proves naught." She smiled, flashing her triumph. "Save that we were meant to be."

His face went all stony.

He looked anything but convinced.

She let go of his hair and slid her fingers over his neck torque. "Know this, then." She laid on her smoothest tone. "It is a great and difficult feat for a living soul to appear to another in such a way. A soul—"

He huffed, cutting her off.

"A soul," she went on regardless, "one already dwelling in the *saoghal thall*—the Yonder World—can achieve the like much easier."

Stepping back, she placed her hands on her hips again. "That is the way of it."

"I still dinna like the idea." He crossed his arms. "And why would Maldred appear to you?"

"Perhaps because he knows everyone else wants nothing to do with him." She lifted her chin, sure of it. "He needs me and knows I will help him."

The Raven snorted.

"The saintliest saint couldn't help that one," he said, frowning again.

"He could not appear to me or any other soul, if the Old Ones wished to deny him."

Ronan harrumphed again.

Crossing the room, he snatched a folded plaid off a chair and returned to swirl it around her.

"I'll no' have you standing naked when we're speaking of the man," he groused, knotting the plaid at her shoulder. "He was said to have been irresistible to women."

Once again Gelis felt a ridiculous urge to dance and jig.

Instead, she stood still while the Raven fussed and straightened the plaid, smoothing and tucking in its folds for her.

She clenched her fists, not quite ready for him to see that each brush of his fingers against her skin sent tingly firelicks of heat rippling across her nerves.

Sweet tingly heat that set her belly all a-quiver and lit a fire in the secret place low by her thighs.

Then he stepped back, looking satisfied.

"That's better." He dusted his hands and glanced around the candlelit room almost as if he expected to see his ancestor leap out of the shadows at him.

"No need to tempt the old marauder—if he is about!"

"He isn't concerned with women." She tried to reassure him, his words reminding her of the spirit's sadness.

The piercing stare Maldred had fixed on her.

"He needs us to help him and"— she drew a breath to present her *coup de grâce* — "he wants to help us."

The Raven's eyes widened. "Howe'er can he help us?"

" 'Tis simple." Gelis smiled. "I am quite sure he showed me where the Raven Stone is hidden."

Chapter Sixteen

❦

*H*is tomb?"

Ronan nearly choked on his surprise. "Then, sweet lass, your gift has lied to you. "Or"—he waved away her protest—"you've falsely interpreted what you saw."

His lady huffed and set her own hand to slashing the air.

"I do know what the inside of a tomb looks like," she minded him, her tone fringing on indignant.

High color stained her cheeks and, as so oft, her braid had come undone. Her hair tumbled to her hips in a welter of red-gold curls, each glossy strand gilded by fire glow and tempting him beyond reason.

There were things a man could do with such tresses.

Things that had scarce little to do with long-dead ancestors and their hoary resting places.

Ronan shoved a hand through his hair and bit back a groan. He didn't want to talk about old bones and burial grounds. Not with her looking so fetching in his plaid that he couldn't think straight.

She, however, seemed determined.

And she'd definitely taken up Maldred's torch.

Her sparking eyes and the jut of her chin proved it.

"I once crept inside the family tomb at Eilean Creag." She started walking around the room, her steps making her breasts bounce. "I was young, and—and I wanted to see bogles. They hid from me, as ghosts are known to do, but I *did* get a good look at the tomb."

Ronan folded his arms. "That changes naught. Maldred wasn't buried in a tomb. He—"

"I know what I saw." She halted in front of him. "He was in a small stone chamber, dark, cold, and airless," she said, emphasizing each word with a finger-jab in his chest. "It could only have been his tomb."

Ronan drew in a great breath and let it out slowly. "You've seen the man's grave, lass. 'Tis a table grave in the family's oldest burial ground. All that remains to mark where Maldred lies is a broken stone slab. It ne'er was a tomb."

"He's in one all the same," she insisted. "And his Raven Stone is there with him. That, too, I saw. He held it out to me and told me to 'free the raven.' "

"He what?" Ronan's heart stopped.

He'd never told her the full tradition of the stone.

And he could tell she didn't know.

If she did, her triumph couldn't be contained.

"He told me to 'free the raven,' " she repeated, pacing again. "I think he was assuring me that by loving you, I will free you of the curse you think you carry. That Dare will then be—"

"He didn't mean me, sweetness."

Ronan turned to the nearest window, hoping the chill

night air seeping through the shutter slats would restore the color to his cheeks.

He was sure all the blood had drained from his face.

He'd felt it happen.

Just as he could no longer deny his lady had truly seen Maldred, wherever the knave held himself.

Even more alarming was the soul-piercing possibility that the maligned old goat wasn't quite the malefactor everyone thought.

At the very least, if his bogle did exist, the centuries might have made him a bit repentant.

There seemed no other explanation.

Not that this one wasn't enough.

Already, the weight of it made the floor dip and roll beneath his feet.

"Ach, nae, lass." He shook his head, the words coming hard as gravel dredged from a burn-bed. "I'm no' that raven."

His chest oddly tight, he stepped closer to the window and reached for the shutters, needing air. But before his fingers could close on the latches, *she* nipped into the space between him and the window arch.

"I don't understand." She grabbed his arms, her fingers strong. "You are the Raven, are you not?"

"I am one of many Ravens." He looked down at her and immediately wished he hadn't.

He hadn't done as fine a job of knotting the plaid as he'd thought. And now, with all her stalking about, the fool knot had loosened and he could see right down the gaping edge of the tartan.

The whole of her breasts gleamed for his delectation, luscious swells, the shadowed cleft between, chill-puckered nipples and all.

Worse, her dusky rose scent cast its usual heady magic on him. Each inhaled whiff shot straight to his vitals, squeezing fast and enflaming him.

Truth be told, he'd run rock-iron hard.

So he blew out a breath, tried to ignore her scent and her breasts, and fixed his gaze on her ear. A delicate ear, yet less a distraction.

"There have always been Ravens in the family," he explained, his voice as strained and uncomfortable as his man-piece. "But there is only one *raven*. A living bird trapped inside Maldred's Raven Stone, sealed there for all eternity. The raven's great power serves whoe'er holds possession of the stone, or so tradition claims."

"Then we must find it and set the bird free."

"Would that it were so simple."

"It might not be a bairn's game, but it must be possible." She beamed at him. "Were it not, there'd have been no point in his beseeching me."

From his place by the fire, Buckie barked once as if he agreed with her.

Ronan ignored him and broke free of his lady's grip. Stepping away from her, he flung open the shutters to stare out at the cold, rainy dark.

"For truth, lass, do you no' think MacRuaris have been trying to do the like ever since the scoundrel and his stone vanished?"

"He vanished?"

Ronan grunted. "So it is said, aye."

He breathed deep of the chill night air, his gaze on the great Caledonian pines beyond the curtain wall. The trees swayed and tossed in the wind, misty curtains of rain blowing past their crowns. Closer, the broad expanse of the bailey lay dark and still, though he knew its quiet concealed a score or more of guardsmen.

Dare never slept. Not even on the longest winter nights.

He frowned.

She'd edged in closer behind him. He could feel her warmth on his back and her attar of roses scent was swirling around him, filling the window arch before slipping away on the rushing night wind.

His entire body stiffened.

She was up to something.

He could feel it clear down to his toes, including the aching ones.

"To think your family has been searching for him all down the ages..." She let her voice tail off, the fading words full of sympathy and well-meaning.

"Aye, they have," he agreed, bespelled by the soft, feminine heat of her, the knowledge that she stood naked beneath his plaid. "At the latest, since the first glimmer of his curse blighted us —"

He clamped his mouth shut, but it was too late.

He could see her eyes lighting even without turning around.

"Ah-hah!" Her voice rang with excitement. "How can you say he disappeared and MacRuaris have searched for him and still claim he's buried beneath a collapsed table grave?"

Ronan set his jaw and kept staring at the wind-tossed pines.

She persisted. "Wouldn't his grave be the first place to search for him?"

"It was."

"And what did they find?"

Ronan braced his hands on the stone ledge of the window and drew a deep breath. Far below, a dog fox trotted along the edges of the trees, cloaked in deep shadow one moment then reappearing into a slant of pale moonlight.

"Well?"

He closed his eyes. "If the clan talespinners are to be believed, the grave proved empty."

"I knew it!" She clapped her hands. "He *is* buried elsewhere and we need only find the tomb."

"The talespinners also say that his evil was so great and his power so infinite that the devil himself envied him." He turned to face her. "'Tis said the Horned One seized the mortal remains and the stone, taking them with him into hell where he tossed both into a bottomless pit."

"Pah-phooey!" She laughed. "I tell you, he—"

Ronan didn't let her finish. "He used the last of his power to curse the family, damning us even in death as the devil carried him away. His capture was our fault, he railed, furious that we'd buried him in such an easy-to-find spot, or so tradition claims."

Gelis shook her head. "I do not believe a word."

Nor do I, Ronan owned, though he kept the sentiment to himself.

"Be that as it may, whether he once slept in the table grave or no, his final resting place has ne'er been found," he admitted, speaking true. "What does remain is his curse. It strikes—"

"I do not believe that either." Her eyes flashed. "I told you at Creag na Gaoith what I think of your curse."

She whirled and started pacing again, his plaid swinging about her knees. "Never in a thousand lifetimes did you *think* a rockslide into happening and—"

"Think you that is all of it?"

Ronan unlatched his sword-belt and laid it and his brand on a chair. Then he removed the large Celtic brooch holding his plaid at his shoulder and set it on the chair with his belt and his sword.

"What happened to Matilda at the Rock of the Wind was only one horror in a long history of family tragedies," he said at last, pulling off his plaid. "Numberless heart-aches have visited us, lass. The kind of pain I strove so hard to keep from touching you."

"Then tell me of it—from the beginning." Gelis claimed a chair beside the hearth and clapped her hands on her knees. "If you think I shall cower and tremble, you are sore mistaken."

He frowned at her, his plaid still bunched in his hands. Turning away, he shook it out and carefully folded it before placing it atop the large iron-banded strongbox at the foot of the bed. When he straightened to face her again, she knew she'd won.

But the hesitancy still clinging to him made her heart clench.

"Please." She leaned forward, letting her eyes plead. "I truly want to know."

He appeared to consider. "As you wish, but it makes grim telling," he finally conceded, looking at her as if he expected her to start quaking any moment.

Or worse, leap to her feet and bolt from the room.

So she leaned back in the chair and forced a calm expression. Never yet had she felt so close to him and it wouldn't do for him to note her quickened pulse and mistake her hope for fear.

Her device apparently worked, because he blew out a great breath and went to stand at the open window again, at last looking ready to speak.

He cleared his throat. "You asked me once if I'm plagued by the *Droch Shùil* and I told you of Matilda's death. How rather than the Evil Eye, my own thoughts sometimes manifest in horrible ways."

Gelis opened her mouth to object, but he waved a staying hand.

"Enough of my kinsmen—and a few kinswomen—have suffered thus," he continued. "Though the instances I know of with surety lie some hundred years or more in the past. Either way, those sad souls had but to glance at a cow and its milk would dry up or curdle. If they crossed a field, its crop withered behind them.

"Their woe was great for they meant no ill and did their best to avoid causing such disasters." He paused, his mouth twisting. "I know of at least one such kinsman who took his own life because of his malady."

"There are many tales of the *Droch Shùil* in these hills." Gelis didn't know what else to say. "So long as the stricken do not use their power to work ill on others, they cannot be blamed. Besides"—she sat forward again—"there are ways to counter the Evil Eye."

Lifting a hand, she counted them on her fingers. "Rowan is one of the surest talismans against the like. Then there are charmed stones, amulets, and a wealth of incantations. Even if you did have—"

"Ach, sweetness. I have told you, what plagues me is far worse." He rammed both hands through his hair and closed his eyes for a moment. "Would that such counter-charms as walking three times sunwise around a milk-blighted cow or drinking silvered water would cure it."

Gelis balled her hands on her knees. "Even so..."

He shook his head. "'Tis no good, lass. The MacRu-aris have been damned since time uncounted. Some of us, like myself and others who have gone before me, must carry a greater share of Maldred's burden."

"Maldred wishes to ease that burden." Gelis's finger-nails dug into her palms. "I could feel it when he appeared to me. He hasn't damned you. I know it!"

"Then I shall prove it to you."

Striding across the room, he went to another of his strongboxes. This one sat near the untidy pile of her own coffers. A bit dented and battered, and with its iron strap-ping showing signs of rust, the chest appeared much older than any of her own or the large one he kept at the foot of the massive oaken four-poster.

His face grim, he bent to lift the coffer's lid. "See you this," he said, pulling out a long quilted leather war-coat of ancient style. "It belonged to my father. And this"—he thrust a hand deeper into the strongbox and retrieved a high conical helm, equally tarnished—"was his as well."

Holding up the objects for her to see, he continued. "They are two of the very few treasures I have of him. Valdar ordered most of his possessions destroyed, so great was his pain when my father died. I hid these at the time and have kept them all these years."

"To be sure, and you saved them." Gelis stood. "You were only a boy and needed your memories—"

He made a choked sound, its bitterness spearing her.

"Memories, aye, but I also kept them as a warning." He put the quilted armor and the helm back in the chest and lowered the lid. "I wanted a reminder to keep me from e'er again thinking ill of another soul."

He looked at her then, his eyes dark. "Especially a soul I dearly loved."

Gelis dropped back into her chair. "I don't understand."

"Nae?" He arched a brow. "Then perhaps you will if I tell you that the day my father rode out hunting and plunged o'er a cliff when a swift black fog descended was a day we'd had a terrible argument. I'd—"

Gelis gasped. "Dinna tell me you—"

"Aye, I did." He took a ewer from the table and splashed a measure of ale into a cup, gulping it down before he went on. "We'd been at odds for some time. I wanted to join his squires at their swording practice and he forbade me, saying I must wait another year. The morning he went hunting, I took an extra sword from his solar and joined the squires anyway, telling them he'd given his permission."

"But he hadn't," Gelis guessed.

Her throat tightened and her heart wrenched for the boy he'd been, the darkness he'd carried so long.

"Nae, he knew naught of it—until he returned unexpectedly, having forgotten to strap on his sword, of all things." He poured another cup of ale, this time bringing it to her and thrusting it into her hands. "Needless to say, he found me in the midst of his sword-practicing squires, swinging a blade nearly as long as I was tall."

He paused, motioned for her to drink.

As soon as she took a sip, he went on. "Ne'er had I seen him so furious. He flung himself from his horse and flew across the bailey to grab me by the collar and drag me into the keep in front of all and sundry. I was shamed and—at the time—vowed that I hated him. When at last he rode out again, I wished he would ne'er return."

"And he didn't." Gelis finished for him.

He nodded. "No one e'er saw him again. Not alive anyway."

"Ach, Ronan." She sprang to her feet and ran to him, throwing her arms around his neck. "You canna—absolutely canna—think it was your fault. 'Tis tragic, aye, but—"

"It was but the beginning, sweetness." He disentangled himself from her arms. "You know of Matilda. My second wife, the lady Cecilia—"

"I know of her, too!" She hastened after him when he paced away. "Anice told me—" She broke off at once and clapped a hand to her lips.

But it was enough.

She knew.

Ronan released a breath. "Anice spoke true, I am sure," he said, seeing no point in lying. "Lady Cecilia was ill content here. She loathed the glen and she hated me. And"—he went back to the opened window, once again needing air—"she ne'er missed a chance to remind me of her unhappiness."

"But why?" His new lady bristled. "How could she not have been glad-hearted to be yours? You—"

"You do me proud, lass." He looked at her, her indignation warming a cold place inside him. "But Lady Cecilia was no' wholly to blame. She was a city lass, a sea merchant's daughter from Aberdeen on the distant North Sea coast. Our dark hills and the quiet of the glen frightened her. Nor did she understand our ways."

"Then why did she wed you?"

"For the same reason you did. She had a father whose

debt placed her in my arms, only his debt was not one of honor." He glanced at the fire, remembering. "The man had lost two shiploads of cargo at sea and when a storm claimed his third and last ship, he found himself facing ruination."

Gelis's brows lowered. "Unless he sold his daughter for a high bride-price."

Ronan nodded. "I...needed a son. It'd been years since Matilda's death and Dare deserved hope." He leaned back against the window arch, his hands gripping the cold ledge. "Some traveling Highlander had made his way to Aberdeen and somehow crossed paths with Lady Cecilia's father. The man was told of a well-pursed Highland clan unable to find a bride for its heir."

"You." She slid a hot glance at him.

"Aye, me." Ronan watched her pace, some detached and surely debauched part of him not missing how his plaid gaped a bit each time she finished her stalk across the room and whirled around again.

He balled a hand to a fist, then unclenched it as quickly.

The whipping of her hips and the flashes of her smooth, shapely thighs were making it increasingly difficult to concentrate.

He cleared his throat, trying anyway. "Lady Cecilia's father sent word to Valdar, claiming his daughter was eager for the match. We were told the fumes of the sea and the city made her ill and she looked forward to coming here. Unfortunately, that was not so."

"Then why didn't she return to Aberdeen?" Gelis wheeled about again, this time giving him a quick glimpse of the bright, red-gold curls topping her thighs.

"Och, saints!" The curse slipped out before he could stop it.

She shot him an odd look, but he rushed on before she could question him.

"She couldn't return because she had nowhere in Aberdeen to go," he explained, half of him wishing she'd stop her pacing while the other half willed her to step even more quickly so he'd be treated to such an eyeful again and again.

He bit back a groan, the pull at his loins almost unbearable.

"What do you mean 'she had nowhere to go'?" She spun around and the plaid dipped, revealing a tightly ruched nipple. "Was her father not there?"

Ronan ran a hand down over his chin, caught between bad memories and the worst rutting-lust he'd ever known.

His heart began to pound as hotly as the heat flooding his groin. "Her father took the coin from her bride-price and rather than repaying his debtors, he caught the next ship to France."

The words seemed to hang in the air, someone else's explanation, while his own voice silently shouted his need, his thoughts centering on *her*.

The comely, sparkling creature eyeing him so heatedly, all bouncing bosom and riotous dishevelment.

She jammed her hands on her hips. "Lady Cecilia blamed you."

"Aye, she did. For that and many other things." He could scarce speak. Blood was beginning to roar in his ears. "Her last words were that 'now she'd be free of me and I'd be rid of her.'"

"And you silently agreed."

"I did." The memory rushed him, guilt damping his lust and cutting off his air. "And it was after we buried her that I vowed to ne'er wed again."

"But you did and I am…other!" She flung herself at him again, this time locking her arms tight around him and pressing close.

Her warmth and all her soft, pliant womanliness chased all else from his mind and his need returned, the force of it tilting his world. He whipped his arms around her, pulling her even harder against him, almost drowning in the wonder of her.

The way she made him feel.

He closed his eyes and inhaled deeply, needing her scent, the essence of her, to cleanse him. A great weight began sliding off his shoulders, but when he looked at her again, it was the brightness in her eyes that undid him.

"Sakes, lass, 'tis naught to cry o'er," he blurted, his voice gruff.

"I am not crying." She pulled back, blinking furiously. "But I might if you don't stop telling me such sad tales and—and admit that you need me!"

"I do need you. More than I would have believed." The admission fell with surprising ease from his lips.

Even more startling, it made him feel good.

Almost giddy enough to shout with the joy of it.

He did tighten his arms around her, but when an unblinking canine stare from the direction of the hearth fire caught and latched onto him, he let go of her.

"Stay here." He put a hand to the small of her back and guided her into the shelter of the window embrasure. "I'll be back in a wink."

Then, he spun around and crossed the room before his wits left him. He cracked the door just enough to peer into the darkened passage beyond.

"Guard!" he called, knowing one would be lurking somewhere.

Sure enough, the Dragon soon appeared. "Aye, sir?" The young man stood erect, the light of a handheld rush torch illuminating his pockmarked face.

Ronan stepped closer to the door, making sure he blocked the guard's view into the room. Then he leaned forward to whisper into the Dragon's ear.

"As you wish, sir." The guard couldn't quite hide his surprise. "I'll be back with it anon."

Ronan kept his back to the room as he waited. Primed as he was, even one quick over-the-shoulder glance at the temptation behind him was too great a risk.

It'd been too long since he'd lain in lust with a woman.

And—he now knew—he'd never before lain in love with one.

"Sir, I have it." The Dragon's voice came through the crack in the door.

Ronan thrust a hand into the shadows, seizing the meat-bone. "I thank you—now see that my lady and I are no' disturbed."

Before the guard could respond, he shut and bolted the door. Then he drew a great breath, put back his shoulders, and marched over to the hearth fire.

"For you," he announced, giving Buckie the bone. "Consider it a bribe."

"A bribe?" *She* stepped out of the window alcove. "For Buckie?"

"O-o-oh, aye, something to keep him occupied." He started forward, pulling off his shirt as he went. "I'll no' have him watching what I'm about to do to you."

Chapter Seventeen

❦

*A*nd what is that?"

The sweet huskiness of his lady's voice slid through Ronan like honeyed wine. He stepped closer to her, letting his gaze rake her up and down.

He almost envied his plaid.

Its soft woolen folds clung seductively to her lush, curvaceous body, the tartan—his very own—molding the generous swells of her breasts and the ripe sweep of her well-rounded hips in ways that were dangerous for a man.

Especially a Highlander.

"So-o-o?" She tossed back her hair. "What are you going to do to me?"

Ronan didn't trust himself to speak.

Not that she needed his answer anyway. The flash in her eyes and the way she bit her lower lip revealed that she already knew.

She stood before him glowing and unafraid, her plaid-wrapped body gilded by firelight. His heart caught and the air around him ignited, his need to have her beneath him almost bringing him to his knees.

"I do have an idea." She pressed him, this time moistening her lips, letting him catch a quick look at the tip of her sweet, pink tongue. "Can it be what I hope?"

Her eagerness pushed him over the edge and he tossed his shirt to the rushes, closing the space between them with three long strides.

Reaching for the plaid, he hooked his fingers into its warmth and stared down at her, his blood alive and his heart thundering. His entire body burned and he craved every sweet inch of her, ached to run his hands all over her naked skin, kissing and licking her everywhere.

"Well?" She wet her lips again.

"Ach, lass," he almost snarled, "I'm more of a mind to show than tell you."

With one swift flick of his wrists, he jerked the tartan off her and tossed it aside. "Do you know what it's done to me, watching you prance about the room, naked in my colors?"

"So it's my own good self in your plaid that brought you around?" She twirled in a deliciously bare circle, her eyes lighting with delight. "And here I thought it would be my golden hip-belt and siren bauble that would sway you."

"You swayed me! And if you think otherwise, then you know naught of a Highlander's passion!" He grabbed her by the shoulders, yanking her close for a hot, demanding kiss.

"I burn for you," he vowed, speaking the words against her cheek. "I have done since that first day I saw you — in mist on a slender sickle of shingled strand!"

"Ronan..." She spoke his name like a benediction, her soul breaking on his need for her.

She was falling into him, spiraling ever deeper into her love for him, losing herself while gaining so much. Her heart trembled and sweet belonging rippled through her, sealing their bond.

"Lass." The endearment made her shiver.

He thrust his hands into her hair and kissed her again, deeper this time, all the desire in him plundering and devouring her lips. She cried out and opened her mouth beneath his, her tongue tangling wildly with his. Leaning into him, she melted with her sighs, let him drink his fill of her breath and intoxicate himself on the taste of her.

"You have no need of adornments," he panted, breaking away to drop to his knees before her on the discarded plaid. "Leave such gee-gaws for a man unable to appreciate a woman's sleek, hot flesh and all her lively allures. It is you, lass, and you alone, who stirs me."

He slid his hands around her hips, digging his fingers into her curves and drawing her close. "Your siren bauble is fine," he assured her, rubbing his face against the softness of her belly, "but it is this I couldn't resist!" He looked up at her, his gaze smoldering as he pressed his lips to her naked skin then dragged his mouth lower, raining kisses across her fragrant female curls.

"Sweet lass—forgive me, but I canna resist you." He tightened his grip on her, grinding his face against her heat. "I tried, I swear, but—"

"No-o-o!" Gelis twined her fingers in his hair, pressing him to her. "'Tis right and good, I say you! Everything between us."

"Then dinna deny me..." He ran his hands up and

down her legs, kissed and nipped the inside of her thighs, circling ever higher until his tongue teased round her most sensitive spot, that one heated swirl splitting her.

"Ach, gods!" she cried, her back arching when he continued to flick his tongue there. "What are you doing?"

"Naught that I willna be enjoying the whole night through!" He licked her then, a long-broad-tongued sweep the full tingling length of her.

Looking up at her, he held her gaze, his own smoldering. "All that I'd heard of you did you no justice," he breathed, the words warm silk against her flesh. "I dinna think I'll e'er be able to sate myself on you."

"Then…" Gelis couldn't speak. Just seeing his face poised so close to her feminine ache sent threads of delicious golden warmth spinning through her.

Desire thrummed the air and he leaned closer again, his mouth less than a whisper away, but she could feel his tongue on her even without touching, the sensation making her heart beat faster.

"You taste like molten honey." He eased her thighs wider apart, licked her more fully. "I canna breathe for wanting you, need your taste on the back of my tongue, your scent branded into my skin."

"Then — ach *dia*!" She jumped when his tongue parted her, its hot velvety tip slipping inside her.

He swept his hands up her sides to knead and plump her breasts, his thumbs sliding back and forth over her nipples as he licked her center again, once more swirling his tongue over and around that sweet wee place that made such intense pleasure pulse between her legs.

"Then what, lass?"

His voice a deep, sensual growl, he pulled back to peer

up at her, his hand replacing his tongue, caressing and rubbing her intimately. "I've told you—I am lost. Tell me your desire, and it is yours, I swear it."

"Then make me yours." She rushed the words, blurting them before his stroking fingers made her burst and shatter into thousands of tiny, mind-numbing pieces.

Already she was spinning, the whole of her world whirling tighter and tighter until nothing remained but that bright, hot-throbbing pulse at her core.

But her heart beat just as fiercely, and even through such blinding pleasure, she wanted more.

"Take me now, this night." She pushed to her feet while she still could. "Unless"—she reached for his hand, the gesture pleading—"unless you fear sealing our handfast?"

"I fear naught but losing you!" He grabbed her hand and upturned it, kissing the soft warmth of her palm. "That, and...hurting you."

"I know there will be discomfort." She reached for him, curling her fingers around his need. "The greater pain would be missing it," she said, squeezing.

It was more than he could bear.

"Then so be it!"

He made to gather her in his arms, meaning to carry her to the bed, but she dropped onto the spread plaid, lying back and opening her arms to him.

"Here, on your plaid." She looked up at him, her eyes glittering in the candlelight. "I'd have you love me in the old way—in honor of our hills and the ancients so that they might bless our union."

"You bless us, sweetness." Ronan bent to tug off his boots, then shoved down his hose, kicking them aside. He stretched out alongside her, certain she was indeed his blessing.

He only hoped he could be hers as well.

But then she circled her arms around his neck and pulled him down to her and all thought fled. Only his need to bury himself deep inside her remained. Burning with it, he shifted, covering her body with his. He kissed her long and hard, almost spilling when she lifted her knees and clamped her legs tightly around him.

She rocked her hips, moving so that his hardness slid across her, the length of him pressing hotly against her slick, wet heat.

He reached down between them, seeking that place again, rubbing and circling until she began to tremble and gasp with pleasure. And always, he kissed her, slanting his mouth over hers and kissing her deeply, sharing breath and letting his tongue tangle with hers until he could wait no more and a great shudder rolled through him, driving him dangerously close to losing control.

"Now, Ronan!" she gasped as if she knew.

"I must, lass." He lifted up to look into her eyes. "I can stop no more."

And then he plunged into her, her sharp cry muffled by his kisses. He froze, holding still for a few tight, agonizingly beautiful moments, then began moving slowly, filling her inch by inch until he'd buried himself so deeply inside her he was sure he'd brushed her soul.

"My Raven..." She raised her hips, intensifying their joining, then cried out when he lowered his head and began suckling her nipples as he started moving in and out of her.

Slow smooth glides, long and deep.

And still he kept a hand just there, his finger circling faster now, in sweet hot rhythm with his pumping hips. His strokes came harder and faster now, plunging deep, while the exquisite tingles streaming out from that other place dampened the dull pain inside her, spinning her closer and closer to a brilliant edge looming ever nearer each time his finger swirled over her.

Then his finger stopped circling and he cried out, a great stinging heat flooding her even as she sped over that glittering edge, shattering and spinning, her own cry blending with his as she slowly drifted back down onto his plaid and the night-darkened room once again took shape and form around them.

"Oh, dear saints," she gasped when she could speak.

"Sweet lass...you are magnificent." He'd stilled on top of her, but he rolled off her now, gently drawing her into his arms to cradle her against him. "But I am sorry for the hurt—"

"The wonder of it more than made up for the pain." She twisted around to kiss him. "And I...I knew what to expect," she added, sighing when he smoothed a hand down over her hip to toy softly with her damp maiden curls.

But then his fingers stilled and the slow, steady rhythm of his breathing let her know he'd fallen asleep. Unfortunately, her arm had, too.

She frowned.

The sharp prickles jabbing up and down from her shoulder to her fingertips made it impossible for her to join him in his slumber.

Nor could she move, for her arm had somehow slipped beneath him and he looked so dear in his sleep, she couldn't bear the thought of disturbing him.

So she lay as still and quiet as she could, her gaze on the moon-silvered window arch not far from where they lay on his plaid on the floor.

The only open window in the room, it let in a draught of icy air, the night cold chilling her and raising goose-flesh on her skin. But if she craned her neck just a tiny bit, she could see the moon through the arch.

Mostly hidden by wispy, wind-torn clouds, it sailed into view every once in a while and some strange some-thing made her watch it.

The same something—she suddenly knew with surety—that was lifting the fine hairs on her nape and causing her gooseflesh.

It wasn't the night cold at all.

Her Raven's naked body warmed her through and through, and the heat of her pleasure in him still pulsed and throbbed inside her.

The chill came from within.

And—she also knew—from whoever or whatever was out in that moonlight and wanting her attention.

She shivered.

The moon slid behind another cloud, its sudden disap-pearance plunging the bedchamber into darkness save for the faintly glowing embers of the hearth fire.

Looking that way, her heart plummeted, for there could be no denying that Buckie had noticed the someone or something out there, too.

The old dog's head was raised, his alert stare fixed on the open window.

Until he realized he'd been seen.

At once, he dropped his head back down on his paws and, she suspected, feigned sleep. Just as she, too, meant to do, not wishing to alarm Ronan if he happened to waken and sense her ill ease.

And she was concerned.

More worried than she'd ever been since coming to Dare.

Now she had far too much to lose.

So she closed her eyes and summoned all her will-power to keep from glancing at the window arch again. Whoever or whatever wanted something from her would just have to wait.

She'd deal with them on the morrow.

She just hoped she could.

She could do it.

Standing on a high promontory on the distant Isle of Doon, Devorgilla tightened her knotty fists and scrunched her eyes to better peer down at the long line of breakers rolling toward the cliffs.

But the night winds were fresh and the seas too choppy for her to see more than the white-crested swells and the little bay of rocks and sand far below her.

"Ill limmer!" She resisted the urge to hobble back the way she'd come and then rummage through her spelling goods until she'd gathered enough of her more potent treasures to blast the long-nosed, white-bearded he-goat responsible for her present plight.

He alone was the reason she stood shivering in the night wind.

If he—whoever he'd been—hadn't made it prudent for her to avoid using her cauldron steam to do her scry-ing, she'd be sleeping soundly on her pallet about now.

Instead, she shuffled as close to the cliff edge as she

dared and tried again to see what she needed on the surface of the dark, tossing waters.

Somewhere on the moorland behind her, a night-bird called, breaking her concentration even as the moon suddenly rode high above the clouds. At once, a wide band of glittering silver stars lit the water, stretching toward her from the horizon, the moon's bright light joining the white-foaming waves to ruin all chance of success.

She needed a shining black surface, smooth and unrippled.

Seeing no choice but to reach for deeper magic, she lifted her somewhat bristly chin and held out her arms, palms downward toward the sea.

Then she started to chant, lifting her voice until bit by bit the twinkling silver swath of moonlight began to draw back toward the horizon.

Encouraged, she splayed her fingers, curling just the tips so that all her power poured down the steep cliffside and into the water, her entire strength then flowing out over reef and rock to quiet the churning waves.

Her arms began to tremble and she couldn't stand very straight in the racing wind, but she remained where she was, mumbling her spelling words more softly now that the black water was stilling.

And then she saw them.

The crone hooted and hopped with glee, her incantations forgotten.

Naked but for the plaid wrapped round them, her charges lay tightly entwined in intimate embrace. The maid's tresses spilled bright across the man's broad chest, and although she couldn't tell for sure because of the tartan covering them, it appeared the girl had flung one leg across her slumbering lover.

The man's arms cradled her, holding her close, and the expression on his sleeping face left no doubt that the girl had finally claimed his heart.

Her own heart tripping wildly, Devorgilla rubbed her hands together. She leaned a bit forward, peering even deeper now, trying to see past them.

She needed to know the rest.

She started chanting again, just a few special words this time, and—lo, her powers still humming—the sleeping couple and their plaid faded away, slowly replaced by tall stone walls, dark and forbidding.

Her little friend sat on a tree stump not far away, his deep russet coat gleaming in a patch of moonlight, his bright yellow eyes fixed on a certain window arch.

The crone's heart swelled and she cackled her relief, more pleased than was good for her that the little dog fox had found his way safely to the blighted glen.

And she could tell from the direction of his stare that his task would soon be completed.

As if he sensed her, the fox blinked and lifted a paw in greeting. But before she could nod benevolently back at him, a great swirl of dark mist whirled across the water, blotting her view.

"Did I not warn you not to meddle, woman?"

"Gah!" Devorgilla jumped, nearly toppling over the cliff edge.

"Shall I take your fool wits if you do not make use of them?" The familiar voice roared in her ears, deep, rumbling, and thunderous.

And then he was there, glaring at her from the mist-cloud hovering somewhere between her and the sea. He raised an arm to point a bony finger at her, his long white hair and beard lifting on the wind.

"Go back to your pallet!" he scolded, the mist-cloud tingeing darker with his fury. "Seek your sleep before you vex me beyond my patience."

He wagged his finger, suddenly looking so grudging beneath his angry, down-drawn brows that Devorgilla threw back her own whitened head and cackled.

Then she caught herself and braced her hands on her hips, eyeing him with all the dignity of her kind.

He glowered back at her, his jaw set with equal stubbornness.

"Their trials are nigh at an end." He put back his shoulders, his chest seeming to swell on the words. "Soon they will know only gladness. Your interfering mischief is not needed."

Devorgilla hooted again. "Can it be that you cannot suffer a crone casting stronger magic than your own?"

Silence answered her.

The ill limmer and his mist cloud were gone.

But his annoyance lingered, crackling in the air around her, and she pulled her cloak tight and turned to begin the slow trek back across the moors to her bed.

And as she trudged along, she hummed a merry tune she hadn't recalled in ages.

This e'en, she'd enjoyed her encounter with the he-goat.

She paused to draw her hood up over her head and tie its fastening string. Then she hobbled onward, a persistent little smile twitching her lips.

The fool man had looked rather fine in his bluster.

Rather fine, indeed.

Chapter Eighteen

❦

Have you seen any mist snakes of late?"

Valdar's deep voice boomed in the candlelit gilt of Dare's family chapel. Beard jigging and eyes fierce, he stood in front of the richly hung altar, his legs spread in a warlike stance. He held his well-honed Norseman's axe, Blood Drinker, clutched in his hand, its blade flashing.

With a flourish, he flung back his plaid, looking anything but a peaceable visitor to the little stone chapel's seldom-used sanctuary.

One reason, for sure, that the other men present were currently ignoring him.

He continued his rant regardless. "Heard of any more platters of food gone a-sailing out our windows? Seen any odd-eyed strangers skulking through the glen?"

Ronan looked up from the carved stone effigy he'd been examining. "There could be a lever here somewhere," he said, ignoring his grandfather's blether. "A secret door or passage we've overlooked. This is the most likely place for a hidden tomb."

"Hah! Tomb-*shwoomb*, I say! We've peered thrice or more at every stone in here and elsewhere for the last fortnight." Valdar's chin jutted stubbornly. "'Tis a wonder we haven't all gone cross-eyed as a great ring-tailed yowe!"

Ronan ran his hand over the cold sides of the tomb, felt along the stone flags at its base. "I cannot speak of such unfortunate ewes, but I once heard of a hidden crypt only accessible by shifting the tail of a dog carved at an effigy's feet. The wee creature's tail was a release disguised to look like stone and—"

"And I say you"—Valdar shook Blood Drinker in his direction—"your gel's *presence* is enough! Her hot blood and high spirits chased away the slitherin' mist devils and all else what's plagued us."

"I'd rather chase them from her." Ronan pushed to his feet, dusted his hands. "Only then will—"

"Pshaw!" Valdar scoffed. "Even you can't deny that the sun's been shining on our glen more often in recent times than in years!"

Ronan's gaze flicked to the wedge of brilliant winter sunlight slanting in through the chapel's half-opened door. "Be that as it may, we'll continue our search."

His grandfather huffed.

"Even the stars are brighter since she's here," he argued, waving Blood Drinker again. "There's no need for us to poke and prod at walls and floors, looking for a tomb that isn't!"

"Gelis says that it is." Ronan folded his arms. "I believe her."

Valdar scowled and shoved Blood Drinker beneath his wide leather belt.

Ronan frowned right back at him.

Then he looked round at the other men crowded into the chapel. Some crept about on their knees, like him, running their hands along recumbent effigies of long-sleeping forebears. Others worked in shadowy corners or the dim, must-filled vault below, using their dirk hilts to tap for hollows, the tips to probe every suspicious-looking crack.

No one found anything.

And not a man complained.

But hours later when he climbed the narrow turnpike stair to his bedchamber, his still-aching ribs and his damnable toes *did* protest.

His head pounded, too. And when he opened his door only to walk into a great, billowy cloud of deep, shimmering blue, his misery knew no bounds.

"By the Rood!" His feet slid crazily and it was all he could do to keep his legs from flying out from under him. "Gelis!" he cried, righting himself. "What goes on here?"

Her face appeared above the welling blue.

"O-o-oh, no!" She jumped up, apparently off a stool, and stood gawping at him. "I wasn't expecting you. Not for several hours."

"So I see." He looked at her from just inside the door, the slippery blue *cloud* making it difficult to enter the room.

If it even was his chamber.

Swathed almost completely in blue, it was hard to tell.

But his lady was there, and in such a grand state of

high-colored disarray that another type of throbbing immediately joined the pounding in his head.

Surrounded to her waist by bunches of blue silk, she appeared to be wearing only a fur-lined bed-robe, clearly unfastened. As usual, her braid had loosened and shining coppery-bright curls spilled free to dance with her every movement.

Ronan swallowed.

Every inch of him stiffened, and not from crawling around the chapel on his hands and knees.

Her left nipple peeked at him from the edge of the opened bed-robe, and if it weren't for the *blue cloud* swirling around her hips, he'd have a fine view of her lush, fiery-red nether curls as well.

He took a step forward, his blood heating. "Perhaps 'tis a good thing I've returned early."

She shook her head, completely disagreeing.

He'd ruined her surprise.

Disappointment sweeping her, she swatted at the reams of blue silk. But her efforts only served to trap her more fully in the mound of tangled cloth.

"Och, aye." His body went even tighter when her *hand-swiping* gave him a better view of her soft curves. Already, he could feel her full, round breasts in his hands.

Saints, he could *taste* them.

"O-o-oh, aye," he said again. "'Tis very good, indeed."

"Nae, it isn't," she quipped, striving for dignity. "Not at all."

He arched a brow, not understanding.

She bit her lip. "I—this"—she grabbed a handful of the silk, holding it up for him to see—"is an awning tent for you. A true Viking one. My cousin Kenneth brought it back from Stromness in Orkney. It's already decorated with my father's black stag and I've been stitching a raven on it."

"Ach, lass, I dinna know what to say." He stared at the length of silk in her hands. "'Tis beautiful." His voice was rough, husky. "The most exquisite embroidery work I've e'er seen."

"Exquisite?" Gelis looked down, saw the magnificent rendering of her father's crest gleaming boldly in the candlelight.

Her breath caught and heat swept up her neck, flooding her cheeks.

"Arabella stitched the stag." The admission tore her heart and she bit down on her lip, almost drawing blood. "'Tis her work you see," she owned, gathering the cloth over her arm, smoothing the billowing folds. "The raven is mine, but . . . he is not yet done."

"Then show me what you have so far."

"Not yet, please." She looked away, shame and embarrassment scalding her. "You wouldn't like it just now."

"Say you." He scooped an armful of the tent silk off the floor and shook it out until her half-stitched raven fluttered into view. "I will love . . ."

His praise tailed off, his eyes widening.

Gelis could feel her face turning bright red. "I told you, he is not yet finished."

"He is perfect." Ronan's heart split wide as he looked down at the awkward, uneven stitches.

Barely recognizable as a bird, the rendering could have been anything between a sparrow and a swan. Clearly, his lady wasn't skilled with a needle.

That she'd tried, and had done so to please him, shook his world.

His vision blurred, the raven's crooked outline wavering as stinging heat stabbed the backs of his eyes and a hot lump swelled in his throat.

"Lass..." The endearment came out like a croak.

She glanced aside. "I knew you wouldn't like it..."

He shook his head, unable to speak.

Then he did what he could, striding forward, blue cloud or no, to pluck her out of the welter of rippling silk and yank her hard against him.

"Your raven is the most beautiful thing I've ever seen." He stroked her hair, holding her so tight he almost crushed her. "And you had the right of it all along, sweetness. You *are* my salvation."

"You're not disappointed?" She pulled back to look at him, her eyes glittering with nontears. "Not truly?"

"I am the most blessed man in the Highlands," he vowed, slanting his mouth over hers in a plundering, bruising kiss. A deep all-slaking kiss filled with hot breath and tongue, more love than his heart could contain.

Reeling with the realization, he swept his hands up and down her back, then lower, splaying his fingers across her hips and clutching her even tighter.

"You could ne'er disappoint me." He broke the kiss to drop to his knees before her, his heart thundering so wildly he feared it would soon burst from his chest. "Truth is, I dinna know how I e'er lived without you."

"Ach, Ronan..." She thrust her hands into his hair, pulling him against the slight curve of her belly.

Her soft maiden curls brushed his chin and he made a sound deep in his throat. A low growl, earthy and feral, it was nearly unrecognizable as his voice. But her sweet female heat proved too close. Her silky-hot lure beckoned until he growled again and buried his face between her legs, first nuzzling her damp curls, then licking and lapping at her. Long, broad-tongued strokes, slow and deliberate, then quick little swirls to flick across her most special place, followed by gentle nips to her most tender flesh.

"Aggggh..." She gripped his shoulders, her entire body going rigid as he swirled his tongue just there. "Ach, gods!" Her passion broke on a great shuddering cry and she slumped against him, trembling and gasping.

Her breath came loud and ragged in the quiet room, each sweet sated gasp blending with the crackle and hiss of the hearth fire and the sound of his own ever-rising growls.

Ronan frowned.

The noises weren't his.

Nor could they truly be called *growls*.

Leastways, no more. Nothing less than a keening wail, the sound was unmistakably a howl.

"Do you hear that?" He pushed to his feet, angling his head to better catch the sound. "Like a dog howling."

He looked at her, hoping she'd heard it, too.

Her knit brow said she had. "Buckie?"

But a glance past the tent silk to the far side of the room showed the dog sound asleep in his favored place before the fire. And his snores were of the old-dog fluting variety, not howl-like at all.

"It didn't sound like any of the other castle dogs either," she observed. "It—"

"It wasn't inside the keep." Ronan strode to the nearest window and opened the shutters.

Chill night air rushed in, fluttering wall hangings and guttering candles. One of the hanging cresset lamps swayed on its chain and went out with a hiss. The icy blast also brought another long, piercing howl.

An ear-splitting one this time.

"By glory, 'tis a fox!" Bracing his hands on the window edges, Ronan leaned forward to peer down at the little dog fox sitting on the tree stump where he had perched over a fortnight before.

As then, he sat proudly, only now he didn't just stare up at the window. Far from it, he repeatedly threw back his head and howled at the moon.

A bright crescent moon riding high above the long belt of dark pines, its silvery brilliance slanted down to glint off the fox's lustrous red coat and the fine white tip of his thick brushy tail.

He looked their way then, his yellow-gold eyes fixing on them for one long and unsettling moment before he tipped back his head and resumed howling.

Ronan shook his head. "Have you e'er seen the like?"

"I may just have..." His lady puzzled, her gaze intent on the little creature. "He looks oddly familiar—"

"God's blood!" Ronan's heart slammed against his ribs, his world upending even as the little fox hopped off the tree stump and disappeared into the wood. "I know where Maldred is!"

Gelis spun around to look at him. "What?"

He grabbed her shoulders, turning her back to the window. "There, that is the key!" He pointed to the moonwashed tree stump. "I canna believe it took a fox howling at the moon for me to remember."

Gelis blinked. "The tree stump? You think Maldred is buried beneath it?"

"Nae, lass, no' the tree stump." He slid his arms around her, drawing her back against his chest. "The key is the crescent moon."

"The moon?" Gelis twisted from his arms. "How can the moon have anything to do with it?"

"A *crescent* moon, and it has everything to do with it," he said, awe in his voice. "The answer was given me a long time ago, had I paid heed."

He slid another glance at the moon, then back at her. "Once when I was very young, Valdar's kitchen stores were nearly depleted," he told her. "A harsh winter kept us from leaving the glen and Valdar's stock of wine quickly emptied. His loss was my delight, as I was allowed to play in the wine vault beneath the kitchens."

Gelis tucked a curl behind her ear, listening.

"The kitchen laddies and I used the empty wine barrels to build a fort and"—he paused to draw a breath—"once, while shoving them about, I came across a strange carving on the floor. One of the stone flags appeared to be inscribed with two crescent moons back to back."

"What did you do?"

"I ran to Valdar, as always," he remembered, his gaze seeming to look backward. "But he laughed, claiming the marks had been scratched on the stone by a barrel."

Gelis's brow puckered. "And you think those two crescent moons mark Maldred's tomb?"

"I am certain of it."

"But why?" She still didn't understand.

"Because, my heart," he explained, excitement beginning to beat through him, "many years later while discussing Druidic beliefs with Torcaill, he mentioned that such a device—two crescent moons back to back—was an ancient Pictish symbol of immortality."

"And Maldred believed himself immortal."

"That we'll ne'er know," he considered, "but family tradition claims he was obsessed with the possibility."

"So you think his tomb is in the kitchens?" She looked at him, wide-eyed. "Beneath the floor of the wine cellar?"

"I do," he agreed, his pulse quickening with the surety of it. "And there's only one way to find out."

Chapter Nineteen

❖

Ronan shoved and heaved and, finally, set another wine barrel to rolling. He frowned as the thing began to trundle away, certain that each new barrel he'd tackled since the small hours was mysteriously larger, more full, and without doubt much heavier than the one before.

Now, with the new morn already growing old, he was also nigh on to believing the wretched barrels were multiplying behind his back.

A sidelong glance at Hugh MacHugh, the Dragon, and others assured him that they shared his sentiments.

To a man, they strained and labored beside him while his lady, Anice, and even young Hector crowded close. Bent and shuffling like a clutch of plague-backed crones, they moved slowly about the wine cellar, their eyes fastened on the dusty floor.

Only Valdar and Torcaill stood apart, their age and rank excusing them from participation. They stood near the stair-foot, Valdar offering ceaseless snorts and grumbles, the druid simply looking on, his softly glowing *slachdan druidheachd* the best encouragement.

"Heigh-ho!" Valdar slapped his thigh then and pointed to a large semicircular scratch on one of the floor's large stone flags. "There be your grave marker! A barrel scrape, as I said, just!"

Ronan straightened and looked around. A score or more of hanging lamps cast a helpful gleam on the floor, but the thin haze from the smoking oil made a soul's eyes water and burn. And with each passing hour it was getting more difficult to distinguish the natural cracks and wear-scratches on the aged stones.

Even so, his grandfather's barrel scrape was just that.

Ronan frowned. "That is a scrape."

"So I've said all along." Valdar folded his arms, looking triumphant.

"We still have at least ten barrels to move." Ronan ignored his grandfather's peacocking and leaned forward to brace his hands on his knees. Weary to the bone, he gulped in a few deep and restorative breaths.

It scarce mattered that the air was stale and smoky.

The two back-to-back crescent moons carving of his boyhood memory was here somewhere.

And he'd find it or turn gray looking.

So he straightened and flexed his fingers before tackling the next wine barrel. But even before he set his hands on this one, a shift in the air lifted the hairs on his nape. When the barrel started to move, rolling away with ease, his heart began to pound.

A flash of silver-blue burst from the top of Torcaill's staff then, the brilliant light illuminating the ancient Pictish symbol etched deeply into the floor.

Two back-to-back crescent moons, just as he remembered.

Only now they glowed with the same bluish light as the druid's wand.

Behind him, Gelis gasped. "The tomb," she cried, hastening to his side. "I knew you'd find it!"

Valdar humphed. "Finding it doesn't mean old Maldred is in there," he scoffed, stepping forward to eye the carving. "I doubt we can even pry up the stone to look beneath it."

"The stone will give way." Torcaill strode over to them, his staff pulsing bright silver-blue. "The time is come. It would open now even if we hadn't uncovered it. Somehow we would have known."

Ronan shot him a look. "Now you say so," he groused, the words escaping before he could catch them.

But the druid only lifted a brow. "Likewise, it was your task to search, my friend. The journey has been good for you."

"Then let us make it better by putting it to an end." Dropping to one knee, Ronan glanced at Hugh MacHugh and the Dragon.

"Come, lads, let us see if we can budge this stone. And Hector"—he called to the boy—"run and fetch a coal spade from the kitchens."

Eyes round, the lad spun about and streaked up the stairs, returning as quickly with the requested spade. Ronan shook his head when the boy offered it to him.

"Nae, lad, you keep it," he said, already using his dirk to pick at the seams where the stone slab was set into the floor. "When we hoist up the stone, I want you to thrust the spade into the crack, see you?"

Hector nodded.

But the moment Hugh MacHugh and the Dragon knelt to assist Ronan and all three men dug their fingers into the groove of loose grit Ronan had freed along the stone's edges, the massive lid shifted, sliding upward and then sideways with the unpleasant screech of grinding stone.

Fully without the need of a spade's leverage.

It *did* remain heavy.

"Now, lads!" Ronan's muscles strained against the stone's weight. "Heave to!"

And at last it came free, revealing an icy black void beneath.

"Hech, hech!" Valdar was the first to peer into the hole. "There is naught down there but—hell's afire!" He jumped back when the Dragon held a torch above the opening. "There *is* something down there!"

"The Raven Stone." Torcaill lowered his staff into the opening, its shimmering light almost dim against the blaze of blue pulsing in the dark below. "Such light can be from naught else."

"And Maldred?" Gelis pushed her way through the little knot of men. "He's there, too, is he not?"

Ronan nodded and reached for her hand, drawing her to the opening. "See, he's there and...blazing heather, look!"

Not believing his eyes, he looked on as the glow from Torcaill's wand stretched toward the shimmering blue stone, the combined brightness revealing what he'd been suspecting for days.

Maldred the Dire's mortal remains not only sat crouched against an enormous carved slab, his precious stone cradled to his breast, he'd died peering up at the opening.

A chill ripped down Ronan's spine and he shook himself, the unexpected clutch at his heart changing everything he'd ever known about his clan's ill-famed forebear.

His lady squeezed his fingers, her touch grounding him in a world set to reeling. *I told you he wasn't the fiend he's painted to be*, he thought he heard her whisper.

But he couldn't be sure. Too loud was the roar of his own blood in his ears.

"I knew it," he said, not missing Torcaill's grim nod. "He had himself buried with the stone. Taking it alive into hiding to—"

"It was an act of deepest penance," the druid finished for him. "I've suspected it for long. He couldn't bring himself to destroy the stone, but he knew its power would be the end of his clan. So he did the only thing he could, sacrificing himself in the old way, for the good of all."

"I'll not have the thing in these walls!" Valdar jammed his hands on his hips. "The stone, I mean," he added, quickly crossing himself. "Maldred can stay where he is. *Requiescat in pace* and all that! But the stone comes out o' the tomb—"

"Begging pardon, sir, but I don't think it is a tomb. Not a real one, anyway," Hector chimed in, his face bright with his daring.

"Eh?" Valdar's brows shot upward. "What's this, laddie? Since when is a stone hole with bones in it not a tomb?"

Hector shuffled his feet, the coal spade clutched in his hands. "I have good eyes, sir," he offered. "Everyone says so and..."

"Go on." Ronan put a hand on his shoulder, squeezing. "Why do you think it's not a tomb?"

"Because..." The boy swallowed, then rushed on, "it's a *circular* space, and the stones lining the walls look like Maldred's old crest stone above the keep door. The heights are about the same, though the stones at the back look a bit taller than the others."

He bit his lip and glanced round as if he expected someone to naesay him.

"I've heard the seannachies," he continued when no one did. "The ones that claim Maldred's crest stone was taken from an ancient stone circle and...and if you look close"—he glanced at the opening in the floor—"you'll see there's a stone missing down there. And—"

"—tradition says, this keep was built atop that circle," Ronan concluded for him.

The boy nodded.

"He speaks true," Torcaill confirmed, glancing up from where he knelt at the opening's edge. "The old crest stone would fit perfectly into the gap in the circle. And"—he used his staff to pull himself to his feet—"Maldred is sitting against the circle's recumbent stone. Even its two flankers are there, still guarding the recumbent."

He smoothed a hand down the front of his robes. "So, aye, the lad supposed rightly. Maldred did choose the circle as his tomb."

"And he can fine well stay there—as I said!" Valdar assumed his most stubborn look. "You"—he wagged a finger in Ronan's direction—"can do what you will with his stone. Just see that it vanishes."

"Dinna you worry." Ronan slid an arm around his lady, pulling her close. "I already know what needs—"

"Sirs!" One of the kitchen laddies trampled down the stairs, coming to a panting halt at the bottom. "The guards at the gatehouse sent me. A great knightly host approaches, riding in fast from the west."

Ronan raised a brow. "Any word who they might be?"

But he already knew.

"MacKenzies." The boy's answer confirmed the worst.

Gelis gasped and Ronan flashed a look at her, not surprised to see that her face had drained of color. Apparently she, too, knew the riders were anything but her kinsmen.

"Sir." The kitchen boy tugged on Ronan's sleeve. "What shall I tell the gate guards?"

Ronan kept his tone neutral, not wanting to frighten the lad. "Tell them I shall ride out to meet with the riders," he said, a chill sweeping him.

When the lad turned and raced back up the stairs, he frowned.

Dungal Tarnach had kept his word.

He'd come for his stone.

And he hadn't wasted any time.

"You can't think to ride out to meet them alone."

Ronan resisted the urge to squirm beneath the fire in his lady's eye. Saints, but she could look at a man. And this look wasn't one of his favorites.

Frowning, he wrapped a hand around her arm and drew her away from Dare's open gate and out of his long-nosed men's hearing range.

"I must go alone." He clamped his hands on her shoulders, willing her understand. But when he sought the right words and none came, he simply spoke the truth. "I have to risk a chance on honor."

"From those who would guise themselves as my kin?" The heat in her eyes kindled. She jerked free of his grip and tossed back her head, her anger almost sparking. "They will skewer you before—"

"Have you so little faith in my sword arm?"

"I have all confidence in your skills with a blade." She swiped a hand across her cheek, glaring at him. "But those are not ordinary men. By your own admission, they—"

"But, my sweet, they once *were* mere men."

He left out how greatly he was counting on that truth.

Glancing aside, he stared for a long moment at the deep pine woods where he knew they waited. For so bitter cold a day, the skies were slowly brightening and several slanting rays of morning sun slipped through the clouds, gilding the tops of the trees and the broad sweep of hills rising behind them.

A few cloud shadows drifted over the high moorlands, shading them inky-blue and softest lavender, colors he'd not seen there in years.

The sight gave him hope.

Unfortunately, it wasn't enough to change his plan.

"I do not like it." His lady raised her chin. "'Tis foolhardy."

"Nae, it is the only way." He took her face between his hands, forcing her to look at him. "And you *will* obey me this time. I'll know you and everyone else safe within these walls until my return."

The words spoken, he drew her tight against him. But she brought up her hands between them, splaying her fingers across his chest and pushing back to peer up at him, her eyes glittering.

"Please." She blinked, her usually strong voice quivering.

"Will you at least tell me where you mean to tryst with them?"

"When the deed is done, aye, but not a moment before," he vowed, lowering his head to kiss her. He slanted his mouth over hers in a devouring kiss, claiming her lips and giving her his passion, trying to show her beyond words that he had no intention of letting her go.

Or of endangering what he now knew they had together.

"Return to the keep and turn a braw face to my people." He pulled back to smooth his hands over her hair and rain light kisses across her face, neck, and shoulders. "Show them what a brave lassie you are," he urged her, nipping the soft skin beneath her ear, then nuzzling her neck again. "Do it for me, for us."

"I would rather ride out with you." She remained defiant.

Ronan shook his head, unrelenting.

Then he stepped back and folded his arms. "Go now. Away into the keep with you or" — he gave her his fiercest look — "I will carry you back inside and chain you to one of the hall pillars."

She bristled. "I will not wait gently," she vowed, but spun about and strode through the gates. "Don't forget I'm a MacKenzie," she called back as she disappeared into the gatehouse arch.

"See that she doesn't leave the keep!" Ronan tossed the order to the guards, then swung up into his saddle and spurred toward the trees, not stopping until the prickles down his spine told him that he'd ridden into the midst of his foes.

He'd no sooner reined in than they stepped from shadows, a band of gaunt, sunken-eyed old men, their dark robes lifting in the morning breeze, their faces solemn.

They didn't look anything like MacKenzies, and Ronan knew a swift surge of hope that they didn't try to cozen him with such a ploy.

"So we meet again, Raven. I greet you." Dungal Tarnach came forward, leaving the others in a quiet circle behind him. "Have you brought our stone or"—he lifted his staff and it glowed orange-red—"must we take it?"

Ronan ignored the threat. "I will bring the stone and—"

"I am rejoiced to hear it." The Holder smiled, his wand sparking. He lowered it at once, his expression almost benevolent. "'Tis overlong that one of your race—"

"And," Ronan continued as if he hadn't spoken, "you may attempt to take the stone, but in a fair trial of strength and will. And not here—"

"So! You would challenge us?" The other's smile faded. His voice rose. "And for that which is rightly ours?"

Ronan lifted his own voice, his hand on the hilt of his sword. "I would challenge you on your honor, if it means aught to you. And"—he raked the company with his stare—"for the safekeeping of this glen and we who dwell here."

Withdrawing his blade, he offered it blunt-end first to the Holder.

"My blade in exchange for yours," he said, following Torcaill's advice to gain the other's steel before his own could be charmed. "We meet in single combat at the Tobar Ghorm before the light fades—unless you fear an honest fight."

The Holder scowled, but took the blade, grudgingly handing over his own.

For a beat, his eyes flickered a faint, faded blue and he looked worried, but he caught himself as quickly. "The Tobar Ghorm is an odd place for—"

"The Blue Well is the only place for honest men to settle a matter of such import." Ronan fixed him with a stare, encouraged when the older man looked away first.

"I can think of fairer ground..." The Holder pulled at his beard.

"You know it must be the well." Ronan broke the quiet when the other man fell silent. "We spoke of the like the last time we met there."

Dungal Tarnach's brow creased.

Ronan waited.

He closed his hand around the hilt of the strange blade, the deep lines in its owner's face and the stoop of the man's shoulders bothering him more than it should.

Even worse, he felt a concession forming on his tongue.

"If you feel unable to accept my challenge yourself," he heard himself saying, "then I will face your best sworder in your stead."

Dungal Tarnach hesitated, but his gaze flicked to a younger man standing nearby. Stocky, fierce-eyed, and ruddy of complexion, the man strode forward now and took Ronan's sword from Tarnach's hands.

"I will cross blades with you," he announced, his voice ringing.

"Then so be it." Ronan nodded. "If I better you, you tell me how to destroy the stone and then you leave our territories forthwith and forever. If I lose, you take your stone and leave as well, ne'er again setting foot in these hills."

"It is agreed." Dungal Tarnach returned the nod.

The other Holders looked on in silence, but finally inclined their heads as well.

It was enough.

And more than Ronan had hoped for.

Chapter Twenty

❦

Hours later, in one of Glen Dare's darkest corners, on a wooded islet in the middle of Loch Dubh...

"The stone, if you will, Raven?" Dungal Tarnach stood beside the Blue Well, his hands outstretched. "I will hold it the while."

He indicated a cleared circle of deturfed ground not far from the well. "As you see, we have made preparations for your challenge."

Ronan nodded, not about to show his relief.

He'd forgotten the wild tangle of dead heather and blood-red bracken crowding the well's little clearing.

But he wasn't about to relinquish the Raven Stone.

"The Tobar Ghorm can safekeep the stone." He crossed the naked, hard-packed earth and stepped around the Holder to set a heavy leather pouch on one of the tumbled stones guarding the well shaft.

Straightening, he looked round. "I trust it won't be touched until we finish?"

Dungal Tarnach frowned. "How do we know yon sack holds our stone?"

Another spurt of hope shot through Ronan. "I would think you'd sense its power."

"You doubt our strength?" The older man lifted an arm, pointing at the leather pouch.

At once its ties came undone and the pouch fell open, its sides slowly peeling back to reveal the Raven Stone before disappearing completely.

More shaken than he cared to admit, Ronan placed a hand over the top of the stone, its sudden glowing blue heat almost blistering his hand.

He kept it there anyway, certain the pain would vanish when he broke the contact.

Just as he was certain—or hoped, at least—that the Tobar Ghorm's brilliant blue water, so deep below the earth's surface, and undeniably blessed, would keep the Raven Stone from the Holders' hands if he failed.

"You are a brave soul, MacRuari." Dungal Tarnach's gaze lifted from the stone. "A shame Nathair will defeat you."

Ronan almost choked.

How appropriate to take up a blade against a Holder named *snake*.

Oddly enough, the irony undid his ill ease on seeing his leather pouch vanish. He threw off his plaid with an eagerness and speed that surprised him, then looked on as his challenger shrugged off his robes with equal relish.

Ronan's own steel already gleamed in the man's hand and a criss-crossing of scars on his broad, muscular chest revealed that he'd held his own in more than one swordfight.

Knowing himself equally branded, Ronan tested Dungal Tarnach's steel, swinging it round, then spinning and dipping, lunging and feinting until the sword felt comfortable in his hand.

Almost sneering, Nathair simply waited.

"Come, have at me." Ronan beckoned him, raising the blade in earnest now. "Show me your best so the devil will be proud of you."

"Save your breath, Raven." The man lifted Ronan's blade. "You will need it."

Ronan beckoned again, eager.

From the corner of his eye, he saw Tarnach and the others move to the edges of the cleared turf ring. They formed a silent, watching circle.

For one horrible moment, he was whisked back into Dare's hall, facing Sorley again. But then Nathair sprang, Ronan's own steel slicing the air to clang loudly against the strange blade in his hand.

The other's strength jarred him, the force of the swing almost knocking him aside. Nowhere near as tall as Ronan, the man was nevertheless built like a steer and, apparently, possessed a stirk's muscle.

Again and again, his steel clashed against Ronan's in a fury of vicious stabs and slashes. They circled and swiped, blades windmilling and drawing back, the shriek and clank of steel on steel loud in the cold morning, though the roar of Ronan's own blood muted the clatter.

Then Nathair spun, first feinting and then springing back around to make a vicious sidelong slash at Ronan's middle. Seeing the arcing flash, Ronan ducked and rolled to the side, the other's blade just missing him.

But something flared in the man's eyes and Ronan saw

his intent. Nathair meant to seize the Raven Stone now, using its power to win the fight. Already he'd maneuvered himself near the well's edge, using furious windmilling slashes to keep Ronan at bay.

"It won't work, snake! You'll ne'er get it!" Ronan lunged, his own blade arcing with even greater speed. "Not you, your brethren, or anyone!"

"Bastard!" Nathair sneered. "The stone is ours."

"Nae," Ronan hissed, "it is no more!"

Leaping forward, he brought down his sword in one ferocious sweep, the force of the blow cleaving the stone in two perfect halves.

"No-o-o!" Nathair roared as the shattered stone shot across the well lip, plunging at once into the Tobar Ghorm. Whipping round, the Holder glared at Ronan, his steel raised high for a deadly strike.

"Yesss!" Ronan blocked the attack with ease, the other's blade whistling harmlessly over his head while his own sword—or rather, Tarnach's—sliced through Nathair's left arm to drive deep into his side, splitting his ribs.

The *snake's* eyes bulged and he toppled forward, Ronan's sword falling from his hands.

It was over.

Another debt of honor paid, if a centuries-old one.

Ronan dragged the back of his hand across his brow, only vaguely aware of the movement around him. The stumbling rush of a score of thin and stoop-shouldered old men toward the edge of the ancient sacred well.

"'Tis over." A relieved-sounding voice, aged and weary, cut through the red haze. "The stone has truly split in twain."

Dungal Tarnach's voice.

But sounding more like the benign-grumbling gray-beards who gathered round Dare's hearthside on dark winter nights than any *Holder* he'd ever known.

"MacRuari! You not only destroyed the stone, you've freed the raven." Tarnach glanced up at Ronan's approach. "Come, lad, see for yourself."

His brow lifting at the friendly tone, Ronan joined them, these bent and frail men who knelt to peer down into the Blue Well.

He saw at once the shattered Raven Stone. He'd destroyed it indeed. Its two halves rested on a jagged ledge deep in the heart of the well shaft.

He also recognized the reason for the old men's wonder.

The awe in their voices and their surprising turn of heart.

Peering into the well, Ronan saw that the split stone revealed the skeletal remains of some kind of ancient, long-moldered bird. But what truly stilled his heart was the raven. Black-winged and full of life, the bird was slowly spiraling upward through the shadowy well shaft.

"'Tis as I knew it would be." Dungal Tarnach pushed to his feet and stepped back, one hand pressed to his be-robed chest as the raven crested the stones lining the well's edge to whir away on glossy, blue-black wings.

The raven circled back once, half-closing his wings to dive at them and sail past in a fast glide before soaring upward again, speeding away across the hills and moors before Ronan and the Holders—a pathetic clutch of stooped, withered old men—could even acknowledge what they'd seen.

"Sakes!" Ronan breathed, running a hand through his hair. He could scarce believe it himself.

More shaken than he cared to admit, he turned to retrieve his sword, but it appeared in his hand before he could. He blinked, not surprised to find Dungal Tarnach at his elbow.

"We will see to Nathair," said the Holder, his gaze flicking over to where a few of his brethren already knelt beside the body. "Though I'd ask your permission to bury him here." He spread his hands and Ronan noted they were gnarled and age-spotted. "Unlike Nathair, the rest of us do not have the strength to carry him far."

Nor, Ronan was sure, did they have the stamina to journey very far themselves.

Their druid wands might work a bit of flummery for them, but their bones were old.

And though he couldn't be sure, he suspected much of their magic had lain with their now-broken stone, whether it'd been in their possession or no.

"'Tis true," Tarnach said then, proving he could still read thoughts, regardless. "The stone fed our power. 'Twas the life force of the sacred raven trapped within. Each beat of its heart craved its stolen freedom and its sorrow bled into the stone, drenching it with the bird's power. Now..."

He looked aside, then back at Ronan. "Two wrongs have been righted. Maldred no longer holds the stone he took from us, and the raven has regained the freedom we took from it. There are many among us who will be gladdened that our craft is now reduced to"—he held out his hand and Ronan's empty leather pouch appeared in it—"a few simple wizard's tricks."

Ronan took the pouch, an uncomfortable tightness beginning to spread through his chest. "You—"

"We are not all as Nathair. We will keep our word." Dungal Tarnach hitched up his robes to turn away, revealing that his shoes were cracked and worn. "We might need a few nights to reach the end of your glen, but then you will see us no more."

"Hellfire and damnation!" Ronan swore against the tightness in his chest. The fool sensation had somehow spread to his throat, sitting there hot and persistent.

And he feared he knew only one way to rid himself of it.

"Have you e'er heard of a Highlander turning away guests?" he blurted, certain the husky, rough-edged words had come from someone else's lips.

"Eh?" Dungal Tarnach stopped in midturn. He looked back at Ronan, his eyes wet and red-rimmed.

Old-man red-rimmed and quite ordinary.

If an old man's tears can ever be called the like.

Seeing them sealed Ronan's fate.

He swore again. But the hot tightness in his chest and throat broke free, something inside him splitting as wide as the cracked Raven Stone, releasing him as surely as the stone had given up its bird.

Fighting back a ridiculous urge to throw back his head and shout his triumph, he reached out to grasp Dungal Tarnach's hand between his own.

"Have you e'er heard of a *MacRuari* turning away friends?" he amended his first question.

The wetness in the druid's eyes glistened. "Ne'er in my day," he replied, his voice as thick as Ronan's. "Though that was more than long ago . . ."

"Nae, that day is now." Ronan squeezed the old man's hand, pumping. "If you are so inclined?"

A tear slid down the druid's cheek. "With the greatest pleasure," he said, nodding.

"Then so be it." Ronan stepped back and snatched his discarded plaid off the grass, eager now to be gone.

He had much to explain.

First and foremost, he needed to tell his lady how much he loved her.

He'd only realized when facing Nathair that he'd never yet said the words.

But a short while later when he left his little skiff on the shore of Loch Dubh and began the long ride back to Dare, those words and any other ones he might have said flew from his mind completely.

He'd but ridden around a steep hill slope before an *onion creel* blocked his path.

An onion creel dressed with a plaid blanket and a tangle of leather straps.

"By the Rood!" He knuckled his eyes, but the basket remained.

Reining in at once, he swung down from his saddle, his feet not even touching the ground before *she* stepped from the trees, Buckie trotting along right beside her.

"Gelis!" He strode forward, catching her by the shoulders. "Saints, lass, I told you to stay at Dare. Do you not know the kind of danger—"

"From a band of ragged, damp-eyed old men?" She laughed, her eyes sparkling. "You were magnificent! And I cannot wait to...greet them properly! And the raven!" She beamed at him, taking his breath. "Who would have thought—"

"You saw?" Ronan's jaw slipped.

"We all saw." Valdar appeared at her side, shoulders back and chest swelled.

Others quickly joined them; Hugh MacHugh, Hector and the Dragon, and even Anice with two of the youngest kitchen laddies clutching her hands. On and on they came, stepping out from behind trees or thickets of broom and whin, until Ronan would've sworn the whole of Dare's household stood before him.

Buckie wagged his tail and barked, not to be ignored.

"Think you we'd let you take on the Holders without us keeping your back?" Valdar plucked Blood Drinker from beneath his belt, brandishing it boldly. "One sly trick on their part and we'd have been on them in a wink!"

He jammed his hands on his hips, looked round. "Faster even!"

And only then did Ronan notice how well-armed his people were.

Steel glinted and shone everywhere and those unable to swing a sword clutched other weapons. Pitchforks and scythes were in abundance, and—if his eyes weren't fooling him—even several long and sharp-ended bone stitching needles tucked beneath Anice's belt.

Hugh MacHugh had his trusty meat cleaver and Auld Meg wielded a wicked-looking iron birthing implement, the proper use of which Ronan didn't care to imagine.

Ronan blew out a breath, shook his head.

His heart began to thump.

And the awful tightness was spreading through his chest again. This time it not only crept upward to thicken his throat, it was also stinging his eyes.

Then he remembered three of Valdar's words.

We all saw.

He cleared his throat, certain of something odd going on.

Something everyone knew but him.

"How could you have seen what happened?" He glanced at Gelis, then his grandfather. "The Tobar Ghorm isn't visible from the lochside."

"So you say?" Torcaill stepped forward and made a great arc with his wand and, for a blink, the Blue Well appeared, its glade peaceful now, even the cleared bracken and heather returned as it'd been before.

"Some wizards' powers never fade," Torcaill added proudly, lowering his staff.

"As Valdar said, we would have come to fight with you," his lady announced, hooking her arm through his and leaning into him. "We watched it all, waiting—"

"Am I to believe your wand would have sent everyone flying through the air to the islet?" Ronan turned to Torcaill. "There has only e'er been one skiff kept at Loch Dubh."

To his surprise, the druid only tightened his grip on his wand and stared back at him.

Gelis slid a telling glance at his grandfather and laughed.

"You tell him," she said, looking about to burst.

And so utterly delectable in her merriment that his heart *did* burst.

"That dog must be hungry," Valdar declared with a shrewd glance at Buckie. "I have some dried deer meat in a pouch tied to my saddle bow. I'll just fetch it now—"

Ronan shot out an arm and caught the back of his plaid as the old man tried to move away. "Buckie can have your entire store of venison...later. I'd hear how you meant to get out to the islet without boats."

"Ach, botheration! Why not?" Valdar hooked his hands around his belt and glowered round. "What's the good of a chieftain's secrets with the whole o' the clan now a-knowing them!"

"Secrets?" Ronan lifted a brow.

"Underwater causeways!" His grandfather yelled the word. "A whole maze of 'em zig-zagging just below the water's surface and leading from every side o' Loch Dubh out to the islet. I discovered them when I was a laddie and my own skiff ran aground on one."

Ronan glanced at the loch. "For the pilgrims of old," he said, guessing the reason. "They used them to reach the sacred well and you"—he slid an arm around Gelis, drawing her close—"meant to use them to rush to my aid."

"That was our plan, aye." Valdar's chin came up. "Had I known the outcome, I'd ne'er have revealed—"

Ronan cut him off. "Is there anything else you haven't told me?"

The old man's eyes lighted. "Ach," he blustered, taking a sudden interest in his fingernails, "just that what I've been meaning to say to you for a good long while now."

"And that is?"

Valdar slid a look at Gelis. "Only that I told you so. That lassie is what you needed, just!"

"And I couldn't agree more." Ronan took her face in his hands and kissed her.

"But he's wrong about one thing," he breathed against her ear before releasing her. "I not only need you, I *love* you and will for all our days."

"Oh, Ronan!" Gelis flung her arms around his neck, clinging tight. "I love you, too," she cried, lifting her voice above the cheers, barks, and shouts rising around them. "We will *always* love each other. Into forever and beyond!"

And as soon as the words were spoken, a great dark form circling high above them dipped one wing in approval.

Epilogue

✦

CASTLE DARE, THE BAILEY
MIDSUMMER EVE

Isn't it magnificent?" Gelis glanced up at the new heraldic crest above the keep door. "It takes my breath," she vowed, her heart catching as she stared at the recently mounted stone slab.

Ronan made a noncommittal humph, but dutifully tipped back his head to follow her gaze.

A gift from the Black Stag, the stone peered down at them, benevolent and proud.

Carved on a polished sea rock taken from Eilean Creag's shoreline, the stone's center bore a great incised swirl representing the Corryvreckan and lauding Valdar's long-ago bravery against the deadly whirlpool. Equally meaningful, flanking engravings of a raven and a stag stood out in bold relief, bracketing the swirl and honoring the joined future of both clans.

"It *is* magnificent," she repeated, the portent of the carvings warming her.

"Aye, full magnificent," Ronan agreed, no longer looking at the crest stone at all.

Gelis laughed and flicked her braid at him.

"You, my Raven, are that and more," she teased, the heated look in his eyes making her wish the night's revelries were behind them.

As if he knew, he put his hands on her shoulders. "I can scarce believe—"

"What?" She pulled back to look at him. "That Maldred finally rests in a new tomb inside the family chapel? I think he's pleased."

Sure of it, her gaze went to where his erstwhile crest stone graced its original place in the pagan circle now standing free beneath the shimmering night sky.

"That, too, would make him happy. To know—"

"I was not speaking of him." Ronan pulled her close, sliding his arms tight around her. "I meant I can scarce believe how much I love you. If we should live a thousand lifetimes, I will search for you in each one. I—"

"Ach, Ronan, I love you more—I vow it!" She flung her arms around his neck, kissing him.

"Hot meats!"

They broke apart as a kitchen lad rushed past, a huge platter of steaming roasted beef and mutton hoisted on his shoulder.

Ronan stared after him. Then he looked at her, his eyes glinting wickedly. "I am ravenous."

Gelis shivered. The look and his tone left no doubt about the nature of his craving.

"Even so . . ." She flashed her best smile. "There is more to this e'en than the dip of my gown's bodice or the swing of my bauble chain. Whichever"—she winked—"you were eyeing just now!"

"I was admiring you, no' your fripperies." He caught her to him again. "But I won't toss you o'er my shoulder and race abovestairs with you until the time is seemly!"

Tingling at the prospect, she trailed a finger down his chest. "If two of our guests keep sparring, we might not have to wait long."

"Hmmm?" He blinked.

"There." She frowned at a table set beneath a gaily decorated Viking tent pavilion.

"I thought they'd get on so well." Her gaze lit on two pinch-faced, white-haired guests. One sported a long-beard and was male and the other could be described as a bit grizzled, bright of eye, and female.

"Come!" She grabbed Ronan's hand and pulled him in their direction. "If we do not do something—"

"He will not accept your offerings." Devorgilla of Doon's peeved voice rose as they neared. "Somerled only—"

The crone snapped her mouth shut when the little fox on her lap took a bit of roasted mutton from Torcaill's out-stretched hand.

"Some might say he has more sense than you." Not quite able to keep the gloat out of his voice, the druid held out a second morsel.

This, too, was accepted.

Torcaill's eyes lit with triumph.

Devorgilla's lips thinned to a tight, petty-looking line.

"You've turned his mind with tidbits," she snipped, her knotty fingers clutched possessively in the little fox's lus-trous fur.

"He has the wits to know what's good for him. You would be wise—"

"I *am* wise." Devorgilla slid her arm around Somerled, drawing him close. "Enough to know I have no wish to dance with you!"

"Oh, dear." Gelis started forward, but a firm hand held her back.

"Wait." Ronan leaned close. "Torcaill can handle her."

"Now, see here, woman," the druid began, proving it, "it is not every day that I extend a hand in peace. This day I offer it in respect as well. Your wee friend knows that and is honored. Can you not—"

"I have been reaping respect since before you lifted your first wand!" Devorgilla's chin jutted. "I've no need—"

"Then respect and admiration." Torcaill sat back, stroking his beard. "And," he added, his voice deepening, "I was wielding my wand long before the first bloom of girlhood ever touched your fine cheeks."

The crone's mouth formed a little O and she clapped a hand to her face as if to test his words.

"Aye, very fine cheeks," the druid confirmed, nodding when the crone's fingers strayed upward to pat her frizzed gray-white hair.

"I'm still not for dancing with you." She huffed and lowered her hand. "My ears haven't forgotten you called me foolish and unskilled."

A particularly wild Highland reel started up then, the burst of screaming pipes and fiddles putting a glint in her eye all the same.

"Tsk, tsk…" She wagged a finger. "You were quite ungallant!"

"Then we are quit!" Torcaill sprang to his feet, pulling

her up with him. "You cannot deny you called me an old goat and a buzzard."

He stared down his nose at her until her eyes twinkled with mirth.

"I did call you that, right enough," she admitted, letting him guide her into the center of the dancers.

"A lass can err..."

Her words floated back to Gelis as the two began to jig and twirl. "I did not make an error with you." She leaned into Ronan, her heart filling. "I knew from the start that we—dear saints, look!"

She pointed at the whirling pair. "Do you see them?"

Ronan blinked. "I do, but I can hardly believe it."

Even so, the night's silver-cast light shone clearly on a tall, straight-backed young man so handsome and proud he could only be Torcaill. His beard and hair gleamed as dark as Ronan's own and his shoulders looked nearly as wide. Gaunt and gray no more, he tripped the reel with more vigor than any other man dancing.

And the blushing maid in his arms laughed brightly, her own hair no longer grizzled and white, but auburn and glossy. Her eyes sparkled as he whirled her around, her flying skirts not black but blue, their hems lifting to reveal well-turned ankles and fast, perfectly stepping feet.

Until a cloud passed over the moon and the illusion faded, leaving them as they were before.

But still they twirled and jigged, smiling and laughing the while.

An uncomfortable heat swelled in Gelis's throat. She swiped a hand across her cheek and blinked back the non-tears no self-respecting MacKenzie would shed.

"'Tis said this is a festival of lovers." She lifted her

chin to counter the wobble in her voice. "If they leap over the bonfires later—I shall believe it!"

I believe it now—every e'en we share is a loving festival...

Gelis blinked, not sure she'd heard the words.

"You are as happy, my lady?"

That, she did hear.

But the uncertainty in the beloved voice took her by surprise.

"Tell me," he pressed. "Are you as content as those two...as we saw them just now?"

He stepped closer, the intensity of his gaze scorching her.

Her shoulders bumped into something hard and solid, and she started, only now realizing that he'd led her into the quiet of the little stone circle.

"Well?" He braced his hands on either side of her, trapping her against one of the stones. "I need the answer, sweetness."

The hitch in his voice undid her.

Her heart nearly leaped from her chest.

"Och, Ronan! I will tell you how happy I am!" She flung herself at him, slinging her arms around his neck. "Happier than these stones are old," she gushed, indicating them with a toss of her head. "My love for you is greater than the breadth of the sky or the depth of the sea! Even the number of waves rolling to shore, the sands and all the—" She broke off, his creased brow worrying her.

"What is it?" She angled her head, a great fear gripping her. "Do you not feel the same?"

She had to know.

He tightened his arms around her and kissed her long,

deep, and hard, his passion dispelling her ill ease until he broke the kiss to look at her.

His brow was even more troubled than before.

"You know I feel the same." He paused. "There's jus' one thing—"

"You have regrets?" She rushed the words, the look on his face almost laming her.

"Aye, I do." He watched her closely. "I regret I ne'er seduced you."

"*Didn't seduce me?*"

He shook his head. "Nae, I didn't. No' properly. 'Twas you who—"

"Ahhhh...but you did!" She laughed, relief almos' splitting her. "I was seduced the very moment I saw you And"—she grabbed his face, kissing him soundly—"I swear if Valdar hadn't sent his man to fetch me, I would have come looking for you myself!"

"Ach, lass." He squeezed her, the thickness of his voice saying so much. "Then shall we say that we were both seduced?"

"Um-hmmm..." she agreed, this time not bothering to blink back her nontears. "Seduced and forever bound."

About the Author

SUE-ELLEN WELFONDER is a card-carrying Scotophile whose burning wish to make frequent (free) trips to
the land of her dreams led her to a twenty-year career with
the airlines. Bilingual, she flew international all those
years, working her flights as foreign language speaker.
Her flying career allowed her to see the world, but it was
always to Scotland that she returned.

Now a full-time writer, she's quick to admit that she
much prefers wielding a pen to pushing tea and coffee.
She spent fifteen years living in Europe and used that time
to explore as many castle ruins, medieval abbeys, and
stone circles as possible. Anything ancient, crumbling, or
lichened caught her eye. She makes annual visits to Scotland, insisting they are a necessity as each trip gives her
inspiration for new books.

Proud of her own Hebridean ancestry, she belongs to
two clan societies: the MacFie Clan Society and the Clan
MacAlpine Society. In addition to Scotland, her greatest

passions are medieval history, the paranormal, and dogs. She never watches television, loves haggis, and writes at a 450-year-old desk that once stood in a Bavarian castle.

Sue-Ellen is married and currently resides with her husband and Jack Russell Terrier in Florida. Readers can learn more about her and the world of her books at www.welfonder.com.

More sensual Scottish romance
from Sue-Ellen Welfonder!

Please turn this page for a preview of
A Highlander's Temptation
Available in mass market
October 2009

The Legacy of the Thunder Rod

❖

Along the west coast of Scotland lies a chain of islands of such beauty and grandeur even the most ardent romantic is hard-pressed to describe their majesty. Curving bays of glistening white sand and glittering seas of every hue vie to take one's breath while jagged, spray-strewn skerries and sheer, impossibly steep cliffs compete with gentle, grass-grown dunes and long-tumbled ruins to stir the soul.

Ruled for centuries by the pagan Norse, the Hebrides is a place of legend, each isle steeped in ancient lore and tradition. Sea-gods, mer-folk, and fabled Celtic heroes abound, their mythic tales spun with relish by silver-tongued bards in the long, dark cold of deep winter nights.

But not all such tales are widely known.

Indeed, some are kept secret.

And one of the most *intriguing* secrets to be found in the vast Sea of the Hebrides belongs to the once-proud Clan MacConacher.

Broken, small in number, and ill-favored with the

Scottish crown, the MacConachers dwell far from their erstwhile seat in Argyll; their straight-backed, long-suffering ranks reduced to scratching out a living on a rocky, windswept isle surrounded by reefs and rough seas.

An isle they cherish because it is all that remains left to them, and, above all, because MacConacher's Isle lies well beyond the reach of the dread MacKenzies, the powerful clan that ruined them.

Not that the MacConachers wish to forget their doom-bringing foes.

Far from it, the present chieftain is young, bold, and of fiery spirit. Keen to throw off his clan's mantle of shame and sorrow, he has only two burning ambitions. He lives to restore his family's good name and fortune. As he also plans for the day he can wreak vengeance on Clan MacKenzie.

His least concern is his clan's most precious possession, the Thunder Rod.

Given to an ancestor by a Norse nobleman, the relic is a polished length of fossilized wood, intricately carved with runes and still bearing bits of brilliant color. Clan elders claim the rod was either a piece of wood torn from the prow of Thor's own longboat or, perhaps, crafted by a great Viking lord for his lady to keep in his remembrance when at sea.

Roughly the size of a man's forearm and rumored to hold great magic, its particular powers do not interest the braw MacConacher chieftain.

Until the stormy morning when the black winds of fate present him with an irresistible opportunity to settle a long-simmering score.

Now, at last, he can use the Thunder Rod.

If he dares.

Chapter One

❧

EILEAN CREAG CASTLE
THE GREAT HALL AT MORNING,
AUTUMN 1350

What do you mean you wish to see the Seal Isles?"

Duncan MacKenzie, the indomitable Black Stag of Kintail, slapped down his ale cup and stared across the well-laden high table at his eldest daughter, Lady Arabella. His good humor of a moment before vanished as he narrowed his eyes on her, his gaze piercing.

Arabella struggled for composure. Years of doing so helped her not to squirm. But she wasn't sure she could keep her cheeks from flaming. Already the back of her neck burned as if it'd caught fire.

So she moistened her lips and tried to pretend her father wasn't pinning her with a look that said he could see right into her soul, maybe even knew how her belly churned and that her palms were damp.

Or that all her hopes and dreams hung on this moment.

"Well?" He raised one dark brow.

Arabella plucked at a thread on her sleeve, then, realizing what she was doing, stopped at once. She looked up, somehow resisting the urge to slip a finger beneath the neckline of her gown or perhaps even loosen her bodice ties. Faith, but she needed air. Her chest felt so constricted, she could hardly draw a breath.

She did manage to hold her father's stare. Hot and bold MacKenzie blood flowed in her veins, too. And even if she'd spent her life quashing any urges to heed her clan's more passionate nature, this was one time she meant to do her name proud.

So she angled her chin and firmed her jaw with just a touch of stubbornness.

"You heard what I said." She spoke as calmly as she could, her daring making her heart skitter. "The seals..."

She let the words tail off, the excuse sounding ridiculous even to her own ears.

Her father huffed, clearly agreeing.

"We've plenty of such beasties in our own waters." He made a dismissive gesture, his tone final. "You've no need to journey to the ends of nowhere to see them."

At once, a deafening silence fell around the hall's torch-lit dais. Somewhere a castle dog cracked a bone, his gnawing all the more loud for the sudden quiet. Everywhere kinsmen and friends swiveled heads in their puissant chieftain's direction, though some discreetly glanced aside. Whatever their reaction, no one appeared surprised by the outburst. Those who called Eilean Creag their home were well used to his occasional bouts of temper.

"If it is such creatures you wish to study, I saw one just yestere'en." He sat back in his carved oaken laird's chair, looking pleased. "A fine dog seal sunning himself on a rock down by the boat strand."

Arabella doubted every word. She did tighten her fingers on the handle of her spoon.

This wasn't about seals and she suspected her father knew it.

His continued stare, narrow-eyed and penetrating, was more than proof.

Arabella started to lower her own gaze, but caught herself and frowned instead. And rather than returning her attention to her wooden bowl of slaked oats as she would have done perhaps even just a few days ago, she sat up straighter and squared her shoulders.

She only hoped that no one else heard the wild thundering of her heart.

It wasn't every day that she dared defy her fierce-eyed, hot-tempered father.

Indeed, this was the first time she meant to try.

Her contentment in life—she couldn't bring herself to use the word happiness—depended on her being strong.

Firm, resolute, and unbending.

"I'm not interested in Kintail seals, Father." She cleared her throat, careful to keep her chin raised. "And there *is* a need. Besides that, I want to make this journey. The Seal Isles are mine now. You gave them to me."

"I added them to your bride price!"

"Which makes them my own." She persisted, unable to stop. "It's only natural I should wish to see them. I can make a halt at the Isle of Doon on the way, bringing your felicitations to your friends the MacLeans and the *cailleach*, Devorgilla. You can't deny that they would welcome me. After that, I could perhaps call at—"

"Ho! What's this?" Her father's gaze snapped to a quiet, scar-faced man half-hidden in shadow at the end of the table. "Can it be a certain long-nosed loon of a Sassu-nach has been putting such mummery in your head?"

Arabella bit her lip, not about to admit that her head had been fine until a courier had arrived from her younger sister's home a few days before, announcing that Gelis had at last quickened with child.

A pang shot through her again, remembering. Hot, sharp, and twisting, her bitterness wound tight. Just recalling how the messenger's eyes had danced with merriment as he'd shared the long-awaited news had upturned her world.

It'd been too much.

The whole sad truth of the empty days stretching before her had come crashing down around her like so much hurled and shattered crockery.

She refused to think about the cold nights, equally empty and warmed only by the peats tossed on the hearth fire and the snoring, furry bulk of whichever of her father's dogs chose to scramble onto her bed of an e'en.

Setting down her spoon, she fisted her hands against the cool linen of the table covering and swallowed against the heat in her throat.

To be sure, she loved her sister dearly. She certainly begrudged her naught. But her heart wept upon the surety that such joyous tidings would likely never be her own.

"Faugh!" Her father's deep voice boomed again. "Whoe'er heard of a lassie wanting to sail clear to the edge of the sea? 'Tis beyond—"

"Hush, you, Duncan...." Stepping up to the high table, her mother, Lady Linnet, placed a warning hand on his shoulder. "Bluster is—"

"The only way I ken to deal with such foolery!" Her

father frowned up at his wife and, for a telling moment, all the fury drained from his face.

The mirror image of Gelis, only older, the lady Linnet flicked back her hip-length, red-gold braid and leaned down to circle loving arms around her husband's broad shoulders. Blessed with the sight—another gift she shared with her youngest daughter—Lady Linnet's ability to soothe and banish her husband's worst moods wasn't something Arabella needed to see at the moment.

The obvious love between the two only served to remind her of the intimacies she'd never know.

Burning to call such closeness her own, she winced at the sudden piercing image of herself as a withered, spindle-legged crone humbly serving wine and sweetmeats to her parents and her sister and her husband as they reposed before her, supine on cushioned bedding and oblivious to aught but their blazing passion.

Arabella frowned and blinked back the dastardly heat pricking her eyes.

Her mother's voice, clearly admonishing her father, helped to banish the disturbing vision. "Ach, Duncan." She smoothed a hand through his thick, shoulder-length black hair, sleek as Arabella's own and scarce touched by but a few strands of glistening silver. "Perhaps you should—"

"Pshaw!" He made a derisive sound, breaking free of her embrace. "Dinna tell me what I should and shouldn't do. I'd rather hear what that meddling lout who calls himself a friend has—"

"Uncle Marmaduke has nothing to do with it." Arabella spoke before he could finish. "He is a better friend to you than you could wish. Though he did mention that he's here because a south-bound trading ship—"

"A vessel said to be captained by an Orkneyman you know and trust." Her uncle sipped slowly from his ale cup, his calm chasing her fears and giving her hope. "Word is that the trader is large enough to take on your girl and an escort in all comfort."

"Hah! So speaks a meddler!" Her father smacked his hand on the table. "Did I no' just say you were the cause of this?" He roared the words, glaring round. "Aye, there's a merchant ship set to call at Kyleakin. Could be, the captain is known to me. I ken most traders who ply these waters!"

"And I *ken* when you are about to make a bleeding arse of yourself." Sir Marmaduke set down his empty ale cup and leaned back in his chair, arms casually folded. "A pity you do not know when to heed those who care about you."

Duncan MacKenzie scowled at him. "And I say 'tis a greater pity that you dinna ken when to hold your flapping tongue!"

The words spoken, he flashed another look at Arabella. "If you're of a mind, I'll take you to see what wares the merchant ship carries. There are sure to be bolts of fine cloth and baubles, perhaps a few exquisite rarities. Maybe even a gem-set comb for your shiny black tresses."

Pausing, he raised a wagging finger. "But know this, when the ship sails away, you will no' be onboard!"

Arabella struggled against tightening her lips.

The last thing she wanted was to look like a shrew.

Even so, she couldn't help feeling a spurt of annoyance. "I have coffers filled with raiments and I've more jewels than I can wear in a lifetime. There is little of interest such a ship can offer me. Not in way of the goods it carries."

She took a deep breath, knowing she needed to speak her heart. "What I want is an adventure."

"*A what?*" Her father's brows shot higher than she'd ever seen.

He also leapt to his feet, almost toppling his chair in his fury.

Out in the main hall, several of his men guffawed. On the dais, one or two coughed. And even the castle dogs eyed him curiously, their canine eyes full of reproach.

Duncan MacKenzie's scowl turned fierce.

"A little time away from here is all I ask." Arabella ignored them all. "I've grown weary of waiting for another suitor to make his bid. The last one who dared approached you over a year ago and—"

"The bastard was a MacLeod!" Her father's face ran purple. "Dinna tell me you'd have gone happily to the bed of a sprig of that ilk! We've clashed with their fork-tongued, cloven-footed kind since before the first lick o' dew touched a sprig of heather!"

"Then what of the Clan Ranald heir who came before him?" Arabella uncurled her fists, no longer caring if anyone saw how her hands trembled. "You can't deny you've called the MacDonalds good allies and friends."

Her father spluttered, frowning.

Lifting her chin a notch higher, she rushed on. "He was a bonny man. His words were smooth and his blue eyes kind and welcoming. I would have—"

"All MacDonalds are glib-tongued and bonny! And you would have been miserable before a fortnight passed." Her father gripped the back of his chair, his knuckles white. "There isn't a race in the land more irresistible to women. Even if the lad meant you well, sooner or later, his blood would have told. He would've succumbed, damning himself and you."

Arabella flushed. "Perhaps I would rather have chanced

such a hurt than to face each new day knowing there won't be any further bids for me."

Mortification sweeping her, she clapped a hand over her mouth, horror stricken by her words.

Openly admitting her frustration was one thing.

Announcing to the world that she ached inside was a pain too private for other ears.

"Why do you think I ceded you the Seal Isles?" Her father's voice railed somewhere just outside the embarrassment whipping through her. "Soon, new offers will roll in, young nobles eager to lay claim to our Hebrides will beat a path to—"

"Nae, they will not." She pushed back from the table, standing. "You've frightened them away with your black stares and denials! And there isn't a man in all these hills and isles who doesn't know it. No one will come. Not now, not after all they've seen and heard—"

She broke off, choking back her words as she caught glimpses of the pity-filled glances some of her father's men were aiming her way.

She could stomach anything but pity.

Heart pounding and vision blurring, she spun on her heel and fled the dais, pushing past startled kinsmen and serving laddies to reach the tight-winding stairs that led up to the battlements and the fresh, brisk air she craved.

Running now, she burst into the shadow-drenched stair tower and raced up the curving stone treads, not stopping until she reached the final landing and, throwing open the oak-planked door to the parapets, plunged out into the chill wind of a bright October morning.

"Ach, dia," she gasped, bending forward to brace her hands on her thighs and breathe deeply. "What have I done...."

Shame scalded her, sucking the air from her lungs and sending waves of hot, humiliating fire licking up and down her spine.

Never had she made a greater fool of herself.

And never had she felt such a fiery, all-consuming need to be loved.

Wanted and desired.

Cherished.

Near blinded by tears she refused to acknowledge, she straightened and shook out her skirts. Then she tossed back her hair and blinked hard until her vision cleared. When it did, she went to the nearest merlon in the battlements' notched walling and leaned hard against the cold, unmoving stone.

Across the glittering waters of Loch Duich, the great hills of Kintail stretched away as far as the eye could see, the nearer peaks dressed in brilliant swatches of scarlet and gold while those more distant faded into an indistinct smudge of blue and purple, just rimming the horizon. It was a familiar, well-loved sight that made her breath catch but did absolutely nothing to soothe her.

She'd lied and the weight of her falsehoods bore down on her, blotting everything but the words she couldn't forget.

Not her own words, railing against how long it'd been since a suitor had come to call for her. Or the gleefully announced tidings of a courier, keen to share his lord and lady's good fortune.

Nor even her hotly defended wish to see the Seal Isles.

O-o-oh, nae, it hadn't been any of that.

It'd been her sister's words when last they'd visited.

Innocently shared accountings of the wonders of marital bliss and how splendorous it was to lie naked with a man each night, intimately entwined and knowing that he lived only to please you.

Exactly how that pleasing was done had also been revealed and thinking of such things now caused such a brittle aching in Arabella's breast that she feared she'd break if she drew in too deep a breath of the day's chill, autumn air.

Worst of all were her sister's repeated assurances that Arabella, too, would soon be swept into such a floodtide of heated, uninhibited passion.

Everyone, Gelis insisted, was fated to meet a certain someone. And, she'd been adamant, Arabella would be no different.

It was only a matter of time.

Then she, too, would know tempestuous embraces and hot, devouring kisses the likes of which she couldn't begin to imagine.

As for the rest... it boggled the mind.

And ignited a blaze of yearning inside her that she feared would never be quenched.

Frowning, she flattened her hands against the cold, gritty stone of the merlon and turned her gaze away from her beloved Kintail hills and imagined she could stare past the Isle of Skye far out into the sea.

But still she heard her sister's chatter.

Her insistence that the feel of a man's hands sliding up and down one's body, his fingers questing knowingly into dark, hidden places, brought a more intoxicating pleasure than the headiest Gascon wine.

Arabella bit down on her lip, sure she didn't believe a word.

What she did believe was that she had to be on the merchant trader when it set sail from Kyleakin.

And what she *knew* was that—if she made it—her life would be forever changed.

THE DISH

Where authors give you the inside scoop!

♥ ♥ ♥ ♥ ♥ ♥ ♥ ♥ ♥ ♥ ♥ ♥ ♥ ♥ ♥

From the desk of Sue Ellen Welfonder

Dear Reader,

My editor absolutely thrilled me when she told me this book's title: SEDUCING A SCOTTISH BRIDE (on sale now). After all, seduction plays a strong role in romance, and Scotland is the heartbeat in every book I write.

SEDUCING A SCOTTISH BRIDE conveys the grand passion shared by the hero, Ronan MacRuari, also known as the Raven, and his heroine, Gelis MacKenzie, youngest daughter of Duncan MacKenzie, the hero of DEVIL IN A KILT. The title also alerts readers that the book is Scottish-set. Of course, with Scotland being my own grand passion, readers familiar with my work already know that they'll be going to the Highlands when they slip into the pages of my books.

Passion and a vivid setting are only two of the magic ingredients that bring a book to life. I enjoy weaving in threads of redemption and forgiveness, a goodly dose of honor, and always a touch of Highland enchantment. Another crucial element is hope.

Heroines, especially, should have hopes and dreams. Lady Gelis bursts with them. Vibrant and lively, she's a young woman full of smiles, light, and laughter. Her greatest wish is to find love and happiness with her Raven, and even when terrible odds are against her, she uses her wits and wiles to make her dreams come true.

Lady Gelis also believes in Highland magic and takes pleasure in helping her Raven solve the legend of his clan's mysterious Raven Stone. And, of course, along the way, she seduces Ronan MacRuari. Or does he seduce her? I hope you'll enjoy discovering the answer.

Readers curious about my inspiration for the Raven Stone (*hint: a fossilized holly tree in the vault of a certain Scottish castle*), or who might enjoy a glimpse into the story world, can visit my Web site, www.welfonder.com, to see photos of the special Highland places they'll encounter in SEDUCING A SCOTTISH BRIDE.

With all good wishes,

Sue-Ellen Welfonder

♥ ♥ ♥ ♥ ♥ ♥ ♥ ♥ ♥ ♥ ♥ ♥ ♥ ♥ ♥

From the desk of Larissa Ione

Dear Reader,

In PLEASURE UNBOUND, the first book in the Demonica series, you met the three demon brothers who run an underworld hospital. There's Eidolon, the handsome, dangerous doctor. Wraith, the cocky half-vampire treasure hunter. And Shade, the darkly confident, insatiable paramedic.

Shade was a favorite of mine from the beginning, so naturally, I had to torture him a little.

Okay, a lot.

See, before I became an author, I was a reader, and as a reader, many of my favorite romances were those in which the hero and heroine are forced together by some external force. So when I started thinking about DESIRE UNCHAINED (on sale now), the second book in the Demonica series, I saw the perfect opportunity to employ a favorite plot element.

Shade was less excited by my decision . . . but then, his life was on the line, and the only way out of the mess would be death. Either his, or Runa's.

Yes, fun was had by all in the writing of Shade's book!

Oh, but it gets better—or would that be . . . *worse*?

Because not only do Shade and Runa have to deal with being forced together, they also have to

go toe-to-toe with a madman bent on revenge . . .
which is another of my favorite plot elements.

   In real life, the need for revenge comes from powerful emotion that drives people to unbelievable
acts. We watch the news and wonder how someone
can snap like that. And if humans can lose it so im-
pressively, imagine what an insane demon can do!

   Speaking of demons, I've put together a down-
loadable compendium of all species in the Demonica
world, available on my Web site, www.LarissaIone.
com. The guide, available to all Aegis Guardians,
aids in the identification of demons and includes descriptions, habitats, and pronunciations.

Get yours now, and happy reading!

Larissa Ione

www.larissaione.com

From the desk of Leanne Banks

Dear Reader,

There are some personalities so powerful that they
refuse to die. Sunny Collins, late mother of Lori
Jean Granger, is the mother who keeps on giving.

Advice, that is. But it's not the typical, stand-up-straight, brush-your-teeth, study-hard-in-school kind of advice. Sunny wasn't exactly the typical mother, either. Here's a taste of her advice so you'll understand why she's unforgettable . . .

"High heels weaken men's knees."

"Dogs are generally more devoted than men are."

"When you're a teenage girl, think of dating as a visit to the candy store. Remember you can visit more than once, and make sure to try everything that looks interesting."

"The true test of a man's ardor is if he will go shoe shopping with you on Black Friday."

"If you must do a nasty chore, listening to rock and roll will help the time pass more quickly."

"Sanity is overrated."

"You will always be my little sunbeam."

You'll find more advice from Sunny in TROUBLE IN HIGH HEELS (on sale now), SOME GIRLS DO, and WHEN SHE'S BAD. Enjoy!

Best Wishes,

Leanne

www.leannebanks.com

Want to know more about romances at Grand Central Publishing and Forever? Get the scoop online!

GRAND CENTRAL PUBLISHING'S ROMANCE HOMEPAGE

Visit us at www.hachettebookgroup.com/romance for all the latest news, reviews, and chapter excerpts!

NEW AND UPCOMING TITLES

Each month we feature our new titles and reader favorites.

CONTESTS AND GIVEAWAYS

We give away galleys, autographed copies, and all kinds of fun stuff.

AUTHOR INFO

You'll find bios, articles, and links to personal websites for all your favorite authors—and so much more!

THE BUZZ

Sign up for our monthly romance newsletter, and be the first to read all about it!